Dan X
Daniel, Mark, 1954-
Pity the sinner /

CYF $22.95

PITY THE SINNER

Pity the Sinner

Mark Daniel

St. Martin's Press ⚏ New York

PITY THE SINNER. Copyright © 1993 by Mark Daniel.
All rights reserved. Printed in the United States of America.
No part of this book may be used or reproduced in any manner whatsoever
without written permission except in the case of brief quotations embodied
in critical articles or reviews. For information, address St. Martin's Press,
175 Fifth Avenue, New York, N.Y. 10010.

Library of Congress Cataloging-in-Publication Data

Daniel, Mark
Pity the sinner / by Mark Daniel.
p.   cm.
ISBN 0-312-14027-4
1. Horse racing—Great Britain—Fiction.   2. Jockeys—Great Britain—
Fiction.   I. Title.
PR6054.A469P58   1996
823'.914—dc20   95-26259   CIP

First published in Great Britain by Michael Joseph Ltd.

First U.S. Edition: April 1996

10   9   8   7   6   5   4   3   2   1

For Lucy Farmiloe
with love and honour

PITY THE SINNER

Part I

SNOW MAKES THE DOWNS plump as pillows. It caused all racing to be abandoned today, so I spent the afternoon in undressing the house. I made a hash of it.

It is nowhere near twelfth night yet, but my daughter Polly has gone to ski with schoolfriends for the rest of the holidays. I am alone. The tinsel and the holly mocked me with their blasé presumption of jollity.

This has been a stiff Christmas of silent sulks and grudging thanks. I gave Polly the skis and the outfit and £500 spending money. She gave me a pair of shooting-stockings. I do not shoot. Not now.

It is a task like murder. If 'twere well 'twere done, 'twere well 'twere done quickly. I bundled together the Christmas cards and flung them into the fire. I pricked my fingers on holly leaves. In tugging at one strand of tinsel, I brought down a Holbein lithograph. My Lady Surry has a crack across her stern and lovely face.

I removed the old familiar bobbles from the Christmas tree and packed them away against another year. The tree itself I took outside. I put a match to it. It went up with a woomph.

It was early evening as I packed up the crib. The baby Jesus has only been there for three days. Now he is back in his box. The Wise men have not even arrived. I returned Joseph, the ox and the ass to their tissue bed. Only the Madonna remained, kneeling on the straw. She gazed down with immutable, endless love.

I am not devout, but none the less I stroked that little plaster figure and said 'Sorry'. I was not talking to the Virgin.

And now I must sit in this haunted house for which I fought so desperately, with no one save the ghosts of that night for company. For the first time in sixteen years, I have picked up a pen rather than a bottle. You are my company on this soughing night.

Come with me to hell. I have to go back there nightly.

3

Come with me and tell me with your hand on your heart that you would have done other than I.

Oh, I know. Theoretically it's all straightforward. Thou shalt not, and that's all there is to it. So we look at the newspapers, see horrible crimes, and we say how disgusting or how mad or how bad the perpetrators must be. Tut tut and pass the Cooper's Oxford, dear. Peace is nice, war is bad, murder unthinkable.

Until war is declared, of course. Then it's bash the Argies and let's stay up late to watch some pinpoint devastation.

And murder too is not unthinkable. I can show you that.

Perhaps I did wrong. Perhaps you would have done otherwise. Perhaps in fact as well as in theory, you would die and permit others to die, sooner than kill.

I want the absolution of sympathy. Murder is a very lonely business.

THE JOCK-STRAP ELASTIC snapped at my waist. A bare millisecond's judder. Not bad for thirty-six.

Thus the warrior girt himself for battle.

I stood. The breeches whispered up my legs, cool as barley. I left them unfastened. The sweater next. I plunged into a tunnel of green and emerged crumpled into the yellow light. I pulled the warmth down over too much chest and large, erectile nipples which used to earn a lot of jeering back in the old days. The green sweater had sleeves striped pink, the registered livery of Mrs Jack – 'call me Daisy, dear' – Bartleet, a builder's wife who probably thought livery meant hungover, but what the hell, she was rich, and blonde and bubbly as spume on a brook. She wore flash-frozen fireworks on her fingers and bobby-sox on her feet. She was my owner.

Glenn's voice said, 'Come on, pull the other one. Premature senile dementia, you ask me . . .'

At my left, Dave's burr: '. . . quick to come into himself, so they had him insured for a packet . . .'

A lordly voice smacked at the exposed rafters: ' . . . think I'm a fucking dwarf or what? Jesus, Val . . .'

And beneath it all, the familiar burble of murmurs and frou-frou of cloths.

Cotton socks, then, my own idiosyncrasy, laddered but Jermyn Street. Sometimes I wore tights, sometimes long-johns, but on a day like today, just fine cotton lisle and boots thin as bin-liners.

I did not have a ride in the first two races today, so I pulled my cover-coat on. I put my hands in the pockets. In the right-hand pocket, I touched paper. I knew what it was. The very touch of it made my heart sink. But just as the bereft lover will listen to the same sad Janis Ian track over and over, so I had to slump down on the bench, open out the letter and read it all again.

It came from my wife's solicitors. It was illiterate and couched in specious jargon. It said 'whereas' and 'as previously indicated' and 'hitherto', but for all its flounces and flummery, its message was clear. Katya wanted every penny that I had ever saved. She wanted my past and my future. She intended to squeeze me until the pips squeaked.

I folded it and sighed and wondered where all this hatred and bitterness had come from. As subjects for speculation go, it proved a trifle less rewarding than what song the Sirens sang or what name Achilles assumed when he hid himself among women.

My steps were heavy as a diver's as I made my way out of the changing-room, acknowledging greetings with a nod and a grunt, and into the cold grey daylight and the hushing breeze.

I looked out over the winners' enclosure, hoping to see a smiling face in a rich frame of auburn. Instead I saw a scowling face and spiky short hair so blonde as to be almost white. Something in my stomach gulped and I damned near dived back into the weighing-room for sanctuary.

For an absurd moment, I was affronted and outraged. The racecourse was my territory. How dare she trespass upon it? Reason returned to inform me that anyone could pay for a member's badge and stroll about the racecourse. She had no interest in racing, but Newbury was not far from her new home, so I had to admit there was no reason why she shouldn't be here, though I could think of no reason why she should, save to gloat or to proliferate tales of her misfortunes and of my failings.

I took a deep breath. I tried to saunter casually across the winners' enclosure. As I did so, she turned away and started to walk slowly towards the back of the members' stand. She was perhaps twenty-five yards away. I called 'Katya!', but it came out wobbly and high-pitched, so I tried again. 'Katya!'

The authoress of my misfortunes and the mother of my child turned. Her eyes rolled heavenward. Her lips twitched. Her shoulders sank. I came up to her. I said, 'Hi. Surprised to see you here. How's Polly?'

'Very well, thank you, Neil.'

'You . . . you haven't brought her with you, then?' I asked stupidly.

'No, Neil. She's with a childminder actually.'

'Can we – I mean, as you're here – could we have a word?'

'I don't think we've anything to discuss, have we?'

'Well, I got the letter from your solicitors this morning. I just thought . . .'

'The solicitors will deal with it, Neil.' Her eyes were hard and staring as those of a cheap doll. 'I have no desire to hear all your lies again, and I was rather hoping to watch this race. Still, if you want to talk, I suppose I can't stop you. Just don't expect me to pay any attention. Anyhow, as a matter of fact, I have people to meet. I can't see any point in this, but all right. I'll meet you here after the first. I suppose that's all right with you?'

It was more than all right. It was the first time that Lot's wife, now a pillar of salt, had conceded that once she fucked and loved. A lot.

She had granted me an audience.

'Sure. Thanks. I'll be here.'

She turned again. She walked around the stand to the lawns with her head held high. Occasionally, she cast a smile of syrupy sweetness at a passer-by. Otherwise, her expression was stony and disdainful. She wouldn't like anyone to think that she was actually with this man.

'Now,' she hummed meaninglessly as she took up her position. She scanned her racecard, then the jockeys' board, then the sky. 'What on earth will win this, I wonder . . .'

I gritted my teeth. I murmured a silent prayer for self-control. I then did something for which I have never shown natural proficiency.

I walked away.

Diplomacy was needed here. I was pleading for my life.

Pavlovian reaction clawed at my gut. I was still shaking at the echo of that voice. It had given me instant dysentery. My eye now made grotesques of the familiar. Nick Roeg had

7

directed this racecourse. Every eye and every smile seemed knowing. I retired to the loo beneath the stands and practised deep breathing while outside urinals sizzled, wool rustled and heels rapped and clanged.

'Hng,' a gruff, autocratic voice was stifled by a cigar between the teeth. 'Oh, he'll do it. Fit as a fiddle. Not often your trainer says "Go for broke", but Louis said absolutely. Operation's been a hundred per cent success. Pulling like a bloody train.' The man grunted. 'Twice the horse, he says. I got him at fourteens. You'll still get a hundred to eight out there, you shop around.'

'Thanks, Dad.' The other voice was youthful and enthusiastic. This had been weaned on gobstoppers and silver spoons. 'No, I'll see what I can get. Looks the part, I must say . . .'

The clothes whispered. The shoes clattered. For a second, an ox-blood brogue was visible beneath the cubicle door. I pulled the racecard from my pocket and scanned the list of runners in the first race, a novice chase. And there he was.

Lestrange, he was called; nine years old, a colt, br., trainer L. Lauderdale, Wantage, Berks, owner Colonel H. R. Furnivall.

I remembered him vaguely, a black, to all intents and purposes, but blacks are such pigs that no one likes to admit to owning them. Lestrange had known success over hurdles, but, over the past two years, had run down the field in every sort of contest. They had tried bringing him back to hurdles, tried blinkers, various distances, even, on one occasion, run him in a bumper at Gowran, but all to no avail. Three weeks ago, however, I had beaten him into third place at Worcester when he had blown up just before the last. He had been bowling along quite nicely until that moment and had never, according to Chaseform, fallen in his life. All in all, a lively prospect if, as his overheard owner said, he had been tubed or otherwise operated upon.

I glanced at my watch. I had seven minutes. I stood, unbolted the door and strode fast from the cubicle.

This looked good, felt good. It was in such haphazard ways that the gods reward their depressed devotees, I told myself.

Say I could get £1,000 on Lestrange or at a hundred to eight – that was twelve-and-a-half grand, for God's sake.

I could use that sort of perk.

Jockeys are not allowed to bet. Jockeys, being human, just occasionally do. I scurried round to the front of the stands and searched for familiar faces unblemished by beatitude.

There was no shortage. Indeed, the blissful serenity to be observed on the countenances of plaster saints was scarce to be seen in these parts. Probity and self-righteousness, however, may insidiously creep into perfectly pleasant, venal souls. I could take no risks.

The face on which at last I settled belonged to a woman, but only just. Only just belonged, that is, to only just a woman. The face looked like a beach-ball after the collie has had a good game. It loosely lolled on a short, squat body. The dugs were so pendulous as to constitute a paunch.

Brown felt hat, brown face (horsehair had escaped where the dog had bitten), brown waistcoat, brown coat, sensible shoes . . . Tory Crispin-Burnett seemed a reluctant woman, disdaining entirely the softer vanities of female display.

It had not always been so. Once, Tory had had suitors aplenty, if only because of her inherited wealth. Her father, I had been told, had been in textiles, and had developed many a fancy cloth used by the *haute couturiers* of the pre-war years. Tory, therefore, had been wooed by swanny swains whose eyes and hands, no doubt, wandered wistfully towards the young mannequins even as they murmured their proposals.

She had developed a fierce contempt for all such slender, sybaritic toddies. She spat at those who complimented her and glowered at those who smiled. She had used her millions to set herself up as one of the first women trainers. At first, she trained only her own horses, but her success-rate had been so high and the stories of long-priced winners so many that, in time, owners flocked – or slunk – to her standard.

'Hello, Munrow,' she greeted me with much grinding of teeth. 'Looking for a ride? Bad luck. That boy of mine is good.

9

Should've accepted the job nine years ago. No chance now. Clapped out. Like me.'

'Speed,' I said softly. I glanced over my shoulders. 'Celerity. Alacrity.'

'Yes, yes. I should think I know more about it than you. My horses shift.'

'Yes, darling, but can you?'

'No. Why?'

'Punt,' I said without opening my mouth. 'This one. Lestrange. Louis Lauderdale's.'

'Arsehole.'

'Maybe, but . . .'

'How much?'

'A long one.'

'Commission?'

'Sod off. A present.'

She seemed to be fighting a coughing fit, but this was Tory's version of laughter. 'Better be a good one,' she blinked. She wiped her mouth with her sleeve.

'You get there on time, it will be.'

She nodded. She made a noise like slipping shale, and she was off, barging, sidestepping down the steps, head down. I watched as she scampered like a rodent through the racegoers on the lawns, through the rails and into Tattersall's, where I lost her amid the eddies of flesh and wool.

The horses were at the start. I unwound my binoculars' strap and raised them to my eyes. I adjusted the focus.

There they were, circling, some going liberty light, some trudging, heavy headed. My boy was one of the former. Perry Scott had the ride, probably, I thought with a sinking heart, because of an association between Perry and the good Colonel Furnivall. Perry was a nice chap and a good enough man to hounds, but the only reasons for his professional licence were his family's friends, who had provided him with too many wins as an amateur, and his family's too-close association with Lloyd's, which had left him needy. He rode beautifully, with long leathers and a long rein.

10

Marcel Marceau climbs mountains beautifully, but I'd not want him above me on the Eiger.

They were lining up now. Perry sat tall in the saddle. The peak of his cap was turned upward. He was chatting to his neighbour, every inch the young buck, while his mount danced like a lifeguard on sharp pebbles.

I suddenly did not want my money on this horse.

I lowered my glasses and scanned the crowd below. Tory had just come back through the rails. She had stopped, and was shoving something into a shoulder-bag which looked more like a wine-sack. Tory never looked happy, but she did not at the moment look agitated, frustrated or annoyed.

She had laid the bet.

And they were off.

Particularly Lestrange.

Usually, when watching my elect horse, I pray that it should move faster. My prayers, though heartfelt and frequently vociferous, usually go unanswered. On this occasion, I fervently muttered the usual arcane spells – 'Oh, fuck's sake . . . What do you think you're *doing*, man?' but this time in the hope that Lestrange would go slower. The spells had their usual result.

Lestrange had Perry Scott and my hard-earned grand on him. Neither had any restraining effect.

The horse was fit all right, pulling like a train – everything of which my unseen informant had assured me – but this train was a runaway, and Perry no Casey Jones. In racing terms, he was being carted.

I watched as he fought to gain control of one side of the horse, only to give up as the first fence loomed close. Lestrange took it flat and fast and on the forehand, with Perry, very wisely, clinging on to the saddle-tree for dear life.

The horse landed, stumbled slightly and resumed his urgent flight from whatever equine bogies pursued him. He was full of life and making a game of terror – a terrifying game, in no wise different from a young man's driving too fast or running before a gale for the hell of it.

Somehow, after the first circuit, he was still upright and still pulling, some twelve, fourteen lengths ahead of the pack.

It couldn't last.

Well, it *could*. That's the trouble with steeplechasing. There's always the theoretically possible miracle. The horses ahead may crash, the front-runner may win off the pace . . . As in every walk of life, such miracles do occasionally happen, turning paupers into millionaires, millionaires into paupers.

But not today.

They were catching him when he hit the first in the back straight. He was only four or five lengths ahead and had skewed over the last two. He must have been able to hear his pursuers. He must have known that the game was up.

His attempt to rise to the fence was like mine to rise to the fiftieth sit-up. The muscles which so lately had been full of oxygen were now hot and hurting. They just wouldn't do their job.

He stayed on his side of the fence. Perry jumped it solo. He sort of lazily rolled and plummeted, and with him went my heart, my hopes and one thousand of my pounds.

Perry got up when the field had passed. My heart and hopes – and pounds – stayed down.

She said, 'Hold it. Just hold it, right there. I don't want to talk about this. Just get this straight, OK?' And her fingers flexed fast by the moss-green cashmere. I had given her that coat. 'I've heard all your bloody excuses. I've heard all the clever, wriggling arguments, all the boring old crap. I'm not going to be bullied again. I'm past that.'

There was that edge to her voice, that familiar, hateful, serrated cutting edge which made the dog hide behind the sofa and the begonias wilt and my bowels contract. Her English had always been good, but there was no trace now of the Danish lilt which once had lulled me.

I glanced quickly over my shoulder. The second race was about to start. Late punters were climbing the stands to unwind the straps of their binoculars, to cast a last wistful glance at their racecards, to reassure themselves with barks and yaps and growls. Their breath was Pernod in water. They were preoccupied, but none the less this was no place for one of Katya's shrieking sessions. She, I knew from bitter experience, would not be constrained by the crowd or considerations of propriety. Her temper was constrained by nothing.

'Look, OK,' I soothed with raised and halting hands, 'I'm not trying to bully anyone. I'm just trying to establish some basic premisses.'

'Just trying to establish basic premisses,' she mimicked. Her blonde head rocked from side to side.

'All I'm asking is, can we just accept that we both have Polly's best interests at heart? That's all I'm asking. You know, OK, we have our disagreements, you can't cope with me. Fine. But we have that bond. We have that in common, willy nilly.'

She studied the stands over my shoulder. 'Actually no,' she said.

'No what?'

'I'm not sure that you do.'

'Sorry. Do what?'

'Have Polly's best interests at heart.'

'Oh, come on, doll, Christ's sakes, I love that child and you know it.'

'Oh, as far as you're able to love anybody except yourself, sure.' Her eyebrows were raised. She smiled a razorshell. 'But frankly, coming back late, never at home, driving without her properly strapped in . . .'

'Once!' I snarled, then closed my eyes and did some heavy pranayam breathing.

Katya had listed my sins in a letter to my mother and to various of my more influential friends. Now the many accidents and eccentricities that make a man, a life, were boiled down into a foul fumet of vices and failings unrelieved by virtues, good intentions or good deeds. She had lived with me for five years, yet she preferred to believe the evidence of that document to that of her memory. She had me off pat.

13

'. . . failing to strap up the baby seat . . .'

'Once!' This time my voice was quiet and husky. 'I was learning to be a parent, just as you were. Anyhow, look, I'm not going to get into a slanging match. I love Polly and she loves me and she has every right to see her father. There's no point in fighting that.'

'We shall see.'

'Yes, OK, we'll see,' I nodded, as ever shocked and numbed by the intensity of her pain yet compelled to defend myself from it. 'But we don't have to do it all through solicitors, for Christ's sakes. OK, so you're on legal aid, but, I mean, you know what that interim order cost me? Just the hearing, preparing the statements, all that? Counsel and so on? Six grand. Six grand, and if we'd just sat down and talked, it could have gone to you or to Polly.'

'To your little tarts more likely.'

'Come on,' I sighed. 'There are no "little tarts".'

'Oh, no. Of course not. So who's the floozie? I saw you arriving.'

'God's sake,' I muttered. 'She's a friend, that's all.'

'Oh, yes, a friend who just happens to have legs up to her armpits. Buy her that suit? Arabella Pollen, isn't it? Very nice. What? Was she on a day out from school when you met her? Jesus. Fucking eternal teenager.'

'You don't want me, Katya,' I growled, 'so why should it worry you that I see anyone else? No. No, OK, sorry. Don't answer that. Look, you know my position . . .'

'I do, actually,' she cooed in a 'good-boy' tone. 'You're a pauper, of course. Like hell you are. I've seen what's in the knitting account, thank you. You're obviously no more honest than you were . . .'

The course-commentator broke in like a staccato oboe, 'And they're away.' The crowd rumbled and hushed.

I lowered my voice. 'I've got a year or two more riding, if that. My only asset is the house. I'd never have bought it if you hadn't given me your assurance that you were committed to the marriage . . .'

'It wasn't me that wasn't committed, actually, Neil.' She turned towards the course.

'You that ran out.'

'Because I had to.'

'Because you wanted . . . ' I started through gritted teeth, then, 'Oh, shit.' I hit my thigh because I had to hit something. 'Forget it.'

She was pretending to take an interest in the two-mile hurdle, so I joined in the charade. I looked down at her out of the corner of my eye. She had been pretty – goddamn it, she still was pretty, but not to my eyes. There had been too much pain, too much anger.

'Look,' I said, 'if you'll just let me keep a hold of the house and the yard, I can set up as a trainer, keep paying you an income. Few years, could even be a really good income. You make me sell, I'm stuffed. That's all my savings, damn near all my patrimony. What do I do then? Get a job selling horse feed or something? It's to no one's advantage. It'll cripple me, but that'll get you the down-payment on a mortgage, set you on your feet, whatever. I keep up the twelve grand a year I'm giving you now . . .'

'You owe me more than that, Neil.'

'I owe you fuck all. I owe Polly. You haven't lifted a finger in three years, and then you run out. Don't give me that "you owe me" number.'

'I suggest you talk to your solicitors,' she literally sang, *cantus planus*. Shit, *planissimus*.

Her skirt, which reached down to mid-calf, was of a fringed dark-green fabric which looked like felt. Her jacket was of frogged maroon velvet. Her hat was black, with a couple of wedge-shaped, egg-speckled feathers in the brim. The coat fitted loosely; loosely flowed. The overall effect was good if unadventurous; school marm scoops the pools, sort of thing.

But the face – oh, Christ, it hurt to see it, to think that I had in some measure caused that vicious red gash which was her mouth, those dark eyes which looked over made-up but weren't, that tight, tremulous set of the jaw, that pallor. She had adopted resentment of her feckless, bankrupt father, resentment of past lovers whom she had chosen with the acumen of a carrion-crow, resentment of judges, doctors and teachers – and she had turned it all on me. But then she had time. Resentment is a luxury of the patience-playing classes.

The horses rocked by with a sound like dribbling taps. I vaguely noticed that Tommy Phelan had one full of running and going well within himself, that Sam Reeves, in his usual monkey-on-a-stick crouch on the favourite, was not going to take this one. The animal was well-positioned, had it all going, but had his ears back. Sam was already at him. Vaguely noticed, allowing the mind to do its own thing, clocking the form without thinking.

'The law's a blunt instrument,' I said, without lowering the glasses. 'Its decisions are crude and absolute. You and I can think and talk, we can be flexible . . .'

'I'm not interested, Neil,' Katya hummed. She swivelled further than the horses had gone. She was watching grass and rails with baited breath.

'I can make money, love. As a trainer. I can – I'm already tithing to Polly. A fund. Charlie Vane and Eledi are in charge. I'll give you a good income . . .'

'Until you have a fall, until you meet someone. Forget it. I want out. I won't be dependent on you. You might as well get this into your head, Neil. I want security. You know what it costs to rear a child? Private education, all that? Seventy-five thousand. It said so in the *Mail*. That's the minimum. You've got it. I'll have it, thank you. Sell the house.'

'You're not thinking!' I wailed. 'The house represents everything – my past and my future. What the hell do you expect me to live on?'

She shrugged. 'Your problem, Neil.'

My breathing was short as sobs, I lowered the glasses so that the air could cool my eyes. 'I – oh, shit,' I said eloquently. 'And you can't earn? You're thirty, for Christ's sakes. You're fit, aren't you.'

'I have a small child.'

16

'Sure. We have a small child, so for the next few years . . .'

'No, Neil. That's it.' She was back to singing nursery credos again.

'Three years. Seventy-five grand. A pretty nice form of prostitution. Have you not an ounce of dignity, woman?'

'No,' she said happily. 'You took it away. You have only yourself to thank. The law is on my side. There's no point in talking about it. That's it.'

The crowd seethed. The seething subsided. Tommy Phelan took the race in a typical flailing, gangling finish. Sam Reeves was nigh tailed off. The crowd slipped like lava from the stands. Katya wound her glasses straps precisely.

'There we are,' she said. 'So. That's all clear. You screwed me. Now it's my turn.'

'I . . .' I shook my head. I scrabbled for words beneath the murky maelstrom of anger. The passing crowd gave me some cover. I cast diplomacy to the winds. 'You didn't look after me. You didn't work when I was broke. It was I that drove the tens of thousands of miles, risked my neck in all weathers. I paid staff to do everything – everything – and you sit – you stand there saying, "I'm a victim. I'm a victim. The nasty man done wrong to me." Anything done to you, you did to yourself, Katya. You fucking consented. You're a grown-up, whatever your victims-all support groups say. You had a choice. You exercised . . . Jesus, I mean, one moment you're an independent woman and as good as me. Next, you're the eternal victim and the world's beastly to poor little you and owes you a fucking living. You can't have it both ways.' My voice was rising now, my vision smudged. 'So which one is it, then, Katya. Which one is it?'

'Well,' she said, and turned to me with a smile, 'you'll have plenty of time to work that out, won't you? And please don't shout at me.' She turned away with that savage sweet smile, the smile of a hostess to a gatecrasher. 'Goodbye, Neil.'

I was left mouthing 'Bitch, bitch, bitch!' as she strutted off into the crowd.

I had leisure for resentment just then.

I had been going out with Katya for two years before we married. We married because Polly was on the way, but anyhow, my biological personal organizer had been beeping insistently and urgently. When I consulted it, it told me 'Propogate, spawn, be fruitful and multiply.'

A salmon of moderate intelligence, thus instructed, sets off at once for his home stream. He passes, no doubt, many choice and fragrant estuaries, but he is not to be diverted. Home is the home of his fathers; which makes a salmon of moderate intelligence a damn sight brighter than I.

I was, I suppose, uncertain as to just which my home stream might be. My mother's family were alienated. My father's waters – the world of racing – seemed somehow too brackish, seemed, to be honest, beneath me. No. Not me. Beneath my conjectural issue.

But, being Danish, Katya was classless. She was fun, she was well-turned-out, she spoke the Queen's English with crisp consonants, open vowels and an indolent drawl. My mother's world found her acceptable. My fellow jockeys found her worthy of gravelly cheers and whistles which she accepted and reciprocated in tomboy kind.

She was an unlikely Gilbert Osmond, the best of all worlds which proved the best of none.

It is hard for me to remember now, but she was fun back in those days before marriage and childbirth. Occasionally ill-tempered and moody perhaps, but sprightly as water on a griddle and full of giggles and gossip. But she was living in London then and I in Berkshire. She always had an adoring public, and there were few evenings when we did not dine out. That she was spoiled I knew, and that sex for her was more sporting than sacramental. At the time, I found her vanities amusing and her levity refreshing.

When she told me that she was pregnant, I felt only the slightest *frisson* of alarm. Then I realized I urgently wanted the child, and Katya had become a nice sort of habit. My mother said,

'She's sweet, dear. Eyes a bit close together, but you can't have everything, and perhaps just a little bit the demand-fed baby.'

We married quickly and quietly – an irrelevancy, we said, a bit of paper merely. It was only for the child's sake. It would make no difference.

But bits of paper are no longer bits of paper merely once words are written on them. They are books then, letters, certificates, treaties or declarations of war. The word breathes life into paper; the paper makes the fleeting word irrevocable and potent long after the writers and their passions are past.

That bit of paper initiated hostilities. Katya gave up her flat and moved into my rented cottage. As a jockey, I was, of course, away a great deal of the time. When I was home, I was home all day. Katya found neither arrangement to her liking. She became belligerent and brooding.

The pregnancy proved a difficult one, but I could give little help and support if we were to buy the house which Katya constantly pressed me to buy. I was blamed for not owning a house and for failing to take Katya out dancing, yet I was blamed too for my frequent absences and for obsessiveness about my work.

Polly was born in May. Her arrival was the signal for the break-out of war.

Some seek solace in drink. My weight barred that route for me. Some find peace in other women. I tried that a couple of times, but was always acutely and conscientiously aware that my therapy was another human being with her own frail dreams and hopes and terrors.

I took to the one vice to which a jockey should be immune. I gambled. If the big winner would come in, everything would be all right. Katya would be happy.

But Katya, I was discovering, would never be happy. She was a depressive and an emotional terrorist by nature. I had never really known her before, so I don't know whether it was hormonal changes or merely the loss of a starring rôle which turned hatred from a part-time indulgence into a full-time job.

I had been taught that sulking, shouting and blackmail was disgusting, irresponsible and irrelevant. I therefore raised a disdainful eyebrow as she ranted and shrieked, sometimes smashed things, often sighed. These acts and moods seemed to me as unrelated to the justice of her cause as bombs to that of republicanism.

I told her so. She screamed some more.

Further fuel for my resentment was furnished by her lack of motivation, or, in less trendy terms, her bone bloody idleness. She had been running a small business when we met – a good augury, I thought. But the business quickly atrophied, and Katya sat morosely playing a patience called 'sausage', resenting my every labour, my every success.

And finally, I had to admit, she was uncultured. This sounds pompous, I know, and unjust, but it rankled all the same. I had not looked for a high-priestess of Western culture, but I had hoped for a few pleasures outside bed. What had at first seemed a fresh and youthful reaction against sacred cows turned out to be a profound ignorance and blithe unconcern as to those cows' natures and welfare. She would gaze for a moment upon a great house, a great yew, a great racehorse and announce with a shrug, 'I cannot be bothered with all this old stuff.' Of the Giotto panels in the Capella dei Scrovegni she could muster only, 'Christian shit' and 'God, it doesn't even look like a camel!'

My mother gave her a large and rich Helen Allingham which had hung in her nursery and in mine. Katya had not even told me of the gift until she had flogged it to a Bond Street gallery and spent the proceeds on designer clothes. Such things hurt.

Oh hell, there never was a chance. This bore no relation to my home stream.

My version of events has as much claim to be just and true as her Gothic affidavits. We did not speak the same language, and that, in retrospect, was that. To her, horses were 'silly, dirty old animals', and Durham Cathedral 'old, cold and ugly'.

20

Sex was a matter of bouncing to orgasm and beauty defined by cost and novelty.

Something had to give, and something gave, and because these were our natures, we could not, for a long time, understand.

So now in the courts she asserted power which she had never enjoyed in our marriage, and I just shook my head, bemused, as ever, that anyone could find it in her to hate so much.

The hell with it. It was gone.

All, save for its final and its only good product: my beloved daughter, Polly.

I tried not to think of Polly.

This is where it gets embarrassing. This is where I reveal myself to be no hero. But don't leave me because of that. Please.

The house was a dead asset. Solicitors' fees had gnawed deep into my income. The odd winner was not going to answer the case. The odd loser, on the other hand, just might.

So I sought out Daniel Quinn.

I saw him by the winners' enclosure. He was tall, he was glossy, he was good-looking in a smooth, menacing sort of way. He was large and strong for his sixty-plus years, though his cheeks had started to sag into dewlaps and there were creases from his eyes to his jawbone. His hair was aluminium shavings, his skin copper. He walked the racecourse with the air of a farmer amid his herd, grey eyes flickering this way and that, appraising his stock. His coat was of camel hair. It was adorned with a lean golden blonde in black jersey and silver fox. She looked sophisticated. She was of an age. She did not look stupid. None the less he wore her like an accessory.

I followed them.

They led me into the stands. They led me up the escalators. Various people greeted me. I nodded, vaguely smiled. Quinn took his blonde into a bar overlooking the course. He deposited her at a table. Somehow, like a hot knife in ice-cream, he passed through the massed expectant drinkers lining the bar. He leaned forward. Gold flashed amid silver hairs at his wrist. Gold flashed on his saveloy fingers.

A yellow-haired barmaid with a deflated face was at once at his disposal. He smiled. She nodded several times. I could feel as much as hear the rumble of his voice. The barmaid nodded a bit more, fumbled with the foil on a bottle of Taittinger.

I eased forward. I said 'Excuse me', to a couple of tweed backs, and 'Sorry. Excuse me', to a sheepskin coat and a silk scarf with horseshoes on it. Their owners turned, looked down and round, affronted, but they made way for me. By the time I reached the bar, the yellow-haired barmaid already had four champagne flutes set out on a tray. I leaned forward casually. My forearm rested in a pool of beer. A man reached over my shoulder. He waved a fifty-pound note. He hollered, 'Two gin and tonics and . . .' Quinn's barmaid ignored him.

'Mr Quinn,' I said. I did not look at him.

'Neil!' His hand was heavy on my shoulder, quickly clasping. The smell of after-shave and cigar-smoke. 'Splendid to see you.' He showed me his teeth. They looked very white, very sharp. 'How's it going, then?'

'Lousy,' I shrugged.

'Yes, yes, I heard about Katya. Bad luck. Really bad luck, but these things happen. Happened to me twice. Always horrid.' He thrust two twenties at the barmaid. 'Hold on to the change, love,' he purred.

She simpered and damn near curtsied.

'Two gin and tonics and . . .' the man behind me shouted. I could feel the bulge of his belly against my back, the heat of his breath on my ear. He growled, 'Oh, for Christ's own sake.'

'Well,' Quinn picked up the tray. 'I hope things'll improve, Neil. Few winners will perk things up a bit, eh?'

'I . . .' I looked up at him. I swallowed. I didn't like him, but I liked me a whole lot less. 'Look, things are really bad, Mr Quinn. Really tough. If there's anything . . .'

'Of course, of course. Word to the wise,' Quinn was backing away, smiling regally to the mob. 'I'll give you a call. Sure we can come up with something. You know me. Not one to let an old friend down. Don't you worry, Neil. Be in touch soon.' He stepped on the toes of a woman behind. She gasped. He turned and bowed. 'I'm so sorry, madam. Do excuse me. No. Don't worry, Neil. I'll see you right.'

And he was gone, to slap another camel-hair or cashmere shoulder, to sip champagne with those powder-dry lips, to fondle silver fox, to make another deal in which those small figures on the grass beneath – racegoers, punters, trainers and us lowly jockeys – would be shuffled and sorted to his taste and his advantage.

Who was Daniel Quinn? Nobody really seemed to know. Katya had introduced him to me three or four years back. He was one of those men whose line of business seemed simply to consist of being rich. 'A businessman', it was said, 'an entrepreneur', 'a mover and shaker'. They said that he had made his pile in property, in theatrical productions, in stallion shares, and sure it was that he had backed a few West End hits, owned shares in some of the finest animals. I fancied, however, that research at Companies' House would reveal little about Quinn. A few directorships, perhaps. Little more. He owned things and bits of things, people and bits of people, lots and lots of things of manipulable size, not vast, unwieldy complexes subject to public scrutiny.

There were rumours.

'You really want to know?' In the billiard room at Kilcannon, Charlie Vane had spoken in a voice made deep and loud by vintage port and cigars. He had been on a break of twelve. Heady stuff at our standard. 'Basically . . .' he had stretched forward for a shot at the pink. Incredibly, the ball burbled in the jaws of the pocket and went in. Charlie preened and chalked his cue. 'Basically, he's a very, very nasty little London spiv who got lucky. Remember Rachman? Buys up slum properties with sitting tenants, cuts off the services, brings in big dogs, starts floods, intimidates the tenants, eventually gets vacant possession, right? Pretty fellow. His name's entered the language. Rachmanism. Some immortality. Anyhow, he'd have gone down for centuries if he hadn't had a convenient heart attack and hopped the perch. Well . . .' he squinted down his cue at an easy red, 'well, that heart attack was more than convenient for Mr Quinn and all. He was a streetwise little yob who worked as Rachman's lieutenant. And with all the publicity, Rachman had taken to buying his properties in the names of a few trusted nominees . . .' Charlie struck the cue ball and miscued. The white skedaddled about the cushions. It smacked into the yellow. 'Arseholes,' Charlie announced. He lurched slightly on his way to the scoreboard.

'Yes, so there happened to be a couple of streets in the name of Daniel Quinn, his blue-eyed boy. Rachman dies unexpectedly, Quinn finds himself sole owner of a stretch of Soho. This is not in the rules of the average game of Monopoly. So the squalid little villain becomes the real estate owner, cleans up his act, improves his elocution, buys the clothes in Savile Row, marries a nice country girl, who leaves him, marries a Swedish model, who quite reasonably tops herself, plays the property market, makes himself indispensable to the rich and foolish who think a touch of villainy is glamorous. Bingo. There's Quinn for you.

'Thing is – bad luck – he likes to control people. Same as with his master, Rachman. Business is gambling. You minimize the risks, but it's still gambling. But you break the rules, make sure that people jump when you tell them to, you're not gambling any more. You're backing a stone cold certainty. Fixes races. A few hundred in a jockey's pocket, you can lay a few thousand against him. That's Quinn's sort of bet. And then there's that threat implicit in his past. People say, "Don't tangle with him. He was in with the London firms, the Krays, the Maltese, all that." So on the one hand you've got the smoothy, personal friend of the high-rolling jetset, on the other, you've got the nasty little toerag from the wrong side of the tracks. I wouldn't touch him with a bargepole.'

But I had touched Quinn, allowed him to touch me. Back then, when Katya was shrieking and shaking, back then, when I sought the crock of gold that would bring us happiness, I had accepted a few thousand here, a few thousand there for hooking the odd favourite to make good my gambling losses, because I am not a hero, just a damn fool with a desire to have smiling about me and to show my dependants a good time, because I am growing old, because I was sick at the time, and . . .

OK. Because I'm a venal shit, if you will. In the unforgiving eyes of the law, the cold gaze of public opinion, that's the truth of it. But I don't see it that way.

There again, what shit does?

In my defence – ah, hell, I was going to say that I've never bullied like Quinn, never forced my will on those weaker than myself for my own profit. But Jiminy Cricket jumps up to wag his bloody accusing finger and to remind me of the owners who have trusted me, the trainers who have laboured for a victory, the grannies in Bude and Budleigh Salterton who have included me in their each-way Yankees. No, I haven't bullied, and yes, my sins have always been committed in a good cause, but sins they have been.

The best I can say is that I am a small player and that the City and the racecourse are crammed full of people who think nothing of such deals on a far larger scale.

So the existence of sharks consoles a piranha.

Me, I chose Bugsy Moran for my Valentine. I bought Betamax. I won the ship's lottery on the *Titanic*.

I call it bad luck. Others suggest that I simply have prodigious and unerring discernment. Bookies lay confidently against horses that I pick. Travellers change flights when they see me boarding. It's a gift, of sorts. Inverse prognostication, or some such.

Had I not fallen at the Island fence in the third race on that dark, rain-smoky Thursday afternoon, I might not have known for another few days that I was richer by £80,000 which I sincerely did not want. Perhaps – ah, hell, who knows? – perhaps, had I not been thinking about Katya's intransigence, I would have put the clumsy old fool right for the fence and we'd have sailed over. We might even have won. He was able enough on his day.

But as it was, with the jingling and creaking and drumming of the field all about me and the driving icy rain showing me how it felt to be a pincushion, I was spitting curses as we galloped down to that plain fence on the home turn, and suddenly the fence was too low, the heels of the animals ahead too far beneath me, and although I shook him up and gave him a crack and sat into him and shouted something like 'Waaargh!', I knew that we'd stood off too far.

His tucked-in forelegs smashed into the birch. The fence puked gouts. I was jolted forward. The horse grunted. The wind was forced from him with a gasp like a tyre that hit a tack. His arse rose beneath me. The grass was ripped backward fast. The mane was torn from my hands. As he plunged steeply downward, I was flung forward. I scurried for a split second on air, then did my best to twist so that I would land on my shoulder.

I did not quite make it. My chest hit the spitting grass, then my jaw, then my hip. A diorama of muddy equine legs span and squelched about me. I tumbled a couple of times. I then slid. It was like being worked over by a very, very good boxer. The blow to my head blinded me and shook my brain and scraped my jaw and cheek. The haymaker to my ribs jerked the air from my lungs. The clout to the hip was a final insult added to the injuries.

For a few seconds, all was darkness and pain and confusion. I rolled up tight. I screwed my eyes up tight. I felt my mouth tugged back off my teeth in a terrible *rictus*. A kettle-drum thumped in my temple, a faster snare in my chest, and all about me the thudding hooves of the landing horses, the cymbal hiss of their breath, the triangle tinkle of their bits as their riders shook them up and urged them on contributed to the crazy tattoo.

The sounds receded. They became indistinguishable from the patter of the rain on my cap, my boots. I was suddenly bitterly cold. I knew from experience that my collarbone had gone, but I uncurled slowly for fear of a sudden shooting pain that might indicate further damage.

No. I was bruised, but every bit did what it was told. The toes waggled, the legs straightened. The ribs were unbroken. The kidneys felt devilled and I'd probably piss blood for a day or two, but the tastes in my mouth were of bile and soil, not blood.

I pulled myself to my feet just as the ambulancemen reached me. Myself felt heavy. My feet felt frail. A hand took my upper arm to aid me. An amiable red face at my shoulder wrinkled in concern.

'You OK, Neil?'

'Yeah, yeah. I'm fine,' I patted the older man's shoulder. I spoke absently, partly because Atlas seemed to have stepped on to ice and was wondering whether to drop his burden, principally, however, because my mount was lying very still and stiff beneath the battered fence. His damp body steamed. I waded unsteadily over. 'Oh, shit,' I murmured.

'Nothing to be done, I'm afraid,' the ambulanceman spoke softly. 'Must have broke his neck.'

'Poor old sod.' I squatted at the horse's head. I punched away the smearing of my vision. It only seemed to make it worse.

He'd been a good old sort, Kilmainham, a burly, boisterous, overgrown adolescent to whom life had been one enormous game. I had schooled him from the first. I'd tried to tell him that this business could be serious.

I wasn't really the person for the job.

Kilmainham had said 'Phooey,' just as I would have done, and bounded blithely on. He had won twice over hurdles for me, twice over fences. His owner, a Birmingham builder's wife, would be heartbroken.

I have few soppy illusions about horses. I've been around too long for that. But even the weariest old tart must feel some distress when a client croaks on the job. Having a horse

– any horse, not just the familiar old friends – die under you must be a little like that. A moment before, you were sharing the heat, then that physical bond of muscle, bone and will united to one end is suddenly and irrevocably riven. It leaves you feeling very lonely.

The rain bounced off Kilmainham's unmoving eye, gathered and ran like tears down his cheek. I gave his ear a quick tug, then nodded and stood. 'OK. Someone give us a hand with the saddle?' I sniffed and stared up at the sky so that the rain could cool my hot eyes. 'Right. Be on our way.'

I bent to pass under the rails. The stands rasped as someone won, someone lost. Suddenly darkness slid over my vision like a lock of hair over binoculars, and I had to stay like that, bent almost double, a thumb in one eye socket, a forefinger in the other, waiting for balance to return.

The reflection that the earth moves at 1,000 miles an hour round the polar axis, at 70,000 miles an hour about the sun and at about 1,000,000 miles an hour round the galaxy, usually causes me some mild surprise. Not just now. I felt that it had put on a spurt.

'Come on, Neil, lad. Easy does it.' A hand took my either forearm. Light came back as I was eased into the blood wagon. I blinked. The sweat was cold on my brow and at my sides.

Doors slammed. I slumped on to the bench. We were off, bouncing on the rough turf. I rocked and clutched my head. I said, 'Oh, God, Maisie, I told you we should have booked a stateroom.' Then I fumbled for a kidney-bowl and retched.

The doctor was mugging up on form in the *Sporting Life*. He looked up briskly, then returned to chewing his pen and considering more important things than me. He was insultingly young and blond.

'So,' I said jovially. I tried to saunter.

'No,' said the doctor.

'What d'ye mean, no?' I smiled. 'Come on. Just a bit of a bump, Christ's sakes.'

'Forget it, Neil. I saw you. I had a twenty on your fellow. I took close interest in every elegant stage of your descent. No bloody way. To start off with, I suspect . . .' He slammed down his pen and stood. He gestured me towards the black vinyl couch. He flicked on his pen-torch. 'Hmmm. As I thought. Want me to ask how many fingers I'm holding up? The answer will be two. You know the form, mate. Concussion, mild or otherwise . . . Now. Where does it hurt?'

'Where doesn't it? Shit, doc. Just bruises.'

'We'll see. Get that sweater off, will you?'

I shrugged. I wished I hadn't. I crossed my hands and grasped the sodden hem of the polo-neck. I pulled. I said, 'Ow, fuck,' and stopped pulling. 'OK, OK,' I slumped forward, 'bloody thing's gone again. So what? Just strap it up for us, will you, and we can forget all about it. Portugal Place is going to walk the last . . .'

'I'm inclined to agree, Neil, but without you. Sorry.' He had eased my arms out of the sweater and was now prodding my collarbone. 'How many times has it gone now?'

I winced and hissed, 'This is the ninth.'

'God, you guys,' the doctor sighed. 'Ever thought of having the whole damn thing out? Wire it up instead? Pete Straker did that. No. Sorry. It's a couple of days' holiday for you, Neil Munrow. We'll pack you off down to the General . . .'

'It's all right,' I shook my head, 'I've got someone who'll drive me.'

'Just so long as you don't drive yourself.' He returned to the desk to write notes for his colleagues downtown. He lent me a blanket to put over my shoulders. The *Life* caught his eye again. He pushed back his chair. As I reached for the door handle, he droned, 'You sure Portugal Place'll get the trip?'

'I won't be on him,' I shrugged. 'What do you bloody think?'

'God, I really thought you were a goner.' Isobel Dewing threw back a weight of best-bitter hair which could have snapped

29

her neck when wet. When wet, it looked like weather-forecasting seaweed. When dry, as now, it splayed and sprayed and slyly shifted like seaweed fronds in water. It took a while to settle. She puffed on her cigarette. She let out the handbrake. The car slowly jumped the first of the hospital's sleeping-policemen. 'You rolled like a woodlouse,' she said.

'It didn't feel like rolling,' I told her; 'more like being done over by graded bruisers.'

'I thought the poor animal was going to land on you. He looked vertical from the stands.'

'I missed that bit, thank Christ,' I shuddered. She spoke of a jockey's nightmare. 'Ah, well. Poor old feller.'

It was still mid-afternoon, but the lights in Newbury's streets made it seem twilight. Christmas was coming. The orange from the shops, the red and green from their windows and from the traffic lights, the white of the headlight beams, all scattered and splodged on the wet windows in a blotter of light.

'Jesus.' Isobel wound down her window to chuck the cigarette out. A soupy 'Silent Night' oozed in. 'Not that I'd like you to think I gave a damn or anything, but the heart does tend to jump around a bit when you're watching someone you know being turned into a jigsaw puzzle. The wives must be as crazy as the men.'

'Most of them don't watch. Should have heard the doctor back there. Bespectacled beetle, goes, "Oh, yeah, you're one of those mad hari-kiri bastards." I say, "I pay, don't I?" He says, "Yeah, sure, but usually we get the feeling we're achieving something. You guys, it's like gardening. You weed and you weed, but the weeds just keep coming. I mend you lot and I mend you lot and you just keep coming back that much worse. It's galling." "Yeah, but we're a damn sight fitter than most of your patients," I told him, "and one thing's for sure, we don't come to you needing Valium."

'"Oh, great idea," he says, "have a war on the National Health, why not? Write a prescription for neurotics – two circuits of Aintree between meals." "Yeah," I say, "OK, but would it work?'' He shrugs. He says, ''Goddamn us for sick, demented animals. Yes. Yes, it would work. The moribund die. The living haven't got the time.'' '

'Why women live longer than men,' Isobel pronounced.

'Why they used to, sure.'

'You talk too much. By the way, where exactly are we going?'

I said 'Um.'

The choice was between London, where Isobel was based, and my place in the Wiltshire downs. If I said London, I had no guarantee of a bed. Isobel and I had not yet jumped that hurdle. We had examined it. We hadn't found it too daunting. Just, at the moment . . .

'Wiltshire, I think,' I told her, 'if that's OK with you. I'll buy you dinner at the Dove. You free to stay over?'

'Yep. S'pose so. Sounds OK to me.' She forced a tape into the machine, turned the wheel to her right and leaned back. She hummed. Rod Stewart, for Christ's sakes.

I had had few secrets from Isobel even before we met. She was articled to my Gray's Inn solicitors. She had therefore read every gruesome detail about me in Katya's affidavits. She knew that I drank like a fish and was, to boot, consistently menacing, inattentive, unreliable, unfaithful and profligate.

She must have drooled.

She had read her fair share of affidavits from embittered spouses. She sprinkled the whole with a fair dose of sceptic's salt and concluded that I was a human being. 'Thing you discover in this business,' she told me, 'there are no heroes and no villains. Most heroes wear Y-fronts and do disgusting things to the smaller furry species of mammal in their spare time, and most villains love children and dogs and roast partridge. Except for the very, very few genuinely evil people, of course, and maybe there's the odd psychopath who's inherently good. I've given up that sort of judging. *Tom Jones*. You ever read it?'

'Yup.'

' ''A single bad act no more constitutes a villain in life than a single bad part on the stage,'' ' she quoted.

I said, 'Thanks.'

I found this consoling. I couldn't face much judging.

We had met by arrangement at Paddington station. Eight o'clock in the morning and bound, bleary-eyed, for a child-care hearing in Oxford. My solicitor, a senior partner whose meter ticked over at £175 per hour, had suggested that I might save some money by travelling down with his articled clerk rather than with him. Counsel would take care of things, he said, and Isobel could telephone should there be any problems.

I had been startled by his concern for my financial welfare until I remembered that he had played as an England wing-three-quarter and that there was a World Cup match at Twickenham that afternoon. So I told her on the telephone that I'd be beneath the departures' board. I was five nineish, I said, darkish, big eyebrows, perfect hoofshape scar on my left cheek. I'd be kicking passing beggars in a brooding sort of manner and carrying *Private Eye*.

She was stunning, she said, then, no, what? Twenty-six, long, thick, sort of brownish-reddish hair, gormless grin, um . . . not fat . . . um, actually she'd be looking like death warmed up at that time of the morning. She had a party the previous night. She'd be carrying a briefcase – oh, shit, she'd find me.

I found her. I recognized her back instantly. The hair, perhaps, but I don't think so. More to do with what my father would have called the 'cut of her jib': the shoulders held well back, the small pearl earrings (clips not pins), the soft suede coat above a plain black dress. All somehow tallied with the voice that I had heard.

'Enjoy your party?' I had asked, and she had turned, and if that was what death looked like, warmed up or otherwise, I have been much in love with easeful death. No wonder Romans died like Romans.

Oh, she was no headturning, heartstopping beauty, but she was tall – a good two inches taller than I, and her eyes were wide and wide-set and pale blue-grey with dark rings about the irises and her mouth was humorous. Maybe it was the loneliness and the anger that I felt just then, but looking at her made me want to do all sorts of very imprecise things which had to do with weeping and kicking up leaves and crumpets and cuddling.

Then I took in the long legs and returned to normal.

So I grumbled at her on the train. I delivered my most telling and sensitive dicta as to the treachery and mendacity of women. I complained about the cost of solicitors and about the tea, which British Rail, rather alarmingly, call 'Leaf Tea'. She smiled. She did *The Times* crossword.

'Lincoln in the fifties, always on the bottle,' she mused.

'What the hell are you talking about?'

'Sorry. Clue.'

'Oh, So, what's the procedure exactly? Today, I mean.'

'Hmm? Oh, well, I deliver you to the court, make sure you meet up with counsel, then dash off across town to file your residence application . . .'

'You be gone long?'

'Shouldn't be, no. So counsel meets up with your wife's representatives and negotiates to have this ridiculous claim for supervised contact dropped. I mean, they'll know perfectly well they haven't got a chance. Whatever you are, you're not a child molester and there's no suggestion of violence . . .'

'More fool me. Considering all the flak I'm getting, I might as well have chinned her. At least get some satisfaction.'

'You don't mean that.'

'Oh, not really,' I sighed, 'but sometimes – ah, grrr!'

'I know,' she soothed, 'but no one's going to believe all that crap, so your wife's people should see sense. If not, we gird our loins for battle. Don't worry. It's only an interim order. The court'll grant you contact.'

'Thank God. Christ, I miss that baby.'

'I know. It'll be sorted out OK.'

'Mmm.' I leaned my forehead on the glass of the window and watched the environs of Reading speeding by. 'Label,' I murmured.

33

'What?'

'Lincoln in the fifties. Label.'

'Oh, of course.' She wrote with a flourish, then tapped her teeth with a slim pen which looked like a present. 'Want another?'

I smiled. 'Go on,' I nodded and leaned forward. 'Shoot.'

We had that puzzle finished by the time we reached Didcot and, in between clues, she had told me a bit about herself. How she had attended Cheltenham Ladies' College, Lord help us, then spent a couple of years teaching at the American School in Milan, then a bit of modelling, then – oh, hell – her jetset spell, I mean, this Italian designer guy, bodyguards, yachts, holidays in the Far East, the lot. Then she didn't know, he was too much into himself, eroded her confidence, and anyhow, some sort of deep-seated Cheltenham Ladies' College Calvinism kept nagging at her.

She came back to England, decided to take up law, flat broke, but . . . But you know, what's attractive in a twenty-one-year-old ain't so darned fetching as you near thirty, and she'd always thought she'd like, you know, to stop drifting, get a qualification under her belt, make a serious go of it; so here she was. And she kept thinking it should be 'perspicacious' but there weren't enough letters . . .

Before the hearing, counsel conspired in corners, and it was agreed that I could have unsupervised contact, subject to certain conditions, with my Polly, to include at the least the following weekends . . .

Katya glared at me across the court foyer. She had made herself look hideous as a gesture of independence. She wore no make-up, a shapeless shirt and baggy cords. As a concession to her terrors that I, whom she had known for six years to be a harmless loony, might have turned into a blood-soaked psychopath since her desertion, I agreed that I would have a responsible person to stay overnight when Polly was with me.

*

34

'So what's a responsible person?' I asked Isobel in the taxi back to the train.

'I don't know. It's up to her to prove that the person isn't responsible. I mean, don't ask Keith Moon, that sort of thing.'

'What about you?' I asked.

'What?'

'I mean . . .' I backtracked fast, 'I mean, would someone like you be deemed a fit person?'

'Why not?' she giggled. 'Hell, no one's responsible full-time. We all have our binges, our black moods, our crazy days. It's a form of words, that's all.'

'You like children?'

'Rather too much,' she admitted, 'and rather too irrationally. I go and stay with my sister from time to time. She's got three. Cures me for the next month.'

'Don't suppose you'd like – I don't know – dinner, the theatre, one of those things, one of these days?'

'As a potential nanny, was it?' she smiled.

'No!' I protested. I had lost the knack over two-and-a-half years of marriage. 'No, I just thought – oh, stuff it. Forget it.'

'Ummm,' she cocked her head and made much of considering, 'let's see, shall we? I suppose it's allowed. I'm curious about you, I'll admit, but . . .'

Her curiosity had so far extended to three dinners in London and this day off to see me engaged in my trade. She had remained good-natured while, occasionally, I had punched walls and cursed and generally behaved like a melancholic maniac.

The trouble with grief – it's not constant pain. It's a gamut. One minute I'd be walking contentedly about the house that I bought for my daughter, the gardens in which we had chuckled and played, the rooms in which we had hugged and talked gibberish; the next, the pain pounced out at me and jabbed with unerring aim and acuity and it would burst from my mouth in obscenity.

I did not miss Katya. I was happier without her shrieking, her depressions, her lassitude, her daily fits of violence, but God in heaven, I missed that beautiful, smiling little girl.

35

When I saw her born, to my astonishment, I reeled, thrown back against the wall so hard that my teeth clunked together.

Never had I seen such a monster.

Oh, she was tiny, but to me in that moment she appeared huge. There was so much of her who, until then, had been a unified concept – 'a baby'. There were eyes which saw and blinked, a mouth which opened to make little burbling sounds, tiny hands in oversized gloves which flexed and clawed, a tiny, perfect monster of a million working parts, independent of me yet mine, and my dependant.

I did not give her my heart. She wrenched it from my chest with violence like an executioner. For the first time in my life, I knew what it was to be sweetly violated, ravished and glad of it.

And then as she grew, she giggled and chuckled and wriggled, and her eyes were mine, and I became the sort of neurotic father who woke his child up simply in order to ensure that she was alive. She took to summing up the seminal, the essential in things. 'Mmm' she would astutely observe when pointing at a cow, or 'woovwoovwoov' at a dog, and when she saw a horse, she would bounce up and down and click her tongue. And she delighted in chasing me with her walker or spraying me with the hose so that I would yelp in mock dismay, and sometimes, when I came into the garden, she would simply fall over on to her back so that I could pounce on her, growling.

I astonished myself by turning down after-the-last drinks and rushing home from the sports, just to spend a few minutes with her before she went to bed. I astonished myself by being quite happy when I woke up to find the weather too bad for racing. I astonished myself by saving a little money.

Uxorious I would never be. Philoprogenitive, I discovered, I unquestionably, mysteriously was.

But all this time, as the new house neared completion, Katya had grown worse.

She had always been volatile and prone to black moods. She had always resented her father, who, she claimed, had

36

abused her when she was a child; she had always, when in these moods, projected all that built-up resentment on to me in fits of fury which at once invoked in me terror, anger and, above all, pity; but I was the husband, the ever-present representative of all males. I could not help her.

After Polly's birth, these fits of violence became more and more frequent, the spells of sulky lethargy longer and longer. I tried, I really did try, to cheer her, but she did not want cheering; she wanted, she needed, an emotional slave who would dance slowly to her glooms, cavort to her joys. I could not be that.

So one day, two months ago, I had returned home to find her gone. And now the house echoed.

Houses, rather, for there were two; the rented cottage where we would stay tonight and the farmhouse and yard into which I had sunk all my savings and most of my leisure time over the past year.

I had dozed and mumbled a bit as the Shogun sped down into the bare downs. I awoke properly only when familiar landmarks started to flicker past.

'D'ye mind if we go up to the farm first?' I turned down Reinhardt and Grapelli doing 'Them There Eyes' as Isobel steered the car past the old brewery in Tisbury.

'The new place?' Isobel shook her head. 'No, I can't wait to see it. Why?'

'I've got to feed the animals.'

'What have you got up there, then?'

'Left here and left again at the top of the hill. Just – careful here. It's a bitch of a bend – just Bossy, Lord of the Isles, and Bracken, my dog.'

'But your postal address is still the cottage in the village, isn't it?'

'Well, I sleep down there mostly, because it's warmer and the roof isn't finished here, but I've only got the cottage till the 31 December so I've been moving furniture up piecemeal. Basically, every evening when I get home, I've been going up to the farm and working on it – putting locks on the doors,

37

replacing rotten boards, priming, painting, plastering. Couple of lads from the village have been helping. I mean, you should have seen it a year ago. It's still not ready, but it's coming together.'

'And what was Katya doing all this time?'

I shrugged. 'Sitting at the kitchen table sulking and playing patience and reading Danish memoirs.'

'So what did she do with her time?'

'Christ knows. That's what so galling. I mean, I have spent every spare bloody moment up there, getting the place right, working first thing in the morning, last thing at night, so that we'd have a home and a business for when I hang up my boots, and she's done bugger all. And now she wants the lion's share of the whole bloody thing.'

'Well, she's looked after Polly. Give her that.'

'Sure, I'll give her that. Though with plenty of help. But no, she's a good mother. Before that, though, you try getting Katya out of bed for anything less than a bomb alert. Bloody incredible. Right, the track's up to your left at the top of the hill . . . Go easy. It's roughish.'

I understated.

My great-uncle Edwin, the only senior member of my mother's family who acknowledged us after her marriage, owned a tumbledown castle in County Carlow. We went there for an annual holiday of fishing and walking the Black-stairs. Edwin's driveway, half a mile of pits and bumps and potholes, broke sumps, exhausts and axles with remarkable efficiency.

'That, sir, is a gentleman's drive,' Edwin would tell those who complained. 'If you're going so damn fast that you bust up your barouche, you're going too damn fast for my land. Scare the horses, squash my otters, God knows. Frankly, sir, bugger your barouche.'

His wife, Lady Mary, by the by, used to travel in an ancient Daimler with her umbrella ferrule pressed to the nape of her chauffeur's neck. 'I don't like jolting,' she explained.

Well, I now had a gentleman's drive, too; a narrow, bumpy

track which wound up between steep banks and wild plum trees, up through two gates and fields, up beneath an old copse called Swain's Hanger and so to my Fox Farm. The quality of the road surface was comparable to that of a runway after low-level bombing and extensive strafing.

So our teeth jolted together and our heads hit the roof, and Isobel said 'Roughish? Bloody hell!' and she changed down and said, 'Is that it?'

And yes, that was it, just beneath us, its pale brick walls washed by pinkish light, and bright above the dusk which suffused the valley; the house which, just eleven months ago, I had bought for the future, but was already a thing of the past.

It was a hotchpotch. It had started as a two-roomed cottage, then an artist had moved in in the forties and had extended and extended in a random sort of way as the need or the fancy arose. He had created a grand carriage-sweep. He had built a long, jutting drawing room with a flat roof. He had built a studio – a big creosoted barn which you reached through the front hall. In the kitchen and the study, he had introduced large bow-windows so that he could sit in the window-seats and watch the play of light on the valley below.

Isobel parked. She leaned back with a sigh. From around the corner at our left, Bracken happily lolloped. He trotted to the driver's side and snuffled at the window.

Isobel opened her eyes. She said 'Oh!'

I undid the seatbelt and laughed. 'He has that effect.'

I opened the door and stepped out, and the big shaggy setter was snuffling and drooling at my trousers, his soft brown eyes narrowed in a smile. He sat, and his banner of a tail swept a triangle in the gravel. His forepaw struck out at my crotch like a club. He laughed. Saliva clogged with gravel dibbled from his maws. His breath stank.

'Isn't he beautiful?' Isobel's door clunked shut and she walked round.

'And doesn't he stink? Don't you, old boy?' I dropped on to

one knee to hug him. 'He's a kind old lad, aren't you feller? He's a lovely boy.' Bracken nudged my collarbone with his head. I yelped and fell back.

Isobel's hand was on my shoulder. 'Are you OK?'

I exhaled noisily. 'Whew, yes. I'm fine. Just watch this creature when there's a bitch on heat around. He gets over-enthusiastic with girls, wrong time of the month. And there's about as much arguing with him as with Mike Tyson.'

I stood, dusting gravel off my arse. 'And that,' I pointed, 'is the Boss.'

The shaggy, mud-mottled brown horse had trotted over to the fence by the lawn and now snorted and tossed his head, demanding. I led the way over to him. The grass was heavy and spangled and splayed.

'This is a racehorse?' Isobel suspected a practical joke.

'You better believe it,' I crooned. I reached up to pull Bossy's ear. 'Lord of the Isles. Remember?' I turned my head to look at her. Her cheeks were already pink.

'Something,' she frowned. 'What, exactly, did he do? He was good?'

What, exactly? A great, greedy, beautiful animal, impatient for battle and glossy as chicken stock, an over-enthusiastic, clumsy jumper with feet like ice-buckets, but on his day he had carried me, a long-haired burly little aspirant, to glory, and shown me for the first time what real equine power and courage could be.

What, exactly? How exactly to tell of that afternoon at Prestbury Park – God, fourteen years ago now – and I in only my second Cheltenham Gold Cup? How exactly to explain my nerves as Coco Collins, his trainer, flicked me up into the saddle with, 'If he gets round – and that's up to you, Neil – if he gets round, lad, he'll win this.' Twelve to one, a brilliant erratic novice ex-point-to-pointer beneath a not-so-brilliant erratic amateur rider, and the great Rent Boy hot favourite and bidding for his third in a row . . .

Crazy, yet Captain Collins knew his stuff and he meant what he said, so, although it was the hottest, clearest Gold

Cup day in living memory, and the sunshine lay on my shoulders like a sleeping pet, I shivered as the girl who did Bossy released the clip and he bounded away from the parade.

Jesus, that day. The sheer thrill of it, the sudden certainty that he that day was borrowing my mind and I his strength and that we were both blessed by benevolent gods, that nothing could go wrong; the sudden awareness of what power really meant as an animal fell ahead of us, beneath us and, cool as assassins, we extended our leap by four, five feet to avoid the flailing legs; the sensation of flying at the water; the knowledge, at the top of the hill, that we were right, that the race was ours . . . How to tell all that?

So Bossy made up my mind for me – my father's world or my mother's – professional jockey or estate manager. I went for professional jockey, and injury and long drives and mud and muscular aches and banting, moments of glory, years of slog, and kissed goodbye to prosperity and to Cirencester Agricultural College.

And I did not regret it. I could not regret it, for all that I was nearing the end of my career now and prospects were bleak. Because Bossy had shown me that miraculous power three times more, and because there had been other horses which I love and honour still. And there had been companionship and adventure and the smell of the horses and of saddle soap and sweet hay in clear air; and above all there had been membership of a clan.

Much of that, I owed to this dear old clumsy nag who had showed me what was possible.

And of all this, I could only tell Isobel 'Ah, he's an old darling. We did a lot together a century ago. Won the Gold Cup, the Hennessy . . .'

'He did?'

'We did, didn't we, fellow?'

I pulled the headcollar from the gatepost and very gently slipped it over his ears, and I kissed his snip and led him along the fence to the gate. I unlatched the gate and he shoved at me with his nose, which hurt. 'Silly old bastard!' I crooned, and I liked the shifting warmth of his neck at my shoulder.

We trudged in companionable silence through the orchard and across the lawn to the little pink yard with the water-pump at its centre and its bare strands Zephirine Drouhin still doodled on the walls. I had mucked out Bossy's box and laid a new bed first thing this morning, so all that I had to do now was to swap his New Zealand rug for a lighter blanket, pour hot water on his bran mash and throw two slices of a hay-bale into the corner of the box. I never did like haynets. Then, in the darkness of the box, I patted him goodnight and shooed Isobel out in front of me.

'Funny,' Isobel mused, her hand on Bracken's head. 'I mean, an old champion. Picture – I don't know – a hero, an athlete, a heavyweight champion, and now his arms are all withered and his breathing is short and his balls hang down to his knees, but, you know, you know that once . . . It's like a relic.'

'Fetishism. I know. Why people spend fortunes on the real Rembrandt, not the reproduction. Still gives me a kick. I mean he – and I – we're in the history books. Always will be. Silly, I know. Not that he's geriatric, I can tell you. I hunted him in October. Still got a buck in him, still won't be headed. He can't stand to see anything else ahead of him.'

We strolled back up the path to the house. I unlocked the front door and stood back to allow Isobel to pass.

Milton Dupree, RA, had used an artist's ingenuity about the house. The fireplaces were beautifully marbled, the studio floor painted to look like marble tiles. The drawing-room mantel was supported by painted columns made of broom-sticks. Every window was backed by bright-red shutters with bright-red knobs, and this weird, neo-classical porch through which we passed boasted cement columns, again cast on a bound clutch of broomsticks.

'Hang on,' I told Isobel as I entered the hall, which was also the dining room. I doubled back through a door at my left and down two steps. I tinkered.

'What's that?' she called.

'Generator. Hold on.'

'You've got your own electricity?'

'Have to,' I dusted off my hands and pushed back the hair which always flopped over my eyes. 'They quoted me thirty thousand pounds to get the mains supply up here. So I've got two of these old things – one for the house, one for the yard.' I flicked a switch. The generator started its usual consoling throb. I stepped up into the hall and switched on the lights. I shut the door behind me.

'So,' I took her arm, 'it chugs on until you switch off the last appliance last thing at night. After that, I'm afraid, trips to the loo and so on are lit by oil lamps and tilleys. I'm looking into wind-power. There's always a wind up here, but I'd need an invertor and a few huge batteries. I've got my name down for army-surplus tank batteries.'

'This house,' announced Isobel, 'is mad.'

'I know,' I grinned. 'Even the position is loopy. It's not elegant. It's not compact. I still find myself walking into airing-cupboards and broom-cupboards, but it was built to live in, not to conform to this or that principle. Every room has a peculiar feature and a view, and there's – I don't know – such a sense of space.'

I showed her round. Upstairs, there were two bathrooms and four bedrooms. The first of the bedrooms was Polly's nursery. I had painted and stencilled it with nursery rhyme characters. The Tomy baby alarm pouted in the power-point, unfulfilled.

'Don't worry,' Isobel sat sidesaddle on the rocking-horse, 'she'll be back.'

'I know,' I nodded glumly. 'I hope so.'

'Think positive.' She stood with a brisk nod and a positive-thinking sort of *moue*. She led me out of the room. 'So, you're pretty much furnished?'

'Pretty much, yup. Then there's this sort of spare room . . .' I showed her into the twin room which gave on to the drawing-room roof. I turned and clattered down the corridor, 'And our – my room, here.'

There was a large and ornate wooden bed which I had bought at a local house-clearance, a cheval mirror, a big wardrobe, and a dressing-table, bare save for a bottle of Essence of Limes. The walls were white. This was a welcome to whoever might impose her colour on them.

Somewhere in my asinine, ever-optimistic mind, I hugged to myself the notion that there might be such a person – a person with a life of her own who wished to share, not to possess, to accept the consequences of her own actions, not to blame and to whine, a cheerful travelling companion who improved the view rather than insisting on drawing down the blinds.

Man survives because hope springs eternal. Men are doomed because hope springs eternal.

I strode across and drew the long blue velvet curtains. I pointed. 'And there's another bathroom through there.'

'A touch of your *en suites*.' Isobel peered in. 'Very choice. Yeah. You're pretty much set up, I reckon. Few more carpets, pictures, you're made.'

'Yes. I'm . . . I wasn't going to put in anything small and valuable – pictures, trinkets, you know – until I was in residence. Damn fool burglar who comes up here with a bloody great furniture van – mile-and-a-half right of way and so on, but there's always the opportunist. Carpets and things, well, they come as I earn them. They did,' I corrected ruefully.

Downstairs again, I led her through the hall to the study, through the study to the kitchen, then back out through another door into a corridor which doubled back to the hall again. I opened doors to left and right. 'Hot press, broom-cupboard, workman's – well, you know, hammers and things – and then, down here . . .' I opened a door at my left, '. . . you've got the utility-room, boots and whips and so on, because you can get out into the garden this way – the old boy used to keep his dogs in here – and then . . .' I shut the door and led on through the hall and down three steps to my left, 'the drawing room.'

Isobel stepped in. 'Now that,' she said, 'is a lovely room.'

It was, too. It was a long, thin room, as yet still uncarpeted.

At our left was the marbled broomstick fireplace, at the end a sunroom crawling with clematis and winter jasmine, at our right the huge bow-window overlooking the terraced lawns and the fields below.

Isobel walked down the room, touching the weary old sofa, the walnut tallboy which my mother had given me, the sofa tables, the console tables, and the inlaid walnut grandfather clock, the finest piece in the house. Her feet rattled on the bare boards. Her voice rang. 'No, Neil, you've got to keep this.'

She stood in the sunroom now, and her contours were fuzzy against the pink and orange light as she gazed out across the valley.

'If you possibly can,' she said, 'you've got to keep this. It's you.'

'Oh, don't worry,' I said sadly. I sauntered into the room and slumped down on the sofa. I looked down at my inter-linked fingers. 'If there's any way – any way at all – I will.'

Isobel said, 'It's fureezing. Want a hand?' as I fumbled with the cottage keys.

'Nope,' I said stubbornly, though in truth, trying to get the key in was like trying to rape a mermaid. 'I'm OK. Hold on.'

I was still unsteady on my feet. When at last the key turned and the door swung inward, I staggered into the heavy velvet curtain inside. I righted myself. I stood back to allow Isobel in. 'Right, top of the stairs, second on your left,' I told her. 'Bathroom's next door. I'll get fires lit and so on.'

Isobel, for some reason, kissed my scarred cheek and ran straight up the steep stairs two at a time. She had to unbolt the child-gate at the top. I closed my eyes and breathed deep. I turned to my right and wandered into the drawing room.

It was a cottage, lush and plush as cottages are now expected to be. It had a huge fireplace in the drawing room, and beams and thick carpets and Laura Ashley curtains and deep-mullioned windows. The owners were a lieutenant-colonel and his wife, at present posted to Germany. A few names dropped and a few weighing-room stories had persuaded him that I was a good chap to talk about in the mess. She, who had tutted at me and suspiciously eyed my boots, had been so sorry for a heavily pregnant Katya that she too had at last consented. Now he had been given a teaching post at the Infantry school. They wanted vacant possession on New Year's Day.

We had taken the place so that we could look for a house to buy, and, the month after Polly's birth, we had found the farm. On Sundays and out of season, I had worked on the new place whilst Katya sat pouting and playing patience at the cottage kitchen table. I scrubbed and rendered, painted and carpeted. The nursery was the first room to be completed. I fumigated the interior and then replaced the flat roof of the drawing room. I oversaw the re-wiring. I haggled over bills. When I came home, I played with Polly and cooked dinner, and Katya sat pouting and playing patience at the kitchen table.

And for that, she wanted my house.

Oh, she had a new man, and he owned three wine shops in the Windsor area, which was three more wine shops than I had, but she was not so rash as to move in with him. I had hoped for some mercy, but Katya's solicitors announced in this morning's letter that she wanted blood and right now. I earned, in a good year, perhaps forty, forty-five before tax, prodigious travel expenses and telephone bills. The house was all that remained.

I was thirty-six and nearing the end of my career, but I was back where I had started.

'Hey, you,' Isobel clattered down the stairs. She found me still staring blankly at the black window. 'What happened? I thought you were meant to be lighting fires . . . Come on. I'm all tidied up and I'm famished.'

'All tidied up' meant that she'd brushed her hair and pulled on a black angora sweater. She looked very clean and young. 'I'm sorry, love,' I murmured. 'I was miles away.' I walked to the fireplace and started to roll newspaper.

46

'Here, no, leave that to me or we'll never get out.' She rummaged beneath me for firelighters and kindling. 'You just get logs or coal or whatever, then run a comb through your hair and we can be off.'

'OK,' I said, 'I'll only be a minute.' I threw the newspaper into the fireplace. I turned towards the back hall where my boots and the headcollars were. 'I'm sorry . . .'

'Hey?' said a voice behind me. I half-turned. She was squatting on the hearthrug, a length of split pine between her hands. 'Are you OK?' she asked softly. 'We don't have to go out.'

'No. Don't be silly.' I flapped away the very thought. 'I'm fine. Just a bit dopey. Bit of fresh air'll sort me out . . .'

I was in the back hall then, kicking off the brogues, fumbling with the gumboots as though they were on the bottom of a well-used, cloudy bath. I set them upright. They fell over. I breathed, 'Oh, fuck it, fuck it all . . .' as I jerked them upright again, grabbed the right one as it toppled and forced my stockinged foot in. My trouser cuff caught. The other boot deliberately and maliciously prostrated itself. I hopped and blinked and tugged. I almost whimpered, 'God damn it all to hell!'

Then a hand was on my shoulder and her voice said, 'Neil?' then 'It's all right. Come on. Come and sit down,' and it must have been the knock on the head, but something in me crumpled as I turned and looked into those clear, concerned, black-rimmed eyes, and – it must have been the knock on the head, a symptom of concussion or something – but the lava in my eyes erupted and a huge sob punched me in the gut and I squeaked, 'Sorry!' and my lungs wheezed like an airlock as I rushed for the warmth of her, the darkness of her, as all the pain burst from me in hot convulsive jerks, 'Sorry, sorry, sorry . . .'

And she said 'Shhh, shhh, shhh.'

'It must have been the knock on the head,' I said. 'Bloody silly. Shakes you up a bit. Don't worry. I feel better now.

47

Here.' I tipped up the half-bottle of Clicquot. 'Sorry. Only had the half-bottle.'

'If you apologize just once more, I shall kick you. So, what's the plan?' Isobel, now ponytailed and wearing a pair of my cavalry twills and a baggy lumberjack shirt, poured milk on to muesli. We were having breakfast at nine in the evening because that was all there was in the house.

'Well, I ought to see Jack Gaynor,' I grimaced. 'Osteopath.'

'Whereabouts?'

'London, I'm afraid. Wimpole Street.'

'Suits me. Unless . . .' She raised her eyebrows and smiled. 'Wouldn't like me to linger, would you? Come back, I mean; hang around for the weekend? I quite fancy a mucky country weekend, if you could stand it. I've got tomorrow off and quite a bit of holiday to use up before the end of the year.'

I nodded slowly. 'I could stand it. Not much fun for you. I haven't really got any plans now that I'm off riding for a day or two. Thought, nip up to town . . .'

'I could get some clothes while you're being wrenched about.'

'. . . then just – I don't know – get on with work on the house. If the weather holds, you know, refelt the drawing-room roof. Boring for you, but . . . Best I can offer is some pruning. I'm not much good with roses.'

'Oh, me, I'm a demon with the secateurs.' She tipped her bowl, scooped and slurped. 'Sounds good to me.' She mopped her mouth. She pushed back her chair, stood and swung round in one easy movement. She was nice to watch.

'I don't know why I bother,' I glumly told her arse as she bent to retrieve croissants from the oven. 'Working for Katya basically, but you know. I've started. Don't like to give up.'

'Ah, you can't think like that.' She straightened. She threw a steaming croissant on to the table before me. 'She may drop dead tomorrow . . .'

'God grant,' I murmured.

'No, come on, Neil. You don't really mean that.' She sat. She wriggled forward in her chair. 'I hate kitchens like this,' she said. 'Can't tell the fridge from the cooker. Designer yuk. No, come on. She's the mother of your child, and even you admit she does that well enough. No, it's just – well, the house is a labour of love. You can't just pack it in.'

'Hmm,' I nodded. I broke up the croissant and supped coffee. 'And no more of this domesticity. Take you out for that dinner I promised you. There's a new place out Tisbury way . . .'

'Sounds good to me.' She reached forward and touched my forearm. 'You've got a deal. You all right, Neil?'

'Ah, hell,' I nodded. 'I'm fine. Just tired and . . .'

'Course you bloody are.' She pushed away her plate and she stood. 'I'm whacked and I haven't been pummelled half to death today. Right. I'm away to bed. You be OK to lock up and all that?'

'For God's sake,' I snapped from habit, 'I'm not a bloody invalid.' Then I remembered who she was, shook my head and smiled. I took her hand. 'Of course I'll be OK, love. You got everything you need?'

'Yup. Thanks.'

She looked down on me without expression. Then she quickly ruffled my hair, gently removed her hand from my grasp and turned away.

I heard her climb the stairs, heard the creaking of the boards and the rustling of clothes or bedclothes. I thought for a second about waiting five or ten minutes, then finding some excuse to enter her room. Why not? Because I could not stand a knockback was why not, and because she would know that and would feel that she had to be gentle. Because lovers that first night are meant to be all fierce fine frenzy and I was all mewling melancholy.

So I took hot chocolate and C. S. Lewis to bed with me for warmth and stimulation.

I finished neither.

The weather held. I drove to Swindon station over the downs through the sort of day that an equatorial magician would keep in his garden for an occasional plunge. The sky was sheer and the palest of pale blues. Larks shot up and down as though on yo-yo strings. Villages snuggled close about their manors and churches in the folds of the hills.

On the train, we signally failed to master *The Times* crossword. It sneered a gap-toothed sneer at us. We did not care. It was one of those days when a childish excitement takes over, when the muscles are taut and it's easier to grin than not to. We speculated as to our neighbours' purposes and identities. We talked a lot of rubbish.

We took a taxi from Paddington to Wimpole Street. Isobel waved goodbye and took it on to her flat in Camden. We would meet at Paddington again at three o'clock, dodge the worst of the rush-hour.

I missed her when she was gone.

Jack Gaynor microwaved and manipulated me. Unlike the doctor at Newbury, he was used to patching up jockeys, even had a word or two of praise for my condition. For my age, he said, which spoiled it somewhat.

I left him with a smile and a wave and joined the parcel-carrying crowds. I was feeling good, which was strange. Normally, when weather or injury prevented me from riding, I repined. Today I was glad of the holiday.

I had over two hours to spare. OK, so I'd join the crowd, do a bit of shopping, go to Penhaligons, get some Bluebell bath essence for Isobel, potter around Hatchards in search of books for Polly, that sort of thing. First, however, I needed money. I was setting off for the nearest branch of Lloyds when I saw a jaunty, white-haired little man strutting along the pavement opposite. He led a poodle. He wore a bright Fairisle pullover of the sort in which Katya and her mother had specialized.

I remembered Katya's words about the knitting account. I frowned. I took a taxi to Fleet Street.

A doorman manned the door for me. I entered Mammon's temple.

Slaughters' bank is old-established. It is old-fashioned. It is respectable, solemn and serious and much patronized by the nobility and the gentry. I had an account there because my mother, who had been of the nobility, had had an account there, as had her father who was a duke, which is as noble as you can be without getting silly.

Slaughters' is what Westminster Cathedral would like to be. The floors and the many columns are of coloured marble, the vaulted ceilings of mosaic, featuring a lot of gold. There are grand memorials on the walls in honour of the employees of the bank who gave their lives for their country in the two World Wars. There are no racks of leaflets offering you budget plans or mortgages or power through plastic. There are just nice young men in black frock coats, grey cravats and sponge-bag trousers and venerable commissionaires in Ruritanian full-dress uniform. Whispers ring at Slaughters'.

My account – Katya's and my account, I should say – was in the name of Katya Jansen Ltd.

When I had met Katya, she had been running a small company which made hand-knitted sweaters for children – Arrans, Fairisles, that sort of thing – designed by Katya and her mother and knitted up by a host of worthy women about the country.

After our marriage, Katya had allowed the business to atrophy. Her mother, the firm's principal talent, had died of cancer, and Katya saw no reason to work while I was earning good money. This was galling, particularly since her independent enterprise had been one of her principal attractions. There were still knitters on the books, however, and Katya's smart friends still occasionally asked for a Katya Jansen shawl collar or toggle sweater for their godchildren, so the company remained in existence.

Its turnover was quite surprisingly high.

Jockeys, as has been noticed, are not allowed to bet. Jockeys, as we have already discussed, are most definitely not allowed to receive money from the likes of Daniel Quinn for services rendered, and it would not take even the most plodding of Mr Plods very long, in the event of an inquiry, to connect the odd deposit with the odd recent winner – or

51

loser. Such payments were therefore made discreetly into the children's knitwear account. If Katya had not cleaned it out, I should have, by my calculations, some £3,000 in it.

I never was much good at calculations.

'Yes, sir, how can I help you?' asked the Nice Young Man behind the bars. If tropical fish have methodist preachers, they look like this fellow.

'I was wondering,' I started and my voice echoed about the vaults, so I swallowed it and started again softly, 'No, I was just wondering if I could know the balance of our account.' I slid the chequebook under the grille.

'Certainly, sir. Forgive me, but if you have some proof of identity? Dreadful impertinence, I know, but with things the way they are . . .'

'Of course,' I fumbled for my wallet. I pushed across a driving licence. 'Of course.'

'Thank you, sir. One moment, please.' He nodded. His chin became his Adam's apple. He retreated through a door. Slaughters' had computers. They even had money, but they didn't like us to see such things. Naked cash might shock us.

He returned a minute later. His air was no more or less deferential than before. A Slaughters' client is a Slaughters' client and entitled to be so by birth. Money has nothing to do with it. 'Here we are, sir,' he intoned. He folded a *With Compliments* slip and slipped it under the grille.

I said, 'Thank you.'

I opened it out, upside down.

I turned it over.

I read £82,352.49.

I said, 'Um.'

Then, because it was the only cogent and decent thing that came to mind, I said it again.

'Um, no. I think there's some mistake,' I said as softly as I could. 'If you could just check it again.'

The guppy yuppy nodded again, again retired to the Nasty Room where BUSINESS was done.

Even then I was fantasizing. A grateful someone had given

me a present. A demented someone had died and left me a fortune. A bookie had written a bet wrong . . .

But no. There was an error. There had to be. No one gave presents of that size. Nobody had died, nor had I been summoned to any will-readings.

Maybe Katya had for some strange reason deposited her lover's money here? No. That too was unthinkable. She would never take the risk that I might discover and withdraw it. No. The computer was on the blink. My dreams of avarice had telekinetically affected it. The young man would come out and say 'I *am* sorry, sir.'

The young man came out. He said, 'I *am* sorry, sir, but I can find no error. Should there have been a deposit or something?'

'No,' I stared at him. 'Er, no. It's just . . . Sorry, when was this – when was the bulk of the money paid in?'

'I anticipated your query, sir.' The young man gave a self-congratulatory smirk. 'The sum of £80,000 was paid in yesterday.'

'This is crazy,' I murmured.

Suddenly fear and elation battled for control of me. My breathing was short. I said, 'Look, I'm sorry. Could I have details of the – um. Could you tell me who paid this money in and . . .' The words became a trickle and dried.

'Certainly, sir.' I thought that this time I detected the faintest trace of a sigh underlying the Nice Young Man's obliging words. He evanesced once more.

Just think, though. If this money really were mine – pay, say, £50,000 to Katya. No, to Polly, and let Katya have the interest for the next ten years. Then £20,000 into an insurance scheme for Polly's education – Jesus, that still left me a clear ten grand to plough into the house and the yard. I'd be up and flying.

But what if anyone found out? Jump jockeys just don't receive sums like this. They don't receive any sum larger than a grand or so without arousing curiosity . . .

No. Forget it. Take a grand out for Tory, another for

shopping and leave it be. The bank would discover its error within the week. Swallow fantasy. Sit firmly upon all rising hopes. Miracles happen, but not to me.

'I thought I remembered this one, sir.' Fishface's words rumbled like an underground train beneath my hopes and fears. 'A *man* came in late yesterday evening and deposited the *sum*.' He made both 'a man' and 'the sum' sound like particularly virulent bacteria. 'It was a cash draft, and the docket was signed in the name of a Mr Trevor Verulam.'

I did some more staring, some more frowning, some more idiotic gulping. The name meant nothing to me. I could swear that, in all my vast and varied acquaintance, I had never knowingly encountered a Trevor Verulam.

'A cash draft?' When at last words emerged, it was a sort of yelp. It was like farting at a funeral. The clerks started and stirred as though Prince Charming had been doing some unseen snogging upstairs. A man at my right turned in disapproving surprise as my voice slapped at the columns. 'You – you mean I can just – just withdraw the lot? Right now?'

'Yes, sir,' the piscatorial preacher was patient. 'Did you wish to?'

'No,' I gulped. 'No, just – I'll take two thousand please, in cash.'

I was shaking my head in bewilderment as the notes were counted and elastic snapped round them. My prayers had been answered. My daughter's future and mine could now be assured. An unknown benefactor, an angel, had rewarded my dubious virtue and then flitted discreetly back to heaven.

Sure, and tell that to the stewards of the National Hunt Committee.

But some part of me – the part that made me spend twenty pounds on the National Lottery whenever I rode in Ireland, the part that was looking forward to Christmas although I knew that it would be cruel and lonely, the part that still vaguely believed in heaven and hell – wanted so much to believe that there were benign magical forces yet at work in the land, that this crock of gold was mine by right.

Thirty-six years told me that it could not be so.

I pocketed the money and stepped hesitantly back into the street. A gowned barrister bumped into me. I got tangled in the lead which connected a redhead and a Cavalier King Charles. The barrister sniffed at me. The spaniel growled.

I made it to Penhaligons. I bought soaps, essences, oils and candles, then hailed a cab. I was impatient to be back with Isobel. I needed to talk to her. I therefore wasted an hour in pacing the station concourse.

She arrived running just three minutes before the train was to leave. She was chic in tweed trousers and yellow cashmere. She carried a bulging grip. She was grinning.

I grabbed her arm. I snatched at the bag. 'Come on, for God's sake,' I steered her towards the platform, 'it's about to leave.'

'All right, all right,' she pulled her arm from my grasp. 'There are other trains, Neil.'

She suffered me to take the case from her. I ran on ahead of her, opened the first of the train's doors. A whistle shrilled from somewhere down the platform. Pigeons scattered amid the smutty smoke. 'Come on,' I muttered as Isobel strode briskly up the platform, 'Come on,' as she clambered up on to the train.

'What the hell's up with you, Neil?' She led me now through First Class. 'I'm here, aren't I?'

'Yes, OK. I'm sorry.' I hit someone's *Daily Telegraph* with the grip. The train jolted forward and stopped. 'I was worried, that's all. Something odd's happened. I'll tell you.'

'Well, I need a cup of tea,' she announced as we stepped though into the buffet. The train had started moving imperceptibly. All I knew was that the stationary trains were now moving backwards. 'Then you can tell me all about it.'

We found aisle seats on either side of a table. I sat beside a blonde little girl with pink plastic earrings who was colouring Goldilocks green.

'So,' Isobel snapped the plastic cover off her polystyrene mug. She fought with the little plastic container of UHT milk, 'Why all the agitation?'

I cast a glance at her neighbour, a plush, bespectacled brunette in an Indian print shirt. She held a Doris Lessing like a shield.

I leaned forward with clasped hands and I murmured the story. Isobel said 'Oh, shit. I don't believe it.' The childish fantasies leaped up into her eyes as they had in mine. 'There's no possibility . . . ?' she asked. 'I mean, this Trevor Verulam might have been working for someone you'd done a favour for?'

I shrugged. 'Well, it's possible, of course, but come on. It's hardly likely.'

'Nothing about this is likely.' Isobel sipped and made a face. 'But there the money is, in your account. It must be something to do with Katya. Has to be. Talk to her. Mind you,' she smiled, 'it makes a fair nonsense of her claim that she's broke. Unless she's got a damn good explanation, her demands for money are going to look bloody silly.' The dream flickered across her face again. 'God, to think that you could just have removed all that cash. I suppose I ought to be glad you didn't, but boy, would it have taught her a lesson. Take her a suitcase full of tenners. "Well, Katya, you wanted the money. Here's eighty thousand in full and final settlement." She'd gawp. She'd sign, then she'd go to the bank and find she'd been paid off with her own money. Poetic justice.' She giggled, then, 'No. You did the right thing. It'll help with the divorce, that's all.'

I looked at my watch. 'I could ring her now.'

'Why not? Get it sorted out.'

I left her to the crossword and to tea. I lurched, ran and staggered back up the train to First Class. I fished out a telephone card and tapped out Katya's number.

The ringing in the Berkshire house seemed very distant. I thought of my little Polly there, hearing it, calling 'Telfo!' and rushing to pick it up, and felt that ache, that longing to hug her and kiss her, to feel her little warm hands exploring my face – eyes, nose, mouth – giggling as I took her hand in my mouth and pretended to eat it . . .

56

There was a long silence, then Katya's voice, friendly and brisk. 'Hello, I'm sorry. We're not in at the moment, but we'll be back soon and will call you if you'll leave your name and number after the beep.'

'We . . .' She spoke of my Polly and herself as lovers. This, for now, was her whole identity – suffering mother, aggrieved wife. My child was a prop necessary to that role.

The Ansafone whistled. I said, 'Hi, Kati, hi Polly, darling. Love you. Listen, love, I'm on the train. What's happening in the knitwear account? There's a whole lot of money there, and I'd like to know how much of it is mine. Can you call me? I'll see you both soon. Bye.'

I laid down the receiver, unaware that I had just made the greatest error of my life.

The horse was watered, the dog was fed. We had almost finished the roof. Another roll of felt would see it done. There was dinner with Isobel ahead, and tomorrow Polly would be with me. I was unconcerned about stray fortunes as Isobel and I returned to the cottage that evening.

I switched on the Ansafone. A couple of farts, a couple of whistles, then, 'Neil, call me, would you?' – the familiar voice of 'Uncle' Dave Wonnacott, an old jock and still one of the best horsemen in the game – then, 'Neil. Hello, there. Daniel Quinn here. So sorry to beard you in your lair, but a little problem has come up. Do you think you could give me a call when you come in? Thank you so much.'

'A little problem has come up . . .' The phrase was as intimidating as 'I'll see you in my study after prayers.' I'd have chosen a Christian Brother for my headmaster sooner than Daniel Quinn.

I frowned a bit, as much as anything because Quinn had never called me at my home. He was habitually cautious. I might exchange the odd word with him at the racecourse, but all other communication was through pale, furtive, ferrety or bovine young men in lightweight suits and with brown envelopes beneath their arms.

'Sounds mysterious,' Isobel called, and those long, denim-clad legs appeared step by step down the stairs. 'Problems?'

'No, no,' I smiled weakly. 'Er – how about tea?'

She looked very clean, very healthy with her hair pulled back in a ponytail and that broad grin making pippins of her cheeks.

'Don't worry,' she touched my shoulder, 'I'll make it. You attend to your mysteries.'

I smiled vaguely. I nodded. I flicked open the *Directory of the Turf*. Quinn was listed under 'Owners'. Two addresses were given – a flat in Campden Hill Square and a manor in Gloucestershire. I tried the country number. A fat male voice intoned, 'Harcourt Manor, may I help you?'

'Yes, um, is Mr Quinn available, please?'

'Who is speaking?' The voice sounded like an owl in a hollow tree.

'Neil Munrow,' I said. In the kitchen, Isobel clattered china and sang 'Always'.

'One moment, if you please, sir.'

I waited. With the receiver tucked beneath my chin, I patted my pockets for cigarettes. There were none. I cursed and scanned the room. The packet was on top of the television. The telephone-lead would not reach that far.

There were a couple of clicks. The line went dead for a moment, then I heard the sound of water, like someone touching the roof of his mouth with his tongue. Astrud Gilberto was singing 'Corcovado' somewhere in there. That fitted. Quinn's style was shop-soiled *Casino Royale*. I pictured an indoor pool, complete with lissom doxies in or out of bikinis.

'Neil,' the word slithered through the receiver, 'good of you to get back to me so soon. I am sorry to bother you. How's the shoulder?'

'Fine,' I croaked. I found myself nodding. 'Be all right in a couple of days.'

'Good, good. What I like to hear. Listen. Silly mistake. Easily sorted out . . .'

The voice had somehow found its way from my ear to my

gut and was crawling through it, growling. I wanted to sit down, but the chair had been moved to the window. I could not remember why. I suddenly knew what Quinn was about to say.

'Silly, I know.' Quinn's vowels were flat, his tone almost cheery. 'Would you believe it? Yesterday, well, of course I was worried after what you said, anxious to help. Of course I was. Never let an old friend down. I'd had a bit of a winner, so I said, you know, pay what I've won – eighteen grand – into poor old Neil's account. We'll – we could always find a way for you to pay us back, you know, instalments, the odd little favour . . .'

'That's – that's very kind of you. I mean, really . . .'

The ice in his glass chuckled. Astrud sang

> *Quiet nights of quiet stars,*
> *Quiet chords from my guitar . . .*

I wondered why she expected noisy stars, then wondered why I'd never wondered it before. Isobel trilled

> *Not for just an hour,*
> *Not for just a day . . .*

and muted trumpets squawked in my gut. My heart was over-drumming.

There was a little snapping sound from Quinn's wet lips. 'No, no. Like I say, a friend in need. No, the silly thing is, the idiot thought I said eighty, not eighteen. Would you believe it? Now, I love you dearly, Neil, but eighty grand, you will admit, is a little over the odds.'

He paused, expecting a laugh. I gave him one. 'Her her,' I said. 'A little. Sure. Sorry.'

'I am sorry if this puts you out,' the voice was a bowed double bass, *legato*, 'but could you possibly just sort it out for me? Best thing, just withdraw the cash – what? You racing on Monday?'

'Yes,' I was keen as a boy scout. 'Yes, I will be.'

'Any chance you could withdraw the cash on Monday morning – no record that way – and bring it to the sports? Don't worry about the interest. Call it a lucky bonus. So, what? Keep the eighteen. That makes sixty-two, doesn't it?'

'Yes,' I almost whimpered. 'Sixty-two. That's fine. No problem. Thank you very much. Really.'

'Nonsense, nonsense. Just sorry about the cock-up is all.'

There was another long pause while Stan Getz pushed out thick, sweet, sinuous sound. I licked my lips and tried to think of something natural and light-hearted to say. Isobel came in. She pushed out the dialling codes book and placed the mug on it. I smiled weakly.

'No,' I said at last. 'Damned embarrassment, eighty grand suddenly turning up in my account, Jesus. I'm rich for three whole days.'

'Enjoy it,' Quinn laughed. It was a sound like a heavy lorry reversing.

Isobel's eyebrows were raised. I nodded at her. I frowned and turned away from those large, clear eyes.

'No,' Quinn went on, 'but I suppose it is serious. What shall we say? Car park's easiest, wouldn't you say? Say midday in the Owners' and Trainers' car park? I'll look out for you. You know my car?'

'Maroon XJS, right?'

'That's right. Still the same old thing. OK. Just, you know, bring a suitcase. I'll make sure you get it back. Fine. As I say, sorry about this . . .'

'No, no, I mean, God. Thank *you*.'

'Not a bit, not a bit. You just have a good weekend and I'll see you on Monday. Ridiculous situation, isn't it?' The glass and the ice tinkled again. 'Thank you so much for your trouble, Neil.'

The telephone clicked and droned. I looked down at it, bemused and affronted for a second that it should do such a thing.

Isobel was sitting gape-legged on the sofa, her hands wrapped round her mug of tea. She smiled. 'All well?'

'No.' I slammed down the telephone and strode across the room to pick up the two things which suddenly seemed more desirable to me than any other things on earth: my cigarettes and a chair. I carried the chair back to the telephone. Even as I sat, I was tapping the cigarette from its packet. It waggled between my lips as I spoke. 'At least, it may be OK. It should be.'

I clicked the lighter and inhaled deeply. I pulled the telephone towards me and started tapping out the number. 'I've discovered where that bloody money came from, anyhow,' I said, and the exhaled smoke burst into clouds in the light from the lamp on the seaman's chest. 'Come on,' I breathed into the telephone. My fingers fluttered on my thigh, 'Come on . . .'

The telephone trilled twice. When it was picked up, there was a lot of fiddling about. There were a couple of sharp bangs. There was a woman's voice in the distance. Otherwise, there was silence.

I took a deep breath to steady myself. 'Hello?' I said gently. 'Hello? Polly? It's me, Daddy. How's my little girl then?'

A little voice said 'Yes.' My heart oozed.

'Did you know that I love you and miss you more than anything?'

'Daddy.'

'And I'm going to come and see you tomorrow, and we'll go out somewhere lovely and I can't wait . . .'

'Fishes,' said Polly. 'Daddy fishes.'

The pertinence of this observation escaped me. Polly loved watching fish. Perhaps there was a wildlife programme on the television to which she wanted to draw my attention. She was like that, my Pol, informative and succinct to the point of obscurity.

There was rustling. Katya's voice said, 'No, that's what I told him . . . Are you going to let Mummy have it, darling? Say bye bye . . . Thank you.'

Polly murmured, 'Bye bye, Daddy.'

'God bless you, my love,' I moaned. She knew how to hurt.

'Hello?' Katya's voice was loud.

I gritted my teeth. 'Hello, Kati, love.'

'Oh. Hello,' she said unnecessarily, just to demonstrate her disappointment. Her voice was now officially dead. I could imagine the grimace at her companion.

'What can I do for you?'

I looked across at Isobel, who was studying a coffee-table book about Venetian palaces. I spoke as casually as I could manage. 'Did you get my message this afternoon? About the Slaughters' account?'

'Yes, thank you.'

'It's just – there's been a cock-up. Some money's just been transferred through my account by mistake . . .'

'No, actually, not by mistake. I've talked to the bank about it. And it's *our* account, in case you'd forgotten. And who is Mr Trevor Verulam, Neil?'

'I don't know, something to do with . . .'

'What are you doing, Neil? Raising money against the house, illegally, without my permission? Or . . .'

'No, I . . .'

'Or some little thug, one of your "acquaintances", paying you for pulling horses and you hoped I wouldn't notice?'

'No, for God's sake, I . . .'

'Well I have noticed, Neil, I am glad to say. You made a serious mistake there, didn't you? Bad luck. So now you may be able to keep your ridiculous house. Well done. We'll just call it full and final settlement, shall we?'

'No, listen!' I barked.

'I have no desire to listen. You're going to tell me a load of bullshit because you're trying to steal from your own daughter . . .'

'I am not I am not I am not,' I chanted.

'And I've caught you out. That's fine. Full and final settlement. Thank you very much, Neil. Very responsible of you.'

'Listen, for God's sake, woman!' I roared. 'Just, for a second, listen. That money came from . . . It's not mine. It's a mistake. Please. Believe me. I could be in serious trouble if I spend – if you take a penny of it. You can have – look – have ten of it. Keep ten grand just till things get settled. Eighteen of it is mine.'

'No, thank you, Neil. I think I'll take the lot. Care to dispute it in court? Say I'm entitled to half your estate. Could be more, just say half. Well, not even including this money, like I said yesterday, that's seventy grand. Then there's the contents. OK. Keep your bloody furniture. I don't like it anyhow. So I'm provided for. Thank you. Then we'll see what the court says about Polly's share.'

'No, Katya!' I howled. 'You mustn't! That money isn't mine!'

'That's not what the bank says, Neil.'

'Look, I'm sorry. You really can't have it.'

'Too late. I transferred it to my account this afternoon. Don't worry, I'll think about it, but some of it will stay in my account and some will be invested for Polly.'

I slumped forward and rested my forehead on my hand. Sweat or something wriggled down my spine. 'Katya, that money has to go back. Keep the eighteen if you must, but sixty-two has to go back by Monday.'

'Why? What for?' she sang. 'You must think I'm mad, Neil. Half that money is mine anyhow, legally. It's a joint account, in case you'd forgotten.'

'No, no, no,' I begged. 'Please, Katya, understand. These are not pleasant people. If I owe them sixty grand, Jesus, they'll kill me.'

'You should keep better company, then, shouldn't you? I'm sorry. Our daughter comes first, Neil. I'm not prepared to discuss it. We're very grateful. Now, I've got company, so I'll say goodbye.'

'Katya, listen!' I almost sobbed.

'Goodbye, Neil,' she said blithely, 'see you tomorrow. Polly will be ready at eleven.' And again the telephone did its clattering and droning routine.

I just let the receiver fall. I covered my face and moaned, 'Oh, Jesus God Almighty,' into praying hands. Quinn would break a leg for five thousand pounds. I just did not have that many limbs.

'It happens,' I shrugged. 'I'm sorry. It shouldn't, but it happens to all of us. It's in the nature of the business.'

'I just can't believe it's so – so easy!' Isobel winced.

I sighed and sipped my brandy. We sat in the bar of The Dove, a little hotel with a fine restaurant which also served as the local boozer to a raucous, rumbustious crowd. I had been trying to wipe that vexed, brooding look from Isobel's face throughout dinner. It had resisted the cleaning power of jokes and gossip. Explanation now offered my only hope.

'Oh, it's crazy,' I admitted. 'Other countries, you've got no bookmakers. Everyone benefits. The Tote pumps money back into racing – better facilities, better prize-money, owners do better, trainers, us, lads, everyone, and there's no bloody point in fixing a race. Here, because they've got a huge and powerful lobby in Parliament . . .' My head swivelled as the burble in the far corner shattered into laughter. 'Here, the lion's share of the twelve billion gambled on racing every year goes into the pockets of bookies, private businessmen who not only contribute precious little to us guys who make the sport but also compete in laying odds. So say there's a hot favourite, but a couple of bookies don't want to get burned, they get together, offer the rider more money than he's going to make all year, cash, no questions asked, just to go a little slow . . .' My lips twitched. I did not need to finish the sentence. I laid down the glass. Isobel still looked cordial as a deathmask. She said nothing.

'Oh, I don't bloody know,' I said, exasperated. 'All I know is, when I was at school, only time I got beaten, I was a flash little bugger and I'd left twenty quid on top of my locker. It got nicked and I reported it and my housemaster beat me. Guy who'd nicked it was just tipped the wink and the money miraculously reappeared; but I got the beating. I thought that was unfair until I thought about it. Like, with staff around, small boys, what was I doing putting temptation in their way?'

Isobel nodded. 'I think I like your housemaster.' Her eyes scanned my face. They were still worried. 'It's mitigation, OK, but . . .'

'I know, I know, no excuse, and I'd have been as po-faced as anyone ten years ago, but – everyone treats morality as just so simple. Perhaps it is, perhaps it should be, but the reality . . .'

I felt that I was fighting for my life beneath that quizzical statue's gaze. Thoughts were shooting like squibs about my brain. I tried to catch just one, to hold it down and analyse it. I reached into my breast pocket and tossed my wallet on to the table.

'There. You're walking along the street and you find that lying in the gutter. Is it so simple? Do you trust the police? Did your Sunday school make an impression on you? Are you rich or poor? Is the wallet a rich man's or a poor man's? Have you got family who could really use the cash? It's just a set of scales, really, isn't it? You've got a small child, you're broke, the wallet obviously belongs to a bloated plutocrat, you've no real religious conviction, the scales tilt one way. You believe in heaven, the wallet contains a family's weekly housekeeping, receipts from the supermarket, pictures of the kids, you've just backed a nice winner, the whole thing tilts in the other direction. So some guy comes up to me, says, "Just give this horse an easy race, you're ten grand richer." Sure, fuck it, I mean, I don't want to, but, you know, I can break my neck tomorrow. I'm getting on. There's Pol to be looked after. Shit, it's just sometimes the scales are all weighed in one direction. I think, "who does it hurt?" No one much. Not a major tragedy for anyone, so why not?'

Isobel spoke very clearly, emotionlessly. 'I understand.' She could have been one of those machines that tells you to fasten your seatbelts.

'Yeah, but . . .' I flapped my hands uselessly, then realized they had nowhere to go and allowed them to slap down on my thighs. 'It's the old thing, isn't it? He who rides a tiger cannot dismount. Is that right?'

65

Still her eyes were marbles. I stood and gathered up our glasses. I took them back to the bar and nodded once to the barman. He poured a large brandy for me, another glass of port for Isobel. He raised his eyebrows and nodded towards her. 'Nice,' he said.

I carried the drinks back to our table. I sighed as I sat. I felt old. 'No, you deal with the likes of Quinn, you're never going to be able to back off with outrage. It's a bit like, you know, so the guy screwed you when you were pissed and you'd never have done it sober, but now that you have, what the shit, you know, might as well do it again. It's sort of unconvincing really, you suddenly say. "How dare you? I am pure and virtuous," when last night you were willingly tied to the bedposts and doing things with frozen scampi. You kind of lose the moral high ground that way.'

'OK, Neil, OK,' Isobel halted me with an upraised hand. 'I said I understand. God knows, it happens everywhere, and like you say, this business . . .' She tossed back her hair and crossed her legs. Her stockings hissed. She did not like this new aspect of me, but she had taken it on board. 'But listen. This money – I mean, this is an accident. OK, worst comes to the worst, won't Quinn let you work it off?'

'Christ, how?' I gulped at my drink and shivered. 'Yes, in theory. But that many fixed races – I mean, reputation matters in this game. You're a bit sharp, sure, that's one thing. You're a known crook, though – who wants you on their animals? And believe it or not, it's not easy to hook a horse unobtrusively. But yes,' my shoulders slumped, 'yes. That's what I'll have to offer. That, or sell the house and pay him back from my share. If he'll wait that long. Plus interest. Oh, Jesus, love, he's not going to like me.'

'But when you explain . . .'

'I can't, goddamn it!' I heard my voice. I glanced quickly over my shoulders. The landlord was polishing glasses. The locals were all in a huddle. I shuffled forward and leaned on the table. I spoke softly. 'No, how can I? I say, well Katya took it – what happens? He puts pressure on Katya to get it back. Jesus, they can have her, but Polly's there. This man – I don't know – maybe it's all just mythology, but he certainly worked for Rachman, and you just have to meet him to know that he can be a nasty bit of work. Pretty rough associates. No. I'm just going to have to say, "Sorry. I blundered. Didn't dare tell you on the phone, but I thought . . ."'

I scrabbled for some convincing excuse. I could not find one. 'Oh, Jesus,' I closed my eyes and watched burning scraps of paper rising behind my eyelids. 'He is not going to like me. Christ, I'd not exactly be friendly with someone who did me out of eighty grand, and I don't go in for murdering people.'

Isobel too had leaned forward. Her hair touched my hand. Her lips moved just inches from mine. 'Can't you just raise a mortgage or – I don't know – go to family with your cap held out?'

'Nope and nope.' I waved to Scot Wiggin, a local landowner, as he left with his fat old springer. 'Nope to the mortgage because Katya won't let me. Nope to the family because all my relations – all those who have money – are tight, pompous arseholes.'

'Oh.' A conjuror's thread tugged at Isobel's mouth. She sighed. 'Well, look, what's Katya going to do with all this cash? She can't just blow that much. So why not tell Quinn the truth, say, "Look, I'm sorry, but feel free to threaten Katya, just don't hurt her, and, if really necessary, I'll pay by one means or another."'

I pushed back my chair. I clasped my hands together. I looked down at my jodhpur boots. They were scuffed and mud-mottled. A sort of low growl pushed up from my gut.

'No.' I shook my head. 'No. I'd like to, but I'll still not do it. I don't want that lump of shit going anywhere near my Polly. I don't even want him to know where she is. Once he's got that, he can hold it over me for ever. My weak spot. No, I'll talk to him, see what he wants. I've no bloody choice.' I tossed the drink back in one.

'Oh, *God*!' Isobel ground out the invocation in a strangled scream. She rapidly stood, slung her coat over her arm and shouldered her bag. 'I want to get out of here.'

'Hold on.' I called after her, but she swept on. The door closed behind her with a rattle.

I had to rush to the bar to pay the bill with much fumbling for pens and bank cards. When at last I reached the car park, it was raining hard. Isobel sat in the passenger seat, smeared by the squirming water on the window. She stared straight ahead.

Rain wormed under my collar. It flattened my hair, trickled down behind my ears, snagged my eyelids, smudged my vision. I had to stand in a puddle and knock on the window before Isobel unlocked the door. She straightened. She resumed her staring.

I climbed in beside her. The car rocked. I put my forearms on the steering wheel. I wanted very much that she should like me. I looked at her silhouette gilt by the light from the carriage lamps about the pub's front doors.

'Look, I'm sorry,' I said huskily. 'I can't undo it. I would if I could.'

'It's just . . .' she was a hesitant robot, 'I don't know if I can cope with this. It's just . . . It's too much, all this sordidness, all this money-grubbing, all this unpleasantness. OK, so it's not your fault, but it's the world you live in. I don't like it.'

'Oh, God,' I prayed. I bowed forward and rested my forehead on the steering wheel. 'Nor do I. Sport, glamour, fresh air, sporting glory, good, healthy stuff – you start wanting all that, and it just creeps up on you. End up like this. Like you start a marriage – all lilies and roses and choirs and champagne and hope, and suddenly it clouds over. Promises are broken. You've got sulks and emotional blackmail, battles for possession and supremacy, and you just sit there and wonder how it happened, how the foie gras turned to shit and the Krüg to piss. You'd have thought . . .' I shook my head. 'Oh, shit.' I turned the key. The engine, like a stubborn old man, made much of considering before assenting. The wipers swept up the diamonds.

'What?' Isobel's voice was a muffled drum.

68

'Oh, I don't fucking know,' I snarled. 'You'd have thought you'd learn with age, but you don't. There isn't that much age available. Jesus, I mean, what are we doing here?'

'Is this metaphysical speculation or do you mean *we?*'

'Yeah. Us. Christ's sakes, Katya was sweet and sexy and gentle once. Now look at her. Sweet? Sweet as a docker's armpit. Sexy? Sure. Sex for her means lying on one side with her legs clamped together and you just lie there behind her, she plays with herself, says "Stay still," goes off wherever she goes. Great. You feel like a device, something sold in a shop with no windows.'

'I don't want to know,' Isobel croaked.

'So here we are,' I stormed on, 'and you know, I'm attracted to you. You, for whatever reason, must think I'm an interesting specimen or you wouldn't be here. You're a friend. You're sexy and kind. I want to help you. I want you. Physically. And then what? Does it all turn to shit? Is that all we are? Complicated machines whose sole function is to turn good ingredients, nature's fucking riches, into turds?'

'I don't know.' Her voice was shaking now. 'But I've learned, even if you haven't . . .'

'Because if that's what it's all about – ownership, bloodsucking, stealing my time and every good thing I've got to give – I don't want it. I would like a travelling companion. I want to go to Greenland's icy mountain, she wants to go to India's coral shore, fine. We'll meet by the tide of Humber and not fucking complain. Just drop back into step and tell our tales. Is that so unrealistic?'

'Shut *up!*' Isobel hurled the words at the windscreen.

I shut up and struggled to regain control of my breathing – too much that had been confined had burst from me.

'You talk too bloody much, Neil,' Isobel was saying, and her voice shook. 'Listen,' she gulped, 'just listen. I – I spent six years, just like you, with someone who wanted to own me, to put me down, everything I tried to do. Blinded me with glamour. Married twice already, but I was nineteen, bloody silly, knew better than my parents. Stefano stole my

69

time, my pride, everything. I have my own life now and I don't want ever again to be held down or owned by anyone, do you understand? And for Christ's sakes stop being so sorry for yourself and so bloody vindictive. You're not perfect, Neil. Far from it. And don't go that way,' she yapped.

'What?' I braked. I turned to her. She looked wary. In the dull light, snails' trails gleamed on her cheek, her chin.

'Go on. Up to the farm.' She spoke fiercely.

'What?'

'Fuck it, just do it, will you?' She raised a hand to her forehead. Her fingers unfolded.

I shrugged and drove on up the road, up the dark and winding track. The trees at our right were bare beggars, clawing for sunlight. A barn owl arose from a post-and-rail fence and floated across the road, a curd of a bird.

Isobel spoke again. Now her voice was tremulous. 'Christ,' she sniffed, 'you don't think I'm going to share your marital bed with you, do you?'

I said 'Sorry,' and tried to appear cool. I think, though, that I put in a quick skip as I strode over to open the first gate.

We did not turn on the generator. I locked up. We clattered through the dark hall and through the study to the kitchen, where I found a hurricane lamp. The flame bowed and danced as it grew, and the walls closed in on us. Black shadows slid like scalpel blades across the floor and walls. The ceiling shuddered.

'Tea or something?'

'Yup. Good idea. Mind if I go up?'

'No, sure. Of course. Only be a second.'

I lit a candle on the table and handed it to her, and that was the only moment which was less than businesslike, less than matter-of-fact. There was something about the action, about our isolation in the flickering light, which recalled some ritual in which I had never participated. I stared at the rivulet pleats of her shirt, at the deep cavities in the flesh at

70

her throat, at the eyes which now were mere hollows. Her face was a golden skull, her hair mere darker darkness.

Screenwriters say 'beat', to indicate the passage of such time; one beat's rest; a heartbeat. Leave it to the actors to decide how long it should be.

So. Beat. Somewhere between a second and a century.

And then, 'Right. See you up there,' she said, and her hair dropped over her face like a clump of snow from the eaves. She turned away. Her skirt rustled as she padded, barefoot, I now realized, to the doorway and into the blackness beyond.

I put the kettle on the oil-fired stove. It spluttered and hissed. I just stood there, staring at that black doorway and wondering.

I was afraid.

I was afraid because I felt that a divinity or a devil was shaping my ends and I didn't know which. I could not believe my luck – oh, not at getting laid; so much was easy, even for a scarred, short-arsed old sod like me – at finding someone so lovely, so soon; someone, furthermore, with whom I felt entirely at ease. I had not known this before.

So much of our lives, I suppose, we display when wooing. You meet for the statutory dinner or theatre and your tail is spread and magnificent. I'm a doctor, I'm a lawyer, look at my suit, my tie, my friends, my eyes, my wallet. And she, I'm a floozy, I'm a banker, look at my frock, my legs, my tits, my eyes, my close connections with a former flatmate of the Princess of Wales, my witticisms, my maybes.

And thus arrayed, thus magnificent, we are invulnerable.

Me, now, I know that my armour is good. It is at once practical and decorative. It repels arrows poisoned by perception; it attracts, if not awe, at least smiles, appreciation and, in the right people, submission. Subtly chased with the tale of my ancestry, it is more luridly adorned with my personal triumphs and more charming sins. It speaks at once of status lightly borne and of gentleness barely concealed. I do not blame people for liking it. I made it. I like it a lot myself.

71

Then there is the inner coat of mail – intricate, impenetrable. This helps with the goodbyes, with treacherous friends and clinging lovers. It feels good to throw off the outer carapace. I can move more freely. I can feel the wind. You can like that too, if you will. Some do, some don't.

But Isobel had had time for neither. She was unimpressed by my racing triumphs. She had not even heard of my horses, my owners, my friends. She had seen me angry and melancholy, concussed and bitter, yet she wanted me.

For a moment, standing there in the kitchen, I found myself doubting my own perceptions. I saw her as glamorous, witty, capable, desirable. I might be wrong. Perhaps I had deceived myself through wishful thinking. Perhaps in fact she could not find a man more interesting that a stammering half-pint, striped-shirt City man who thought that manhood meant drunkenness and hands up skirts. Perhaps she was desperate. Perhaps she just slept around . . .

But no. She was what she seemed.

And that scared the hell out of me.

The gods had been incredibly kind to me in my time. They had also been savage. Surely if now they gave me what I had vainly searched for for years, it was merely to mock me by snatching it away.

I made tea.

I switched off the hurricane lamp and trudged almost wearily upstairs in darkness. Isobel lay beneath the duvet with her head propped up, her hair splashed over the pillow like the wind's breath on a relief map. Her eyes were closed. I laid the tea on the bedside table. I stretched and yawned, which was not, now that I think of it, polite.

'Come on, for God's sake,' she said without opening her eyes. 'I'm freezing.'

I nodded needlessly and went through into the bathroom. There was no toothpaste, but there was soap. I had a piss and washed as briskly as I could.

'*You know the greatest art in life?' my mother's voice, quoting some dispossessed Central European uncle, I think. 'Gratitude.*

*You look around you everyday – count your blessings – and say
"Thank you," and you'll never be unhappy. There is just so much
to be grateful for.'*

I pulled out the plug in the basin. I looked upward. I said,
'Thanks,' then I moved back into the bedroom. I sat on the
edge of the bed. I undressed with my back to Isobel. I slid
beneath the duvet. I ran a hand down her ribs, her flank and
she turned on to her side so that I could cocoon her. 'God,'
she shuddered, 'you're *cold*.'

I kissed the nape of her neck and her shoulders. I breathed
in the scent of her hair. I stroked and squeezed and again felt
disbelief. With all this to give, the girl must be demented. Her
skin was hot and smooth. She said 'Mmm,' and she turned to
me.

For a while, then, things went as these things do – kissing,
caressing, fondling, exploring, and everything at once familiar
and new in the darkness. Suddenly she kicked back the duvet.

'Come on,' she said, 'do it.'

'What?' I was startled.

'Fuck me. Come on. Hard.'

'I . . .'

'Fuck me,' she ordered again. 'Now. Come on. I want to
get it over with. Are you a man? I want it. Now. Hard. I want
to feel how you want me.'

Bemused but willing, I complied.

Isobel was repetitious. 'Oh, God.' She kissed my left pectoral
again and again. 'Oh, God, oh, God, oh God. That was good,
good, good!'

I kissed the top of her head. My left arm curled close about
her back which was now smooth and warm as *boudin*. The
candle had burned down and guttered in the last hour. Now
there were just two square blinds of dark purple where the
windows had been.

'What,' I sighed contentedly, 'was that all about?'

*'Like this,' she had said as she rolled over on to elbows and
knees, and 'no, against the wall,' and 'look at it, look at it!' though*

she could have seen nothing as she lay on her back, and held her legs high, and 'Oh, God, yes, we're doing it, so good, so good!' as the slurping and slapping increased in speed . . . I had never ridden a finish that hard.

'Mmm?' Her flat palm roamed about the sparse hairs on my chest. My ribcage still rose and fell. My heart thudded fast against her cheek.

'Well, all that "get it over with" stuff?'

Her voice was small now. 'Just that,' she said. 'I didn't want the preliminaries. I didn't want time to think. I just wanted to be . . .' I felt her shrug.

'Yes?' I teased.

'You know.'

'Oh, so suddenly we're all coy.'

'Yes, well. OK. It's true. You know I've been celibate for a year?'

'Really?'

'Yep. And before that, Stefano. Last two years, perhaps three times. He liked to sleep on the other side of the bed. He thought it was dirty.'

'Madonna complex,' I sighed. 'Goes for you 'cos you're tall and elegant and English Rose. Ideal. Only two sorts of women in his mind. Mother, who doesn't do such things, and whores. Must've got the shock of his life with you. Jesus.'

'Don't you like it?'

'What do you think?' I squeezed her.

'And, you know,' she mused, 'ten minutes max. I mean, slow and gentle is nice, but the seventies, all that mutual regard – I mean, am I really such a freak? Sometimes I just want . . . Well, a woman just likes . . . Well, I like . . . just hard, like that.' She worked her head into my shoulder and again kissed my chest with a loud 'Mmmah!' She flung herself on to her back and lay on my arm, staring up at the ceiling. 'God, I'd forgotten what it was like.'

'So you didn't take matters into your own hands during your year off?'

'No,' she shook her head. 'Just switched off.' She raised

74

herself on to one elbow. Her hair dropped on to my shoulder. Her fingernail drew DNA on my chest. 'Do you think . . . ?' she started.

There was a long, dark silence. My mind was bobbing, my body sinking deeper and deeper into the mattress. 'What?' I said at last.

'I don't know. I just can't believe it.'

'What's that?'

'It just feels so – I don't know – so right. Do you think . . . ? I don't know. Maybe I should go and find some more men, just check that I'm not conning myself. It's like with my flat. It was the first one I went to see and I just felt happy there. And everyone said, "Come on. No way will you find the right place first off." So I saw – what – twenty, thirty others, but I just kept coming back to Castle Road. I was just incredibly lucky, but too timorous to realize it. It can't happen again, can it?'

I pulled her towards me, felt her surprisingly full breast giving on my chest. She was warm. 'You'd better bloody believe it,' I mumbled in her ear. 'And no other men. Not if I have anything to do with it.'

She kissed my lips. Her mouth spread against mine in a smile. 'Really?'

'Well, how do you think I feel?' I propped myself up on my forearms and my eyes were just a foot from hers. 'Three aching years of feeling there must be something wrong with me because, try as I might, there was just gloom and anger and hatred. The worst loneliness in the world, that. And now . . .'

'But I'm not the first. Since Katya.'

'Nope,' I agreed, 'but . . .'

'You are. For me. Since Stefano. You believe me, don't you?'

I considered very briefly. Until an hour or two ago, I'd have sworn all lovers false. Perhaps, like an atheist in the trenches, I just needed to have faith in someone. Perhaps this girl, from whom I had been able to conceal nothing, actually merited my trust. Anyhow, I discovered, I'd sooner give than withhold it.

'Of course I do,' I shrugged. 'Why should you lie?'

'I did try it once, back in August.'

'Try?'

'Yup.' She was combing my hair with her fingers now. It felt good. 'Poor guy. Jamie, he was called. I daunted him. He fancied me at a distance, but it was all too much for him when we came to the nitty-gritty. Oh, maybe that's not fair.' Her head hit the pillow beside me. The pillow gasped. 'I think – you know, with Stefano, I mean he was a bully, made me feel that everything I did was trivial and stupid. The only weapon I had was sex – or rather, not letting him have it. Maybe I was a bit cold, from habit. I don't know.'

'Cold?' I laughed. I was still smarting from the heat of her. 'You? Jesus!'

'Oh, not with you. You sort of open up. You aren't proper or embarrassed or anything. You like to play, but . . .' She stretched and creaked. The sound built and burst in an explosion. 'Oh, hell. Do you think they're playing with us, Neil?'

'Who's that, darling?' I was drifting again.

'The gods. Are they giving us one another only to snatch us apart? Jolly good jape. Tee hee. Got that girl Dewing again.'

Her thoughts so precisely echoed mine that I had to turn and wrap my arms round her and hug her to me as though she might suddenly be swept overboard.

'No.' My voice shook my breastbone. 'Goddamn it, they'll not prise you from me.'

Then I thought of Daniel Quinn and a missing £80,000. My hand started working and I whispered, as though to drown the thought with sensation and incantation. 'Never, never, never, never . . .'

Thirty-six years told me to beware, but this time I was going to believe the fairy tale.

So light comes when the tunnel seems darkest, and you just have to hope that it is not an oncoming train.

I had just one weekend more in which to be happy. I knew it. I resolved to make the most of it.

Katya had rented a place far more suitable to her nature and her class than my mucky farm. She had taken a nice little half-timbered house in Datchet, not three hundred yards from the Thames.

Here lived DJs and television personalities and advertising executives. Here too lived women who sweated Youth Dew, whose flower arrangements consisted of two sprigs of blossom and a twisted bough and whose lawns and carpets were indistinguishable to the touch. They were the sort of people who knew about diet but did not like food, who burbled freely about freedom of speech for their televisions but would faint at a fart – the sort of people who met for a drink at the gym. There were a lot of hairdressers' salons and ethnic restaurants in the High Street.

Enough, Munrow. They were people.

It was just that I did not want my Polly growing up in such a place. I wanted her to know natural history, to run and to ride and to collect warm eggs. I wanted her to know stillness.

But Katya had decided, and the law said that Katya, because cloven not crested, had this right to ordain my baby's future.

I felt uncomfortable walking up that garden path overlooked by weigela and, on every side, by windows blinded by cataracts of net. I sort of shuffled and stamped on the doorstep for something to do. The bell sounded like an ice-cream van. Unsurprisingly, it was not Katya who answered it, but a dumpy adolescent girl who made a noise like a gang-bang with her gum. She slouched in the doorway.

'You'll be Mr Munrow,' she predicted.

'I am he.' I bowed.

'Ms Munrow says sorry, but she's 'ad to go out, but . . .'

And here she came at a gapelegged trot, her arms extended for balance, her eyes laughing but her lips pursed in fierce concentration – my darling, my life.

I sidestepped past the sloven. She shrugged and went 'cha-cha-cha'. I dropped on to one knee, and Polly came into my arms.

Oh, shit, I know. I too have seen it a thousand times in Canadian made-for-TV movies. I too have thought, 'Yuk,' and, 'come on, leave it out,' and other such tasteful, world-weary dismissals, but that was before this beautiful little monster ripped my heart from me.

On seeing those bright, grey-green eyes, on hearing her say without surprise, 'Daddy,' on feeling the warmth of her plush cheek against mine, those little legs scrambling for a foothold on my thighs, the passion and protectiveness which welled inside quite simply threatened to choke me.

I hugged her close, stood with her, swung her around, kissed her ears, her eyes, her lips, her wispy swirls of dark hair, and I realized that all this time I had been wandering around with an open, aching scar. She made me whole again.

When I looked up, I had to blink a lot, and my voice was rough. 'Right. So, where's her bag, then?'

The sloven shrugged again. Her corn-sack tits arose for a moment as high as her navel. She pointed. 'Right,' I said again, and kissed my Polly and she – oh, little things for little minds – kissed me back and said, 'Daddy' and worked her crown into my neck as though to burrow a cosy niche there.

'Right. We'll be off, then. Back at five o'clock tomorrow.'

'Yeah,' cha-cha-cha. 'She asked me speshly to say five o'clock. No later, if that's all right.'

Even this superfluous, presumptuous message could not rile me. Not now. I bent to pick up the canvas bag of clothes and nappies. I turned and left without another word.

Drivers heading westward on the M4 that day were lucky to escape injury. Polly said 'Rabby,' and I must sing another chorus of 'Run, Rabbit, Run', or 'din-don,' and it was '*Frère Jacques*', or 'Pony' and it was 'Yankee Doodle'. She rocked her head in time to my cracked and husky singing. And then, 'Whassa?' she would say, and I must swivel round to see where she pointed. 'That's the church,' I would tell her, and she would nod as if I had merely confirmed her suspicions in the matter. 'Cher,' she would say. Or I would say, 'Those are horses, darling,' and she would break the news to me, 'Daddy *ride* horses.'

One way or another, I must have spent half that journey looking backward.

We drew up outside Fox Farm just after twelve-thirty. I pulled Polly from the baby-seat and hoisted her high. She pointed at Bossy. 'Bossy horse!' she cheered, and clip-clopped with her tongue. 'Daddy house,' she pointed solemnly. 'Where Polly's car?'

Polly was still too short to propel her little plastic car, so I had to push it for long distances while she practised to be a road hog, calling out 'beep-beep' and 'broom broom'.

'After lunch, darling,' I told her, and the wind lifted her hair from off her brow. 'First we have some lunch, then you have a little sleep, then we'll go out in Polly's car and see the animals, OK?'

'OK,' she was obliging. 'I want food.'

Bracken licked her feet and she giggled as I carried her in through the back door. I sat her down as we entered the kitchen. Isobel sat reading *The Times* at the pitch-pine table. 'There,' I said. 'Polly, this is Isobel.' 'Hi, kiddo,' Isobel winked. She turned back to the paper. 'She looks like you,' she mused.

Polly stood still for a few seconds. She studied Isobel fiercely. She frowned. 'Go 'way!' she ordered.

'No, Polly!' I laughed. 'That's not very nice, is it?'

She turned and clutched my knees. She hid her head beneath my crotch.

'Leave her be,' Isobel said calmly. She turned a page. 'She's not a people-pleaser. Good. She'll look at me, make up her own mind, get used to me. Buggered if I'll woo her. She'll come to me in her own sweet time. Cottage-pie in the oven.'

Isobel was right. Slowly, and with almost regal condescension, Polly came to suffer Isobel to pick her up, cut up her food, even, on one occasion, to change her nappy. Having been without me for six week, she was jealous of my every movement and would cry if I left the room. We went to see the animals at Longleat, however, and Polly allowed me to take her one hand and Isobel the other so that we could swing her. Isobel jumped up to a grazing giraffe which raised its head and clouted her hard on the jaw. Polly found this hysterically funny. So, I admit with shame, did I. It took Isobel a little longer.

Polly came into our bed at six o'clock the following morning, and on the Sunday afternoon, as the three of us sat on the sofa watching *Lady and the Tramp*, Isobel caught my eye and grinned; so I reached across Polly to kiss her. Polly looked up contentedly and hit Isobel's bruised jaw. 'No,' she said, 'go 'way, Isobel,' then she chortled at her own joke and nestled further down between us.

So I kissed her. And I kissed Isobel some more, too.

Katya was 'out' again when I dropped Polly off on Sunday evening. I drove straight from the sloven's 'ta ra, then,' to a chrome and copper pub up the road where I slapped my tonsils hard with whisky. I slammed the glass down on the bar, climbed back into the car and returned to a double yellow line just across the road from Katya's house.

I lit a cigarette and played scales on the steering wheel.

It was ten minutes before the trug-mouldie slouched from the house as though downhill. I watched her buttocks chomping denim as she plodded down the street. I waited until she turned the corner, then I climbed from the car. Once more I unlatched the gate.

Katya had not seen me coming. So much was obvious from the undisguised rustling and banging after the doorbell had shrilled, the coy coo of 'Wait there, darling!', the promptness with which her little blonde-topped form appeared in the frosted glass of the door.

She was almost smiling as she opened the door, but the smile congealed and decomposed, high-speed. The dark eyes narrowed. 'Oh,' she said, 'it's you. Yes?'

'Look, Kati. Sorry to bother you.' I spoke quickly as if the flood of words might prevent the door from closing. 'I just wanted a quick word. I hoped you were in.'

'Yes, well.'

'What?'

'Yes, well, I'm in, aren't I? As you see. Come along then. Let's get this over with. Polly needs her bath.' She stepped off the doorstep and pulled the door to behind her. 'So. Right.'

I swallowed a bit. I wanted to spit but must conciliate. I had not prepared a speech. 'Well, obviously . . . It's about this money. At Slaughters'.'

'Well, that's simple. The answer's no. Is that it? Right, then,' she half-turned, 'thank you, Neil.'

'No, listen.' I reached out a hand towards her shoulder, but thought better of it. I raised the hand to cover my heart instead. 'No. You don't understand, love. That simply isn't my money. You remember Quinn? Dan Quinn? It's his money. He just used my account – our account – as a sort of . . . he just lodged it there, temporarily. He never meant to pay me that sort of sum.'

'Are you sure?' Her smiling mouth was in quotes. 'How interesting. How very, very interesting. So Dan never intended to pay you. How interesting. No, no. Please. I think this is really fascinating, Neil. So you're quite sure that no money was paid to you?'

'Well, yes,' I admitted, 'like I told you. Eighteen grand. I offered you that.'

'You're full of generous offers, aren't you, Neil? I'm overwhelmed. No. Come on, Neil. I do know you, you know. I do know you. There. No. I think that's enough. You can't try it on with me. That money was paid into our account. You owe me that much. It's all very simple, really, and I must get back to Polly. Of course, if you want to distress her by making a scene, I can't stop you, but I warn you, I will call the police. Now. Thank you. Good.'

She strutted on to the doorstep, pushed open the door and cried 'Coming, darling!'

'Katya . . .' I almost whimpered, '*please*. This means real trouble, real danger . . .'

'Don't over-dramatize, Neil,' she hummed. 'It's very undignified and very boring. Now.'

'Kati . . .'

But she turned her head and nodded once like royalty acknowledging a joke from the crowd. 'I must get back to my child,' she said, and pushed the door back behind her. 'Hello, darling!' she sang for my benefit, not for Polly's. 'I am sorry.'

Through the frosted glass, I saw her blonde head dropping, and little arms arising to clasp her.

'*My child* . . .' Glass is thin, transparent and frangible. I have never hated a substance so much. I would not now see Polly until she came to stay for four days just after Christmas.

The good times were done. There was battle ahead.

My mother, Lady Sylvia Vane Stradling Demoubray-Stirling, only daughter of Gawain, 14th Duke of Galloway, ran off with the groom, or so the Demoubray-Stirlings would have it. In fact, she chose to marry the son of her father's factor. Certainly the young Iain Munrow helped in the ducal stables when a boy and must have ridden to hounds with tan rather than champagne boot-tops. By the time that he married my mother, however, he had risen to the rank of captain in a good Scottish cavalry regiment, ridden for Britain in the 1948 Olympics and won the Foxhunters' twice and the Grand National once. He was already acknowledged to be the finest steeplechase rider of his generation when my mother, having rejected many a nobler, limper hand, took his.

He was an exceptionally good-looking man with more than a touch of the Galloways in his features. Blood, however, proved thinner than the ink on birth certificates. That my mother was, perhaps, marrying a distant cousin did nothing to endear him to her legitimate family.

Twenty years earlier, such a union would have been unthinkable, twenty years later, unremarkable, but at that time, it was just possible (my mother renewed her acquaintance with him during the war while working in London for SSAFA), yet sufficiently unconventional to affront the stuffed shirts.

And my grandfather, alas, had a shirt to mock Jane Russell's.

The Galloways were not always thus. The early dukes had fun, in a recherché sort of way. Attainder, execution, massacre, battle, cattle-raids, the pox and surfeits various accounted for the high turnover of the Dukedom's incumbents.

Gawain Galloway, however, was rich, mean, unsporting and humourless. He regarded my mother's marriage as a betrayal. He, and his son Douglas, disowned, disinherited and disdained her.

She did not care, or not, at least, very much. What she had not banked on were the inevitable corollaries of my father's passionate and courageous nature. 'He loved life' – it is too often said of those who love only life's bonbons or selected highlights. My father loved the lot – the slattern as well as the lady, the villain as well as the lord, the blood and mud as well as the white damask and linen, the ale as well as the claret. He was damned if he'd miss a minute of the game.

And when the game grew tawdry, when war was done and the turf became, like tennis, a mere business, when eccentricity was proscribed and lust called sin, he pepped the game up for himself. He organized coups. There were mistresses, there was gambling. And there was drink.

He was not, God bless him, an unhappy sot. In the daytime, he was a gentle and exuberant man, an enthusiastic teacher and a sportsman. At night, he simply stewed himself. Dinner-guests at our house in Lambourn were well used to it. He would sit in his armchair, often with his lame hedgehog in his lap, and announce, 'Everyone is to have a good time. Drop the latch on your way out, will you?' He would then pour and down two enormous tumblers full of whisky and, like Socrates, talk volubly until the poison hit. A stroke pole-axed him in the paddock at Goodwood when I was sixteen.

And that left me to carry on the family's cavalier traditions.

I wasn't making too good a job of it.

*

There was a moment, early on that Monday morning, when I thought that perhaps there would be no racing, not that cancellation would have done me much good. The light from the window was shrieking white, but when I leaped from the bed and pulled back the curtains, it was to find the fleshly furls and folds of the valley encrusted with rime, not fat with snow. The frost would fade.

I turned back to the bed as if to report to Isobel, but both sides of the duvet were flung back in plump lapels. She had left in the early hours, a blur which had drifted briefly towards me in the bruise-black of daybreak. Her lips had been cold on mine. 'I've got to be off,' she had whispered. I had rolled over to cling her hand to my breast, to nuzzle into hers.

'No, darling.' She had kissed my ear and gently pulled free. 'Thank you for a wonderful weekend, and look after yourself today. Let me know how things go, OK? Love you.'

There was a hole in the air where her warmth and her scent had been. I lay there, slowly surfacing from sleep, as her heels clicked downstairs, as doors quietly opened and closed, as her car gave an embarrassed cough before consenting to sing. It sang like Leonard Cohen.

And I was alone in the house on the hill.

So I had lain there like the condemned man, watching the light come up in the sky, while breezes sped purring over the garden like a fleet of Rolls Royces.

I wanted to be up and on my way early. I had no very good reason. I was just happier moving than still.

In the twilit bathroom, in a bath which smelled of bluebells (I smiled to see that Isobel had left the bottles), I tried to read a Nigel Balchin which I had found downstairs. My eyes scanned whole paragraphs like blocks of colour. My mind could comprehend just the tone of each, not its constituent elements.

I washed and shaved quickly. I pasted on the Clarins moisturizer – and if that makes me a nancy-boy, well and good, but I spend my days wind-whipped and have no desire to look like a camel's scrotum by the age of fifty. Many's the conversation I've heard in the jockey's weighing-room about the relative merits of Guerlain, Clarins and Decleor, and Max Gordon, the formula-one driver, swears by Guerlain, so yahboo to the macho Tarzan of the typing-pool.

I dressed fast in jeans, polo neck (grey cashmere, a Christmas present from Katya) and leather jerkin. Downstairs, I made coffee and tried to stop my fingers from drumming and my feet from dancing an ungainly puppet's jig. To step outside was like diving into a hill loch fed by wriggling icy streams. It was good then, like a cigarette after a swim, like silence after disco, to walk down to the yard and into Bossy's box, to feel the heat and the slickness of him, to smell that rich, sweet, clean cocktail of equine dung and piss and sweat and hay.

Perfectionism is consoling. In forking every last strand of wet straw into the barrow, banking the remainder about the edges of the floor, sweeping thoroughly, tossing the fresh straw and reconstructing the banks, I found the sort of contentment which makes craftsmen smiling men. I forgot for a moment about the day to come; here, at least, I was in control. I could make things good.

I didn't seem to be very effective at that out there.

When at last I leaned on the pitchfork and surveyed my work with a happy grin, the fear of what the day would bring flooded back. My stomach keened at me like a fretful dog. My rectum twitched. They did not want to be involved. They fancied that they might get hurt.

They were right.

I had thought that I might go through the charade – drive up to London, call in on Slaughters', ask for the money, express dismay at finding it gone, then drive back with expostulations of innocent bemusement.

The thought had been tossed aside, barely used. I would never win an Oscar. I had learned that at Steward's Enquiries.

'Ah, thought as I'd be findin' you down 'ere.' The voice behind me was deep. The rumbling West Country brogue curled like a woolly caterpillar. I was the sort of voice you'd like to hear in fever or hysteria. It warmed and soothed.

'Hello, mate,' I said before turning to see Dave Wonnacott's tall, lean form, fuzzy at the edges against the sky.

'Uncle' Dave was the senior member of the jockeys' brotherhood. With his tinsel hair and castellated teeth and a face much crosshatched with wrinkles, Dave was the natural confidant, adviser and consoler of young jocks in their losses in races and in love. The arm on which he rested his weight on the doorframe, the legs, one straight, one bent, seemed mere spaghetti. Dave was rumoured to live on a single Cornish pasty and a glass of cider a day. When I saw him, I always thought of the clichés about wire and whipcord.

'I gave you a call,' he said.

'Yeah, sorry. Lot on my plate.'

'Why I called. Just wondered how you was keepin'?'

'Thanks, Uncle.' I smiled, as ever warmed by his kindness. 'No, I'm fine. Bit shaken that first night. Otherwise great.'

'You sure, now?'

'Sure I'm sure. Why?'

'Oh, I dunno.' Dave stepped into the box and looked about him. 'Lovely job. Make a good lad, you would. No, I just had a feeling, that's all. Silly, but you know, you here all on your own, and me just down the road. Laura was worried, too. You know her.'

I knew Laura. Dave's wife was pretty and round and reliable as a Morris Minor. She believed that food solved all problems and gentian violet all injuries. She thought racing silly, but men were like that.

'See you're back today,' Dave crooned. 'In the saddle, I mean.'

'Yup. No chance of a result, but.'

'Always a chance of a result,' Dave said, from habit, I think. 'Anyhow, a fee earned is bread and butter on the table. A winner is jam. Can live without jam.'

'Uh, uh,' I told him. 'Errant wives live on Tiptree's best. The bread and butter they take for granted.'

'Ah, little Kati'll be all right, don't you worry. She's just all worked up and unnecessary, you know, like a filly's had a scare, squeakin' and squirtin'. She'll calm down.'

'You reckon?'

'Sure. sure. Don't you worry. And Neil . . . Word of advice, that's all, and don't take me wrong, but, you know, there's all sorts of bitterness and nastiness at the moment, but it doesn't help if you shoot your mouth off, slag off Kati, all that. It'll get her riled for one, and – well . . .'

'It's unattractive,' I supplied. 'Yeah, don't worry, Uncle.' I laid a hand on his upper arm and together we walked out into the yard. 'You're right. And things have improved this last weekend. It's strange. I'm not so tied up in it all, so full-time obsessed. Just a couple of problems to get out of the way and I can look to the future.'

'Good, good,' Dave nodded. He inhaled deep and released all that cold air with a satisfied sound like a man who has at last found a bush in the desert. 'And a very nice girl I'm sure she is. Laura'll be pleased. Tell you what. Why don't you both come to dinner next Saturday, let Laura give her the once over?'

We drank coffee in the kitchen. I watched the clock above his head. The hands did what clock-hands must, for all my telekinetic concentration.

And so I thanked him again and we parted and I locked up, wished Bracken farewell and climbed into the Shogun.

As I coasted the rise, I turned back for a last look at the house which had held my dreams and ambitions for the past year. For a moment, it crossed my mind that I might never return, but I looked at Bossy, at the staggering post-and-rails fence, at the tiny village smoking way below, and I told myself not to be so bloody ridiculous.

This was England. This was the twentieth century.

God help me.

I was still telling myself that it was the twentieth century, and finding precious little consolation in the thought, when I reached the racecourse. On the road above, I crouched low in my seat to scan the car park.

The police were already here at the exits and entrances.

Their motorbikes slouched at the diagonal. I recognized a few jockeys' cars on the scuffed and furrowed grass. Otherwise, there were just kennel-coated attendants, swinging their arms and stamping out the cold.

The lights changed. I turned my attention back to the road. Only then did I notice my nearside neighbour.

It was a perfect cartoon double-take. A tanned face and a buttoned beige glove happened to my eyes. I let out the brake and eased forward, my gaze now fastened on the rear lights of the frozen-food van ahead.

Then I saw and my stomach gulped and my head jerked sideways.

Quinn was not ten feet from me. His window was open. His gloved fingers slowly strummed on the chrome of the window-frame. His thin lips undulated. He nodded as though listening.

I faced front fast and tried to look unconcerned.

I had also seen the man in the passenger seat. That too did more for my digestion than a bowl of bran.

There was no reason why Keith Gurdon should not be there; he was an ex-jockey. I was pretty sure that he had ridden for Quinn in days gone by. Quinn was just being nice, giving the old chap a day out for old times' sake.

And Robert Maxwell was on a sponsored swim for his pensioners.

Keith Gurdon should have made me feel good. There, but for the grace of God, I could not go.

Keith had started out brilliantly, a good-looking West Midlands boy with strength, intelligence and a phenomenal sense of timing. This was – what? – some ten years before I rode my first race. Then a whole load of things must have happened at the same time. He got famous, he got laid, he got pissed and he got greedy.

First, he left Dick Lennox, the trainer on whose back he had risen. Giles Bowles, a gross, drooling ex-trainer, took the young Gurdon under his wing, and, it was rumoured, into his bed. Bowles told Gurdon that he was too good for a retainer. Bowles would act as his agent instead, pick his rides for him, manage his affairs. Like many a rock-star, Keith believed his press and went it alone.

He had never been popular in the changing-room. Now, as a cocky little scavenger of the best rides, he was cordially hated. On the track, he was squeezed out, jostled and turned over. Off the track, like many a pretty boy before him, he was taunted and teased. Much was made of his relationship with the disgusting Bowles.

Keith's physical strength saw many an attacker, on and off course, looking stupid, and, had he been blessed with good humour, he might in time have triumphed, but Keith was mean-spirited and petulant. He responded in his own ways.

He became a criminally dangerous rider, thinking nothing of cutting the legs from under you or putting you through the wings just for the hell of it. He drank too much, and he had to prove himself a ladies' man. He pawed owners' wives and daughters. Sometimes, no doubt, he got lucky. More often, he got his. He impregnated Sir Austyn Edgerley's sixteen-year-old daughter. Edgerley, a former amateur champion with a taste for theatricals, very publicly and permanently added interesting angles to Keith's formerly boringly perfect nose and jaw.

So he drank, and was hated, and didn't get the rides. When I first met him, Keith was bitter and, quite literally, twisted. A mare had finished Edgerley's work for him. His face now appeared to be tugged to the left side. His nose turned to the left; the skin over his cheeks was tight to the left; his sneers and his smiles were all, literally and figuratively, sinister. He looked as though he went everywhere with a plate of glass pressed against that side. He was already wrinkled, then, but then, as now, his hair was an incongruous yellow, the yellow of urine-stained sheets.

Keith sat alone in the changing-room. Jockeys' language is not renowned for its refinement, but Keith's made even us hardened oath-swearers wince.

There is a nervous disease called coprolalia, or shit-speaking. Its sufferers suddenly and for no apparent reason start spitting out obscenities. My mother's gardener's one-eyed wife was one such. 'Oh, I can never resist a pastry bugger shit fuck one lump or two?' she once trilled over the tea-table.

Keith Gurdon had consciously developed coprolalia. He shit-spoke diarrhoetically.

His sinister sneers were evident. His sinister smiles you saw only when he attempted what was now his principal rôle: that of corrupter. He it was that first suggested I should stop a favourite. I, a rookie, laughed in his face. He it was that drooled to me about the women he had had, the joys which awaited me should I yield. He put me off sex for a week. So I, on the up and up, rapidly joined the brotherhood that regarded Keith in much the same light as an unexpected nasty smell – something unpleasant to be ignored or shooed away.

At the end, I almost felt sorry for him, this sorry, ugly, disillusioned little man who so recently had been the brilliant, strutting cock-of-the-roost. He had developed the shakes, I noticed, and was frequently to be seen sitting wet-eyed and trembling in the corner, dribbling filth to himself.

The end came at Stratford, at an open-ditch which, to my terror, Keith did not seem to see. He was length and a half ahead of me, and sagging and rolling in the saddle on a washy chestnut. El Cid in his last battle must have looked more vital. Keith would not have scared a pony-club camp.

The horse hit the fence. Keith flew, with not a flap of the hands, a kick or a curse. I lost sight of him as I put my mount right, got him to put in a short one, took the fence sedately – and there, beneath us, was Keith, staring upward entranced, his toothless gums bare and gleaming.

Horses are good at avoiding bodies, but mine never had a chance. He hit Keith as he landed, he stumbled, and for a moment we were all tangled up with Keith as he rolled and flailed beneath us. Then we were clear. We had taken Keith a good three yards with us.

That little ride cost him six broken ribs, a punctured lung and a kidney nigh pulverized.

90

To add insult to injury, I won the race.

So Keith hung up his boots and was seen no more, and the turf grieved not. I knew nothing of his antics since, nor had any desire to do so. I shuddered to think of the employer who would find his CV or his interview technique appealing.

But here he was again, still yellow-haired, still leering, and with Quinn.

I steered the car through the gate and over the turf to the rear of the car park. I parked next to Tony Pennington's sponsored Rover. It was empty, but it was as near to company as I could find.

Quinn's XJS drew up at my off-side.

I unsnapped the seatbelt and climbed out. I stretched a bit. I strolled round to the boot to pull out my coat. Keith's door was the first to open.

'Well, hello.' His voice was thin as a cat's.

I looked up. 'Hello, Keith,' I smiled. I straightened and held out a hand. 'Long time. How's it going?'

'Oh, all right,' Keith swaggered. He wore a puce nylon blouson, a check shirt, grey Terylene trousers. He took my hand, let me feel his strength. His skin was suede. 'All right. Miss this fucking business, but still, yeah, doing OK.'

'Good, good. Good to see you.' I watched Quinn's silvery curls arising above the car. I did not like the speed and smoothness with which he moved. I did not like his height. I did not like the breadth of his shoulders or the crispness of his red-and-white-striped shirt, which he was covering with a jacket against the December chill.

'Neil!' Quinn cooed. I nearly did. He strode round the car, that big brown hand extended. 'Thank you for being so punctual.'

I kept the smile painted on my face. I nodded. If I'd been a dog, I'd have rolled over on my back with my legs in the air. Out of the corner of my eye, I saw Keith hunch his shoulders. The nylon of his blouson swished.

'So,' Quinn said. He rubbed his hands together. 'Bloody cold, isn't it? Right. I am sorry about all this. Still.'

I found myself wiping off his handshake on the seat of my trousers. 'Um,' I said. 'Um, Keith knows about all this?'

'Oh, yes. Don't worry. Keith is privy to my every thought, eh, Keith?' Quinn's glance was conspiratorial. Keith's would have scared a gargoyle. 'So.'

I wished that he would stop saying 'so'. There did not seem to be much in the way of cogent small talk in answer to 'so'. I took a deep breath. 'Right. Yes. Listen. We've got a problem, I'm afraid.'

'Problem?' Quinn's eyebrows jumped. 'Oh, dear. Bank being troublesome?'

'No, no,' I shuffled back a few inches. 'No, but . . . I mean, I didn't know that that money wasn't mine, and – well, it's not there any more.'

I glanced quickly all about me. The police still chatted at the gateway, three hundred yards away. A car-park attendant was my nearest neighbour, but he was a good hundred yards off, and holding a steaming polystyrene mug in one mittened hand while beckoning a car with the other. I looked back at Quinn.

'Not there?' he was saying, and his words were flattened by a DJ smile. 'Come on, Neil. You're having us on.'

'Er, no.' I shrugged. 'It's – gone.'

'Ah, fuck it, Munrow,' Keith miaowed. 'What are you fucking us about for, eh? You've got the fucking dough. Give it to Mr Quinn, fuck's sake. Don't mess about.'

'I can't.' I shook my head sadly. 'I'm trying to get it back, but – it's gone.'

'You're not trying to tell us that you spent it, are you, Neil?' Quinn frowned.

'I . . .' I could not involve Polly or Katya, so I struggled for the right word. It was there, all the time, right beneath my nose. It came out simply. 'Yes.'

'Well, that's all right.' Quinn's teeth were gritted, but still he smiled. 'I must say, I can't see quite how you should mistake my money for yours, but OK. Perhaps you're used to receiving mysterious payments of eighty thousand pounds. How these modern jockeys live, eh, Keith?'

'Yeah.'

'Not like your day, eh?'

'Nah.'

'Still, there we are. Neil just happens to receive such payments regularly, so he didn't notice . . .'

'No, I . . .' I started.

Quinn swept on. 'So he's bought something. Well, that's not too bad. It can be sold, can't it? Maybe make a small loss, but we've got eighteen thousand leeway, haven't we? Have to come out of my little present, Neil, but then, I think you'll have to admit, it is your mistake. So, what was it? Let me guess. A Sung vase? I wouldn't blame you. I love Sung. A little Gainsborough? Never know. Might keep it myself. A horse? Or a house. Is that it? A little hideaway somewhere. Somewhere you can take your charming little daughter. Polly, isn't it?'

'No!' I rapped, then, 'Yes. Yes, but no, no I haven't bought anything. I mean, I own my house, and that's worth – what? I mean, I bought it for a hundred and twenty thousand and I've done a lot of work, but . . .'

'Yes?' Quinn prompted.

'Well, I'm not allowed to sell it or mortgage it or anything until Katya's share is determined . . . But I should . . . I mean, whatever happens, I should get sixty, maybe seventy out of it . . .'

'Neil, Neil, Neil,' Quinn sighed. He shook his head like a parent watching a child making the same mistake for the millionth time. 'That will take time and time is money. No, no. This will not do. So you're telling me that – what? In three or four days you have simply spent eighty grand, is that it? Just frittered it away? Nothing to show for it? That's what you're asking us to believe?'

His voice was rising now. Crimson swarmed up his neck. His mouth was a trap which had snapped shut. He gazed down at me with loathing. He repeated, 'Is that what you're asking us to believe, Neil?'

'Is it?' Keith stepped closer. I could see the blackheads

93

which clogged the wide pores of his cheeks, the oyster flesh which lined his sagging eyelids. I could smell his sweat and the tobacco on his breath. 'Come on, Neil. Tell us.'

'No,' I said, and my arms sort of rose and fell in a fledgling flap. 'Well, yes, sort of.'

Quinn's fleshy cheeks shook. He breathed in through his teeth with a hiss. A leaf skittered up his nicely tailored grey tweed trouser-leg. He closed his eyes for a second, then this shoulders slumped. 'Neil,' he said equably, 'you are going to have to do better than that. It seems to me that you have come here to tell me that you intend to steal from me. I can't be right, can I? You wouldn't be thinking along those lines, would you?'

'Better not,' Keith snarled. He reached forward and pushed the knot of my tie sharply tighter. 'Better fucking not.'

'No, indeed. You had better not,' Quinn shot his cuffs. 'Do you know how much eighty thousand is, Neil? In – shall we say? – *real* terms? Do you? Do you know, for example, how much it costs to have someone topped? Two thousand on the cheap, ten maximum for a pro who won't squeal. Eight lives, we are talking, Neil. Eight human lives. So. We weren't thinking of stealing from me, were we?'

'No . . .'

'No, because that would not be wise, not with a small daughter, not wise at all. So, what are you saying, Neil, hmm?'

'I was thinking – look, I can sell the house, in time,' I pleaded, 'and in the meantime, I thought, I mean, perhaps I could do some work for you. Some races. I mean, you have a good punt . . .'

'Eight lives' worth of work, Neil?' Quinn looked startled.

'Just . . . Oh, shit. I don't know. Whatever it takes.'

'Whatever it takes,' Quinn repeated slowly. 'Whatever – it – takes.' He nodded to Keith. 'That's a lot of work for a jockey, wouldn't you say, Keith?'

'Too fucking right,' Keith ran a hand down my left cheek. 'Too bleeding right.'

A Rolls pulled up on the other side of Quinn's car. Quinn did not even turn. 'Well,' he said, 'I think something might be arranged, don't you, Keith? Eight lives worth of work, but I'm sure you can do it. Oh, and by the way, Neil, just in case you were thinking of being clever, please remember this. That money, *my* money, was paid in by one Trevor Verulam.'

'I know.'

'Yes, but do you know who Mr Verulam is?'

'No,' I almost whimpered, and a shudder corkscrewed through me.

'He's a notorious race-fixer. South African, as it happens, and a warned-off person. You will, of course, be aware that a person warned off in South Africa or anywhere else is not permitted to have dealing with trainers or jockeys anywhere in the world? The information, therefore, that you are in receipt of large sums from such a person would unquestionably end your career as a jockey and as a trainer.'

I nodded wearily. I might have expected as much.

The Quinns of this world cover their risks. He had very thoroughly set me up.

There would be no running to the police or to the Jockey Club, complaining of coercion. Eighty thousand pounds from a disqualified person had been withdrawn from my account. My livelihood would be snatched from me before the authorities had stopped laughing.

'So,' Quinn said again. I liked it no more than I did five minutes ago. He walked to the boot of his car and reached in. He shrugged on his camelhair overcoat. 'I think that we can make some sort of deal, Neil, despite everything.' He slung his Zeiss binoculars over one shoulder. He slammed the boot down. He ran his fingers twice through his hair and turned back to me, now every inch the man of substance once more. 'Keith,' he said, though his eyes were on me. 'Give Neil his present, would you? Welcome aboard, Neil.'

He tossed Keith the car keys and turned away. I watched him go. Leaning forward as if into a stiff wind, he strode towards the stands. Halfway across the car park, he was hailed by someone dispensing champagne from the boot of a Continental convertible. He veered and joined his friends, his hand outstretched as it had been to me.

'Well now,' Keith said, 'here we are.'

I thought this remark unnecessary.

'I've been looking forward to seeing you again, Munrow.' Keith shoved both hands hard down into his blouson pockets. 'Cocky little Neil fucking Munrow, eh? Young fucking champion and so fucking high and holier than fucking thou. Look at you now, eh? Oh, God, it warms my fucking heart, it does, to see you begging for mercy, offering to do anything, no matter how bent, just so's the nice Mr Quinn'll leave you alone. Fucking lovely. Saint Munrow. Joined us poor bloody sinners now and no mistake.'

'Get on with it, Keith,' I sighed, 'I'm riding today.'

'Oh, yeah, you're riding, of course. Mister Munrow is riding. Mustn't get in the way of that. Little fucking shit!' he suddenly spat, and his upper lip curled upward. 'Just because we're a duke's grandson, all that, good education, lah-di-fuckin'-dah. Not very impressive now, are we? All right. Lord Munrow is riding. All right. Here.' From his right-hand pocket, he pulled a small box. 'Present,' he said. He thrust the box into my hand and stood back with a smirk.

I looked down. The box was of black velvet. A jeweller's box. I frowned. I opened it slowly as if it might explode.

It contained a gold signet ring.

'I think you'll find it a perfect fit,' Keith twanged at my shoulder. 'And Mr Quinn says you wear if full-time or else. Ever see you without it, there's eighty fucking grand to be called in, right off. His way of reminding you you're his, that's all.'

I pulled the ring from its slot and examined the motif. It was a large Q. A rat crouched in its centre. Its tail formed the letter's tail.

'He must be fucking crazy,' I snapped, 'if he thinks I'm wearing that . . .'

I raised my right hand to throw the damned thing away, but Keith grasped my wrist. God, but his reflexes were quick.

'I wouldn't,' he sneered. His face was just inches from mine, the smell of his breath sweet and strong. 'Remember what he said about your little baby girl and all? You're his animal, Munrow, his fucking animal, get it? You wear this or the deal's off. Gives him a good feeling, see? Quinn's rat. Nice idea. That way you never forget. Eighty fucking grand and your family. I think it's worth it, don't you?'

He had pulled my arm down as he backed. I unfolded my fingers and looked down at the symbol of slavery. Every ounce of my arrogant nature, every hour of my upbringing, every least element of my beliefs, told me to fling the filthy ring away from me.

But I had a debt to pay. I pulled my family signet – a leopard on a sheaf of straw – off my little finger. I replaced it with Quinn's mocking brand. As Keith had predicted, it fitted perfectly.

'There,' Keith grinned, 'not so hard, eh?'

'No, Keith,' I closed my eyes as I put the old ring into my jacket pocket. He would never know.

'Nah. And here,' Keith took my right arm, 'just to make sure.'

He led me to the XJS. He climbed into the passenger seat. He was holding the ring between his index finger and his thumb.

I cannot believe it, but I just stood there as he smiled his smeared smile, reached for the handle and, still gripping the tip of my finger above his left shoulder, slammed the door shut.

It was like someone put a bomb in a paint-pot. The green of the grass and the mountain-sheep-fleece sky were spattered then blotted out by the scarlet of pain.

In dreams I have heard again the click as the car-door opened again, the slap of my hand on my leather jacket, the clunk as the door swung shut. In dreams I have started up as I heard that powerful engine growl bass and hum tenor as it reversed just inches away. In dreams I have heard my shrieking, keening, crooning and babbling as I knelt on the sodden grass and hugged my finger as though it were a small sick animal, not me but mine.

I don't look forward to dreams like I used to.

Then the heat fled and the pain found its source. It did not diminish; it was just localized now, and concentrated, and I was cold as a distant star.

I opened my eyes to look at the finger. It was more like some bent and wizened seed pod. The bone was broken so the finger tip hung loose on twin tendons. The nail was split. Half of it was doubled back and dangled on a thread. There was blood and ripped skin and blackness in there. Crooning, I laid it down in the spangled grass. The cool would have helped, but to touch anything with those exposed nerves was agony.

I burbled urgently. I rose to my feet, that hand loosely flapping. The grass and the cars and the buildings and the sky shot upwards as though they were all great canvas backdrop which had suddenly been raised. I lurched, but I stayed upright. The world settled again. I staggered towards the stands.

Horns blared at me. I barged into several cars. I did not care. I needed relief for this pain.

It's strange. I must be more accustomed to pain than most. I have fallen, been kicked and dragged and have broken most of the principal bones in my body, but that was always when the adrenalin was pumping, and adrenalin is one hell of an anaesthetic. There's an inverse law of pain too. The bigger the injury, the closer to the vital bits, the less the agony. Extremities hurt like hell.

One of the policemen saved the day. Gauntleted and helmeted, he ambled over to me, expecting to arrest an early drunk-and-disorderly. 'Come along, now,' he said, but I yelped and held up the crushed finger. I whined, 'A doctor. For Christ's sakes.'

The policeman said, 'Oh, my God,' and I heard him gulp. Then all was sweet consoling bustle. Mother authority picked me up and bore me solicitously to a doctor who clicked and clucked and injected ice into my hand. He threw away that needle. I never got the chance to tell it that I loved it.

*

'It wasn't too bad,' I told Isobel on the telephone that night. 'He was OK about it. I mean, he was annoyed, but, you know, he's prepared to wait.'

'Oh, thank God,' Isobel sighed, and I heard her bed sigh too as she sat. 'After all you told me, I was imagining all sorts of horrors.'

'Yeah.' I looked down at the bandaged hand. 'No. No need to worry. All well.' All was far from well. I had spent the last half hour in telephoning trainers to tell them sorry, I could not ride for them tomorrow. The finger was tightly strapped to its neighbour. Physically, I was able to ride, but the tom-tom pain was too intense to allow concentration.

'Where are you?' Isobel was cheerful.

'At the cottage.' I shivered. The grate was empty, and the room was all the colder because the cleaner had been in my absence and had straightened magazines and removed coffee-mugs. I did not think that I could cope with fire-building. 'I miss you,' I said, and meant it.

'I miss you too. Can I come and be the gardener again this weekend?'

'Please.' I nodded fervently. 'Look, I was wondering. Seeing as you're a responsible person, what are you doing over Christmas?'

'Christmas I have to spend with my mother.' She was firm. 'Christmas starts out being for children, then it's for mothers. She needs her whole brood about her.'

'Yeah, sure. No, but when do you have to go back to work?'

'Not till New Year. Oh, you mean *after*. No, that's fine. I could join you, say, what? The twenty-seventh? That'd be fine. When does Polly come?'

'Twenty-eighth,' I told her, and the windows rattled and a door at the back of the house slammed as a sudden gust of wind hit it. 'Pick her up in the morning, then I have her till New Year's Day.'

'Fine by me. I can go on a diet. I'll need it. No. I'd like that.'

'You going out tonight?' I asked, and felt absurd because I ached liked an adolescent, wanted to hear her tell me no.

'Yup. Dinner with a guy I met at a party. Works for Credit Suisse or one of those. Dullish, I should think. Don't worry, I'll probably be back before I change into a pumpkin. We'll see, anyhow.'

'Yeah.' I nodded. I felt old and idiotic. 'Have fun.'

'You?'

'Hmm?'

'What are you up to?'

'Just go to bed, I reckon, and dream of fornication. I'm whacked.'

'Dreams are allowed.'

'Thanks.' Again the door at the back banged and the latch rattled. 'Well . . . I miss you. I think I said that.'

'You're mad. I could do with you, actually.'

'Got a problem?'

'You could say. I just bought this slinky new body . . .'

'I quite liked the old one.'

'And it's making me feel . . .'

'Go on.'

'No! You know what I mean.'

'I love it. You're all prim and proper till I get you to bed.'

'Yes, well, that's different. No, I'm just raunchy. That's the problem. More you get, more you want. With me, anyhow.'

The wind had rallied its forces. It swooped and scampered around the house. Again the door banged.

Keith walked in.

I had allowed myself to relax, bathing in warm nonsense and privacy. The appearance of that leering face, that lank yellow hair here in my house was like a mallet-blow to the chest. My feet, which had been on the sofa, hit the ground fast. I stood.

'Look, I'm going to have to go,' I said briskly. I did not want Keith or Quinn to know of Isobel's existence. There must be no intimacies or endearments.

'OK. What's up?' Isobel asked, and there was concern in her voice.

100

'Nothing. Just someone turned up. Can't talk now.' Keith had helped himself to a glass of vodka. He perched on the arm of a chair. He was smiling at me. I glowered.

'Everything is OK, isn't it?' Isobel said.

'Yes, yes. Absolutely fine. Must dash. See you.'

I did not wait for a reply. I slammed down the receiver. I turned on Keith. 'What the fuck are you doing here?' I roared. 'This is my bloody house. Get out of here before I break your filthy neck.'

'Neeaow, neeaow,' Keith spoke like a children's TV presenter, 'let's not be fucking silly. Start off with, you couldn't take me even when you was fit, so easy up with the fucking threats, eh? As for now – sorry about that little accident with the door.'

I recognized the truth of his words. Short of calling the police, there was precious little I could do to remove this excrescence. I stopped advancing on him and contented myself with opening and shutting the one fist which would open and shut, and with some deep, growly heavy breathing.

'What do you want?' I snapped. 'Haven't you done enough harm for one day?'

He resumed his position on the sofa. He pulled a tobacco tin from his pocket and started rolling a cigarette with orange-stained fingers. He took his time. 'Just a word, just a little chat, Munrow. How many days and nights in a first-class fucking hotel could I have for eighty grand, hmm? Work it out. Say two hundred a night – that's five nights for a grand, and five eighties is four fucking hundred. Four hundred nights in the effing Dorchester or something you owe us, and this, though nice in its way, isn't the effing Dorchester, now is it?' He giggled. 'Nah. Half an hour of your time, a drink or two? Say knock fifty off your debt, OK? Still got Mr Quinn's ring on, have you?'

'Fuck off,' I said, because I was still wearing the damned thing. I had howled at the doctor when he tried to cut it off.

'Have you?'

'Yes. OK. Now get out.'

'No, no, Munrow. We're having fun, me and you, we're socializing in your *desirable* gentleman's residence. All right for some, eh?' His wave took in the room. 'Silk curtains, nice rugs, pretty pictures. Wish I lived like this.'

Good. So at least Keith thought that this was my only house. I would not disillusion him.

Keith slumped into the armchair so that his legs dangled over the arms. 'You know, I never did work out why you didn't like me, Munrow. So fucking high and mighty, you were, in with all the big boys, the Strakers and the Murphys and all those cunts. Had no time for the lowlier fucking species like me. Is that it, Munrow? I was beneath you? You never know, if you'd deigned to smile, have a word, courteous sort of thing, we might have been good friends, had some good times . . .'

'I didn't like your language, I didn't like your manners, I didn't like your morals, I didn't like your looks.' I walked over to the drinks table and slopped Glenfiddich into a tumbler. The doctor had told me not to drink. I silently toasted Hippocrates.

'Well, well. Let's just think about that, shall we?' Keith said in a nasal twang behind my back. 'My language – OK, for the high and fucking mighty, perhaps it's a bit on the rich side. Sorry about that. My manners – yeah, well I didn't go to a fancy public school, did I? My morals – ooh, no. I was a naughty boy, wasn't I? Hooked the odd nag while you was straight as a fucking dye, weren't you? But then, I was ten years older than you, wasn't I, Munrow? And now? Ten years on. Pure as the driven snow are we? "Please, Mr Quinn, I'll do anything you fucking want just so's you'll let me keep your money." Jesus, you make me puke, Munrow. I've seen you fucking pulling them, watched you on the video time and again. And looks – yeah, well, time was I was a nicer looking lad than you, Munrow, but we have accidents in this business. You're no beauty, but I was just unlucky, that's all. Some crime in that, is there? Just turn on a man 'cos he had a fucking accident – is that what they teach in your fucking Sunday schools? Cheap little cunt.'

I felt a twinge of guilt as he spoke. No amount of provocation could excuse a character like Keith's but perhaps our routine dismissal of him as a twisted, homosexual little crook had contributed to his corruption. Perhaps a smile or a word of greeting might have saved him. The camaraderie of the weighing-room is strong. It must be a horrible place in which to be isolated.

But more, I felt fear as I listened. I had, thanks to a comfortable youth and a good education, an easy manner which won me the odd girl and made me friends. But aside from that – none of my making – how far was I from Keith's condition? As he said, I too had pulled horses. I too was now in Quinn's thrall. I too was broke and facing the future alone.

'I'm not going to discuss this, Keith.' I strove to be convincingly forceful. I strode towards the bureau in the corner. 'Just tell me what you want and get the hell out.'

I unlocked the drop-front of the bureau. I lowered it slowly. Keith still lay slumped in the armchair with his back to me. 'And if I don't . . . ?' he sniggered.

'If you don't . . .' I snapped the stock and the barrel of the twelve-bore together. I was pushing in the cartridges as I turned. 'If you don't . . .' I used my right forearm to raise the barrel. The click made Keith turn. His distorted grin froze. His glazed dark eyes opened wide, then narrowed. 'I can still use a gun, Keith, even with one hand. And don't think I wouldn't. After what happened this morning, I would take great pleasure in seeing what sort of pattern your brain cells make on the wall. Manslaughter, it would be, at worse. An interloper on a windy night – an interloper who, I'll lay odds, has a record. Am I right? Justifiable homicide, they'd make it, wouldn't they? And remember this, Keith. From now on, you want to talk to me, you ring first and make an appointment. My house is my house, and no little turd walks in here without my say-so. Try it again, and I swear – I *swear*, do you hear me? – that you'll be greeted with this little darling. So. Spout and out. Now.'

'Oh, tough little shit,' Keith's eyes swivelled. Their whites were dirty. He stood and dusted down his trousers. 'You wouldn't fucking dare,' he raised his jaw.

I pulled the trigger.

I astounded him – his clamped-down face suddenly opened and he flung himself to one side like a goalkeeper – but I astounded me a hell of a lot more.

The barrel bucked. The stock jerked into my hip. The gun skewed from my grasp and fell to the carpet. The blast shook the sedate furniture, slammed at the windows, battered at the door and walls and made the bottles and glasses jingle on the tray. And afterwards, as if to soothe and say sorry, it rang and sweetly sang.

I had aimed at the armchair. I had scored a direct hit. The pattern of shot had not had time to spread far, but it had punched a great hole in the chair's side. It now spewed ill-digested shredded wheat.

I, as often happens to the man with the gun, recovered first. I crouched to pick it up. Keith lay huddled to the left of the chair. He clutched the peach curtains to his face. He was shaking.

'Right,' I said in as deep a voice as I could muster. I walked towards him. I looked down on him. 'What's the message?'

'Fucker,' he whimpered, 'fucker, fucker, fucker. I'll do you.'

'No, you won't,' I said softly, 'because I know you. You want to be everything that I am, or failing that, you want me to be reduced to you. You could no more do me than a sinner could do his god. Get up.' I kicked him. I knew that I was making a dangerous enemy. 'Tell me your message and fuck off out of here.'

Keith got up. He got up slowly and inelegantly. His eyes were wet and staring. He blinked incessantly. His hands were shaking and a tic had started up. His left ear seemed to want his mouth for company. It tugged, but his mouth stayed where it was. 'All fucking right,' he croaked, still crouched. 'Listen, sonny boy. Saturday. That thing of Smythson's. Addle something.'

'Addlestrop.'

'Whatever. It loses.'

'Get out.' I astounded myself again by being genuinely savage. 'Just get out of here and don't come back.'

'Oh, I'll be back,' he leered. He pushed back his yellow hair. 'Mr Quinn won't be pleased with you, Munrow. You'll be hearing from us.'

'Piss off,' I gestured with the gun. 'Tell Quinn, OK, I'll stop the bloody horse, but if he can't control his little gofers, I might just get so angry that I bring him and me down together.'

'You . . .'

'Out!'

'Fuck . . .'

'Out!' I yelled.

Keith spat and sneered, but he left.

I waited in the back doorway as he shuffled round the corner. I slammed the door, shot the bolts and walked fast through to the study window. I watched him climb into some sort of pale, pristine Ford which smelled of hire car. Only when he had driven away did I lay down the gun and throw myself on to the sofa to give vent to my spleen in comfort.

'Clothilde?' Isobel mused. She turned the piece of china in her hand. 'Fascinating. No, I think they're lovely.'

Laura Wonnacott preened. She touched her spare, immobile purple curls with a forefinger. 'Oh, I like them. It's a bit of an interest, isn't it? You need a bit of an interest, don't you. Dave's got his birds. I've got my little ladies.'

Dave had just taken me on a guided tour of his birds. He had fondly identified Reeves and Amhersts, copper, silver and golden pheasants, quail, blackgame and partridges. I had said 'Really?' and 'Yes,' quite a lot.

I had not eaten save for a slice of toast for breakfast. Even the rarest and loveliest fowl was therefore immediately undressed and oven-dressed by my mind's eye.

As for Laura's 'little ladies', to whom Isobel had been

introduced the while, they were all remarkably pink. Some of them wore tu-tus, some frills, furbelows and picture hats. They wore the sickly simpers of one who has eaten a slug at a royal banquet and they held roses or lilies or baskets very fastidiously, as one might hold an unidentified pair of knickers. They were painstakingly modelled by – as I am sure the sales spiel would have confirmed – 'master craftsmen'. They were called things like 'Clarissa', 'Marybelle' and 'Florinda'. Laura had sixty-four of them, ranked as if Busby Berkeley had just called 'Cut!' on eight specially lit shelves.

'Can't see what she sees in 'em myself.'

Dave sat in an armchair and stretched those long, thin legs. He wore tartan slippers. I was in my stockinged feet. Only Isobel, enjoying the peculiar rights of the stranger, had been permitted to retain her shoes. 'But I'll tell you something; she's got an eye for an investment, my Laura. Some of 'em's worth twice what you paid for 'em, bin'ey, my dear?'

'Well, you know,' Laura cocked her head, astute, 'a thing of beauty . . .'

Isobel said again, 'Well, I think they're lovely,' and sank on to the sofa. Laura perched at the other end; her knees were superglued.

The girls had glasses of dark brown sherry. We men had peanuts and cans of ale. There had been no question about this. Our drinks had been decided at the same moment as our genders. On the stereo, Phil Coulter's piano sort of bubbled beneath his string section like an Alka Seltzer in soup.

'Sorry to hear about your bit of bad luck,' Laura told me.

I frowned. 'Which bit was that?'

'This afternoon. Dave said . . .'

'Oh, yes.' I gulped beer while I adopted a suitably innocent and chagrined expression. 'Yeah, well, I made a right cock-up of it, didn't I? All my own darn fool fault. He'd have won, I reckon, but I just couldn't get him settled, and when he hit the plain one on the bend, it just seems to knock all the stuffing out of him. Pity. He's a good sort. He'll win something good one of these days.'

'Well, he's well bred, isn't he? Class horse.' Dave was sage. 'Sassoon out of – what was she called?' – Village something. Won some good things on the flat. Would have been a nice one, though, today.'

I shrugged. 'Ah, well. It happens.'

'So,' Laura turned to Isobel, 'how are you coping with these horse-obsessed men, love?'

'Oh, I just profess ignorance and disinterest,' Isobel caught my eye. 'I'll have a small bet on the National, I like the horses, but that's it. I refuse to get caught up in it.'

'Quite right, too.'

'But it must be pretty hellish for you, wondering every day if Dave's going to come back with this or that bit missing. I mean, first time I ever saw Neil in action, he broke his collar-bone and got concussed. A few days later, it's a little finger smashed. OK, there aren't that many bits that really matter, but it must get pretty exhausting . . . ?'

'Oh, I don't think about it,' Laura smiled fondly up at Dave who had unfurled himself in order to fill their glasses. 'If I go racing, I get together with the other wives in the restaurant, never watch a race, and I switch off the telly as soon as I see a horse. Funny, really. Sometimes, I'm hoovering or something, and I look across at the blank screen and think, "In there, there's Dave and Neil and the rest of them all battling it out," and I could turn them on and make them all real if I felt like it, but I'd sooner not.'

'You're lucky,' I said, 'Dave bounces. At his age, he should be looking for a hip-replacement, but I've seen him take some crashing purlers and he just gets up and dusts himself off.'

'Ah, yes,' Dave smiled, 'I've been lucky. Parachute training helps, I suppose. Mind, you've not had it so bad, Neil.' He drained his beer and licked spume from his upper lip. 'No. It's not the falls that worry me, not the horses, it's the bloody humans. You can get an uppity horse, you can get a non-trier, you can get one too gassy, but it's one in a million that's a genuine vicious rogue. Odds b'aint so good with the humans. Bastards.' He spoke with uncharacteristic sorrow and bitterness. He shook his head. He looked up, blinking. 'Sorry,' he said, 'just gets to us sometimes, you know? Sorry, Laura, love. Sorry, Isobel.'

'Don't be silly,' Isobel grinned. 'I've heard a bit about the villains from Neil.'

'Too many of 'em about,' Dave sighed.

'I should think you should be sorry, Dave Wonnacott.' Laura folded plush hands in her lap. 'Swearing and all with Neil's nice young lady friend here. I'm sorry, Isobel, dear. Don't know what's come over him. Come along, now. If you'll give me a hand, I think it's time for supper.'

Isobel obediently followed her out. I was left with a slumped and brooding Dave, an empty beer-can and Coulter doing things to 'Danny Boy' which Danny Boy should not in decency have allowed.

'Oh, I don't know,' Dave said at last, 'sometimes I just think, you know, I love this game, I've had a lot of fun, I've won a few, lost a few – overall, I've done all right. But there's always some bugger doesn't want to play the game, always . . .' He stood, his fingertips in the pockets of his cords. He strolled to the fireplace. 'I'll tell you. It's like . . . I mean, you know what sport is. You take your chances. You and I go off to Bally-nahinch like last year, fish for two weeks, catch one black brute, so what? We'm had a good time, haven't we? Or – me, a good day's shooting, go out with a dog and a friend, get all muddy and cold, come back with two brace of woodcock if you're lucky. That's sport, just skill and judgement and chance. But there's always some bastard wants the odds stacked, wants to guarantee success. Fat banking bastards, sooner shoot a guaranteed two thousand tame birds than take their chances with the high and the wild. Know what I mean?'

'Too bloody well.' I too stood.

'And we get 'em too, in our business,' Dave told his feet morosely. 'I mean, there'm enough to go round, bin there? I don't see no one starving. But there's always someone wants more. One person like that ruins all the good times, pollutes everyone else.'

'I know,' I walked over to the fire and stood beside him. I rested my foot on the fender. For a moment, I wanted to tell him all about Quinn. I could have done with a father confessor just then. But I thought of what such a confession might entail for Polly, for me, for Dave, and I swallowed it down again. I leaned my right forearm on my thigh. I looked up at him. 'Someone been leaning on you, Uncle?'

Dave did not answer for a full half minute. The fire hissed and puddered. I just looked into the flames and waited. 'Ah,' Dave slapped his thigh, 'there's always someone trying, isn't there, mate? Just pay no attention. Only thing to do, isn't it?'

'Yup,' I agreed vaguely. My thoughts were muffled by the flickering flame. Then, 'Yup. You're dead right.' I straightened. I kicked the logs. A rash of sparks burst on the blackened bricks. 'Just don't let the bastards grind you down, Uncle. We'll win in the end, eh?'

'Course we will.' He laid a hand on my shoulder. His eyes twinkled again. He looked genuinely cheered by my support. 'Sorry, Neil. Down in the dumps. Silly. No, we stick together, we'll beat the little crooks. Thanks.'

'Dinner!' Isobel hollered from next door.

I said, 'For nothing.'

'For nothing' was right. My reassurance may have worked, may even have been meant, but it was intrinsically worthless as a Philby pep-talk to the Foreign Office.

The good thing about riding races, the thing which keeps us young, is that every day brings new people, new animals, new promise. There are perhaps upward and downward trends, but they are nigh imperceptible and they are reversible. A day of disappointment is forgotten in anticipation of the day ahead, the day after that. Sometimes I have woken up groaning at stiff limbs and bruises which seem to extend from the epidermis to the vitals, but I have never woken up without hope. There are youngsters to be schooled, any one of which might turn into a champion or, at least, a winner, then there is the comradeship of the changing-room, the joy and the constant interest of each race.

There has always been joy in clean battle and in the aggression which it induces, always joy in heroism. We were privilleged to go into battle up to six times daily, and to be heroes before a multitude.

Even when riding a pig, with nothing in prospect but a bumpy plod cross-country and endless arses ahead, there is always the hope that you might coax or force an extra few lengths from the beast or that all your rivals might fall. Even when participating in Quinn's sort of race in which victory was not on the cards, there was the consolation of a fat cheque at the end of the day.

Not now.

This morning I had lain in bed for a clear half hour, just staring at the ceiling, burdened with the hopelessness of the slave. My veins had been full of lead. There had been no prospect of triumph or riches today – or for more years than I had at my disposal.

The only physical certainty is death. The only spiritual death is certainty.

The thought that Isobel would meet me at the course and that we would dine here tonight had cheered me for a moment, but only for a moment. Isobel must watch from the stands as I did Quinn's dirty work. Dave would be there with me amid the creaking and thudding, puffing and jingling. His experienced eyes would be on me as I did – whatever I must do to prevent Addlestrop from winning.

For prevent him I would. Suicidal heroism is not for the fathers of two-year-old daughters.

So at last I had dragged myself from bed. It had been icy. I had cursed and shifted from foot to foot like a circus elephant. My breath had bounced back at me off the air. It had been a lovely morning out there, but I had felt myself to be a blot on my own view of the world. I tainted and muddied its colours. Perhaps, then, this was how Keith had felt in those long years of isolation and decline. *'Why is this hell, nor am I out of it . . .'*

Some Faustus I was. I was to be rewarded by no shipyard succubi nor infinite knowledge in exchange for my soul. The price had been paid. Katya had snapped it up.

I had driven up to Lambourn and schooled a bold young grey with listless, practised skill and temperance. The viewers could not have known that anything was wrong. The horse did.

My poor shattered finger, tightly strapped to its neighbour, hurt like hell, but I could ride. I was almost glad of the pain. Some part of me at least had the autonomy to protest this outrage. As I walked back to the Shogun, Colin Mather, the giant, pear-shaped trainer with whom I had had a retainer for the past two years, had asked, 'Anything wrong, old chap?'

I had told him, 'Hrmph,' and 'Nothing.' I had slammed the car door.

What had been wrong was Addlestrop's presence in the string. He had been bucking and dancing, bursting with strength and enthusiasm. What had been wrong was that Tony, the head man, had muttered to me that the lads had had a nice touch today and good luck, Neil. What had been wrong was that Addlestrop was a likeable, genuine animal, on only his second run over the sticks, who made up for what he lacked in talent and experience with courage and goodwill. What had been wrong was me.

At the course, where everyone buzzed like live cables in anticipation of Christmas, I simply avoided people, relying on battlements of moody 'Hrmphs' to keep them outside the walls. In the changing-room, Chris Leonard sat on the bench beside me as I sat slumped in boxer-shorts and wristwatch. He looked like a Hitler Youth star. He had the manner of a fawn. He gushed, 'Neil, bad luck about the finger. Listen. She said yes! I mean she will move in. Isn't that incredible?'

'Incredible.'

'I really want to thank you. I mean, you were right. I was only thinking of myself, and I *was* reacting to her as if she was my mother.'

111

'Yeah.'

'Only this is – well, she doesn't like this business.'

'This business is what you do,' I growled. 'You're good at it. What's she doing with you if she doesn't like half of you?'

'Yes, but she says it's not really me. I'm just playing. I mean, I don't have to do it.'

'So give up.'

'No, I mean, I don't want to do that, obviously. I'm just saying . . .'

'If you give up because of her, you'll hate her and she'll despise you,' I snapped. 'If you don't, she'll nag you and blame you when the money isn't coming in. It's a straight life-choice, and if I were you, I'd get what you can out of little Carol and move on. You can't change human beings. Get that into your head. Get it into hers if it has the capacity. No, we're not predestined, but our virtues are our vices. Her softness and protectiveness are inextricable from her need for maternal domination. Your need to ride has to do with your need for us, your need to be away from her, to reject her protectiveness. Never try to control another person. End of lecture. Fuck off, will you, Chris? I feel shitty.'

'Oh. Oh, sure, OK,' he said with the affronted air of one who, having once received advice, owns the giver. 'Sorry you feel that way.'

Strangely, I would have given him precisely the same advice had I been happy. The medicine was unpalatable only when undiluted. Chris Leonard faltered away.

The older boys understood. We had been together too long. They left me alone.

So we slouched out into the paddock. I talked to Addle-strop's owners, a keen, jolly little software man and his ema-ciated, blonde-skullcapped wife. She made eyes at me. I assumed that she made eyes at anything more masculine than Marilyn Monroe. I assumed that it meant nothing to anyone save her husband. They gave me different instructions in perfect concord. I smiled vaguely. Colin Mather's smile was immobile as a grilled sole. He hoisted me into the saddle. 'He'll take this,' he said simply.

It was the parody of it all that got to me. Here was no romantic brigandry, here no horsemanship. I was riding out, dressed in livery, on a lovely, valuable animal, to test his speed and skill against those of others in the fresh air.

Bollocks.

I was going to hook the poor beast in an exercise as cynical as pheasant-shooting or property-development.

I had become a salaried shit.

But I sat forward and into him because I loved him, as all of his kind. And I rode him gently, despite his gecking and bowing, to the start. And I joined in the chorus of no, wait, sirs. And we were away.

And it felt so good to have an animal laid out, full of running, beneath me. But it was parody, all of it. The air was used, the pocked grass dirty.

The horse was bred and trained to win. Together, we were a mighty natural force with one purpose, one end, but I must fly in the face of nature, I must interfere with the just course of history.

It was blasphemy.

The pace was sluggish, but that was not Addlestrop's fault. He pulled like a train in the back straight. I tucked him in on the inside rail at the middle of the leading group. Michael Wessel, the South African, was on my outside on a giant brown animal. Chris Leonard, in blue and yellow, crouched low on an ugly dun ahead. Dave, presumably, was somewhere amid the other group of which I was just vaguely aware on the opposite side of the track.

I bent Addlestrop's neck a bit, made him concentrate. The hooves all around me rumbled like casters. The breeze brought the smells of pine and of grass above those of leather and horse-sweat. The plain fence bounced towards us. I shut out of my mind the creaking of the saddles and the burble of the other feet. I heard only the rhythm of my mount's stride.

One, two, three, and.

Silence.

Up, stretching, clipping the top of the birch with a sound

113

like a zip, and down, instantly a double handful, and away, once more amid the puffing and the grumbling.

'Easy,' I breathed to Addlestrop. He twitched his ears once in response, the equine equivalent of 'Easy, yourself', and struck out with his off fore as if to kill a snake.

We were still lying third in our group as we passed the stands and headed out into the country again. Chris's animal had dropped out of it and, for an alarming moment, we had actually found ourselves in front, but Addlestrop had tried to take the open ditch too much on the forehand and had lost his stride as he pecked on landing. Michael was ahead of us now, and Nick Storr on the second favourite, Billy Pilgrim, going well at our right.

The pace had increased. Nick wanted to increase it a bit more. It wouldn't be the first time that Billy Pilgrim had won off the pace. Nick clicked his tongue. Billy Pilgrim cruised ahead of us. Addlestrop did not like this. The breeze on my face became a wind. We started to race.

Nick sailed over the fence. Addlestrop, just half a stride behind, would have done so too, but he still thought that he was hurdling. I should have got him back on his hocks, lost a length, perhaps, but got over safely. Addlestrop cared only about catching his rival.

It was a beautiful long jump. It simply lacked height. I felt as though some heavyweight had congratulated me rather too effusively. I mumbled 'Shit!' into rough mane.

Addlestrop sprawled on landing. For a second, I was riding a headless horse. There was nothing but grass ahead of me. Other horses were landing about us, but Addlestrop somehow kept his feet. He planted his forefeet wide. His rump arose. His head and neck reappeared. He snorted.

Dear God, he was ready to race.

Sorry. Not today.

I had my excuse. I made much of picking him up and urging him on, but my right hand was restraining him. He managed a listless gallop, but the other horses and riders were five lengths, six lengths, seven ahead.

I pulled him up.

He tossed his head and snorted again. His eyes followed the animals ahead. I said, 'Sorry, old boy.' I breathed, 'Phew.'

If the noise that Addlestrop made to me could have been spelled, it certainly could not have been printed.

That night, Isobel whimpered, 'I love you.'

'No, you don't,' I panted, then, fiercely, 'No, you *don't*,' and I pushed her head down into the pillow so that I should not see those eyes.

But I did love her, if love means being totally at ease with another, accepting, being accepted, unfeigning, unafraid. Sometimes at night I would awake beside her and my hand would roam over her body. I would shake my head and blink, marvelling that so much was mine. I would fear again that some celestial practical joke was being played.

This trepidation sprang from no grovelling self-abasement, no overweening humility on my part. I had enjoyed beautiful bodies before, sharp wits and congenial, adventurous minds. For all that I am no pocket-Adonis, no rock-star, nor animal magnate, I have never felt unworthy of such good fortune. The sense of such unworthiness came rather from the passion with which she hugged me, the lack of reserve with which we spoke of gardens or of gods, the ease with which we cooked our meals together, never in each other's way, but moving about one another in silence as though choreographed. The sense of unworthiness came from the certainty that here was my soul-sister, and that soul-sisters are rarer than dodos. Here was the friend that I had sought all my life, and now that she was here, I was not ready. Not, at least, until I had done with Katya, done with Quinn.

I was far from done with either.

Christmas drew closer. Shop assistants and television presenters took to wearing red hats with white bobbles. Windsections and electric guitars took their annual holiday. Massed strings and glockenspiels came back and worked overtime in every advert, shop and arcade. Crazy as it seems, I felt that old sense of excited anticipation as trees appeared in cottage windows and in town squares, Crosby crooned and the Advent calendars looked ever more ragged.

I feel it every goddamn year as if by reflex, and every goddamn year, I am disappointed. Christmas means expense, over-eating, torpor, pine-needles to be vacuumed and no cheques coming in, but still somehow I love the sound of the word, still I thrill to the promised miracle, though I know that there will be no snow and no theophany – just socks and tears and too much turkey.

I suppose that, above all, it serves as a punctuation mark – a caesura in the unremitting Alexandrine of the months. 'Next year,' we say, 'things will be different'; 'It'll all be sorted out by Christmas'; or 'See you sometime in the New Year' – when I too will be new and new-born and, like the garden, will have another go at dressing this bare forked frame. This time, I'll get it right.

I spent a Monday shopping in London with Isobel. She led me round department stores which looked and sounded like aching heads. I bought Polly a climbing frame. I sent it down to Datchet so that Katya could set it up in time for the big day. It was waiting for me when I returned to Wiltshire. 'I think it would be wise,' said the accompanying note, 'if you consulted me before burdening us with cumbersome articles, thank you very much.'

I rang. A male voice at the other end said 'Er . . . yes? Sorry, can I help you?' It was a globular voice, full of bubbles. Old Etonian yet insecure. Katya's wine-merchant.

'Hi. That must be Tony Wickham,' I said cheerily.

'Er, well, yes. Sorry. Who's speaking, please?'

'Neil Munrow. Nice to hear you. No need to be embarrassed or anything, Tony. Is Katya about, please?'

'Um – well, no, actually. Well, I mean, she is, but she's in the bath, actually, you know.' I would buy claret from this man. He lied too badly to be a salesman. 'Can I take a message or anything, you know?'

116

'No, thank you, Tony.' I was merciful. 'Just tell her I called, will you?'

I rang back two minutes later. Unsurprisingly, I got the answering machine.

I bought Polly a tape-recorder and fifty books and a toy for blowing massive bubbles and a chart of the heavens and a doll and a picture of daddy in a leather frame and a Jemima Puddleduck clock and a little desk and chair, then Isobel told me to stop.

I won a race at Lingfield. I lost two on Quinn's instructions.

The second of these was at Worcester. I stopped off at a pub just outside Pershore, as much for a Scotch to pinfire the pain as to ring Isobel, tell her nothing much, just, you know.

The telephone was on the bar. While I spoke, I did not even notice the burly young man with an egg-shaped face who took up a position at my left hand. I laid down the receiver and raised the glass to my lips to down the dregs before leaving.

'Mr Munrow . . . ?'

I started and turned.

He faced the bottles at the back of the bar, but he watched me out of the corner of his eye. So soon as he saw my reaction, he swung round and extended a large pink hand. 'Mr Munrow?'

I lowered the glass. I took in the splash of colourless hair, the boyish, stupid face with its little eyes, pink cheeks and doubling chin. 'Yes?'

'Ernest – Ernie Ricketts. Just got back from the races. Bad luck today.'

'Thank you.' I took the hand.

'I thought it was you. Didn't want to bother you or whatnot. It's just – my old dad over there. I know he'd love to meet you if you could spare the time. Just a second, say hello, whatnot. I took him out for the day and thingy, and it'd be a real thrill for him. He knew your father, he says. Army, I think. I don't know. Bit vague these days and you know.'

'Ricketts, you say?' I frowned.

'Yes. I'm Ernest. Sorry.'

'And your dad?'

'Bob. Bob Ricketts.'

I had him now: Bob Ricketts, a cheery, dark little imp in battledress and beret, here with a billycan, here sitting smoking on my father's tank, here standing at the head of my father's mount at the White City. Bob Ricketts had featured in my father's stories, but for me he existed in sepia and in faded white copperplate on the black card of photograph albums. 'Ricketts, Salerno,' 'Ricketts Tripoli,' 'Romeo Ricketts,' 'Ricketts, whoops!'

'Where is he?' I asked the young Ernie.

'Over there.' He nodded. 'Just a moment, you know. Sorry.'

I set off to the corner where the old man sat in shadow on a vinyl bench. Ernie called after me. 'Just get you one in, sir!' I nodded.

Bob Ricketts had very white hair, but his eyebrows were still thick and black. He was taller than I had expected from the photographs. His face was weatherbeaten and heavily wrinkled. His grin was very broad. 'Allo,' he croaked. 'Ernie said as it was you and I said "Nah" but 'e would 'ave it. Yeah. Now, close up, I'd know you anywhere. You've got a look of your old man. Look of your mum, too, but Munrow all right.'

'Good to see you,' I clasped his shoulder. 'I've seen so many pictures, heard so many stories. You were Dad's batman, weren't you?'

'I was, all through North Africa, Italy, right up till we liberated Belsen. And after the war, too. Tried to promote me, they did, and I said, not bloody likely, matey. I'll stick with the Captain. Oooh, but we 'ad some times, your dad and me. Great 'orses, beautiful girls, always the best of everything for the Captain. He tell you how I pinched the Colonel's badges for 'im?' He wheezed a laugh. 'Your dad wouldn't 'ave new regimentals. A badge wasn't a badge till it'd been buffed down so you could 'ardly see what it was, and I wasn't going to spend weeks on my arse just buffing, but the Colonel, old

Macrae, 'e 'ad some beauties as 'ad been 'is father's before 'im. Well, what's a man to do?'

I smiled. I shifted his walking-stick and sat opposite him. 'Yes, he told me about that, and a disgusting story about you picking bits of trooper out of you.'

'That's right! Lor, poor old Angus. Shell lands bang at 'is feet and 'e's blown to smithereens right in front of us, and I gets all peppered. And they still work their way to the surface, all these little splinters, produced one the other day, didn't I, Ernie? Said to you, there's another bit of Angus, didn't I?'

'Always doing that,' Ernie deposited three glasses on the table. 'Disgusting, you ask me.'

''Ad a punt on you today,' Bob Ricketts drank and smacked his lips. 'Thought you'd take that one. The big one. 'Ad a fiver on you, for old times' sakes.'

'I'm sorry.' I closed my eyes for a momentary, heartfelt prayer. 'He just got winded when he hit the last open ditch. Couldn't get him to quicken. Stuffing knocked out of him, you know?'

'Oh, don't worry.' Bob Ricketts was still grinning. 'I 'ad a lovely day. Lovely. Like the old days . . .'

''Ere, Ernie!' a deep voice called behind me. 'I'd watch the company you keep, I was you.'

I vaguely smiled, suspecting a joke. I did not turn. Ernie, however, had turned and reddened. His lower jaw had dropped.

'Ernie. You 'ear me? That man – that man, Mister Neil Munrow – 'e's a dirty crook.'

'Excuse me,' Ernie murmured, and righteous indignation made him shake. His eyes were narrowed. 'I'll deal with this, sir.' He pushed himself up.

I grasped his sleeve. 'No, Ernie. It's all right. Sit down. Let's have no trouble.'

'You come here and say that!' Ernie pointed.

The clatter of talk and laughter close at hand subsided suddenly. On the juke-box, Queen were doing 'Radio Ga-Ga'. Somewhere further off, darts continued to thud.

'Come on!' Ernie yapped, 'You don't insult my friends, Maurice. You just damn well come here and apologize.'

'Buggered if I will.' The voice was like a burbling bottle. The man was drunk. 'That "friend" of yours lost me fourteen fucking grand today. A week ago, Southwell, weasel-faced bastard comes and I lay him ten grand to two Chequestub, and what happens? Hot favourite ridden by your "Friend" gets stuffed. Oh dear, oh dear. Today, same thing. Punter I've never seen before. Fourteen to four, and Munrow's animal's got the beating of the field by a mile, but Munrow's animal decides not to race today, doesn't it? And later, after the last, I see the fat bastard as laid the bet talking to the same weasel-faced bastard fleeced me at Southwell. Twenty-four fucking grand in a week. Thanks a ton, Munrow. You guys sit down and talk to bank robbers and all, do you?'

'Right. That's it.' Ernie kicked his stool back against the wall. His fat fingers flexed.

I stood. I pushed him back. 'No, Ernie. Wait.' I turned.

The man stood swaying slightly, not eight feet away. He wore pale trousers and a blue and red anorak. His shirt strained over the heavy swell of his belly. He was perhaps fifty, plumpish, greyish and unmemorable. He could as well have been a bird-watching bank manager as a bookie.

'I'm sorry that you've been unlucky,' I said sharply, 'and sorry that I've been involved on both occasions. I don't, however, advise you to shoot your mouth off in public places. There are laws about slander, and sometimes people prove impatient for the law to take its course and sort it out for themselves . . .'

The man had mustered a sneer. He opened his mouth, but I swept on. I could not stay here. 'So, I'm leaving,' I announced, 'and perhaps, Ernie, you would be kind enough to restrain this poor chap from following me or from doing himself any further damage. I'll be in touch, Bob. Sorry about this.'

My cheeks were burning and my eyes smarting as I barged past the aggrieved bookie and strode to the door. I could not wait for the cool cleanness of outdoor air.

I drove away fast, but I knew that no matter how fast I drove, Bob Ricketts with his puzzled, hurt eyes and the anonymous bookie with his bitter sneer would be waiting for me when I got home.

I received Quinn's instructions, however, through Quinn's usual minions – young men with plums either in their mouths or already bobbing in their throats. They probably knew little of what they were doing. They approached me once by the news-stand half an hour before the first, once in the car park while the sixth race was being run – to speak just one word – the name of the target horse. Both horses were well-fancied. Colin Mather's lads started to look unhappy. They spoke of a run of bad luck. Colin looked at me just a little quizzically. I saw Quinn only in the distance. I saw nothing of Keith Gurdon. I wore my filthy ring.

It would always be like this, I supposed, and perhaps, after all, for eighty grand it was not such a bad deal.

Like perhaps Christmas would be different this year.

Some hope.

'Hey, Neil, mate, hear the news?' Glenn Bairstow looked up as I walked into the changing-room. He was almost an exact contemporary of mine, the large, bold, effusive type who was constantly having trouble with his weight. He sat in thermal long-johns on the far bench, legs spread wide. Beside him, Dave Wonnacott, already meticulously dressed for his first ride, leaned forward, forearms on thighs, and squinted down his whip. About them, valets bustled and jockeys wriggled into breeches and sweaters.

'Good or bad?' I called. I dumped my kit on the bench.

'None too good, I'm afraid, mate. A star has fallen.'

'It's Georgie,' Dave nodded slowly.

'Blane?' I frowned. I stopped unbuttoning my shirt and walked over to them. 'Georgie? What's happened?'

'Croaked, mate.' Glenn looked up at me from under thick, black eyebrows. 'Bugger, isn't it?'

I never know what to say when confronted by the simple

fact of death. All deaths are the same like all salt tastes the
same. There is nothing new to be said. I just felt sorrow and
incredulity – all the normal things – and something sank
inside me. 'Shit,' I said at last, then I turned and punched a
locker. 'Shit, shit, shit!' I turned back to them. 'How did it
happen?'

'Bloody silly. Just got the call. His brother – you know, the
piss-artist, singer . . .'

'Yup . . . ?'

'Well, 'parently he'd been out all night on the piss out
Gowran way. Someone rings Georgie down at the farm, says
"your brother's just set off in some bloody great powerful car
which happens not to belong to him. He's a danger to himself." Georgie sets off to find him, meets him coming the other
way. Smash. Dunno if the brother bought it too, but Georgie's
a goner.'

'Oh, God,' I moaned. I closed my eyes for a moment to
picture Georgie Blane in life. He had been one of the best, one
of the most beautiful riders of all time. He had been a horseman. He had been a gent. I saw the bright, always appraising
Irish eyes, now still. I saw the clump of dark hair, the sad
cheeks, the quick smile. 'Oh, God almighty,' I prayed as I
swore, 'it's so bloody unfair.'

'Always the way,' Dave was nodding. 'He was only – what?'

'Can't have been more than forty-six, forty-seven. Had
that nice little bay animal, too. Won at Leopardstown, likely
sort – what was the bugger's name?'

'Tramore,' I supplied. 'After all that time scrubbing around
with useless old nags . . .'

'That's right. Bloody bad luck. Gather he had a new girlfriend and all. Everything going right for him at last, and
bang. Whole thing up in smoke. Sod it.'

'Poor bastard,' I sighed. 'Oh, Christ, and there's Joanna . . .'

'And Conor,' Dave nodded. 'It'll hit him hard. Bloody idol-
ized his dad, he did.'

As well he might, I thought as I returned to my dressing.
Georgie had ridden Secret State to victory in the National. He

122

had ridden Lady Waller's two Gold Cup winners, Wampeter and Ice Nine, smooth as snakeskin. He had ridden Vantage, the novice who had taken the King George in style only to die almost immediately afterward in a freak accident.

George had loved his horses with a fierce sentimentality. He had nursed them, wooed them, coaxed them and punished them with the same passion. He spoke of each as a character. A horse that served him well had a meal ticket for life. An ungenuine brute or one that tried it on was taking on the wrong man. Georgie had had the ability to second-guess a horse. He knew what it was thinking before it thought it. He could diagnose weaknesses, sensitivity and fears with greater accuracy than any faith-healer. To watch him was – and remains, thanks to video – a joy.

Georgie had had the retainer at 'Coco' Collin's yard just two stable jockeys before I took on the job. When I started riding, he was already retired. He was farming and training in a small way down in Wexford. But I got friendly and more with his daughter, Joanna, the eventer – not least, I confess, because her father was one of my childhood heroes.

For the first three years of my professional life, I counted Georgie as my friend. Joanna and I would stay with him when there was racing at Gowran or Fairyhouse. No one ever mocked an aspirant's arrogance more gently than he, nor gave better advice.

It wasn't just me. Georgie was always the jockey's friend, always willing to lend a hand at schooling a tricky animal or to guide a young jockey with drink problems in the right direction. He was an ever-present link with the past.

Now gone.

'Georgie may have had his troubles,' Dave said as he walked past me, 'but they all seem so trivial now. You just remember the great days, don't you?'

I nodded. I fervently hoped that he was right.

'We going to the send-off, then?' Glenn swaggered up. 'Have a right royal Irish piss-up in his honour. What say you? Should make a show.'

123

I nodded, though I would never have thought of it. 'Sure. Good idea. Why not? When'll it be, d'you reckon?'

'Three, four days?' Glenn shrugged. 'Come on. Catch a flight out of Heathrow, evening funeral, roll back the following morning.'

'Laura will want to come,' Dave said solemnly.

'Sure. Good. More the merrier. Storr? Oh, no. Forget it. You're too young. Who else is there?'

We looked about the changing-room. The young dumb faces stared back at us.

We thought the same grim thought. We turned on our heels, formed a rank and strode out, shoulder to shoulder.

Our flight in fact grumbled like a fat man out of Luton at four o'clock of a slammed-down evening. It was a day for funerals, grey as wire mesh and speckled with rain.

We were in Waterford within the hour. It was no better there.

Our names, for once, counted for something. They conjured knowing winks, companionable pats and handshakes and impressive service. Confronted, like St Anthony's donkey, with a jockey, hurler or musician at one end of the street and a film-star, politician or billionaire at the other, the Irishman will automatically make his way to the latter group. He will somehow relieve the film-star and friends of their money, and return to buy a jar for his friends at the other end. He loves poetry, the Irishman, in motion or otherwise.

I drove the hired Cavalier to the Ferrycarrig Hotel, a hideous but estimable establishment on the Slaney's estuary. We dumped our luggage, changed quickly into sober suits and knocked back the first of the evening's cocktails at the bar. 'Georgie,' Glenn toasted our fallen comrade. Laura sipped sweet sherry and wept.

Off again, up the thick and flooded river to Enniscarthy and so over the bridge and onward, the river now at our right, past fair Clobemon, home of a thousand drinks and happy faces in better days, and so to Bunclody.

124

Bunclody has – Bunclody is – a broad main street, divided by a stream. On summers' evenings, the locals sit beneath the pollarded trees and watch the water and the traffic going by.

I parked outside a chemist's. We were half an hour early, but already the street was full of black Amies, Costelloe, Lauren and Savile Row. Georgie would have loved the sight.

'Jeez,' Glenn slapped the back of my seat. 'Eledi Heron, no less. Surprised she's allowed out.'

'Easy,' I told him. 'She's all right, Eledi.'

'Uh, oh. Porthos is enamoured. God, there's old Hugh Grey. He still alive?'

'And Simon Waller . . .' Dave waved from the passenger seat.

'Tony Mont,' I nodded towards the television pundit, 'nipping into a bar, surprise, surprise.'

'Not such a bad idea,' Glenn mused. 'Bloody Dan Quinn.'

'Where?' Dave's head had swivelled.

'Where?' I snapped.

'Everyone wants to see Dan Quinn suddenly,' Glenn shrugged. 'OK, so feast your eyes. Over there. By the church. Isn't it?'

I saw Quinn, now in dark-blue cashmere and pale-grey gloves, over by the church porch. As usual, he looked as though he were running the show, vetting the mourners as they arrived. The little finger of my right hand throbbed. I swivelled the ring, just making sure that it was there.

'Bastard,' said Dave suddenly.

Laura said, 'Dave . . .'

We tugged at our coats and pushed at our ties. We walked solemnly across the street and into the hideous modern church. The usher ushed us into an honoured position just three pews from the front. He handed us orders of service with a wink and 'Your racecards, sons.' Glenn slapped him on the back. He coughed and beamed.

Georgie's coffin lay at the centre of the aisle. Strange, if commonplace, to reflect that so many lives, past, present and future, had been and would be touched by that – now so much meat in a box. In the front row at our right, Claire Blane (my cousin, as it happens) stood trembling from head to foot. Conor, a studious, bespectacled youth, held her hand tight. Joanna, with a scarlet velvet hair band, held her head preternaturally high, defying the gods.

Who else was there in that little Irish church?

Well, the list would have set Jennifer's pen a-twitter had Harper's been there.

Amongst the distinguished gathering, I spotted Charles, Earl of Kilcannon, and Mrs Richard Heron, formerly Lord Kilcannon's fiancée. Mrs Heron was attended by her constant companion, the smirking, slinky Angela Clarke. Captain 'Coco' Collins and his slagbag daughter Jessica were in different pews. I was also delighted to see The Honourable Rory Fitzroy-Haigh, over from Italy for the occasion, ex-jockeys Pat Kersall and Jimmy Knight, the Duchess of Savernake, Lord Styles of Tenterden, the Earl and Countess of Fenagh and Myshall, Count Cyril von Weinberg and his lovely bride Marigold (formerly Philippedes), and Mr Jack Clayton. Micky and Jenny Brennan were also in attendance with their charming daughter Kathy, actress Jodie Bentley, Jack Maisey and . . .

Keith Gurdon.

Two pews back and directly behind me. I shuddered. We all saw him. We all straightened our shoulders to make a wall and stood tall – well, as tall as jockeys can reasonably be expected to stand.

All right, so why should he not be here? Keith had ridden against Georgie, hadn't he?

Maybe, but Keith wouldn't attend his mother's funeral unless he was thinking of worm-farming.

Unfair. You don't know the little shit that well.

OK, because Keith was no friend of Georgie's.

So? You were? A kid who worshipped him and screwed his daughter?

No, but . . . Because Georgie was style and grace and honour and affection and Keith is everything opposed to these virtues.

Sure, sure. And you? Suppose Georgie once helped the little

toerag? Suppose Keith too always wanted to be like Georgie? Suppose he, like you, fancied that Georgie became part of his mount and floated where we other mortals plod and squelch? Will you not allow him too his lost dreams?

Yes, yes. All right. Piss off, will you? All I'm saying is, Georgie was always on the side of life, Keith on that of death. There's my answer. It's a fundamental difference between people.

It is? And you, Neil? And you?

I have Polly.

Bacteria have spores. And you?

For a moment, I thought that I had shouted 'Fuck off' out loud. I swallowed hard, closed my eyes and did some deep breathing. The harmonium struck up. It sounded like I felt.

And afterwards, while the more respectable oozed their condolences and scattered, we walked up the street in silence to Andy Redmond's, Turf Accountant and Lounge Bar, unadorned sanctum of the sportsman and the toper. We ordered Guinness and prepared to accompany Georgie at least as far as Lethe.

It was after the third pint that I had to nip out to the loo. I was breathing grateful sighs at the urinal when the door thumped behind me and that cartoon cat's voice said, 'Good to see you, Munrow.'

The sphincters contracted so fast that even the jet of urine was cut off.

'What is it, Keith?' I hastily tucked my cock away. Having seen what this man could do to a finger . . .

'Still wearing our ring, I see? There's a good boy.' Keith touched my shoulder. I shifted it away. 'Don't let me interrupt you, please. Pity about old Georgie, isn't it? Would've been warned off if he hadn't retired. You know that?'

'Yes, Keith,' I said through gritted teeth, 'and trust you to remember just that. He was straight as a die, generous to a fault, and he rode like a dream. That's all that matters to me.'

'Oh, yes. A good little Catholic boy.' Keith leered. I made to walk past him but he sidestepped into my path. 'You're a good little Catholic boy, aren't you, Munrow?'

'Fuck off, out of my way, Keith,' I growled, 'I've warned you once . . .'

'Oh, yes. Sorry. I forgot.' Keith went all Osric on me. 'Just one little thing, Munrow. Quick message from your sponsor.'

'Come on, come on . . .'

'You won't like it.'

'I don't like standing in a fucking urinal with a turd for company.'

'Tough boy,' Keith's lips jerked leftward. 'It's just – some people don't do as they're told, see, and then everything gets all snarled up. You understand?'

'You mean you can't corrupt some people. Thank Christ.'

The urinal hissed into life. Outside in the bar, a glass smashed and tinkled. Keith flicked something off my lapel. 'Have it your own way,' he said. Even in here, I could smell the sweet rottenness of his breath. 'Anyhow, when people step out of line, we have to slap their wrists. You'll understand that, of course. I mean, you have a bet and someone screws up . . .'

'I've done everything I've been asked,' I protested.

'Sure, sure. You've been a good boy, Munrow. Good as gold. No fucking problem. But you're going to have to bring another naughty boy into line.'

'Sod off. I'll not do your dirty work for you.'

'Eighty fucking grand,' Keith mused. 'Lot of money, that. Lot of dirty work there. You'd be warned off pretty fucking sharpish if the world got to know about that, now wouldn't you?'

'So get me warned off,' I snapped.

'Oh, we will, we will, but we still wouldn't have got our money's worth, would we?' Keith stepped back. He reached into his breast pocket. He pulled out a colour photograph. He held it out to me at arm's length. 'I don't know what this fucking means, Munrow, but I do what I'm told, you know. Charming scene, it looks like to me . . .'

I looked down. My back muscles tautened. I started to shake. I wanted to howl. I wanted to do murder.

. . . a lawn in front of a half-timbered house . . . Polly, in a blue
plaid dress and white tights and gleaming patent sandals, hunkered
down to study a daisy, or to 'pick grass for feed horses . . .' Polly
with a zig-zag line across her throat where someone had precisely
cut with pinking-shears. . .

My lungs were like bellows when the last match has burned
out. I tried to suck up air. 'Bastards,' I whispered or whimpered, 'bastards, bastards, bastards . . .'

'There. They said you'd feel better,' Keith twanged.

I looked up at him. 'One day,' I panted and gulped, 'one
day, Keith, I am going to rip the skin off that filthy twisted
face of yours.'

'All in the same boat, Munrow,' Keith shrugged. 'You, me,
Mr Quinn, all struggling to stay alive, you know. You and me,
we're just the same. Have to obey orders or there's trouble.
Mustn't blame the monkey, must we? Only question is, who's
the fucking organ-grinder, eh? Let me get my hands on him.
You and me both. You find him, you let me know. In the
meantime, you've got to do someone. In a race. That way
it's all nice and above board. Put him through the rails for
us, there's a good boy.'

'Who?' It was as much an expulsion of foetid air as a
question.

'Friend of yours, actually. Been very disobedient.'

'Oh, Christ, no,' I covered my eyes.

'That's it, Munrow,' the voice crooned. 'Uncle goody-two-
shoes, fucking Dave. You've got three days. Do a good job.'
He thrust an envelope at me. I opened it with shaking fingers.

There was silence then while neons flashed in my eyelids.
There were two quick thuds as the door swung to and fro.
My shoulders sank. I moaned 'Ohhh . . .' My hands dropped
to my sides. I opened my eyes. I never wanted to have to
open them again.

Keith was gone. There was just the smell of him in my
nostrils, the echo of his words in my ear. The door in front of
me still just oscillated. I looked down at the picture in my
hand, at the little girl, innocent of all save now.

129

No one should have to love so much.

'I hope you and Isobel work out, Neil,' Dave said softly. About us, the motorway service station clattered and the sleigh-bells tinkled. Glenn was filling the petrol tank. Laura had gone to 'powder her nose'.

'Early days, yet, Uncle,' I nodded.

'Yes. Ay, but she's a good sort. A fighter. I like that. Kati was a nice girl, but weak, you know? needed you full-time, always appreciating her, all that, and she had a fierce temper on her . . .'

'True enough, Uncle.'

'No. I hope it works out. I'd like to see you sorted.'

'Thanks, mate,' I washed my smile away with coffee.

'No. It's just . . . Ah, I don't know. Me and Laura, we're lucky.'

'God, you are.'

'And I've done OK. I've got the house, a bit of insurance. Anything happened to me, Laura'd be all right. That's the main thing. 'Course, we never did have young. Perhaps it's all for the good in the end. Laura'd have liked it, though. Still.' He gazed out through the plate-glass window, not seeing the MERRY CHRISTMAS emblazoned on the glass or the cars and lorries parked beyond.

'Come on, Uncle,' I took his wrist, 'you sound like an old fogey.'

'Ah, I dunno. Just – I suppose, Georgie dead . . . one of the greatest, and what's to show for it? Makes you think. And then – ah, well, the river runs on. That's the main thing, eh?'

'That's the main thing.' I nodded morosely.

'Thing is,' Dave sniffed, 'there's got to be a point where you make a stand. Got to be, hasn't there?'

'A point where the slave says no . . .' I dropped into his meditative tone, 'and knows that he'll die for it; so his "no" is like a kind of prayer. There's something bigger and better than me, something . . . oh, shit.' I shook myself. 'Sorry. You're making me as gloomy as you.'

'No, that's good, that is,' Dave beamed, excited. 'That's good. That's right.'

'Just a book I read. Can't remember. Silly stuff.' I looked at my watch. 'Where the hell has Glenn got to?' Then a consoling thought struck me. I wish it hadn't. I found myself talking without thinking. 'Anyhow, Uncle, you say not much to show for it? Georgie's life, I mean. How about us lot then? How about all those friends at the send-off, yesterday? Jesus, isn't that something to show for a life?'

'You're right,' Dave nodded. Again I had restored his good humour. Again I had given him the strength to resist his enemies.

'No, but listen, Uncle,' I tried to backtrack fast, 'there's also got to be a point where you do concede for the good of your loved ones. I mean, you're responsible . . .'

But Dave wasn't listening. He had stood as he saw Laura re-enter the room. He was smiling his broad diamond of a smile. Someone had been leaning on him. He had resisted. He was happy in the knowledge that, whatever happened, at least he had friends.

I had them drop me off at Bristol Temple Meads. I caught the first train to Exeter. There was no reason why I should not. The animals would be fed. There was no one else for me to worry about.

Some people actually fight for freedom.

Brigadier Paul Bertram, formerly head of the Racecourse Security Service, lived in a village called Whimple. I had never been there before, so it took several inquiries of locals – 'Brigideer, eh? Well, there were a general lived up along Boar's Bottom, but 'e'm dead this six seven years' – before the taxi drew up outside a lumpy, white thatched cottage on the plestor, just two doors up from the pub. I asked the driver to wait. Bertram was ex-directory, so this visit was entirely on spec. I hammered with the brass lion's head.

The man who answered was greyer and more stooped than when last I had seen him, but the polished conker toe-caps were the same and the tweeds, if now a little looser, as crisp as ever. The distinctive aquamarine irises were still there too, but the eyes were duller, the whites glazed and webbed like craquelure.

'What's this, then?' He checked me over from head to toe as though he suspected soiled puttees.

'Hello, sir.'

'Um,' he said. He wiped his lips on his sleeve. 'Oh. Munrow! Good. Bit of a surprise. Still. No. Splendid to see you. How's your mother?'

'Fine, sir,' I smiled. 'I'm sorry to bother you. I was just hoping you might spare me the time . . . I needed a little advice.'

'Delighted,' he shrugged. 'No, delighted. Of course. Fat lot of good may it do you, but still. Stay for a bit of something. Basic stuff, but . . . Tell your man to come back – what? Couple of hours? Good.'

He about-turned and marched back into the house. I translated his orders to 'my man', handed him a twenty-pound note and followed the Brigadier.

I walked into a tomb.

I don't know what it was. The furniture was good, well nourished and well groomed. There were yellow roses on the secretaire beneath the principal window, and a silver-framed photograph of the Queen on the Bechstein baby grand. Milky light from the garden touched the rows of racing and military memoirs, the regimental banner above the fireplace, the vast black lacquer coffer by the door. There were no signs of neglect; there was no gloom deeper than that which you expect in low-beamed, low-windowed cottages, yet I shuddered as I looked about me.

It was all so still, so orderly, so predictable. It had the air of a museum montage – *Typical Sitting-Room of Retired Brigadier, late 20th Century*. I knew without looking that there would be the silver-mounted hoof of a favourite point-to-pointer on the desk and photographs of beloved labradors behind that of Her Majesty. Waxworks might sit in those perfect armchairs with their nurses' bosom cushions, but not flesh and blood.

132

'In here,' a voice called. I walked towards it, through a retouched photograph of a dining room and into a white kitchen.

This was better, but only just. Better because plants grew on the windowsill, picture postcards covered one wall and a fat kettle spat and shivered on the Aga. Only just, because even these seemed ordered – unruly schoolboys in the OTC – and there was still this strange sense of walking into something flash-frozen.

Paul Bertram sat slumped and gape-legged. He stared at a space between his feet. He looked up when I entered. He smiled vaguely. 'Ah,' he said, 'good. Nice to see you, Munrow. Don't get up-country much these days, see the old faces. Miss it sometimes. Sometimes I thank God that I'm out of it all. So, how's it all going? Still riding, I see?'

'Yup. A veteran now. Seems like only last year I was a rookie and you were the great panjandrum.'

'God, yes. It flies, doesn't it?' he growled deep, and again resumed his study of the terracotta tiles. The kettle kept up its hobo's monologue. Otherwise there was silence. He raised his head again. 'Um, not today, though?'

'No, sir. Only the one meeting. No rides today.'

'Oh.'

Again Bertram subsided. I was about to cough when a sudden burst of energy shook him. 'Sorry, Munrow. Sorry.' He stood and gestured to a chair. 'Take a pew. Cup of tea? Coffee. Maybe something a little stronger? No? No, sorry. Maggie's out. Walk the dog. Does this course. Flower-arranging. Prinking, I call it. Sort of one old branch, one bit of japonica and some lichen, that sort of thing. I was telling James the other day, you know. I'm of the plonking school myself. Just plonk the whole lot in. James agreed. Absolutely. Still, she enjoys it. Keeps her off the streets, eh? Good. Now?'

I sat, and while he busied himself at the stove, I wondered if there were any point to this visit. The old boy seemed bright in bursts, like a wireless with a failing battery.

I remembered him as tough, tactful and damned near

omniscient. Again and again, there you were, smugly thinking you'd pulled off a nice little stroke and covered your tracks, and there was Bertram calling you over. Word in your ear, Munrow. All right this time, but don't let it happen again. Oh, and I wouldn't be seen in so-and-so's company again if I were you. His intelligence system was astounding. He knew everyone, and everyone, down to jockeys' wives, confided in him. He had been the best because he had been, as it were, a policeman concerned not with convictions but with preventing crime.

He hit the table so hard with the mug that the coffee slopped on to the pine. He did not seem to notice. He sat down with a hiss like something deflated. 'So. What's up, then?'

'Well, sir, it's . . . It's just . . . I'd like to put a hypothesis to you.'

'They all do.' The eyes flashed upward then turned back to the floor. 'All I ever meet these days is short-story writers. Forget the hypothesis, Munrow. You're in trouble and you want to know how to get out of it. All right. Seal of the confessional. Just telling me the story straight. Someone's leaning on you.'

'Er, yes.'

'Hooking them or what?'

'Hooking them and . . .' I sought momentary shelter in the coffee-mug, 'and putting pressure on other riders, turning them over, that sort of thing.'

'Bloody unpleasant,' Bertram nodded slowly. 'You naming names here?'

'I will, but can we just wait, see what you say, first?'

Bertram thrust out his lower lip. 'All right.' He stared dolefully down at his favoured spot. 'So why not go straight to RSS? We've dealt with this sort of thing often enough.'

'They're violent people. I've got a two-year-old daughter. They've taken photographs of her.'

'All right, so theoretically we can talk to the police, get a guard. It has been done before. Bloody expensive. What? Six men full-time, and even then you and your wife and your daughter have to stick together.'

'We're separated.'

'God. Bloody expensive.'

'And they could just wait, take revenge five years from now. I can't live like that indefinitely.'

'No. You say *they*. It's an organization, then?'

'It's a man, but he has people working for him. He'll not expose himself.'

'And there's the catch, isn't it?' Bertram shook his head sadly. 'You'll never get protection if there isn't evidence, and if there was evidence, you wouldn't need the protection because we'd bust the buggers. Still, Julian Honeycombe's not stupid. I can have a word, see if we can't put some pressure on your friends. He may be sceptical at first, but – well, we can only try.'

I gulped, first coffee, then air. I stood and walked over to the window above the sink. 'There's another problem,' I said at last.

'Go on.'

'This someone – this bastard who's leaning on me – he got a warned-off person to pay a silly sum into one of my bank accounts.'

'Hmph. And you took it?'

'No, but it was paid into a joint account. My wife took it out before I could do anything. Now she can't or she won't give it back. She reckons I'm trying to rip her off.'

'Tricky.'

I looked out at a lawn white with gossamer. The croquet hoops had not been lifted. There were three mounds down there beneath the escallonia hedge: the labradors, I guessed.

There was a slow popping behind me. I turned. Bertram was sucking on an empty pipe. He was frowning. He removed it from his mouth and looked down into the bowl as though expecting it miraculously to have filled.

'So you're in hock. Heavily?'

'Very,' I admitted.

135

'Neat. The idea is to trap you both ways.'

'That's right. So if I got to RSS, what happens? I'm warned off, right? I mean, I say, "Look, X is leaning on me," they say, "Bollocks. Munrow's just trying to wriggle out of a bent deal by blaming someone else." They're not exactly going to give my family round-the-clock protection, are they? Seriously, sir. What would you have done if I'd come to you with a story like this?'

Bertram was picking at the bowl of his pipe. He screwed up his face and inhaled on a long 'fff'. The blue eyes flashed upward. 'Seriously?' he mused. 'I couldn't have authorized protection, that's for sure. Not without evidence. I'd have given you a good talking to and I'd have had someone keep a quiet eye on you and your Mister X. I think you'll find that that's what Julian would do, too.'

'Yeah,' I said glumly, 'and meanwhile, if word gets out that I've been anywhere near RSS, my daughter meets with an unfortunate accident. It's not worth the risk.'

'Hmm,' Bertram pocketed his pipe. 'I think you're going to have to call this chap's bluff, Munrow. Stand up to him. It's what I always tell James . . .'

'James?'

'Mmm? Oh, my son. I'd forgotten. You don't know James, do you? No, no, it's what I'm always telling him. Stand up to them, nine times out of ten they'll back off. Threats are just that. You see if I'm not right.'

Suddenly I felt very lonely.

All our lives, we think, ah, well, we can always have recourse to authority, to mummy, to the courts, to the House of Lords or the newspapers. They will right wrongs. They will see justice done. Here, for the first time, was authority telling me, 'Bad luck, old chap. You're on your own.'

Quinn's trap was simple. It was also perfect. He knew my weaknesses, and somehow had attained access to the only truly precious thing in my life – the one thing for which I would die – or, far worse, kill.

Maybe the threat to Polly was just that – a threat. Quinn,

however, had already demonstrated that he was willing and able to do violence. On balance, I could not take the risk. And this time, it seemed, there would be no strong and loving arms to which to run with the plaint, 'It isn't fair.'

Bertram appeared to find the situation funny. He was rocking in his chair. Strange little hiccupping sounds bubbled rhythmically from his stomach. His shoulders arose and fell.

I frowned at him. I moved two steps closer. His face was all downward-curving slits and lines. His cheeks juddered.

'Sir?' I spoke quietly. All the same the word floated about the room like the susurration of a ghost. 'Sir?'

He just sat there, rocking and hiccupping. His stomach shook as though a dog were dying in there under the checked Viyella.

He took a huge wheezing breath. 'It's not – fair!' he squeaked. 'Oh, God. Oh, G-G-G-God, it's not fair.' The tears were sluggish and heavy. They came reluctantly from his eyes, dropped still more reluctantly from his dewlaps. They were old tears.

'Sorry, sir. What's the matter?'

'You!' – a blast on the Eland pipes. 'Oh, it's not your fault. Another bloody workaday little villain – sorry I shouldn't have said that – and there you are with a baby girl and fuck it, why in God's name . . . I'm sorry, Munrow, I shouldn't . . . but I – don't – think – I deserve – this! I'm no – I haven't – *you*, I mean, *you* . . .' His fingers scratched and scrabbled as if on a rockface at his trousers.

'I'm sorry, sir,' I crouched at his side, 'I don't know what I've done wrong, but . . .'

He turned on me, his eyes now more red than blue. 'Oh, there's nothing wrong with you. Oh, God. Oh forgive me. It's just . . . Your everyday passions, for your daughter, for money . . . What's her name?'

'Sorry?'

'I'm – I'm sorry.' His hand patted my arm. 'I have no right to behave like this. It's ridiculous.' Another deep breath, another big shudder. 'Your daughter, for God's sake!' he shrilled. 'Munrow's bloody cherished daughter! What's her name?'

137

'Polly,' I said softly.

'P – early.' He vomited the word. Again he resumed his rocking. 'I'm sorry, Munrow. You'd better leave. I'm sorry. The pub – the pub does a decent lunch. I'm sorry. Please.'

'Can I help, sir?'

'Help!' he howled, 'Please. I'll be all right. Sorry. Please. *Pleeease.*'

I left in silence, trembling at the hurt and the hatred.

It was the pub landlord who explained, over toasted sandwiches of orange cheese and ham-like wet vinyl.

The omniscient Brigadier had not seen that his first son was moving towards suicide. He had certainly not seen that James, his second son, had been disporting himself in the bath-houses of Los Angeles. Two months ago, James had paid the price.

We had all confided in Paul Bertram. His sons had not.

It was an outside ride, a goodish thing, a sturdy, genuine little grey well in at the weights in a decent three-mile chase, £11,000 added to stakes. Deep Midwinter ran true to form, jumped with flair and kept going forever. If he went well here, he'd go for the National. I might even get the ride, which would be nice.

Toby Wesley, the trainer, had known and respected my father. I rode for him whenever I could. He trained a small but classy string near Wantage. He had the cutest eye for a winner of any trainer in the land. With his easy manner and his abundant, prematurely grey hair, you would cast him, at first sight, as coming of long-dog stock – elegant, keen-eyed and sharp – but a Cairn terrier had got in somewhere along the line. You learned that when you talked to him or saw him at work. He had no small-talk, no time for fools, but he had grip. He would worry the best out of a horse. He would persist forever with a talented rogue and would know to the second when the time was ripe. As for owners, he treated them as necessary evils. As long as they paid their bills on time, he would be polite. If they tried to default or to interfere, he would tell them what they could do with themselves and their darling animals. Because he delivered the goods and because he scared the hell out of them, his owners usually behaved.

'Been having some bad results lately,' he told me in the paddock that afternoon. 'Don't like the look of it. Not getting past it, are you?'

'No, sir. Just the luck of the draw,' I shrugged.

'Yes, well, if you fall off this one, I'll know you're geriatric. Cavalry charge, far too many runners, so keep clear of trouble. Your only danger is King's Quest, and I think you've got the beating of him. Take him nice and easy first time round, let him settle. He'll do the rest. Right.' He reached out for the rein as the horse was led in to us. 'There are a lot of punters out there who are hoping for a happy Christmas paid for by this animal. Come to that, I am. He's ready. Win.'

That simple. I nodded. He gave me a leg-up and turned away. Joey, the lad who did the horse, led us out through the crowd, over the strip of tar and on to the turf. 'G-g-g-' luck,' he stammered.

I thanked him and sat forward and we were free, the horse and I, of people and buildings and noise, just hack-cantering smoothly up the strip of pocked turf, with no sounds now but the birdsong from the trees, the horse's breath and the pummelling of the hooves.

I had already ridden in the two races today. In none of them had I had a chance to get near Dave, even had I wished to.

Whether I wished to or not was moot.

One part of me told me that I had no choice. Just get it over with was all. Polly was more important than a hundred Daves. He was a friend, yes, but not an intimate. He had no child, but he would probably throw me into the path of a careering car if he thought that it might save his adored dog. Polly was all and everything, my reason for being, the one thing left of which I could boast, the one thing left for which I was responsible.

Another part echoed Dave's own words. There has to be a point where you say 'no'. But that was with your own life at stake. There's nothing so great – *vide* the Bobby Sands diet plan – about risking or even chucking away a life. Any tuppenny ha'penny crackpot can do that. This was different. This, the endangering of a child's life, demanded real courage.

I did not think that I had it.

'Only obeying orders . . .'

It's a commonplace of liberal morality that obeying orders is no excuse, and smug, commonplace minds at once invoke the excesses of the Nazis as proof positive. Like most commonplaces, it is crap.

Nice, law-abiding citizens always like to think that they would at once have volunteered for the French Resistance rather than goading their bankers and furriers on to cattle-trucks. In fact, of course, they would have worn their swastika armbands with pride precisely because they are nice and law-abiding. The Resistance was in large measure made up of criminals.

But then, that's always the trouble with liberal morality. It is an ethical belch, a complacent, meaningless noise born of a full fat stomach. Where there is fear, where there is a ruthless commander and where no laws prevail, orders is orders.

There was fear aplenty here – fear that had me starting up in bed at night with palms crawling and invisible creatures abseiling on my spine. Quinn was totally without ruth, and no laws prevailed out here in the country where jockeys were expected to contend and accidents to happen.

I knew how to put a man through the wings or the rails. It is not a highly technical business. Basically, a horse is large and heavy and, if used as an offensive weapon against an unsuspecting victim, will do serious damage. I had never done it myself, but had seen it done a couple of times in the old days. Once it had been seen as a macho rite of passage, no less than trousering or whoring. It was always nasty. It almost invariably resulted in broken bones. Sometimes, it was lethal.

You could rank it roughly with drinking a bottle of Scotch before driving down a market-town High Street without breaks. Unfriendly. Irresponsible. Potentially murderous.

Dave was at my offside as we drew up in a rank at the start. The wriggling wind brought a sound like rustling tweed from the stands, now a thousand miles away.

'This should put a smile on your face,' he cocked his head at my mount. 'Looks great, and well in.'

I nodded and mumbled.

'Enjoyed the trip to Ireland,' he crossed the reins at his crotch and gazed down the course with narrowed eyes. 'Nice to have a break.'

'Yup.'

'Isobel here?'

'Nope, Uncle,' I sighed. 'Not today.' My horse was dancing now, tossing his head against restraint. The field was moving forward. The going was good to soft. The hooves made little stabbing sounds. I pulled on my goggles with my left hand. 'Easy, feller,' I crooned, and shortened the rubber-covered reins.

At our left, a bay with a Roman nose decided to panic. He skittered sideways, bored down low, and, having got his head, put in a couple of quick bucks. Chris Leonard kept his seat, but bellowed, 'You bugger!' We all cooed and soothed and stroked.

'All set?' the starter called. He nodded. Somewhere behind me, a high-pitched voice called. 'No, sir! Wait, sir!' but the flag dropped, the tape sprung up with a deep twang and our high-stepping trot burst into a gallop.

For some reason Pat Vigar set off at one hell of a lick and Glenn chose to stay with him. It took the rest of the field about five seconds to realize that we had no desire to join in this game.

There is always the danger, of course, that a front-runner will build up so vast a lead that, even though staggering at the finish, he will win off the pace, but nothing in the two animals' form indicated that they were capable of such a coup. They'd come back to us. So we formed a clump at the centre of the track and played it cool, just bowling along, though still faster than I would have liked.

An ack-ack spurt of divots, a soft-shoe shuffle of panted breaths, a chorus of urgent roars, and we were up and over the first. I was lying third of fourth in the group and I was on a winner. I knew it just as you sometimes know even as you squeeze the trigger that the bullet is bound for the bull. This horse intended to jump cleanly, to run fast and to trounce his opponents. He knew his business. He was content to wait until the real business of racing began.

We took the second sweetly and gained a length. At the third, Chris Leonard's beast, a near-black some nine lengths ahead of us, rose to the fence. We saw Chris jerk. His blue arm arose, clawing at air. The horse vanished and was next seen riderless, trailing a broken rein.

At the fourth, I surprised myself.

I suppose it was just because the opportunity was so perfect. The eyes of the world were on Glenn, still well ahead of us. We were amid a mass of novices. Dave was on my outside. We had swerved out to avoid the cut-up and slippery mud on the inside.

I did not think about it. I did not plan it. As we both slowed on approaching the fence, I gave my boy a quick one down his near flank and swung him hard across. His quarters slammed into Dave's mount. For a split second Dave's thigh was warm on mine.

His horse grunted. Dave's eyes swivelled, wide with alarm but still somehow sad. 'You?' he said.

Our horses took off, all unbalanced, but Dave had no space for the jump between my mount and the wing. We had squeezed him out. My boot was under his as we lurched upward. I raised my foot hard. Dave yelped, 'Oh, *God!*'

His hands flailed, and he was gone, flung sideways at speed like a child from a fairground ride. I saw his shoulder smash into the rail, flinging his feet upward in a ghastly rag doll somersault. His mount just crumpled beside us with a rattle and a thump which shook the earth.

142

'Oh, Christ,' I drooled as I realized what I had done, but a voice inside me shouted and sobbed, 'Sorry, sorry, sorry! It's for Polly! It's for Polly!'

But if Dave could hear at all, it would be his own whimpering or screaming and the roaring in his own head.

And Laura would be happily hoovering and hoping for the best.

But Dave had not bounced. Not this time.

I opened the cottage's front door. Isobel stood on the doorstep. Her hair seemed to blaze in the lamplight. She smiled. She dropped her grip and threw her arms around me. Her kiss was warm and wet, but all that I could manage in response was a half-hearted pursing of dry lips. Her affection was an intrusion on my misery and a mockery.

I pulled away from her. 'Come on in,' I said, and pushed through the velvet curtain into the sitting room. Big Joe Williams was hollering, 'Don't you leave me here' on the stereo, and Sonny Boy's harp sobbing choked tritones between wails like a child's uncontrollable crying. The bottle of Black Bush stood half-empty on the coffee-table. I had bought it on the way home.

'Hey, are you all right?' Isobel asked as I threw myself down on to the sofa again.

I did not look up at her. 'Oh, fine, fine.' I picked up my glass, studied the swirling of the whisky for a second, then tossed it back. 'Just fine.'

'Hi, Isobel? How are things? You look great? How was work? I've missed you?' she prompted. She dumped her case and walked briskly to the stereo deck. The harp wails were reduced to whimpers. 'Come on, Neil. What is this? Stage-set? "I am feeling sorry for myself, please take note." OK, so I'm taking note. What's up?' She removed her jacket, flung it on to a chair and sat beside me. 'And if, after all this spoiled-brat business, you say "nothing", I'll kill you.'

'OK, OK,' I growled, 'sorry. Sure, you're right. Leave it alone. How are you?'

'Neil, you're pissed and in danger of becoming seriously boring.' Those legs, in black tights, curled properly and precisely back beneath her. 'What's up, for Christ's sake?'

'Nothing. Nothing.'

'I warned you,' she said brightly, 'you can't bloody well spread gloom and doom, make me feel lousy and then tell me nothing's wrong. Tell me or I leave.'

'No, I know.' I slapped my thighs in a decisive sort of way. 'You're dead right. I shouldn't be doing it. OK. Good cheer from now on. Sorry. Just a fit of the glooms. Sorry.'

'So, offer me a drink, at least.'

'Sure. Sure. Sorry.' I pulled myself up from the sofa and tottered a little uncertainly to the drinks cabinet. 'Damn silly. No, it's good to see you. Just . . .' I shrugged and pulled out a tumbler. I turned back to her. 'Now. No, everything's fine.'

She flicked over a page of the evening paper. 'Except that you're talking to me like a children's TV presenter and the Queen just died. Otherwise, perfect. So what happened today? You win anything?'

'Yeah,' I groaned. 'Yeah, I won.'

I sloshed whisky into Isobel's tumbler and slid it towards her. I sat again. Isobel was looking at the racing page. There was a picture of me taking the last with an heroic, resolute expression on my face. I had studied that photograph a lot this evening. I had also spent some hours in inspecting my hands and occasionally in appraising my reflection in the mottled mirror.

You read in the papers about people who would mug, torture or murder, and you thought of them as a class apart. You fulminated. Dreadful people. How can they? They need birching, educating, hanging.

I was among them now.

Oh, I had tried to minimize it. All part of a rough game, we all knew the risks, all that, but it was no good. These hands were no longer those of a jockey, a former public-school boy, a lover, a father, they were those of one who had been ready to kill and, worse, to kill a friend. Few things in life are irrevocable. This was. Maybe that was what they meant by mortal sin. For the rest of my days, I could not persuade myself that I was good or worthy of love, because I hated the class of man to which I had been reduced – to which I had reduced myself.

Right shoulder and elbow smashed; right wrist snapped; three ribs gone, one of them puncturing a lung; green fracture of the pelvis; multiple contusions . . .

Dave would live, but he would not be riding races again.

Laura's voice had been awaiting me on the Ansafone when I got home. 'Neil? Oh, dear, I was hoping you'd be back. Oh, heavens, I don't know. I'm off to see Dave. It's so terrible. I just wondered, could you possibly . . . ? Well, the key's on the top of the garage door. I was wondering if you could come down when you get a chance, let Archie out . . . I don't know how long I'll be gone, but I'll call when I know . . .' Her quavering voice had finally given up the struggle, and there was a lot of snuffling, a lot of rapid dog-like panting. 'I'm sorry,' she had squeaked at last, 'I'll call later.'

God grant that she would not.

And those grey eyes which I saw in the looking-glass – Dave too had looked into them with sorrow as the horror had hit him.

'*You . . .*'

He had been expecting it from somewhere, but not from me. This evening, I had searched those eyes, certain that they must somehow reveal what I had become. I had practised smiles and leers, and the face had remained specious. I would have bought a used car from me. I would have left my children with me. I hated myself the more for not bearing a mark of Cain.

And so, in deep self-pity, I had killed and cremated the sporting hero, the hopeful boy and the workaday jockey. All the scrapbooks of newspaper cuttings had gone on to the fire: Neil Munrow's first winner; Neil Munrow smiling at parties; Neil Munrow riding fierce finishes; Neil Munrow with his lovely wife and his daughter. All were cancelled out by the new identity: Neil Munrow, thug for hire.

I had sat and watched the white years curling up, turning brown, then black, then grey. They had given off a lot of heat. It had reddened my face, but it had not penetrated further.

Now there was just one newspaper report that remained; the only one that counted after all those years. Isobel was reading it.

'It says Dave had a crashing fall,' she said. 'Is he all right?'

'Nope.'

'Oh, hell, poor Laura. I must go and see her. Is he in hospital?'

'Yup. Will be for some time. She's with him.'

'Oh, shit. How bad is it?'

'About as bad as if he'd been beaten up by two guys with iron bars. About as bad as, say, a bad car smash. Career's over, anyhow.'

'God, that's terrible. Why didn't you tell me? We must go and see them, Neil. Tomorrow. Where is he?'

'We won't be welcome,' I said, and poured myself more whisky.

Isobel sat silent. Bessie Smith was belting out 'St Louis Blues' with Satchmo's cornet answering back to every phrase above the wheezing of the harmonium.

> *I hate to see the evening sun go down;*
> *I hate to see the evening sun go down;*
> *It makes me think of*
> *All my life go round . . .*

'You had something to do with it?' Isobel's voice piped at last.

'Everything.'

'Oh, Jesus,' Isobel let the paper drop on to the floor. She followed it. She knelt at my knees and looked up at me. 'What happened?'

I shrugged and looked away from her. 'It was him or Polly,' I said. 'Not much choice, really.'

'Quinn?'

I nodded.

'Oh, God, oh, God, oh, God,' she panted like a runner. She rested her forehead on my knees. She was shaking. 'There has to be some way out of this. There *has* to be.'

'"Said the joker to the thief",' I quoted. 'You find it, I'll take it.'

'Well, what's next, Neil?' Her voice was harsh and insistent. 'How much further can it go? Drug-smuggling? Murder? All because one man threatens you?'

'Not me. I'm not worried about me.'

'Polly, then. So anyone can own anyone just by threatening them or their children?'

'In theory, yes,' I swept her hands from my knees and stood. On my way over to the fire, I caught my knee painfully on the corner of the coffee-table. I said 'Fuck.' I did not want to be charming just then. 'So what would you do in the circumstances? Come on. Your child is threatened by a known villain. You're her only defender. What do you do?'

'Me?' Isobel still knelt at the sofa like a child saying her prayers. She did not look round at me. 'I don't know. Tell a lie. Make a blue movie, perhaps, but, beyond that, go to the police.'

'Oh, sure, but Quinn's got that one sussed, hasn't he? I go to the police, say, "Quinn's threatening me." They say, "Oh, sure. Fact is, you received eighty grand from a warned-off person and Quinn threatened to blow the whistle on you, so you're trying to incriminate him. Where's your proof?" I haven't got any, have I? So what happens? I get warned off. Think the police'll mount an armed round-the-clock guard on Polly on the say-so of a discredited person? Like hell they will. So Katya's out shopping one day, a car side-swipes the baby buggy.'

'But surely that's not going to do them any good, Neil? I mean, they'll have lost their slave and they'll run the risk of being done for manslaughter or murder.'

'Oh, sure. They'd sooner it didn't come to that. But the racecourse is a small world, Isobel, and Quinn wants to be top dog. If I go to the police, my story comes out. The police may not believe it, but in the weighing-room, they'll be talking about it: "Neil stood up to Quinn and *he's* come to no harm." No. Quinn depends on their saying, "Neil stood up to Quinn and look what good it did him," like they'll be saying at the moment about Dave.'

'You think he refused to work for Quinn?'

'Or one of Quinn's associates, yes. We're not talking about a world governed by law here. You can't just go running to the police or the Sunday tabloids. It's between him and me, and . . .' I shook my head. 'He's bigger than I.'

'So if there's no law . . .' Isobel said slowly, 'you have to go back to the old way of sorting things out.' She had pulled herself up on to the sofa without standing. She looked down at her hands in her lap.

'I've been thinking that. You mean, kill him?'

'If necessary,' her eyes flashed up at me. She spoke coolly. 'If necessary, yes. But there may be other ways. Like defy him, provoke him, trap him, get him to incriminate himself. Somehow. You can't go on like this.'

'I know it.' I closed my eyes and tried to banish the image of Dave plunging to pain and terror and the end of the life that he loved. 'I know it.'

'You've got to fight him, Neil.' Isobel stood. She walked over to me. She laid her hand over mine where it lay on the stone mantel. 'We don't know that he'll attack Polly, and if he does, we'll have to be ready to defend her. But as it is, you've got just two options open to you – doing more damage, eroding your soul, driving me away, in the end driving Polly away . . .'

'You'd leave?' I stared down at the charred mess in the grate. 'You'd go?'

'I will go,' she said firmly. 'I don't want to, but I'll not stay here and watch you rot. A man hates himself, he can't love anyone else. I've seen it.'

'Hm.' I reached up for the cigarettes on the mantel. I tipped up the packet, tapped out a fag. 'OK,' I turned my back on the dead fire, the pauper paterfamilias-style. 'And the other option?'

'You know that.'

'Top myself, you mean?' I grinned. 'It has crossed my mind.'

'Of course it has. In many ways it's the best thing you could do.' She was incredibly cool. She flicked through compact discs. It made a sound like sarcastic applause in an empty hall. 'Quinn's honour would presumably be satisfied. Polly would get whatever life insurance you have, and you could do no more harm. God, when I think of Dave . . . I am going to see him, Neil.'

She picked out a disc: Buddy Guy. Her words seemed to circle like echoes.

I said, 'I haven't got life insurance. Or rather, I have, but it's all mortgaged to the bank. And anyhow – I don't know. I'm not the suicide type. It's such a – such a bloody self-important thing to do. It's like an orgy. Looks so silly next day. And the thing that stops me . . .' I breathed in deep through my nose. I laughed. 'Ah, God. I couldn't stand to have Katya and her arsehole wine-merchant bring Pol up alone. I've got so much to give her, if I get the chance.'

'So.' Isobel moved away from the stereo to pick up her drink. 'That leaves, you rot . . .' she sauntered over to me, sipped and looked up over the rim of her glass, 'or fight,' she said simply. Mr Guy of Chicago started a tender massacre of the innocents.

'Oh, God.' I reached out to run a finger gently down her glowing cheek. 'It's just a case of where you call a halt, isn't it? *Tosca* is one thing, but hurting other people . . . Shit, why didn't I talk to you before today? Dave could still have been walking. Poor Uncle,' I said sadly. I blinked.

'No. You're the poor one.' She took my hand and held it against her cheek. 'You have to live with it.'

'And you,' I croaked. I cleared my throat. 'And you?'

'If we fight.' She half smiled.

'We?'

'We, but only if we fight.'

I was suddenly filled with a wild ebullience in proportion to my previous gloom. I pulled her to me. I kissed her hard. I almost squeaked with excitement as I released her. 'We fight, my love,' I told her. 'Now let's brainstorm, for God's sake. Let's work out how.'

It was good that night.

We plotted excitedly like students sketching out careers or first novels. Like careers or novels, everything worked out sweetly in the end, 'all things being equal . . .'

All things are manifestly unequal, so why are we forever consoled and enchanted by discussion of the evidently chaotic universe's affairs with that absurd, laboratory-conditions *caveat?* The Worker State, the Happy Ever After, the downfall of Quinn – all are bound to come about, 'all things being equal'. Time will stop if only we speak the right spell.

But Cinderella grows fat and scrofulous and her Prince takes to the booze. Time does not stop. There is no end. Because passions and needs and earthquakes and viruses have never heard about all things being equal.

Neither had Quinn.

Part II

CHRISTMAS CARDS CAME, portraying children with gob-stopper cheeks playing in a marshmallow world. Christmas came, as usual, with sallow children glued to the video and not so much as a dusting of snow to gladden the heart and justify the heating bill. I moved the last of the furniture up to the farm. I cleaned out the cottage and locked up for the last time. On Christmas Eve, I loaded up the Shogun with parcels and bottles. I drove up to Gloucestershire.

My mother lived in a real cottage with a real cottage garden which ran down to the Windrush. Pollarded crack-willows leaned over the stream. They looked like heraldic gauntlets holding sheaves of arrows. Unlike the bastard child of Noddy and Edith Holden which I had just left, this cottage had external walls and shingles frogged with moss, and in-ternal walls which bulged like a nurse's bodice. There was not a horse-brass nor a thick carpet in sight – just small, dark oil-paintings and small, light watercolours on the walls and threadbare, once-precious rugs on the dark boards.

Even I had to duck as I entered the sitting room. My mother sat at her bureau in the far corner. She just looked over her shoulder, said, 'Hello, darling. Good to see you,' and returned to her writing.

I kissed the top of her head. The hair was all buttery white now, but sleek and plentiful. The younger of her two Pekes scrabbled at my knees and panted. The older, Cortez, who now looked more like a worn feather-duster, growled fiercely. 'What are you up to, then, Mama?' I asked.

'Oh, just another servants' hall romance. The count has just nibbled Emily's nipples in the shower, sending waves of ecstatic pleasure coursing through her. Can waves course? Well, they do for Emily. And his strong, nimble hands are soothing away her fears with their insistent caresses.'

'Oh, good.' I nodded approval. I strolled over to the window and bent to peer out past deep mullions at the rain-soaked orchard. 'They're married, I trust?'

'Oh, no, darling. You *are* behind the times. No, they don't have to be married these days. She has to sob a bit afterwards, just to show that she's a nice girl, and they have to get married in the end, that's all.'

'I don't believe it,' I chuckled. 'My mother a pornographer!'

'I know, isn't it fun?' her pen scratched. She continued to speak as she wrote. 'It just seems to flow. Deep down, you see, you have a very ardent, dirty-minded mother with a marked streak of the vulgar in her. I certainly never did anything like this in a shower. I always hated showers. Can't think where it comes from. I get it wrong sometimes. They got rather agitated when I had the last couple do it on his charger. He was a hussar, but apparently it's not possible.'

'Oh, I don't know . . .'

'Well, I just thought it would take some of the work out of it. He was a very languid hero. You know, at a brisk trot . . .'

Laughter burst from me. 'You really do think it out, don't you? No, but difficult, I'd say, and dangerous.'

'Yes, I suppose if the animal bucked . . . Oh, well, I suppose you should know. I should have done more research in my day . . . There.' She laid down the pen. 'I'll leave the sobbing till later. She's just throbbed and exploded internally, which is nice. Let's get some tea.'

Rose Galloway, my mother's literary *alter ego*, had first seen the light some eight years ago, to my considerable surprise and amusement. My brother, Donald, had not thought it funny.

With my father dead, however, my active mother had moved to this little cottage. The garden kept her busy in spring and summer, but in autumn and winter she found an outlet for her energies and imagination in the lucubrations of Rose Galloway.

She was a hit. Twelve books on, she had a devoted readership much given to correspondence. Her success, I think, owed much to her unawed and intimate understanding of the aristocracy and their ways and much to her sheer love of the process of fantasy and of writing. She was also thrilled to

154

be earning a healthy wage which enabled her to go on horti-cultural tours of exotic places twice or three times a year.

'So, darling,' my mother poured water into the teapot while I spread butter on crumpets, 'Donald'll be here at drink's time, so tell me the news. What's that ridiculous girl up to?'

I told her about Katya's attempts to deny me contact with Polly.

'The girl is potty,' my mother announced. 'I mean, I am sure that you're quite impossible, but that is no excuse for gross discourtesy. I could live with Attila the Hun provided that the commonplace courtesies were observed – smile in the morning, go to work, smile in the evening, hope you had a good day's pillaging, good night, Attila, dear. And if you must have lovers, well and good, provided they know their place. And as for using that adorable little girl as a weapon . . . Ridiculous. Wicked. That child is bright and sensitive. She'll need her extended family. She certainly does not need this appalling sort of emotionalism and self-indulgence as an example. Well, just let her try to stop me from seeing her . . .'

I liked that idea. Katya would be a Canute before a tidal wave. 'Anyhow,' my mother sat at the kitchen-table, 'is she being difficult about property?'

'Only wants the lot.'

'Well, she won't get it, will she?'

'Not quite. Don't worry, the silver, the furniture and so on, they're inalienably ours. No, but I'll have to sell the house.'

My mother sighed. Her lips formed a 'b' and stayed that way. Her fingers drummed twice. 'Just when I thought you were settled,' she said at last. 'It really is so infernally unfair. She sits on her arse every day through your marriage, oc-casionally shrieking in an unforgivably vulgar way, and now she wants your money. She didn't ride any of those races, did she? Bloody girls, behave like gorgons one minute then like my heroines the next – "Poor me. I am frail and men are nasty horrid beasties!" – and the law falls for it.'

'I agree,' I nodded, 'but it's not easy for them either. They've got your heroines and Joan Collins for rôle models, Barbara

Cartland's floozies and the authoress. Which do they emulate?'

'Why can't they just be themselves, for heaven's sake?' My mother was exasperated.

'Because, mother dearest,' I smiled, 'they do not have your supreme self-confidence. You are one of the only people I know who never asks why she is loved or seeks to earn love. You accept it as of right. That's very enviable.'

'Well, honestly, all this proving oneself . . . Anyhow, I shall write to Katya, put her straight. Nice enough girl but – I hate to say it – no breeding and certainly no discipline. Is there anyone else?'

'For her, you mean, or for me?'

'Oh, I know about her, darling. My pet policeman down the road checked for me. Old Gerard Wickham's son. Probably about right for her if he's anything like his father. Gerard was wet as water. Red face. Stood on one leg like a stork and showered you with spittle. Made colonel, but God knows how. Probably – yes, there's an example – I mean, he wasn't so much married as devoured by that ghastly woman Denise. No family. American mother, though. That's right. Very highly developed material instinct. I'm sure any son of Gerard's will dance attendance on little Katya. No. You. Have you found anyone to throb and explode with? Frankly, I'd sooner hum and glide, but throbbing and exploding seems *de rigueur* these days.'

'Yup,' I said simply, and my teeth crunched into crumpet. Molten butter ran down my chin.

'I hope she's not small and blonde this time.'

'Nope. Tall and brunette. A fighter and a worker, not a moper. Yeoman stock. You'd like her.'

'Serious?'

'Funnily enough, yes.' The admission still surprised me. 'Just at the moment when I told myself, OK, happiness is not for me, just get laid and make the most of it, she turns up, and all the things in me – you know, industrious, defensive, noisy, silly jokes, anti-hysteria – all the things which were vices to Katya are virtues to her. We get on.'

'Than which, *pace* my dear readers, there is no more romantic assertion,' my mother nodded. 'When do I meet her?'

'Why don't you come over to Fox Farm the day after Boxing Day? Polly will be with me then.'

'Yes. All right. Lunch. Splendid.'

I drained my tea and pushed the cup and saucer away. I pushed my chair back and leaned forward, hands clasped. I hesitated, but not much. My mother was a realist.

'Listen, Mama, when you hop the perch, what do I get?'

'Oh, dear,' she mopped her mouth. 'Not much, I'm afraid. Daddy left nothing, as you know. I suppose it all depends on Rose. I mean, there's the furniture and the pictures, jewellery and so on. They're all yours, what's left of them, and whatever cash I have. That could be – well, at the moment, I've got about forty thousand all told. I live frugally and Rose earns me perhaps twenty if I'm lucky. Say I'm investing ten. In a few years, if I can keep going, that'll be a reasonable sort of nest-egg. Other than that, there's just the house, and I can't go back on that, even though I always did think you were silly there.'

I nodded. Two years ago, when I had wished to buy the house, I had begged my mother to bequeath this cottage entirely to my astute brother, Donald. He had given me £60,000 for my share. The cottage must now be worth a quarter of a million easy.

I bought Betamax.

'So, right,' I smiled up at her. 'No ready money.'

'Not really, darling. I really must have that private income. I mean, what if Rose flops? What if I get incapacitated and can't get to the cyanide pills before those ghoulish sawbones get to me? How much do you really need? To hold on to the house, I mean?'

'Oh,' I waved casually, 'sixty grand or so.'

'Oh, God,' she said.

I said, 'Right.'

'Hello, Marnie, *darling*,' my sister-in-law Rachel was effusive.

She hugged my mother to her. 'Mmmah, mmmah! Lovely to see you. God, it's cold out there. Donny's just unloading children and luggage. Hello, Neil. No, honestly, Araminta has been impossible, wanting sweeties, wanting a wee. We must have stopped six times. Sholto's only just fallen asleep in the last twenty minutes, so he'll kick up a frightful fuss . . .'

I was heading for the front door when five-year-old Araminta walked in. Her honey-coloured hair was piled high. She clutched a doll to her tartan chest. Her shoes left a trail of dark mud. 'Hi, Araminta,' I spun her round. 'Back to the door and off with those shoes, there's a good girl.'

She came obligingly enough with me until Rachel's voice behind me said on three accusing notes, 'Nee-ee-eil?'

At this point, Araminta decided to scream.

'Ahh . . . ' Aquascutum and Burberry swept past me and engulfed the bawling child. Rachel crooned, 'Poor baby.' Her blonde head jerked around. Her pinched pretty little face snapped up at me. 'Just leave the discipline to me, will you, Neil? Minty was so looking forward to seeing Granny, weren't you, Minty?'

Minty, unsurprisingly, bellowed 'Yeeay!'

'How would you feel if a total stranger twice your size suddenly shouted at you?' Rachel twanged. 'There, there. Don't you worry, darling . . . '

'I am not a total stranger, Rachel, dear, and I did not shout . . . ' I cast a despairing glance at my mother. She cocked her head and rolled her eyes heavenward, then frowned as if to say, 'I know, darling, but please . . . ' I shrugged. I walked out through the front door into the blue satin night. On the doorstep, I passed a pretty, bespectacled young woman carrying Sholto, who sucked a dummy. I had once told Rachel that a dummy was the last resort of the idle parent and why didn't she give the poor little bugger a carrot to suck instead. She had lain on her back and kicked her heels and screamed.

I chucked Sholto under the chin. He frowned sulkily at me. The girl at least smiled, which was nice.

There was a bright caul of cloud over the moon, but I

could clearly see Donald's legs and bum at the top of the garden as he reached into the Volvo station-wagon. He wore designer-jeans, which was unfortunate. His bum had developed a double chin. Four large suitcases stood on the grass by the rutted track.

'Don,' I said as I drew near.

He jumped. 'Oh, hello. Yes. Hello, Neil.' He straightened. He dusted off his hands and held one out to me. I took it. We stood at arms' length. 'Doing well, I hope.'

'Yup, Don, fine,' I said. I looked up at his silly white face, now the shape of a seated cook. His dark hair was thin, and slicked sideways over his scalp. His ears were prominent, his lower lip shiny and pendulous as twin pink grapes. 'Children doing well, I see?'

'Yes. Yes. Fine. Thanks.'

'Great.' A cold breeze swept between us like a passing train of ghosts. I looked up, then down, then up the metalled track. 'Right. Let's be getting this little lot in.' I picked up two of the suitcases and lugged them down the path. I heard Donald following.

Don was two years older and four inches taller than I. We had squabbled together, grown together, done all the usual things which siblings do. Like many an older brother, he had been an insecure manikin, a petty tyrant, proud, shy, spiteful, uncertainly strutting.

But his downfall had been his cowardice. Physical courage is no great thing. It is the aboriginal and the unimaginative who do not suffer vertigo, and many a mindless thug had borne home a VC or a congressional medal. The great thing, the rare thing, is the vision and the self-discipline rationally to quiet terror in a greater cause.

Donald had imagination aplenty, but no such self-discipline.

In a household such as ours – my father, after all, had been one of the great race-riders, my mother a noted goer in the shires – cowardice was nigh a crime.

Whilst I mucked out, rode out and fought with the stable-lads, Donald sulked in his room. He hated horses and water. He mistrusted dogs. In a bid at self-justification, he took to despising such things, and for that matter, me.

At public school, he boasted of our maternal forebears but scoffed at our father's fame. By the time that I joined him, he was pretty much universally disliked, save by a small group of blustering, monied slobs. I tried to befriend him, but he had to justify his earlier jokes at my expense. I was soon playing stand-off for school teams and the Artful Dodger in a production of *Oliver!*, debating fiercely, fencing wildly and hunting with the beagles. I was one of those who found pack-life easy.

The blind can understand vision and the sighted can sympathize with the blind, but the fearless cannot understand the fearful. My father was not a brutal man, but Donald's fears seemed to him mere wilfulness. He was of the sink-or-swim school. Donald sank, spluttering, and my father looked on, exasperated and bemused. I swam a stubborn, reckless doggy-paddle and my father smiled. As he drank himself slowly but certainly to death, he taught me, shared his secrets with me, occasionally even grunted approval as I rose to the First XV, took over the schooling of his young animals and found better things to do with stable-girls than fight. He disdained Donald even as Donald approved of us.

Donald saw himself as our mother's champion, though my mother needed no champion. Don wooed my mother's father and brothers who had rejected her and us. This won him nothing but the odd invitation to dinner or to a house-party. Each such dinner became 'the other day' with Donald, and remained 'the other day' for years.

Perhaps predictably, Donald married a very minor title; The Honourable Rachel Walters was the daughter of a third baron – an Edwardian industrial creation. She still had a modest private income. Perhaps predictably, too, he rode the Thatcherite bore and enjoyed a few years of earning silly sums as an estate agent. I, the jockey, remained an acute embarrassment to him, as our father had been in his childhood.

But I knew something which, I think, would have given Donald apoplexy. Three years before he met and married Rachel, a group of friends and I had taken a chalet in Verbier. The pretty young blonde chit who had cooked for us (and had somehow nightly found her way into a twin room where a deal of fun was had by all) was Rachel Walters. She used to creep in in darkness, so the party joke was that the two who first enjoyed her largesse would give way to two of their friends. She knew this, of course, but it did nothing to diminish her enthusiasm. It so happened that I was depressed, young and in love at the time, so I never did occupy one of those beds. Rachel did not know that.

Now Donald was out of a job, and Rachel, so my mother informed me, did not take kindly to having him about the house all day. She drew attention to every pound that she spent, for all that Don had bought the house and made provision for the children's education.

She was not my favourite woman, and she, scared stiff that I might reveal all, illogically treated me like something that came in on her husband's heel.

'You are the enemy of everything we stand for,' she had shrilled at me over a lunch-table last year.

'Ah, well,' I had told her, 'I don't know much about the things that you *stand* for, Rachel, but . . . '

She had thrown a *crème brûlée* at me and left the room like a dried flower arrangement on springs.

'So,' she said sweetly over the fennel soup this evening. 'Another year. Not the best of years for us. How about you, Neil?'

This was a seriously stupid question. I was good, however. I swallowed a mouthful of wine and counted to three as I did some napkin-work. 'Oh, not too bad,' I grinned at her. 'A year of transition, really. Painful, but then so is birth. Onward and upward. Yes, overall, I reckon, things have improved.'

'I saw Katya the other day,' she piped.

'Good.'

'In London. For lunch. Poor thing. She seems in a terrible state.'

'Yes, she does seem a lot,' I nodded. 'She's good at seeming. We men aren't allowed to seem hurt or overwrought. Just shut up and get on. Katya does more self-expressing than anyone I know. I discovered that she had been burdening our postwoman with her every least problem for over a year.'

'God,' my mother sighed.

'Well, what's wrong with that?' Rachel's hair had now started to swing. 'What's so wrong with a postwoman? No, really. She's a human being, isn't she? I should bloody well think she would need someone to talk to. You scared the wits out of her.'

'Oh, is that what happened to them?'

'There. Clever clever remarks like that, nibbling away at her confidence all the time. Do you know?' she addressed the whole room now. Her index finger hooked and freed, hooked and freed the stem of her wine-glass, 'Neil was sleeping with a loaded shotgun in the bedroom. How was Katya meant to live with that – a threat to her life? He could have used it on her. I mean, come on.'

'There was no threat to her life,' I said. My voice thudded like muffled drums, 'and this subject is putting me off my food. But for what it's worth, Rachel, dear, have you ever slept in an isolated country house, woken up in the middle of the night hearing strange noises, remembered stories in the newspapers about burglaries and murders and started to conjure fancies? Because if you haven't, you plainly never progressed beyond Noddy and Big Ears and therefore didn't get to *Moonfleet* or *Kidnapped* or *Coral Island*.'

'Thank God, I didn't, if they made you all morbid like that. Books like that should be banned.'

'Burned, surely,' I suggested.

'Well, I always sleep with a gun,' said my mother, 'partly for foxes . . .'

'Must you?' Rachel flinched.

'. . . partly for protection.'

162

'Ah, that's different.'

'I don't see why,' my mother was blithe. 'According to your theory, this indicates that I cannot wait to go rushing around the countryside drinking foxes' blood and blasting the heads of the locals. I really don't understand this concept of yours, Rachel, dear. If a man getting on a Bristol train tells me that he is going to Bristol, I, trained in psychology, am to assume that in fact he is going to London, is that it?'

'No, of course not!' The hair was swinging all over the shop now, and there were deep channels down her neck. 'This is ridiculous. It is a known psychological phenomenon, that's all.'

'So are hallucinations, my dear, but I do not assume them of my friends. It makes life difficult. You say, "I just saw an elephant." I might momentarily doubt you if we were, say, in St Paul's Cathedral, but as a general rule I would assume that you had indeed just seen an elephant. It makes life so much easier, don't you think? Neil, darling, would you help me with the plates?'

I gratefully threw down my napkin and collected the soup-plates. Rachel poured herself wine as though it were ketchup.

In the kitchen, my mother sighed heavily as she laid down the bowls. 'Oh, dear, oh, dear, that girl.'

'I try, Mama.' I took her hand and squeezed it. 'Her choice of subject-matter is unerring.'

'I know, I know. Half-digested titbits of theory all liquidized into a sort of amorphous mush. It's intolerable.'

'They actually call it "correct" these days.'

'They don't,' she gaped. 'They don't.'

'Oh, yes, they do. There's such a thing as "politically correct". Rachel's it, or tries to be.'

'Politically correct?' my mother shuddered. 'Oh, God, they will be burning books again soon.'

'They are, Mama, they are.'

'Listen, Neil,' my mother donned oven-gloves and squatted before the stove, 'this money business, this settlement, all that. I'll do anything I can, but . . .'

'I know, love.' I took the *pommes dauphinoises* from her. 'Don't worry. *Je me débrouillerai, de toutes façons.*'

'Yes, but listen. I could fork out, say, five without really hurting my income, and upstairs I've got a few tiny things – jewellery and whatnot. They'd have gone to Polly anyhow, in the end, and I don't have much cause to wear them now, even if I dared. We'd probably – I don't know, judging by the insurance valuation – it'd probably come to twenty, maybe more. It's the best I can do, but if it would help . . . '

I leaned over the dish of potatoes and kissed her either cheek very gently. 'Thanks, darling. I think it might help. If it doesn't answer, I'll give it all back to you. I'll not put good after bad.'

'Right, take those in. I'll bring the broccoli. We'll go upstairs for a look after dinner. Quietly. And darling?'

'Mmm?' I had half turned away. Now I turned back.

'Try to keep the peace with dear Rachel. Politically correct? God. I don't know.'

Maybe Donald had second sight. Whatever, he broached the subject immediately after dinner. He had lit a panatella and poured himself a glass of port and now felt sufficiently well-armed to play father. He took up his position on the rug before the fireplace. 'Tell you what, as it's Christmas, I was just wondering, Mummy. Rachel and I were talking about it, you know. I mean, you don't get out much nowadays, and what with the insurance and so on, probably a relief for you. I mean, there are a few pieces – the diamond and ruby necklace and earrings, the sapphire ring . . . '

'That lovely little emerald bracelet . . .' put in Rachel.

'And we were just thinking, you know, if you don't use them – and you've always said that each generation should enjoy things while they can – and obviously Rachel would look great in some of those things, really enjoy it, you know, bit of posh glitter . . . ' He realized that he was begging. He took a deep breath, 'Well, so we've discussed it, and we think it best that we should take over the old family baubles – those that you don't use, anyhow.'

My mother seemed unperturbed by this speech. She stroked the old Peke in her lap. With her other hand she touched the hair at her temple in a curious, delicate gesture. 'Oh, no, no, darling,' she said sweetly. 'No, you know the deal. We really can't go chopping and changing now. You get the house; Neil gets the contents, and that, I'm afraid, includes the jewellery. I am sorry, I thought that was all clear.'

I must confess that no such deal had been clear to me. On the basis of past discussions, I had always believed that the jewellery, much of it inherited by my mother from her grandfather or given to her at her christening, was to be split up as separate from the rest of the contents. My mother was improvising, I was sure, but she was doing it beautifully.

'Oh,' said Donald. He threw back the tiny cone of purple liquid. He walked over to the drinks table and refilled the glass. He was frowning deeply. At my left, Rachel's head swivelled towards me. I did not see her eyes, but I flinched all the same.

'Oh,' said Donald again stiffly, 'I see. So Neil gets all the Galloway stuff. I see. Not that he's ever had the least interest in the family.'

'Nor they in us, darling,' my mother smiled, 'and I have divided the furniture equally up till now. No, you've got Rachel's family. I'm sure they must have some nice jewellery, haven't they, Rachel? Of course they have. And you'll have the house, which is a very nice little nest-egg for Araminta and Sholto. Polly deserves a little something, too.'

'So I'm being punished for marrying well, is that it?' Donald's dewlaps trembled.

'No, darling, but that is my decision and I hope you'll agree that I have the right to decide what happens to my property, hmmm?'

'It's family property,' Donald's chins stretched like a very old concertina.

'And it's staying in the family, isn't it? Now come on. It's Christmas. Let's all be full of goodwill and so on.'

'Goodwill!' Rachel laughed on a rising scale. She hit the

sofa hard. 'God! Neil has done nothing for this family, nothing except bring shame on it. Professional jockey, God! And we . . . and Minty and Sholto . . . Do you realize how much I am having to pay just for us to stay alive? Do you? And you ask for . . . I mean . . .' She saw alarmed and pitying eyes on her. The words trickled to a halt. She inhaled with a wheeze. Her voice wobbled. 'I'm not . . . I'm just trying to be fair. It just seems so *unfair*. Donny's the elder, and Neil can't wear the things, and Donny's the only one who's even bothered to talk to the Galloways. It's just . . . Oh, well,' she fiercely folded her arms, 'I suppose that's typical. All right. We'll manage. Don't worry.'

'We won't,' said my mother. 'Have some more Drambuie, darling. Donald, do top her up. And we'll have to leave soon if we're going to get seats at mass. Oh, listen,' she beamed as 'Good King Wenceslas' bubbled up outside. 'Neil, darling, go and invite them in, will you? And Rachel, would you mind terribly going to the larder and getting the mince pies and things? The tray is laid.'

Rachel scowled. She swung herself off the sofa with a hiss. 'They'll only wake the children,' she snapped, 'but I suppose that doesn't matter . . .'

So we sat there in the drawing room, a happy family gathering, as the singers in scarves and woolly hats and mittens growled or trilled the tale of Wenceslas. I joined in *con brio* on

> *Therefore Christian men be sure,*
> *Wealth or rank possessing,*
> *Ye who now will bless the poor,*
> *Shall yourselves find blessing.*

Donald did not sing. Rachel's face was a visor slammed shut.

They were playing 'Good King Wenceslas' at Katya's place when I telephoned the following afternoon. I had crept up to my mother's room and sat on the candlewick bedspread. There was a smell of lavender. There was a crucifix above the bed. There was a host of family photographs on the dressing-table.

I said, 'Hello? Katya? Hi. Happy Christmas.'

'Oh, right. Happy Christmas. Did you want to speak to Polly?'

'Er, yes, please, love. All well?'

Katya did not answer. A male voice, Wickham's, I assumed, said, 'Go along, Polly.' Katya said, 'It's Daddy!'

There was shuffling then.

'Hello, darling,' I said softly. 'Happy Christmas. I miss you.'

'Christmas,' she said happily, 'Christmas tree.'

'Did you get lots of presents, little one?'

'Yes,' said a tiny voice.

'And are you having fun?'

There was no reply.

'I love you very, very much,' I told her, and my breath became shorter. My voice broke into a whimper. It sometimes did that for some reason. 'I'll see you in a couple of days, OK?'

'OK.'

There was a long pause. 'King Wenceslas' made way for 'The Cowboy Carol'. The man said '. . . ever seen anything so ridiculous . . .' Male and female laughter climbed and descended, hand over hand.

'God bless you, my Polly,' I breathed.

'Yes, Daddy.'

'Bye, bye, darling.'

'Bye, bye.'

I lowered the receiver as though it were made of spun sugar. My fingertips caressed it as I raised my hand.

Receivers get slammed a lot. Sometimes they get smashed. Nice to know they have good times too.

The Christmas tree by the hotel's swing-doors stamped and flounced its tinsel at Isobel as she strolled in, smiling. She was in a black-and-white houndstooth suit – Pollen again – with silly bright buttons, over a black body and black tights. I know that they were tights. She did not wear stockings under skirts so short.

She used a Guerlain moisturizer. I used Clarins. She wore Chant d'Aromes, too. I knew, because I had introduced her to it. Her tan shoulder bag was by Mulberry. I knew these things about her now. Her smile was simply happy. It was there before she saw me.

I stood. Unlike the Christmas tree, the grandfather clock under which I had sat appeared unmoved by the competition.

It was all right, I thought. She was, she really was lovely, and her pace did increase as she saw me, and she held out her hands, palm downward, so that when I took them, she could grasp mine and turn them and bring them up to her lips, one by one, before kissing my cheek and murmuring, as she did so, 'I am going to rape you.'

'I rape easy,' I told her.

She stepped back. Our hands were still interlinked. She said, 'Oh, God, it's good to see you. Put that dimple away or I shall pounce upon you here and now.'

'I love you,' I said inconsequentially, and the smile on my face made me happy too.

'Twit,' she kissed me again. 'I love you.'

'Come on. Sit down. Tell me everything.'

'Have we got time?'

'Sure, sure. Don't have to be there till midday, and it's only down the road. Come on. Want anything?' I released her hands.

She sat. 'No, don't bother. I had a massive breakfast before I left. God.'

'So. Good Christmas?'

'Mmmm, yes. Nice, actually. An uncle I hadn't seen for years, my cousin, Emma. A really good dinner-party on Christmas Eve. Turned into a sort of impromptu rave-up. Fairly exhausting, but fun. And I didn't eat *too* much. Brandy butter sort of leaps down the gullet willy-nilly, but otherwise I was good. What about you?'

'Curate's egg,' I pronounced. 'My mum was on good form. Donald and Rachel were – well, Donald and Rachel. She's gone vegetarian now and swears that Araminta is, too. Araminta doesn't know it. I was privily slipping her turkey and sausages throughout the holiday. She guzzled the lot. Rachel said I was corrupting her.'

'In other words, you spent the whole time winding the poor woman up.'

'Nonsense. Wasn't me that crept in and slipped *Little Black Sambo* into Minty's stocking.'

'You didn't.'

'No, Father Christmas did.'

'You're wicked. Now. Are you set for today?'

'I suppose.' A shudder shook my shoulders. 'God Almighty, but I hope we're doing the right thing.'

'We are. It was a good idea. Don't worry.' She took my hand and squeezed. 'Personally, I think the man's all piss and wind and won't do a damned thing . . . '

'I wish I could believe that.'

'And if he does, at least you're waiting for it. Polly'll be with you. You won't be the first man to defend his daughter from cheap crooks.'

'I know.'

'And maybe – at the worst – he'll send some guys round to beat you up on a dark night. That's the worst, I reckon.'

'Thanks. Yeah, but that I can take. Like falling off a horse plus a bit more indignity.'

'Dave had it worse. Anyhow, it's better than penal servitude.'

'I may have the means to buy a little mercy,' I said.

'What's happened? Family come up trumps?'

'Yup.' I picked up the Woolworth carrier-bag at my feet. I dumped it on the table. 'Feast your eyes on that, me hearties. Shiver me timbers and splice the mainbrace and avast, or whatever. Pull out up the top sheet and spank 'er. It's Cap'n Flint's treasure.'

'What are you gibbering about?' Isobel peered into the bag.

169

She pulled out a maroon leather ring box. 'What's this?' She opened the lid.

'Early Georgian,' I said. 'Diamonds in gold. Rose-cut, so worthless as stones, but the setting could fetch two, three grand.'

'Nice.' Isobel slipped the ring on her ring-finger tip. It would go no further. 'What else have you got in here?'

She pulled them out one by one. Some were in boxes, others merely wrapped in tissue paper. There was a string of flesh-coloured pearls with an emerald clasp and an emerald and diamond spray which had been presented to my great-grandmother by Vittorio Emmanuele. There was a collar of rubies and diamonds and a pair of matching earrings which shrieked of the sixties and a plain star sapphire set in a platinum ring. There was a little gold signet which opened to reveal a tiny gold key which in turn opened a gold-mounted tortoiseshell box, a rattling bracelet of emeralds and a ring which bore a miniature of an Elizabethan gentleman who just might be Walter Raleigh.

'This,' said Isobel, now wearing the ruby earrings and all four rings, 'is fun. They must be worth a fortune.'

'They look it, don't they?' I surveyed the white tissue-paper which now covered the table and the jewels which lay on it like open wounds. 'Perhaps thirty grand at auction. It might help. More to the point, as you say, there's something about gold and glister which catches the avaricious eye. If Quinn knows his jewellery, we're out of luck. If not, these baubles might buy me a few months.'

'Not if you don't do the deed today, as we planned. As long as you're obedient, you're worth a hell of a lot more to him than eighty thousand. He probably wins twenty or more each time you fix a race for him, and his demands on you have been getting nastier and nastier. I guarantee, if you come to him with forty – even sixty – now, he'd turn it down, ask for interest or something. He's got you where he wants you. He'll only cut his losses when he's forced to.'

I nodded. 'Yeah. Or just call in the debt. Ah, well.' I combed my forelock back with my fingers. I exhaled noisily. 'No. You're right. Let's do it. I'm ready.' I caught her eye and sought reassurance. 'You love me?'

'Of course.' She frowned, then relaxed and smiled. 'God, come on. We'd better be going.'

I saw a lot of backs on my arrival at Kempton – backs camelhair, backs tweed, sheepskin and British Warm. They were turned to me as I sauntered in. People veered as I approached and looked interested in noticeboards or smiled at people who did not smile back. I shrugged and swaggered, but ice ran through my gut.

Dave had had visitors, and had talked.

OK, so they hated me, or, at least, felt that that was the thing to do.

They should try looking at it from my point of view. I had done enough hating for the whole damned crowd.

In the changing-room it was worse. There was a lot of rumbling and hissing done by little groups in corners, accompanied by sideways glances and sneers. Only Glenn answered my cheery 'Morning!' as I walked in and dumped my effects on the bench, but he answered only from habit and at once swung himself round so that his back was to me.

I changed in silence. Something in me urged me to protest my innocence. Something in me wept. These were my brothers, and would forgive most things, but not an attack on another of our kind, not, at least, on a beloved uncle.

I was dressed and weighed out too quickly, and must sit alone, waiting for the summons to the paddock, while all about me the usual football-rattle conversations went on – of horses, of women, of restaurants, of good things on the stock market, of cars.

When at last we were free to go out, I scurried to get to the door ahead of the rest. A negligently extended leg in breeches and boots damn near sent me sprawling, but I saw it in time and just contrived to hop over it. Childish, perhaps, but children can hurt children badly, and the child in me was howling.

171

Isobel was right. This could not go on.

This was a handicap hurdle – a cavalry charge with bumps. There were specialist hurdle-jockeys in the field and a smattering of the top chasing boys, but my redeeming demonstration must wait until the big race, the King George VI, at three-thirty. Then the eyes of the racing world would be upon us.

I was jostled and jolted at the start of that race, but no one wanted a tangle of legs at hurdling speed. No one gave me an opening, but at the same time no one tried to avenge Dave. It could only be a matter of time. By accident rather than design, we finished second – five lengths behind the winner, but second nonetheless. My mount, on his first run in blinkers, showed the turn of foot which had won him a couple of decent handicaps on the flat. We passed six flagging animals between the last fence and the post.

There were only four runners in the second, none of them burdened with me, so I changed into my colours for the third, pulled on a cover-coat and strolled out to join the masses.

The masses were plentiful and cheerful after Christmas. There were a lot of red noses and purple cheeks, a lot of ties which looked garish and new and might never see the light again. Two members of the royal family were here, all the top trainers and jockeys and most of the senior stewards. Until Cheltenham in March, there would be no better day for today's work.

I strolled to the racecourse stables, where Gerry, one of Colin's lads, handed me a heavy carrier-bag. He asked me no questions. I had rung him with my curious request this morning. 'It's not a rare commodity in these parts,' he had said, 'and I'll not say coals to Newcastle.'

Like Yonder Peasant on the same day, I trudged, heavy-laden, from the turf of the track to the simmering crowds. The wind pushed at the small of my back so that I kicked as though treading water. The runners were cantering up to the start as I ducked beneath the rails. I worked my way around the afforested islands of punters, each topped with a mountainous bookmaker, in the Silver Ring.

And I saw Quinn.

I stopped and considered him.

He stood on the fifth or sixth step of the Members' stand. He held his glasses at chest-height. He spoke, smiling, to a Japanese at his right shoulder. He threw his head back. He laughed. His curls were pushed up by his collar. I knew that coat. He had worn it on that day when he had met me in the car park and left me to be ringed like a pigeon. His shirt today was pale green, though I suspected that, at close quarters, I would discover it to be green-striped.

His guffaw was a means of transferring his attention to his other neighbour. I knew who his other neighbour was. Clive Sammons had been a run-of-the-mill professional footballer. Having thus demonstrated his histrionic talents, he had resolved to turn his attentions to sport. He had set up a sports goods shop which became a chain. He bought racehorses. He then established a 'club' – a syndicate, in effect, of small investors who wished to own some part of a racehorse. Thousands of people paid up their £100. Horses were bought at high prices, so horses inevitably won. More investors were drawn into Sammons' venture, dutifully paid for veterinary and training fees and enjoyed in exchange occasional days at the sports with badges embossed with 'OWNER' on their lapels or their busts. Horses were bought at high prices, but horses lost.

It was three years before the money stopped rolling into Slammer Sammons' surefire scheme, five before the liquidator was called in. *Private Eye* said that Sammons had paid silly prices for moderate horses. *Private Eye* inferred that Sammons had previously made deals with the owners and breeders of these horses. They pointed out that several of the animals had been owned by Sammons' mistress, Joan Purdey, who had also been his principal trainer. They suggested that some of these horses had been out to grass on Ms Purdey's Welsh hills whilst she was in receipt of massive training fees.

The police could not prosecute, but, there again, Sammons did not sue.

Sammons retained his curling, off-shore wind-blown waves of brown hair and his jolly, youthful smile, but his baby-face was soft and plump now, and his lower eyelids sagged.

I did not know how his investors looked.

I trudged on towards my pre-arranged meeting-place with Isobel. At the entrance to the Members' Enclosure, I found myself executing a dainty little dance with a tweed-suited man coming in the opposite direction. I nodded, said automatically, 'Johnny,' and was almost past him when the idea came to me.

Johnny McIlroy had been a very bad jump-jockey of the pea-on-a-drum variety, but had had the good fortune to finish third in the Gold Cup on an armchair ride. His bouffant red hair was familiar to BBC viewers. He was a pundit, much as newsreaders and game-show hostesses who had had babies become instant obstetricians and paediatricians.

'Oh, Johnny,' I called after him.

His galoshes skidded in the mud as he stopped. 'Neil?' he beamed professionally.

'Don't want an interview, do you?'

'Why? You planning to win today?'

'Nah. Not unless lightning strikes Rousseau and Bertie's thing. Might squeak a place. No. Dark rumours about corruption, race-fixing, that sort of thing. Nothing specific, but hints, and the story may blow within the month. Put your lot ahead of the game.'

He was interested, but not a lot. He shrugged his narrow shoulders. 'Oh. Well. Pretty standard stuff, but . . . You say it'll blow?'

'It should, yeah. Say, six to four it will. Within the month.'

'OK. Why not? Haven't done you for a few months, have we? What? After this one?'

'Fine.'

He frowned at the bag in my hands. 'What on earth have you got there?' he squeaked.

'Dung,' I told him, and walked on.

*

'It somehow seems so bloody childish,' I snapped at Isobel, while above us, the tannoy crepitated and twanged, '. . . and Castellor's a faller at that one . . .' The wind whooshed about, winding up a bolo, and punched. Isobel's hair splayed. She took a step backward.

'Of course it's childish. So is chaining yourself to railings. So is anything that gets you noticed.'

'Sure, sure,' I sighed, and privily damned Cheltenham Ladies' College, 'but in the cold light of day, it just looks so ridiculous. It was all very impressive at night, just talking about it.'

'Neil,' those pale clear eyes challenged mine, 'does Dave's condition look ridiculous, then? Does the threat to Polly?'

'Yes. No. I don't know. No.'

'Make up your mind. Do you think that Quinn is a threat or not?'

I looked down at the ring. 'Yeah, yeah,' I admitted. 'Yeah, he's a threat. I saw him.'

'So did I. Nasty bit of work. Smooth. I find it difficult – I don't know. I expected him to be older. He's so – seventies.'

'I know. Bad enough when the police look young, but when the villains . . .' The wind pushed the end of the sentence back into my mouth, for which I was grateful. 'I've got myself a television interview after this.'

'Good. Should put the lid on it.' She reached out a long hand and laid it on my right shoulder. Her eyes were worried but strangely still. Mine were nervously shifting. 'I'll be here, Neil,' she said. 'I love you.'

A sob or a laugh burst from me. 'Can't think how or why,' I said, 'but thank you. Don't see why you should take all this on. You could have anything – anyone you wanted.'

'I did,' she said, and she kissed me. 'I love you. Don't you understand that?'

'Maybe not,' I admitted sheepishly. 'I'm not sure I've ever known . . . Ah, hell. Pathetic. I just find it hard to believe. Thank you, my love.' I leaned forward to kiss her, but at that moment, the tide of punters swept over us, babbling and shouting. Someone barged into my back and my romantic kiss was turned into something more akin to a head-butt. My lips, which had been headed for hers, hit her jawbone just below the ear.

'Neil, good,' Johnny McIlroy was holding my elbow. 'Hello, love,' he nodded at Isobel. 'Come along. All set? Splendid. Won't be long, love.'

He and the wind pushed me along with the crowd. We turned into a doorway and up stone stairs. On the balcony overlooking the winners' enclosure, he quickly adjusted his hair and his tie. The paper on his checkboard cackled in the wind. 'Now, Neil, sorry, if you can stand . . . That's it. Super. Hold on. Everything OK, Stewart?' he asked the cameraman. 'Great. Right . . . ' He covered his right ear with one hand. He nodded twice. 'OK . . . ' and suddenly he was looking manly and trustworthy, deeply concerned at the sufferings of the world yet able to look upon them without weeping.

'From time to time,' he said, 'there are rumours that all is not well in the world of racing. Often rumours is all they are, but sometimes, inevitably, they have some substance. There will always be the odd villain who wants to stack the odds in his favour and it's up to all of us to be alert. Jockeys in particular can be subjected to pressure and bribes, and it's good to know that most of them are prepared to stand up and blow the whistle on the would-be race-fixers. Among these is an old friend of ours, Neil Munrow. Neil, you say that there's been an upsurge of this sort of thing recently . . . ?'

'*Quint*essentially,' I nodded. 'Yes. I have been repeatedly approached in the last few months with offers of bribes and with serious threats should I not comply.'

'With a request to stop a horse?'

'*Quint*essentially, yes.'

Johnny McIlroy's frown deepened as the interview went on.

I said 'Quintessentially' sixteen times.

'All right,' I announced loudly in the changing-room. Heads

arose sharply, 'I did Dave, and I'm bloody sorry. Maybe you wouldn't have, but that bastard Quinn threatened my daughter and I had no bloody choice, or, at least, I thought I hadn't. Maybe you're better than I am. All I know is, I've had enough, and if you'll watch me in the paddock before this one, maybe you'll change your minds. Right. That's it.' And I sat down.

My speech earned no rapturous applause, just a long embarrassed silence broken only by the rustling of clothing and the breathing of men. I did not look up, just sat there fiddling with my whip and gazing down at the linoleum floor between my legs.

'Well,' said a voice still louder than mine had been. It sang in the walls. 'That sounds fair enough to me. Don't know what the fuck I'd have done if some bugger'd threatened my kids, but I'm no fucking hero. If it's Uncle or your kids . . . God, that bastard, Quinn.'

I smiled gratefully at Glenn, who sat naked from the waist down on the other side of the room. The deed was done now. I was terrified, but I still felt relief. They say that the junkie suffers something like flu symptoms which are only relieved by the hit. I wondered if confession could be addictive too. Two or three of the lads strolled over and punched my shoulder. 'Fucking bad luck,' said one.

'Well, you've blown it now,' Glenn stood. He wriggled into jock-strap and breeches at once. He strolled over to me. 'What you going to do, mate?'

'I dunno,' I shrugged. 'Got no evidence. Can't go to Jockey Club security. Call his bluff is all I can do.'

'Jesus,' Glenn raised his eyebrows, pushed back his tangled hair, 'sooner you than me. He's got some nasty friends, that guy.'

'I know. My only real protection is that you guys know.'

Glenn frowned. 'Sure. I can see that. We'll know what caused that brake failure when we go to the funeral, but surely – I mean, once he knows that you've blown the gaffe – I mean, surely that forces him to act, to save his filthy face, I mean.'

'Yeah, well.' I hit my boot with my whip.

'Oh, I get it.' Glenn whistled. 'Sheesh. Draw his fire, eh? Bloody Nora, sooner you than me, like I say.'

'I wish you'd stop saying it,' I croaked up at him. 'I don't enjoy it.'

'Christ, no. I bet. Sorry, mate. Anything I can do, you know . . .'

'Thanks.' I shook my head. 'Probably nothing'll come of it. I just get warned off, that's it.'

'He can do that?' Glenn whispered. He perched on the bench beside me.

'Yeah, yeah,' I chanted softly. 'He's got me by the short and curlies. Had a warned-off person pay a load of money into my account.'

'You didn't take it?'

'I didn't, no. Katya fucking did. It was a joint account.'

'Oh, shit,' Glenn sighed. 'Shit, shit, shit. Canny fucker. Well, mind your back, Neil. He's got other boys on his payroll. I know that for a fact. If he can do that to Dave . . .'

'Don't,' I shuddered. 'I know. I know.'

But I knew that Quinn would not have me turned over in the course of a race. I was as experienced and strong as any rider around. Anyone trying to do me when forewarned would probably end up with a broken neck. If Quinn wanted to take revenge on me, it would be with bigger, more reliable weapons, and it would be at home.

It was a grim-faced, apprehensive group of men that trooped out of the weighing-room into the swirling wind. The others stood back to let me go first. I tried to swagger, but it didn't come off. I stumbled as I stepped down into the winner's enclosure.

I strode on, ignoring the odd autograph book thrust in my direction. At the entrance to the paddock, Isobel stood waiting. She held out the carrier-bag. I took it with a nod. 'I don't want you at home tonight,' I told her. I did not look at her.

'Go for it,' she told my back.

Colin Mather and his owners looked up as I entered. Colin drew back to admit me into the circle. He frowned at the carrier-bag.

I walked straight past them.

My eyes were on another group. There was a blonde woman in a brown hat and a flared black coat. There was the Japanese. There was Clive Sammons. There was Peter Corrigan, the trainer. And there was Quinn, a co-owner with Sammons. His broad, dark-blue back was turned to me, but I could see a quarter of his profile. His tanned face was creased in a smile. His grey curls bounced in the wind. His right hand waved in some expansive illustrative gesture. His signet ring flashed.

I was unscrewing my ring as I walked toward him. I placed it in my left hand. 'Quinn,' I barked as I approached him, but the wind must have blown the word away. He did not turn. 'Quinn,' I snapped again.

The woman turned. The Japanese frowned at me. Quinn span slowly on his heel. The smile on his face remained frozen there, though his eyes glared. 'Quinn,' I repeated, 'something for you.' I held out the ring. Automatically, his hand closed on it. I reached into the bag for a good handful of specially pre-moistened dung. Whilst Quinn still gaped, his right hand extended, I pulled up the flap on his left-hand pocket and crammed the shit in. Some of it went in. The remainder tumbled down his coat and pattered on the grass.

Then everything speeded up.

Quinn was saying, 'What the bloody hell . . . ?' and pushing at me. The Japanese was tugging at my right sleeve. The woman was yelping something, and I was smearing handfuls of tan dung down the front of Quinn's coat. 'You're a filthy little crook, Quinn,' I panted as his arms flailed about me, jolting my forehead and my jaw. 'You're a disgusting, socio-pathic little crook . . .' Then he attained purchase and one last shove sent me reeling backwards, but not before I had flung a handful of dung at that tanned face. I nearly fell, but supported myself on my right hand. 'If ever I see you again . . .' I gasped.

'No, Munrow,' Quinn wiped dung from his mouth and his chin. His cheeks were crimson. He spoke deep and low. 'No, Munrow, if ever I see you again, it will be in a box.' His teeth were gritted, his eyes slits. His hands flapped foolishly at his coat. For a moment, I thought that he would tear me apart there and then, but the rumble of the crowd reminded him where he was.

Other figures were moving fast towards us. I stood and flicked at my breeches. 'Get stuffed, Quinn,' I said quietly. 'Go back to the gutter where you belong. You're a jumped up, crooked little spiv. It's all right.' I pulled my arm from the grip of a concerned citizen in a cover-coat. My eyes never left Quinn's. 'Just our little joke. A bet. Isn't that right, Quinn?'

Quinn's shoulders rose and fell as he struggled to regain control of his breath and his temper. I smiled sweetly. 'Isn't that right, Quinn?'

I could see his mind working. If he were to tell all now and to have me charged with assault, I would inevitably tell my side of the story. I might have no evidence, but Quinn's every move on the racecourse would be watched from here on. His reign – the latest of many in the history of the sport – would be over. If, on the other hand, he stayed quiet now, he could deal with me in his own way and in his own time – an anonymous tip-off to the Jockey Club, an anonymous knife in the back – and Quinn's nice little racecourse earner would continue.

'Yes,' he said, and his vowels were flattened by his grimace, 'just a joke. A bet, like Neil says.'

'Bloody bad form, if you ask me,' grumbled the man at my elbow. 'Queen Mother here and so on. Brings the sport into disrepute.'

'Must be going, Dan, old chap.' I waved and grinned. 'Such fun.'

Quinn shook like a pressure-cooker.

My legs were not strong as I returned to Colin Mather.

''Straordinary 'haviour,' Colin waffled. 'What were you doin' with that shit?'

180

'Rubbing nice, clean horse-dung in him.' I shrugged, filled with a sudden demented elation, 'Improve his smell.'

'Damn good thing,' Colin's chins spread like an old man's testicles, 'but I'm not going to have the stewards on my back, am I?'

'No, no. Don't worry.'

'Well, I hope not. Now, not much time after all these 'straordinary antics, I've been telling Mr and Mrs Farquharson . . .'

I knew what he had been telling Mr and Mrs Farquharson; that their horse warranted an each-way bet, but nothing too extravagant, that I would just hunt him round the first circuit and see how things stood.

This was a good beta-plus animal whose owners insisted on running him in alpha races. Today, frankly, was too rich for his blood.

So I let the words splosh slowly like stones into a well and I nodded without listening. Over Colin's shoulder, I watched as Quinn, ever a more vivid red, excused himself and stroked his hair and strode with short, rapid steps to the gap in the rails. The crowd drew back as he approached, whether because of his menacing mien or because of the stink, I did not know. It consoled me to think that neither would he.

He raised his right forearm at right angles to his hip. Maybe he clicked his fingers. Either way, a little man scampered from the mass of brown and green, red and black, and bobbed sideways as though one leg were shorter than the other at Quinn's heel.

He had pale yellow hair, the colour of urine-stained sheets.

Quinn was talking fast.

Glenn and I walked like pall-bearers who had just shed our burden. Rain had set in and now speckled the wind. It was like being airbrushed by an asthmatic.

Glenn had understood why I had been reluctant to leave the relative safety of the course and to wander out into this muddy open space where a body might lie groaning for an

181

hour or more, taken only for a drunk, not a dying man. He had taken the whisky glass from me to prevent the former and now accompanied me to the car to prevent the latter.

'Well, I told him. It's done.'

'And well done, mate. Loved it. You've rubbed his nose in it, literally. What's next, do you reckon?'

'Tip-off to the authorities,' I said on a monotone. 'I get warned off. Won't be enough for him. Go for a show of strength. Me, Polly, someone. There's just a point . . . You just have to say "no".'

'Shit, sure. I'll grant you, yep. All right, but . . .'

'You mean what you said?' I looked up sideways at him. 'You wouldn't have . . . I don't know . . . You'd not have stood up?'

'Ah, Christ, man,' he snorted like a horse. 'Who knows? In principle, sure, I'd have put on my Superman cloak and fought for life, liberty and the pursuit of happiness. In fact – Jesus, I'd not choose to be where you are. Me, I've got no kids. It's different. Quinn or me, I'm a stubborn sod, but kids – well, they sort of rip your balls off, don't they?'

'They do,' I smiled down at the turf. 'Jesus, "they fuck you up, your mums and dads"; Larkin told half the story. A child unmans you.'

'Not what I see, mate,' Glenn leaned his elbow on the roof of my car as I unlocked the driver's door.

'What?' I looked up at him.

'Don't reckon you're unmanned. Far from it.'

'Thanks.' I grimaced. 'I did Dave.'

'And Kirk Douglas did a lot of lions and gladiators before he made a stand, and all. Point is, you have a breaking-point. Corruption's just sliding past it and not noticing. Give yourself some credit, Neil. This might be bloody tough.'

'It's the waiting that's the worst.' I clambered into the car and unwound the window.

'Like before the National,' Glenn mused. He thumped the car roof. 'Call me, mate. Keep me posted. I'll bring a brigade over, bugles and that. The cavalry.'

'I'll remember.' I waved and turned the key in the ignition. The engine started up. We didn't blow up. That was a relief. Every minute was to be a relief from now on.

'If he does anything, he'll do it quickly,' Isobel had reasoned. 'The insult will have to be seen to be avenged. He's not going to hang about just waiting while his power is eroded by mockery. His business only works if he can maintain the mystique. So you've got Polly from the twenty-eighth. Guard her with your life. Simple as that.'

Simple as that – the rôle of parents throughout the ages – but guard her with what? I could not have hosts of heavy friends to stay because Quinn would simply stay away. I had to appear exposed and unprepared. That evening, I wandered about Fox Farm, wondering just what precautions I could take. Booby traps would be dangerous to Polly and to me, even had I known how to set them, and I had no desire to be had up for inadvertently fricasseeing the postwoman or the vicar by rigging up the shotgun to a door-operated pulley or some such. No. I would simply have to lock doors and windows, keep the shotgun to hand and rely on my own limited wits.

The clouds were high and the twilight pure purple as I brought Bossy in. Every rustle, every thump or squeal from the fields made me duck and cringe. Once a pheasant broke from the hedge with the whirring and clatter of a broken fan-belt, and a whimper seeped from me as I crouched and covered my head and tried to make myself as small as possible. Bossy regarded me with curiosity and, I thought, disdain. Bracken, as ever at my heel, thought that I was playing and hit me with his right paw. The pheasant laughed like a cartoon witch.

I straightened slowly. Cheyne-Stokes made my breath sound like porn.

Some hero.

Bracken was eating hoof-parings and I was just dusting off my hands after giving Bossy a linseed mash when I heard the car. It droned like a wasp, then the wind pounced, the big trees bowed, the bushes curtsied and they started a quick, frantic dance. A moment later, the sound of the car came back.

I debated with myself. If this was it, on balance, I was glad. I had had no time to prepare, but Polly was not yet here. Matters could be settled here and now. But did I make a break for it and run to the house, where the gun and the telephone were, or remain here and watch? They – whoever they might be – would surely assume that I was in the house. I could outflank my attackers. I had a pitchfork, a curry-comb and a metal bucket, all, theoretically, effective weapons, and, of course, Bossy to provide mobility and a means of escape. I pulled the rug from him, armed myself with the pitchfork, and, feeling faintly ridiculous, crouched down behind the half-door.

Bossy waffled at his mash. The wind howled, charged and hit. The box doors rattled. In the stillness which followed, the bee became an engine which grumbled and hiccupped as it climbed the hill. I heard the crunch of gravel as the car passed my outer wall. Again the wind slammed into the boxes. Bossy stamped on straw and rattled the bucket as he chased the last grains.

Headlight beams swung over the gables of the house. The doodle of wisteria was doubled by its shadows. The lights descended in a fencer's salute. The car appeared briefly between the japonica bush and the corner of the house before vanishing.

It was low and dark.

It could only be Quinn.

I heard the car door shut with chunky complacency. My twisted little finger throbbed its complaint. I heard slow foot-falls on the gravel, then a voice called something. There was a long pause. The lights were on in the study, though the curtains were drawn, so I could see Quinn's tall form as he came round the house. On the other side of the stable door, Bracken growled, then, giving deep, baying tongue, started to canter across the yard.

Anyone can slip on a banana skin, yet it is still comical. Anyone would have reacted as Quinn did on seeing that vast black monster approaching, but his yelp and his rapid retreat still filled me with glee. The fatter the man who slips, the funnier the gag. The more menacing the air of the man who scurries away, the more satisfactory his indignity. The car door shut again. Bracken continued to bark. I was smiling as I pushed open the door and, presenting pitchfork, Dad's Army style, strode across the yard and round the house.

Quinn sat alone in the car. His face seemed very white as he heard my approach and turned, wide-eyed.

He wound his window down just two inches. 'Ah, Neil,' he said. 'Didn't realize you had a beast like that.'

'What do you want, Quinn?' I sneered. It was good for once to have his head at chest level.

'Well, I'd have thought that was obvious,' he shook his head as though despairing of an idiot child. 'After your rather ridiculous demonstration this afternoon, I was hoping that we could sort things out, restore the status quo. I don't like any unpleasantness. I was hoping we could come to some sort of accommodation.'

'Which means I continue to work for you. No, thanks.'

'You must admit that you owe me a large amount of money, Neil. If you can't pay for the meal, you wash the dishes. That is normal business practice.'

'Too many fucking dishes, Quinn, and too bloody dirty. I've told you. I'll pay you back, but not your way.'

'What way do you suggest, Neil?' He was recovering his sardonic cool. 'Stock-market tips? Perhaps you'd like to discover a cure for HIV and offer me the patent? Jockeys, you know, have limited uses. Just tell me. OK. You're all heroic. Just tell me, how would you feel if someone ripped you off for sixty thousand pounds?'

'I'd . . .'

'No, no, just tell me. Come on.'

'I'd be furious,' I sighed.

'You'd expect repayment?'

185

'Sure.'

'And if the thief had no money but worked on the stock-exchange? What? A few insider deals? You wouldn't baulk at that, would you?'

'No,' I admitted. 'No, probably not.'

'And if he went all heroic on you, all holier than thou, all "I can't do that sort of thing", you'd be a mite irritated. You might want to make him hurt a little. And if he came along, on top of all this, and publicly humiliated and abused you, what then? Because that's what you did to me. That's what I got for trying to help you.'

'Bollocks,' I seized on the one thing of which I was sure. 'You set me up deliberately.'

'Don't be absurd, Neil. How was I to know your wife would extract the money? You could just have brought it back to me as I requested.'

He had me thoroughly confused. And hold on – how did he know that Katya had withdrawn the cash?

I didn't get a chance to ask him. He had attained impetus. 'So I think it's time you asked yourself some serious questions, Neil. I tried to help you, quite reasonably sought recompense when you defrauded me, and you reward me by abusing me. You called me a sociopath. I am nothing of the sort. I have feelings. I feel for you, for your child. I would like to help. But your refusal to pay your dues – if I allow that, how am I meant to keep doing business? How am I meant to keep my daughter at school or look after my wife?'

'"Hath not a Jew eyes . . . ?"' I blinked. The echo of Shylock's poignant plaint was so exact that the quotation had sprung from my lips before I could check it.

'Very apposite,' Quinn nodded. 'Just because you play the saint and the nobleman, you feel justified in abusing me. You feel complacent, smug. You can sleep at nights. But I'm owed sixty-two grand. I would have said forty, but interest-rates went up today. You've done yourself no favours. I can't just give it away, can I? I have to act. Do you think I like that? So come on. Let's go inside and work out how we can resolve this matter.'

The prospect of freedom from fear was too alluring, and the man was right. Shylock, in the nature of commerce, had been within his rights. Antonio, like me, had been prepared to accept the benefits but not to pay the price.

'All right.' I lowered the pitchfork. I stood back.

'Is that dog all right?'

'He's OK.' I placed a hand on Bracken's collar. He raised his nose and nuzzled my crotch.

Quinn opened the door and unfolded his body. He had changed into a red cashmere polo-neck and a blazer with deer on the gold buttons. He eyed Bracken suspiciously. He smiled faintly. He said, 'Good boy.' He turned towards the porch.

He was going to have his say. 'No,' he went on as I opened the door, 'it's always been the way in a Christian society. Who are the saints? What have they achieved? St Benedict saw a local girl and fancied her, so he throws himself into a bed of nettles. Oh, good man. Canonize him at once. But Charlemagne, someone like that? Oh, no. He achieved, he improved the lot of millions, but like all achievers, he had to take responsiblilty, he had to fight battles, he had to make moral decisions, he had to crush his enemies. He did good, he even spread the word of God, but he can't be a saint. Oh, no. He's morally questionable. If I had to take my pound of flesh – and you couldn't blame me – I'm the one who would have the sleepless nights while you could smugly say, "Well, at least I did the right thing". Right in what sense? The nice thing, the easy thing, the irresponsible thing? I take responsibility, enforce the contract, I'm the villain. Is that fair?'

He had led me into the study. In my exhaustion I was a zombie, a rabbit transfixed by a snake. His words made sense, echoed, even, my own when holding forth at dinner-parties. I know that there was something wrong, but I could not, just at the moment, think what it was. 'No,' I said, almost grateful for the absence of violence, the prospect of playing with Polly tomorrow without terror. 'No, it's not fair. I agree, but . . . OK. What do you want of me?'

'Oh, much the same as ever, Neil,' he wandered about the room, examining the Chelsea figures on the mantel, the pictures on the walls, even running his finger along the frame of a Herring print and checking it for dust.

I perched on the arm of the sofa, weary now. 'For how much longer?'

'I don't think that need concern you, frankly, Neil,' he opened the door to the kitchen and peered in. 'How many years would it take you to make that sort of money? Three?'

'We can't think of it that way, Quinn.'

'Mr Quinn, I think, Neil.'

'And I'm not doing violence again.'

'That saintly heroism again?' Quinn hissed. He raised his eyebrows. 'You'll eat a chicken but would sooner pay to have its neck wrung, pretend that it never was a living creature? Sweet, but not practical, I'm afraid. Not even ethical if you think about it.'

'Look, I've got some jewellery. My mother's. Maybe thirty grand. If I gave you that . . .' I walked over to the bureau and pulled out the carrier-bag. I tipped it out on to the sofa.

Quinn strolled over. He picked up the ruby and diamond collar and rolled it over his hand. His hand was shaking. 'Charming,' he said. He reached down for Vittorio Emmanuele's brooch. 'Delightful. Yes. That is the right spirit, Neil, but how do I know, if I take this, that you won't just ring the police as soon as I've left the house and report a theft?'

'I'd write you a letter,' I said, then thought. A letter like that would enslave me still more surely to Quinn. 'No. Well, I couldn't do that, but I just wouldn't . . . I mean, what I want – all I want – is peace.'

'Oh, so do I, Neil, so do I, but peace is dearly bought.' Quinn tossed the jewels back on to the sofa and turned away. He moved over to the window and pulled back the curtain. He gazed up the drive. 'I don't think you understand, Neil. I don't think you've grasped the situation. You seem to think that you're suddenly in a position to impose conditions on your employment. It seems to me, however, that you are in a worse position than ever. All that has happened is that you have publicly insulted me.' His shoulders were shaking. His voice grew sharper. 'You openly abused and assaulted me. You, a filthy little professional jockey, have openly abused and assaulted me. And you think – you still don't understand, do you? You have dared to touch me, to make a fool of me. No one does that, Neil, least of all a filthy little runt like you. You will pay and pay and pay for that, till the day you die you will pay for that! No fucker lays hands on me!'

He was genuinely frightening. His large hands scrabbled at his flannels. His lips wriggled and twisted as he spoke. His voice had risen in pitch and volume. Now it was jagged and sharp-edged as a saw-blade. Like a horrible memento of a violent past, the cockney had re-emerged. His jowls shook.

And then it dawned on me.

Quinn was here to subjugate me if he could, but principally his intention was simply to case the joint. And I, thumb in bum, mind in neutral, had allowed Bracken to see him admitted to the house and had allowed Quinn to see the layout. At the same moment, Isobel's phrase entered my head – the flaw in Quinn's argument which I had sought but been unable to find: 'unconscionable contract'. It wasn't just a cop-out. The battered wife had an unconscionable contract, the regularly raped Thai employee, the doctor besought to kill. There was a law higher than that of contract, a power higher than law.

'Get out,' I said softly. 'Get out and do your worst, Quinn. You're so far beneath me that you don't even understand why. You actually believe what you say. You actually believe that you are in the right. Rachman's little gofer. Did you convince yourself that those poor, unfortunate tenants were a lower life-form as you drove them out of their homes . . . ?'

I had got to him. 'That's rubbish,' he stammered, 'he was my landlord, that's all.'

'Not what I've heard, cockney boy, not what I've heard. Out, spiv, out, yob. This is a gentleman's house, not a place for backstreet wide-boys. Go on,' I laughed and flapped my hands at him as though shooing chickens. 'Get the hell out of here, yobbo. Go and play your violent little backstreet games. Off you go . . .'

It was childish stuff, but it worked. He had backed as far as the hall before his trembling rage got the better of him. His fist shot out. I rolled my head from the punch, but it glanced off my forearm and hit my upper lip at half-cock. Still laughing, though I tasted blood on my teeth, I pushed him backwards.

He made room for himself this time, and he didn't telegraph the blow. His eyes were narrow. His bared teeth and the underside of his upper lip were the last things that I saw before the tight, two-fingered karate fist slammed into the bridge of my nose. I staggered backwards, arms flailing, and sat down hard on the bare boards.

There was a lot of blood on my mouth and my chin and my shirtfront, and the straw-coloured walls span like a fairground ride, but I was still laughing as Quinn spat out his last words and slammed the door behind him.

The words clattered about the room and faded to a distant hiss. The wind blew the front door open again. A twig scampered into the warm.

'You will never sleep soundly again, Munrow,' Quinn had snarled and pointed.

He was right, too.

I mopped up the blood. I changed my shirt. I rang Isobel but she was not at the flat. I drank tea because I thought that I wanted to keep a clear mind, then I reconsidered. I decided that I wanted nothing less than a clear mind. I changed to whisky.

I locked up. I cooked iodine crystals in ammonia and a Cumberland sausage. The sausage I ate between two slices of bread. The iodine and ammonia mixture I spread at various strategic points about the house.

This was a trick remembered from childhood. Chemistry had never been my long suit at school, and I still had to ask

Isobel about chemical symbols when we did the crossword, but, in common with most healthy boys, I had always had a considerable interest in things that went 'bang'.

A schoolfriend had taught me the virtues of Ammonia Triiodide. If properly mixed, ammonia and iodine crystals can be reduced to a thick paste. When liquid, the paste is stable, when dry, it explodes if touched.

It is a harmless explosion. All the energy goes into a loud bang and a bright flash. I had found it useful for frightening respectable matrons, including my grandmother, who had cut me out of her will for two years after a roll of loo-paper had exploded in a tiny downstairs loo.

It might give me an edge. That was all.

I cleaned the gun, took it upstairs and placed it under the bed. Then I lay down, still fully dressed, and tried to sleep. If I succeeded, I dreamed that I was still awake. The wind scampered around the house and shook the window-panes. The wisteria tapped insistently. Bracken patrolled, heavy-footed, on the gravel outside. At some point, I got up to go to the loo and pocketed the cut-throat razor as a secondary line of defence. Again I lay down and stared up at the ceiling. Three times I mistook the sound of the wind for that of a car and moved fast to the window, only to see the moon whizzing across a marbled sky and the trees straining and tossing their heads like horses at the sound of a horn.

Then, I suppose, I must have slept, because I was awoken by a violent bang, and I was up and grabbing the gun and my heart was pummelling at my chest wall and my face was hot and red. I flung open the bedroom door and shouted, 'Who's there?'

'Jesus, Neil!' Isobel's voice was amused but breathless. 'God, I thought I was going to have a heart attack! What the hell was that?'

I sighed and lowered the gun. 'A little trick of mine,' I shouted down, 'and don't touch the door-frame.'

Her head peered round the stair-wall. She was grinning. 'I told you to stay away,' I grumbled.

'I know,' she said, 'and I decided to pay no attention. Come on. What's the point if I leave as soon as things get rough? We'll be OK. What have you done to your nose?'

'Quinn,' I sighed. 'Came here tonight. Bit of a brawl. Don't step on that . . . !' I pointed, but I was too late. Isobel had laid her foot on the bottom step.

'God!' she giggled as the echoes rang like crystal and the smoke abated. 'It's like being a demon king in the pantomine. Any more surprises?'

'Not on the stairs, no.' I smiled and shook my head. I laid down the gun and held out my arms. 'Come on.'

Five minutes later, she was gently going down on me as I lay naked on the bed. Another five minutes and she was saying, 'Mmm' and kissing my pubis. 'Now sleep,' she said softly. 'It'll all be OK, darling. Come here.' She pulled the duvet up over us and snuggled up in my arms. 'Everything'll be all right,' she whispered. 'I love you.'

'I love you,' I breathed, and I clung her to me so tightly that I squeaked.

I awoke at five-thirty, grateful that there was a morning. The wind had not died, but still sang chords as it dived and swooped, scurried and worried about the garden and the valley. Beside me, Isobel, who appeared able to sleep no matter what, lay comfortably curled, her cheek on her hands, her hands on that majestic spray of amber hair. A small smile touched her lips. I envied such sleep. It had been many years.

I slid from the bed. Again, as is the way with mornings, I found it difficult to believe in last night's terrors. At night everything is grand and grotesque. In the morning, all is commonplace. The essence of a milk-carton or a table is unequivocal in cold bright light, but when shadows draw in, dear friends become gargoyles, homes become blind, gaping skulls and rectangular furniture develops bulging, moving muscle. Because nothing has eyes, everything has eyes.

But morning mocks such fancy. The birds chatter and giggle about our revels, our passions and our fears. Morning is black-and-white. Night is Eastmancolor.

'Come back to bed,' Isobel creaked behind me.

I turned, bent over and kissed her. She was hot. Her hands clasped behind my neck. When I tried to raise my head, she pulled it down. 'No. Come back to bed.'

I mustered a smile, though I was edgy and irritated. 'No,' I said, 'I must get on.'

'Get on with what? Come on. You owe me one. Give me a cuddle. Please.' She pulled my head down to her breast. I kissed and nuzzled, nipped and sucked. She groaned. Her legs shifted.

'No, come on,' I said, and kissed her nose. 'We'll have a siesta, but I'm just . . .'

'What?'

'I don't know,' I shrugged, 'just edgy. I want to be up and doing. I want the nervous energy. Don't ask me why.'

'OK,' she threw herself down on her side with her back to me. 'Just leave me. I don't care. Send the milkman up when he comes.'

'Isobel . . .'

'No, no. I know when I'm not wanted.' She clamped her hands between her thighs. 'I'll just have to see if I can be self-sufficient. What's that old line? With masturbation you get to meet a better class of person?'

She rolled over on her back and her eyes sparkled as her middle finger hooked and stroked between her legs.

I said, 'Oh, fuck it.'

'Don't you like it?'

'Yes, I like it.' I growled. I knew this conversation of old. 'Of course I bloody like it. It's just that it irritates me because I like it and because I don't want to relax. All the energy's up here,' I tapped my temple, 'and I want it to stay that way. Can you understand that?'

'Look at you, averting your eyes,' she laughed.

'Well, of course, I'm averting my eyes, woman!' I yelped. 'Just *look* at you.'

And for a second I did just look at her. She had kicked back the duvet and lay sprawled, one long leg bent, one straight.

193

Her left hand tweaked at her right nipple; her right hand did its gentle work.

'Damn it, woman, stop it!' I roared in half-feigned irritation. I stepped into boxer shorts, reached for the top shirt of the pile in the wardrobe and fumbled with the buttons.

'You know your trouble?' she teased.

'Go on. Make my day.'

'You're too old to keep up.'

That almost worked, but not quite. 'I'll show you who's too old later,' I threatened. 'In the meantime, I am ignoring you and getting up.'

How could I explain the irritable urgency which possessed me? I wanted to be tidying up or mucking out – anything active and practical and rhythmical and emotionally un-demanding.

On my return from the bathroom, Isobel confessed that she had failed to attain what she had sought. She pouted, but was too unaffected to keep pouting up for long. 'All right, all right,' she said. She scrambled from bed and smoothed on black Lycra leggings. 'So what do we do today?'

'Well, first we prepare lunch. My mother's coming over with the provenance of some of those baubles and to see the house, but her real reason is to inspect you and probably to hang on until Polly arrives.'

'Which is when?'

'Early this evening. Sixish. Katya's driving on to Blandford to stay with some friends. She'll drop her off on the way.'

'God. What's she going to think of me?'

'I don't know and I don't care. Frankly, I don't think she'll have the least trace of jealousy, except of your age and your looks. She hates me.'

'Maybe I'd better tie back my hair, wear no make-up, do a plain Jane.'

'Don't you dare,' I told her. I combed my hair – always a pointless task.

'No, but mothers like sensible-looking girls, don't they?'

'My mother,' I said, 'does not equate sensible with plain.

She approves of making the most of yourself – and she knows her son.'

'And Katya will feel less threatened.'

'In our present circumstances, darling,' I told her, 'I am not concerned to save Katya a mild sense of being threatened. Dress to kill, and the devil take the carpers.'

She stood in just those leggings and a black cashmere sweater. She linked her fingers behind my neck and again she kissed me. 'I love you,' she said. The words tickled my tonsils like syrup.

The day passed slow as a wet Sunday for a child. I prepared partridge and cabbage and *tarte tartin*. My mother arrived, reporting trees down and rivers breaking their banks. The weather forecasters predicted that things would get worse before they got better.

Over lunch, my mother made Isobel laugh. Afterwards, as Isobel prepared coffee, my mother gave her verdict: 'Your face,' she said, 'is a mess. What that poor girl thinks she's doing with you, I cannot imagine.'

'Nor can I,' I told her. 'She's OK, isn't she?'

'A considerable improvement,' my mother pronounced. 'She's very attractive and has delightful unaffected manners. I should think she'd be very good in bed.'

I snorted. 'Would you, now?'

'I would.'

'Yes, well, she's a good friend,' I said. 'We get on well. We agree about most things, and she's tough where I'm a moral coward.'

'Men are,' my mother nodded. 'It's the unattractive corollary of protectiveness. No. I like her. I approve. Mind you . . . ?' She paused. She looked amused.

'Mmm?'

'It's slightly alarming how much you look alike. Maybe that's why she's attracted to you . . .'

'She?' I gaped. 'Isobel? Like me?'

'Of course. Wide eyes, strong eyebrows, broad mouth. I have known some very good relationships between people who could have been twins,' she mused. 'Your great Uncle Alfie was the spit and image of Katerina, and they couldn't have been happier . . .'

I digested the improbable idea that I might resemble Isobel in any regard. I wondered why, if it was true, no one else had remarked on it. This led to the discomforting reflection that, but for Dave and Laura, we had conducted our relationship cocooned from society. We had barely met each other's friends and associates. Quinn's antics and the house had isolated us from the world. It had been love caught in amber. I did not like that thought.

After coffee, my mother demanded the guided tour. In the utility-room, she put a hand on the washing-machine and let off one of my improvised firecrackers. She jumped, frowned, but said nothing save, regally, 'What an interesting idea.' In Polly's room, she walked immediately to the window and ran a hand down the frame. It too cracked and flashed. She nodded. In the master bedroom, her eyes at once fell on the gun propped against the wall beneath the window.

'Right,' she said when we came downstairs again. 'Isobel, dear, will you show me around outside, please? You can stay here and wash up, Neil. I don't want you.'

There was no washing-up to do. Isobel had already loaded the machine. I watched through the window as my mother and my lover staggered and lurched in the gale towards the yard. They were shouting at one another. My mother was nodding.

I went to the generator-room and switched on the electricity so that I could watch *Meet Me in St Louis* on the BBC. The sainted Judy was wishing me and only me a Merry Little Christmas and I was blinking away tears when the two women clattered back into the drawing room.

'All right,' my mother's voice echoed in the uncurtained, uncarpeted room. The boards buzzed. 'Don't blame Isobel. It was, frankly, obvious. You needing money and then all those pyrotechnics. I gather that you're in trouble with some damned Irishman with ideas above his station. Frankly, this concerns me. Isobel has given you precisely the correct advice. Of course you must resist him. But you are, for my pains, my son and Polly is my granddaugher. No heroics, but we must decide what we are going to do for the best.'

'No "we",' I said, and reluctantly flicked off Judy with the remote control. 'Sorry, Mama, but I got myself into this and I'll get myself out.'

'Oh, very admirable,' she scoffed. 'Even Rose Galloway wouldn't write a line like that. Well, she might, but Rose is allowed fatuous clichés. You are not. This is an entirely practical matter which we must address in an entirely practical way. To start with, why don't I take Polly away? We could go down to the seaside, Exmoor or something until the whole thing blows over.'

I looked up at Isobel, questioning. 'Good idea?'

She shrugged. 'I think so.'

'Only trouble is, Polly hardly knows you, but yes,' I said. 'If you can slip away quickly and discreetly – no telephone calls to anyone, all reservations in a false name – that's not a bad idea. It could be a few days' stay. I'll miss her, but Quinn won't chase her if he can get me or Katya – at least, I don't think he will.'

'This Mr Quinn sounds like a very unpleasant little man.'

'Not little, and he doesn't see it that way. He thinks he should be canonized. A businessman, an upholder of the principles of fair play – that's how he sees himself.'

'And all the more dangerous for that,' my mother admonished Quinn at long distance. 'Certainty is so vulgar. Right. That's settled, then. Donald's the only person who will object. No one else'll notice that I'm gone, and Jackie will feed the dogs. I can buy some togs somewhere. What time does Katya arrive?'

'Somewhere round six.'

'Splendid. We'll have a lot of fun, young Polly and I. My work schedule will go for a burton, but *tant pis*. Rather a bonus for me, getting to know my granddaughter. Great fun.'

'Great fun,' I thought petulantly. For all my relief, I was

sad. I had looked forward so much to these five days with my baby, and I couldn't expect her to understand why she would see her father for a matter of minutes and then leave with a relative stranger.

Isobel understood. She sat beside me and took my hand.

So we sat, and we waited.

'There we are, darling.' Katya set Polly down inside the back door. 'Hello, Neil. Oh, Marnie. You're here.' She nodded briskly at Isobel, switched on and off a smile. 'Hello.'

Isobel said, 'Hi.'

Katya unshouldered a shapeless handbag and Polly's large canvas bag. Her short blonde hair looked galvanized by the wind. Her dark eyes were mad. 'You know Anthony, don't you?' She extended a hand towards the night.

Tony Wickham stepped into the light. He pulled at his fingers as though his skin were a glove. He nodded at me, he nodded at Isobel, he nodded twice at my mother. 'Hello,' he said.

'This is Neil,' Katya was saying, 'and Lady Sylvia Munrow, and, sorry?'

I was squatting with Polly pressed hard to my chest. I stood with her. 'Sorry,' I said over her head, 'Isobel Dewing.'

Isobel joined in the general nodding.

'Pretty foul out there,' I said. 'Come on in. Have a cup of tea or something, a drink, whatever. Did you have a good Christmas, darling?'

'Christmas tree, Daddy,' Polly nodded too. It was infectious.

'That's right, darling. You want to see the Christmas tree? Come on.'

I turned and led the party into the hall. 'Yes, it's pretty filthy out there,' Tony said behind me. 'Trees down. Terrible.'

'Would you mind if we rang the AA?' Katya asked.

'There you are, darling,' I kissed Polly's soft cheek. 'Christmas tree. No, no. Please. Use the telephone in the study. You know where it is. And those are Polly's presents.'

'Polly's presents,' my daughter announced. She broke into 'Happy Birthday to You'. She pointed. 'Happy birthday, Isbel!'

'It's not my birthday,' Isobel laughed.

'No. Happy birthday, Isbel!' Polly insisted. She wriggled. I put her down. She approached the tree very tentatively. 'Christmas tree, Daddy!' she shouted, and hit one of the lower branches with an open hand.

'Careful, darling,' Katya bent and pulled her back. 'You will be careful with these wires and so on, won't you, Neil?'

'No, I was thinking of plugging her into the mains,' I said sourly, then, 'No, no. Of course I will.'

'Yes, well, I hope so. She's got a bit of nappy rash, so change her as often as possible. There's Sudocream in her bag.'

'Sore bum!' Polly shouted, and laughed.

'So, who wants what?' my mother drawled. 'Tea? Whisky? Mulled wine? Katya, dear?'

'Well, we should be getting on our way . . .'

'Absolutely not,' my mother sang. 'Polly is not a package to be handed over. She will see her parents behaving in a civilized and friendly way. So.'

'I'd love a glass of mulled wine,' Tony rumbled, somewhat surprisingly. 'Splendid after that drive. Really frightening out there. God. No, super.'

Katya glared at him and sighed. He seemed impervious rather than defiant. He was a large, soft man – an oarsman gone to flab, I guessed – with soft flopping hair and an open trusting face; simple not stupid. An opsimath, I guessed, like so many of his class. He would be wise when he was old.

'Good,' my mother nodded. 'Mulled wine all round.'

She vanished to the kitchen. Isobel struck up a conversation about Chelsea with Tony. Katya stood with her arms folded and her chin raised. Her mouth was puckered as a cat's arse. This, I took it, was her version of disdain.

'I'd better take Polly up, get her into pyjamas,' I said feebly.

'She's all right.'

'I'd like her to have routine. Animals are happier with routine.'

'She's not an animal.'

'I know that, but the same principles apply.'

'Last night, she was up till nine. Did her no harm.'

I sighed, then held my breath and my thoughts.

Polly was playing happily with a duck on a stick whose rubber feet revolved and slapped on the floor. 'Take kack-kack outside?' she asked me.

'No, darling,' I crouched, 'not outside now. It's night-time. Time for sleep.' Being a coward I hoped that I could get Polly to sleep before my mother drove her away. She would not awake when transferred to the car. There would be no painful parting that way.

I picked her up. 'Say night night,' I told her. She set up a complaining wail.

At that moment, the purring wind snapped at the house. There was a 'crack!' and a lot of rustling outside. I carried Polly to the window and pulled aside the curtain. The familiar shape of the giant Scots pine outside had changed. It rocked like a heavy metal fan. One of its lower limbs sagged.

'Dear God,' I whistled. 'It is bloody rough.'

'Tony,' Katya was imperious, 'we can't get stuck here. We really must get going. Will you ring the AA now and then we'll be on our way? Please.'

'Yes. Right. Suppose I should.' He smiled sheepishly at Isobel. He reached for his wallet. 'Sorry, Neil, where is the telephone?'

'Through there,' I pointed through to the study. 'If the lines are still up. It's a naughty night.'

'God, I know. Filthy.' He lumbered to the door.

My mother came back with a tray plumed with steam. 'Here we are, Isobel dear.' She addressed Katya with maternal diplomacy, 'If you could just move your bag . . .'

Katya sighed. 'Katya, actually.' She removed the bag from the coffee-table and laid it on the floor with an unnecessary thump. She was getting agitated and truculent. If she didn't leave soon, there would be an outburst.

'They're going to have to hurry on, Mama,' I said. I handed a glass to Katya, another to Isobel. Polly had forgotten about her protest. She demanded a drink for herself. 'Conditions are bloody awful out there.'

The wind shrieked and slammed at the windows and the walls. There was rattling from the roof and moaning from the trees. There would be a lot of clearing up to do tomorrow.

'Yes, I must get going soon,' my mother spoke vaguely, 'I'll just have this drink to warm me up and then I'll be away. How far have you got to go, Is – Katya?'

'Blandford,' Katya was curt.

'Oh, charming Blandford. I used to stay down there a lot with Iain. Oh, there you are, Tony,' she turned. 'Have a drink. What's the news.'

'They say no one should drive unless the journey is strictly necessary.'

'This is strictly necessary,' Katya droned. 'We're not staying here.'

'No. OK.' Tony was uncertain. He started pulling at his fingers again. 'I'm not looking forward to it, I must say.'

'Nor am I,' Katya sipped her drink, 'but there we are.'

'Treacherous, they say, throughout the South. Lots of accidents. Lots of trees down.'

'Pity the poor sods at Lloyd's,' my mother shook her head. 'So many claims, many of them fraudulent, of course, but what can they do? You're not with Lloyd's are you, Tony?'

'No. No, my father was, but . . .'

'There's no point in making it worse by talking about it,' Katya laid down her drink and pulled her bag on to her shoulder. 'Right. We really must be off. Bye, bye, Polly, darling . . .' She opened her arms, but Polly turned her head from her and hid against my chest. 'Go 'way,' she mumbled.

'That's not very friendly, Polly,' I laughed. Inwardly, my heart rejoiced. 'Be nice to mummy.'

'No.'

Katya leaned over my arm to kiss Polly, who struck at her playfully with a tiny, chubby hand. There were tears in

Katya's eyes as she stepped back. 'Right. See you on Friday,' she said. 'Goodbye, Marnie. Isobel. You will remember about the nappy rash, won't you?'

Isobel smiled brightly.

Tony hastily downed his drink and, with waves and thanks, followed Katya through the glass door, into the back corridor and out into the hurricane. Polly gave me good reason not to accompany them to their car. I took her into the kitchen instead. I waved as the headlights came on and the car started up.

'Right,' I watched the tail-lights shrinking and vanishing as the car crested the hill. I turned to my mother. 'I'm not sure it's any safer out there than here, but you'd better take her. Quickly. You won't try to make it to the sea tonight?'

'No, no. If I can get as far as Mere and find a pub, I'll set off again tomorrow morning. Don't worry, Neil, darling. She'll be OK. I've reared two, you know.'

'I know.' I kissed Polly again and again, aching to see her go. 'Come on,' I said, but my voice sounded like sandpaper. 'Let's do it. Isobel, darling, you transfer the car seat to Mama's car?'

'Sure.'

'Polly go 'side?' Polly asked me.

'Yes, darling.' I kissed her cheek, her ears, her eyes. 'Yes. Polly's going out with Granny. In the car. Polly's going . . .'

'And Daddy?'

I opened the back door. The wind had been lying in wait for me. It pounced. I lurched sideways on the doorstep. Behind me, my mother and Isobel tactfully bothered themselves with Polly's bag and Polly's mug.

'Daddy?'

I said nothing. I walked round to my mother's Polo, just hugging Polly tight and feeling the wispy warmth of her scalp against my lips. Bracken danced beside me.

'Dad*dy*?' she shouted above the wind.

'Yes, my baby?'

'Daddy come in car?'

I opened the back door of the car and placed her carefully in the baby-seat. She blinked those beautiful, trusting, lagoon-clear eyes at me.

'No, darling one,' I mumbled. 'Not now. Daddy'll see you very soon.'

She started to cry. Her face crumpled and she wailed like a musical saw. Great hiccups shook her like punches. I fastened the straps brutally. I kissed her. I crooned in her ear 'I love you, my own darling baby girl. I love you.'

The hatchback was slammed down. I stepped back and shut the door. The wind howled. The trees gasped like an untuned radio. My hair was tugged back off my brow. My tears were dried almost as soon as they fell. I could see Polly in there, crying her heart out, nigh inaudible now.

'It'll be all right, Neil darling,' my mother shouted at my elbow.

Those words might have consoled me once, but parental reassurance no longer sufficed. That was my job now. I was failing in it.

'Go on, love,' I yelled back. The wind put in a big one, and all the trees and rose-bushes cackled and kicked and revelled. 'Get out of here!'

'Take great care, darling, won't you!' She gulped up the last words. She touched my arm. I did not know whether I would ever see Polly again. It had not crossed my mind that my mother must be thinking the same of me. She walked round to the driver's door. The light came on inside and Polly's crying was for a moment clear. My mother tucked herself into the seat.

'And you!' I yelled as the door swung shut and the light went out. The wind crashed over us like a breaking wave. 'Go,' I murmured, 'go, go, go.'

The engine coughed and hummed. The headlights came on. And their beams met others.

The other beams came from the hilltop above and scanned the sky. Within a few seconds, I knew, they would swing downward and dazzle us.

I said 'Christ!' I lunged forward to the door handles. The car was already moving. 'Someone's coming!' I lunged forward as the door opened. 'We're too late! Stop!' The car rocked. Polly was still howling. I grappled with the straps on her seat. My mother said, 'Well, bugger them.' Her seatbelt clicked and swished. She was up and out.

'It's all right, darling,' I sobbed as Polly's hands reached out for me. The buckle resisted me, then gave. 'It's all right, Daddy's here.'

I lifted her out. Too late. The lances of light had sideswiped the house and now caught us on their point. We were petrified by light. My mother still stood at the front of the car. She looked set to wag her finger at an army. I swung round. I handed Polly to Isobel. 'Take her inside, darling. Quickly,' I shouted. Isobel's hair was streaked across her face. She said, 'Neil . . .'

'Go on! Run!' I pointed.

She did as she was asked. The headlight beams followed her. Her shadow was half the height of the house. The car's wheels crunched like cornflakes. The gale buffeted at my eardrums. It wasn't the XJS. It was a big saloon, a BMW.

The car crunched to a halt. The passenger door opened. The light came on. Katya, moving at speed, her fists clenched, eyes glaring, blind as moonstones. She strode towards me, then veered towards the back door where Isobel had just gone. 'Devious *bastard*!' she shouted. She was unhinged and unsexed by her anger, as so often before. The voice was a man's, and a madman's.

I ran after her. Bracken, plainly thinking all this coming and going highly amusing, cantered at my side. Somewhere at the periphery of my vision and consciousness, Tony climbed from the car. 'So sorry,' he was burbling.

'Katya!' I caught up with her at the door. 'What's the matter, for Christ's sakes?'

The wind whipped back her hair. She tried the door handle. 'I'm calling the fucking police. You can't stop me! Let me *in*!'

'What are you going on about?' I reached for her shoulder.

She span round. She spat soft clouds of poison gas. 'I'll break the door down,' she said, *tremolo*. 'Tony is here. Tony is a witness. I want my child. You've done it this time, Neil. You've really blown it. That's it.'

'What are you talking about?' I yelped.

'No. It's no use. Thank God we came back. Get out of my way, Neil. Sorry. It's the police.'

'I'm not in your way, woman, and what the fuck are you *talking about?*'

'Yes, Katya, dear. Do calm down.' My mother came around the corner and stood behind me. 'What *are* you talking about?'

'Don't try,' she sneered and pointed, 'just don't try. You're in it, too, and that long-legged bitch. Tony, we're locked out. You'll just have to knock the door down, if you don't mind.'

Tony said from the shadows of the garage, 'Steady, Kati, darling. I'm sure there's an explanation.'

'Thank God for reason,' I moaned, and the wind moaned with me. 'We can all go inside and perhaps someone can tell me what the hell all this hysteria is in aid of. I have told you before, Katya. There is an explanation to everything and everything is comprehensible if only you will leave that Gothic Chamber of Horrors which is your imagination and gently, quietly ask questions. We are people, not monsters. Now . . .' I said, having delivered myself of my lecture. I walked, bent almost double, round to the front door of the house. I hammered on the kitchen window. I shouted, 'Isobel! It's all right! It's Katya! Let us in!'

For a few tense seconds I stood there while the trees behind me creaked and groaned. At last Isobel emerged hesitantly from the study. Polly was in her arms and crying again. I tapped on the window, 'It's OK.' I exaggerated the movements of my mouth. 'It's Katya!' I pointed towards the back door with a stiff finger. She vanished.

I strode back, shoved by the wind. Isobel nodded. The tight muscles at her brow and her jaw relaxed. 'Now, Katya.' I made the most of my transitory authority. 'You may re-enter my house on one condition, and that is that you do not distress Polly by a vulgar display of emotionalism. I will answer any questions and any charges, but not amid shrieking and insults. Understood? Good. Ah,' I said as the door opened inward. 'Thanks, darling. Katya and Tony are back. What was it, Tony? Tree down?'

'Ah, yup. Yah, more of a branch. Just round a sharp bend. Almost hit the bloody thing. I think, you know, two or three of us could shift her, if you've got a chainsaw handy.'

'I have,' I shooed him along the corridor. 'We'll see what we can do when we've got this little lot sorted out.'

'Darling!' Katya had snatched Polly and was kissing her repeatedly while glaring over the top of her head at me.

'I don't understand what in hell is happening,' my mother flapped nothing visible from her shawl and her skirt, 'but it is all far too exciting for me. I suggest large whisky and sodas all round and a roaring fire. That is indeed a very naughty night. And that child,' she swept past Katya, 'should be in bed.'

'So that's where you were taking her, was it?' Katya was still sneering at my mother's back, but she reluctantly followed her through to the front hall.

'Yes, actually, Katya, dear. That is precisely where I was talking her. To bed.'

'I *saw* you,' Katya trilled. 'It's no good lying to me. Tony, I'm going to ring the police, then whoever can get us out of here. I'm taking Polly. I'm not leaving her here. That's final. That's it.'

'I shouldn't think you'll have much luck with either call.' My mother walked down the steps and into the drawing room. She sat on the sofa and patted the space beside her. 'Now do sit down and stop being absurd. Neil, darling, where is that whisky?'

I clattered over to the sofa-table and slopped Black Bush into five tumblers. 'Here you go,' I leaned over the sofa-back with two of them.

'No. Thank you,' Katya said stiffly.

'Tony?' I proffered Katya's glass.

Tony said 'Yes. Thank you, Neil. Do with that. God, what a night. Now, what is all this damned brouhaha, Kati?'

'Yes,' I walked over to Isobel where she stood by the fireplace. I handed her a glass. 'What are we meant to have done?'

'I *saw* you, Neil!' She cast her eyes heavenward. 'Why keep pretending?'

'I'm not pretending anything,' I shrugged.

'Oh, for Christ's sake,' she sighed, 'so Polly wasn't about to leave in Marnie's car?'

'Certainly she was.'

'And as soon as we came back, you snatched her out and tried to pretend we hadn't seen it?'

'Yes, as soon as you came back, I snatched her out. No, I did not pretend anything.'

'Oh, no, of course not. I *saw* you, Neil! You handed Polly to your – your little friend there, and she ran back to the house and locked the door. What was the plan? Come on,' she looked to my mother, then to Isobel, then to me. She smiled a Margaret Thatcher smile. 'Come on. Might as well tell me now. What was it? Marnie, what was it? You take her to – where? Bristol Airport? Heathrow?'

Light dawned. Isobel and I said 'Ah.' Isobel added, 'Oh, for God's sake.'

'That's enough from you,' Katya yapped.

'I don't think so, Katya,' Isobel strolled over to the sofa and looked down at her. 'Neil's right. You do have a lurid imagination. You really are so damned anxious to justify your behaviour that you invent monsters where there are only people, and in the end, that makes you the only real monster. Neil loves that child. He is hardly going to distress her by abducting her, but because you in your twisted little mind see yourself as the eternal victim, you're prepared to spread hatred and anger and unpleasantness. I'm not defending Neil. He can do that for himself. But he doesn't eat babies, and only a sick mind would believe that he did. Sick and self-obsessed and idle. And your manners leave a hell of a lot to be desired, too. I'm going to get some food going, Neil.'

I grabbed her hand as she passed. She pulled it gently away.

'Very sweet,' said Katya, but her eyes followed Isobel's long black-stockinged legs up the steps to the door. 'So. Forgetting the insults for a minute, perhaps you'd care to explain exactly what you were up to? And no lies, please, this time.'

'Neil felt threatened,' my mother explained simply. 'So we agreed that I should take Polly away with me to a B & B somewhere where the not-very-nice people couldn't find us. When we saw the headlights, Neil reasonably thought that it might be the not-very-nice people and his first thought, quite naturally, was to get Polly to safety. Simple, really.'

'Oh, for God's sake,' Katya released Polly.

Polly ran over to me, hit my crotch and chortled.

'Do you believe this, Tony?' Katya slowly shook her head. She smiled.

'Oh, if Lady Sylvia says it's so,' Tony said vaguely, 'I'm sure it's so. Who are these people, Neil?'

I liked this man and his glass was empty. I like to see my friends happy. I strolled back to the sofa-table and picked up the bottle. 'You may remember,' I said, 'that Katya found eighty thousand pounds in our joint account and, despite my pleas to her to leave it alone, withdrew it.'

'This is . . . ?' Katya jumped to her feet. Her eyes were wide. Her lower lip visibly shook. Her fingers plucked at her black sweater. She gulped. 'Christ, Tony. We've got to get out of here.'

My mother frowned up at her. 'Not much chance of that, I fear, dear.'

'What do you mean "not much chance"?' Katya's voice quavered. 'We just have to . . . We've got to get that bloody branch cut up. Then, if we all pull at it . . . It's not that big. Come on.'

'What's up?' Tony held out his glass and peered past me as I topped it up. 'Kati? What's all this about? A few thugs? I know about the turf. Can get rough, eh?'

'No,' Katya insisted. 'No. We've got to get out, take Polly with us . . .'

'No,' I snapped. If Polly's with you, she's in danger. She stays with me. That's what the court-order says. That's what's going to happen. I'll help you pull that branch away, but Polly stays here or goes off with Mama. That's the deal. And no, Tony. That eighty grand was paid into our account by a big, bad, rich villain who doesn't mess about. What would you do if someone nicked eighty grand from you?'

'Bloody hell. Send the boys round, I suppose; not that I know any boys, but I've got friends who do. Put on a bit of pressure, at least.'

'Yeah, and you're a nice guy. Mr Quinn isn't. He also somehow knows that it was Katya who removed the money. What happened, Katya?' I turned on her. 'He ring you, tip you off, say, "get up to the bank fast", and you, just thinking greed and vindictiveness, do as you're told?'

'You can think what you like, Neil.' She held her chin high. 'I did what I thought was best for my child.'

'You did what you thought best for *you!*' I bellowed and pointed. I closed my eyes for a second and gulped up breath. 'OK, OK. So Quinn wants his pound of flesh and we can't just keep running, so it's sort of poetic justice, really, Katya being here. I begged her to leave that cash alone, and she refused. So now she's scared. Big deal. So am I. And now I'm going to take Polly up to bed and, without overstating things, may God have mercy on your souls. Come on, little one.' I bent and pressed Polly to my chest. As I passed Katya, I said sweetly, 'And you and Tony can discuss the situation. If you want to leave, I'll help you, but you leave alone.'

'But I thought you'd sorted this out!' Katya keened. She rocked back and forth from her hips. 'Yes. Don't worry, Tony. He's just overdramatizing. He does this sort of – He's sorted it all out. I know he has.'

'You thought I'd be enslaved by a bully?' I raised an eyebrow. 'Yeah, well, you thought wrong.' I climbed the steps and for once in my life made a decent exit. 'Twice,' I said.

'Twice,' echoed Polly, and the door swung shut behind us.

'So, Aurora took pity on this old, old man . . .' I told Polly, and softly stroked her brow. Her eyes were wide and serene. She was back where she belonged, with her rocking-horse and her cot and the stencilled pink walls on which I had worked with such hope and pride. 'And she turned him into the first grasshopper . . .'

'Eek, eek?' Polly grinned. 'Grasper go, eek, eek?'

'That's right, little one,' I smiled down at her. 'And now every morning as she rises in the sky he squeaks out his once strong song of love, and she blushes to hear it, and her fingers caress and warm the grass which gives him shelter, and I'm getting carried away, and I love you, and it's time for sleep.'

I leaned down to kiss her, but found myself gathering her to me and breathing in the scent of her as though my life depended on it. She was so very tiny, so very warm, so very much alive, and replete with potential as an unexploded bomb. 'Don't worry, my little one.' It was a husky squeak. 'I'll never leave you. You're mine. I'm with you always.' I laid her back down in her cot. 'Love you,' I smiled and blinked and kissed her.

She was unmoved by all this fetching emotion. She just sucked her thumb and twiddled her hair and stared up at me. She had confidence in me.

She must have inherited my brains.

I pulled up the side of the cot. 'Good night, darling,' I whispered. I turned to pad away.

'Nigh, nigh see you in the morny!' she shouted after me. 'Daddy? Daddee!'

'Yes, Polly, love?'

'Nigh, nigh see you in the morny?' she asked, just checking.

'Yes, darling,' I crooned. 'Night, night, see you in the morning.' The door hushed shut over the thick carpet. I whispered, 'God bless,' and made the sign of the cross for the first time in years.

Passing vampires may have flinched. I doubted that it had hurt Quinn much.

'I'm sorry.' Isobel was at the sink. She scoured an orange Le Creuset pan as though it were Katya's face. 'I just cannot stand that sort of – it's like all these professional support-group floozies, you know? They don't seem to have heard of free will, for God's sake. Oh, no, they're victims all, all "products of their backgrounds", not one of them prepared to get off their bloody fat arses and take responsibility for their own lives. I mean, sure, they've had a hard time. So? I've had a hard time, you've had a hard time. I see it, it's like a child born to one parent, a back-street kid: sure, it's bad, but then, a privileged child: daddy gets drunk – Jesus, you lose your favourite doll – because you're used to security, it hurts just as much. I don't know. Where does responsibility start – I mean, take it back to Adam and Eve, blame them, or what?' She banged the pan down on the draining-board. She pulled a dripping sheaf of implements from the sink.

'I know,' I soothed. I had never seen her so agitated. 'I know, but take it easy, darling. It's one night, and we're stuck with it.'

'Oh, yes, yes. Don't worry.' Her hands dropped to her sides for a moment, then rummaged furiously beneath the suds. 'Don't worry. It's only a moment with me. No, but it's like the playground, isn't it? Always blaming. You know, "He started it!" "No, she hit me first!" I mean, what's the fucking point? Oh, stuff it.' She plucked out the plug and leaned back against the draining-board. Her gloved hands dripped foam which slapped on to the vinyl floor. 'I'm sorry, I'm sorry, I'm sorry. It's just – I suppose I could have been like that, and it annoys the hell out of me to see it. God, Neil. How did you come to marry the woman?'

'I don't know, to both questions.' I shook my head. I was genuinely bemused. 'Strange, but my memory of the whole thing is just a blur. It always is with unhappiness, far as I'm concerned. Too much pain. Too much shrieking. But she

211

wasn't always like that, you know. At least, she didn't seem so. I don't know. I have to accept my share of the blame, don't I? It's just – you and I, we have a disagreement, we can discuss it, we sort it out. She can't do that. It's always deepest black or purest white with her. And if you and I have a disagreement, I say something wrong, you know, few hours, whatever, it all seems trivial. Not with her. Something's eating her up from inside, so she's the only person I've ever known, the tiny offence actually grows and grows the longer she thinks about it. I don't like to think . . .' I leaned my elbow on the vinyl surface, my forehead on my hand. A buzzing handshake joke went off in my head. 'Ah, hell, I hate to think that I made her the way she is now.'

'You didn't.' Isobel snapped off rubber gloves. 'She did. You can't – well, you can with torture and brainwashing, but – no, you can't make anyone anything. You've got a lot of virtues, and each one has its own obverse. That's what I like about us. We have no secrets. We're both disillusioned in the best sense. I no longer expect anyone to be perfect. God forbid. Just, on balance, you're OK. We want the same things. We get on. Once, I confused sex with romance and told myself this was the basis of a relationship. Now I look for a friendship, common standards, common aims, and everything else – bed and so on – is just a bonus.'

I said, 'Oh, God,' partly because I had never thought to hear a girl like this speak my mind, more, because the irony, as ever, was rich. Those guys up on Olympus have great scriptwriters. Sick, but sensational. For the first time, I was loved by a lovely and beloved woman and an adored child, while outside, the wind swooped and slammed at the house and one man, maybe more, planned that I should be permanently injured or permanently dead.

It is some consolation to know that you will be mourned and remembered.

Not much.

It wasn't as bad as I had thought, all told. Katya announced

212

that she was staying. Isobel had made a Beirut peace with her. They watched one another like snake and mongoose, but the while spoke trivia politely enough. My mother was my mother.

Tony Wickham proved the star of the evening. Three or four large whiskies may have helped, but he entered into the Defending the Homestead game with gusto. He had read the right books, seen the right films. Most of his proposals were too fanciful by half, but his bullish defiance towards Quinn and his kind was reassuring. Where Katya moped and pouted, just like the old days, Tony, apparently oblivious, joked, chatted and cheered.

Over bowls of sloppy chilli mopped up with bread, we watched the television news. The weather was the lead. Bridges were closed or down, riverbanks breached and buildings damaged throughout the South. A wall had fallen on a boy in Cambridgeshire. Two old women had drowned in their beds on Severnside. A man in London had been hit and killed by a flying tile, a man in Devizes by a pub-sign, a motorist in Hampshire by a tree.

But the wind was far from sated. It took a deep smoker's breath and blew harder than ever. Thank God the roof had been finished.

It was Katya who, thank God, first announced that she didn't know about anyone else, but she was going to bed. She wanted to be away first thing tomorrow morning, and if Tony could tear himself away from all this ridiculous Boy's Own nonsense . . .

Tony reluctantly did so, but not before he had bent over my mother's hand and clapped me on the back. With Isobel, he was more subdued. I thought for a moment that he was going to clout her, too, but instead he clapped his hands and bowed a bit, said, 'Bloody good. No, pleasure meeting you. Dinner. Great. Right. Funny old evening. Night, then.'

I showed him and Katya up to the twin room which gave on to the drawing-room roof, the room opposite Polly's at the far end of the corridor from my own. I equipped them with towels, a torch and a tilley-lamp. Katya had already kicked off her shoes and was sitting in the far bed when I came to wish them a good night. I did so awkwardly.

Isobel and my mother were climbing the stairs as I descended, and we spent the next five minutes in hunting out spare toothbrushes, toothpaste tubes, cleanser and so on. To her, too, I gave a torch and a tilley. Hers was the little oblong room which overlooked the drive immediately opposite the head of the stairs.

She gave Isobel a cheek to kiss and said 'God bless, dear,' with genuine warmth. She came to me. 'You do get yourself into messes, darling, don't you?' she sighed. 'Oh, well. Life will never be boring, Isobel, dear.' She kissed me. 'Good night, darling. Don't worry. The old sleep lightly, if at all. You relax and leave it to Bracken and me.'

Isobel and I returned downstairs. I switched off the drawing-room lights, then moved to the kitchen to mix up more of my 'demon-king' paste. I checked every door and window in the house, then returned to Isobel where she sat at the kitchen table. The pages of an old *Tatler* barked as she turned them. 'Well,' I shrugged, 'what more can I do?'

'Nothing,' Isobel smiled up at me. 'We don't know if they'll come, still less how. Maybe you should have installed burglar alarms, heat-sensitive lights, all that, but basically, if someone wants to get to you, he can get to you. You work in public, you . . . Anyhow, efficient alarms just make brighter burglars.'

'And we need mains electricity,' I pointed out.

'We've done what we can, we're going to feel very silly tomorrow morning if nothing happens.' She stood, her fingertips in her jeans back-pockets. 'I'm for bed, too,' she said. 'You?'

'Yeah,' I said glumly. 'Might as well. I'll just paint the floors and doors with this muck. God, if a mouse comes in tonight, he'll get the shock of his life.' I picked up the hurricane lamp. 'Primed and ready,' I said. 'Try to stay awake. I'll only be five minutes or so.'

'I'll do my best.' She smiled. She took the lamp. She ran the fingers of her other hand down my scarred cheek. 'I love you, you know.'

'I still can't quite believe it,' I shook my head. 'You were customized for me. The gods are bloody kind.'

'I know,' she said, then qualified it. 'Sometimes. Sometimes they really are.'

I pottered about the house, spreading the black paste on door-frames, window-frames, stairs and floors. There was not much, so I had to choose the right spots by inspired guess-work. A battalion could march through the house without causing a single explosion. An unlucky rat could make it sound like the Somme. I switched off the kitchen lights, and stood in the darkness, waiting.

You get used to the steady, idling black-cab chug of a generator. After a while, indeed, if you notice it at all, it is reassuring. You would be alarmed by its absence, much as townies complain of the stillness of the countryside. This was the first time since I had turned it on this evening that I had consciously heard it. I had to listen hard, for the wind's assault was relentless, but there it was, a deep sound like a contented cat driven over cobbles.

In a matter of moments now, it would stop.

I have often wondered if it is possible to hear your heart stop beating. You've been running, say, or fighting. The heart is thumping. Then comes the fatal blow or the heart attack. There must be some time, surely, between the cessation of the heartbeat and the switching off of the brain and its faculties. You'd be lying there, the heart drumming ever more violently, and suddenly, horribly, you could actually hear it stop.

It was like that here. The last electric current in the house was switched off. Just for a minute, the generator, unaware, kept up its work. Then, without warning, there was silence.

Silence, that is, given that all the black hounds, tormented souls and banshees of Celtic myth were holding their Sabbath

215

outside, but it seemed like silence just then. The house's life support had been switched off.

I tiptoed up the stairs and along the corridor to my room. Every sound, every creak of the boards and rustle of my sweater against the wall, was loud now.

When I opened the door, the wind wailed triumphantly and bounded into the room. The curtains bellied and flapped like washday. Shutting the door was not unlike forcing a reluctant animal into the stalls.

I turned to Isobel. The flicking lantern beside her made her skin seem tanned. The duvet was a snowy sunset. Otherwise, the room was in darkness.

'You opened a window?' I whispered.

'Just the little one at the top. Come on. Get in here. I'm not sure whether it's freezing or whether it's just that bloody wind making me feel that it should be. All I know is, I need my hot-water-bottle.'

'So I have some uses?'

'Limited, but unquestionable.'

I removed my boots, socks and trousers. I clambered quickly in beside her.

'You're going to sleep like that?'

'Yeah,' I puffed. 'I'm not planning to sleep much, and anyhow, reckoned I should be ready.'

'Well, I'm ready.' She rolled over so that she looked down on me. Only the white of her eyes glinted in the dark tent of hair. Her naked breasts, mysteriously fuller than when we had met, spread on my flannel shirt. She was very warm.

'As always,' I smiled nervously up at her.

'That's right,' she nuzzled at my neck. Her hand fumbled at my boxer-shorts. 'Ever ready, that's me.'

'We can't,' I protested. 'We've got to . . . No, darling. We've got to stay alert, Jesus, they could be here at any minute. And my mother . . .'

'Mothers have some experience of this sort of thing,' she breathed in my ear. 'By definition. And if I'm going to face my doom, I'd sooner do it happy, wouldn't you?'

'Sure, but . . .'

'And the wind makes me feel all raunchy. Don't know why.' She raised a breast to force a nipple into my mouth. 'Just suck my tits a bit,' she crooned. 'Don't worry, I'm not going to demand anything more.'

She had no need to. As ever, the touch and the taste and the smells of her, the urgency of her caresses, the limber looseness of her limbs as they wrapped about me, strained against me, all served to dictate to my already tense body far more efficiently than could any request.

What started gently became fast and fierce. There were fifteen, twenty minutes then, in which she held herself open and lay still as stone, and all, for me, was darkness and slippery sensation until the feverish shaking started, the bobbing and bucking and groaning. I pursued her, would not let her go, until she was yelping out her pleas yet coming back for more.

Then we were together again, and she was out of it, gone, still drooling 'no . . . no . . . no . . .' as all that aggression and fear in me was transmitted into lust. The soles of her feet were before my face, and she pushing back at me as hard as I slammed into her. I turned her over and slapped that beautiful arse as hard with my hand as with my stomach. She pardoned and shared in my every lowliest lust. We were children playing again. It was a rough game, but good.

'My legs have gone,' she giggled afterwards. 'I have no legs.'

'Sh!' I said – one brief cymbal stroke.

I kicked back the duvet and strode to the window. I had heard heavy feet on the gravel out there. I gestured to Isobel to turn out the light. Once in darkness, I could see quite clearly the bucking, boring, straining trees on either side of the drive, and Bracken, directly beneath me, sinking down into the flower bed with a long, deep grunt. I sighed.

'OK?' asked Isobel from the blackness.

'Yeah. Yeah, just Bracken.' I turned back to the bed and climbed in. As I did so, I felt for the gun beneath the bed. The stock was cold, the barrel . . .

217

'I'm not going to sleep,' I said.

'Mmmm,' Isobel hummed happily.

'I mustn't . . .'

'Mmmm.'

But she slept, and so, soon after, did I.

I awoke instantly and totally.

Cold fingers played scales on my sides. Rabbits thumped their alarm at the base of my skull. I lay curled on my right side. I opened my eyes very slowly.

He was just inches away.

I could not see him, for it was pitch-black in here, but I could hear his short, clogged breathing. He tried to quiet it by breathing through his nose, but there was a little click with each inhalation. His clothes roughly rustled. There was a smell too, of wet wool and of stale sweat.

My stomach whimpered.

I could not move.

My mind had seized up. I was shaking. Even had I been able to move, I did not know how best I should do so. To reach for the gun – to move at all, particularly while his eyes were accustomed to the dark – might be to draw his fire, his blade, his club – whatever weapon he must surely carry. He moved closer. For a second, I could actually feel the warmth of his breath on the back of my one exposed hand. My shaking was so violent that I was sure he must feel it.

He padded very softly and slowly down the bed and round its foot. His hand felt his way. I knew from the slow-puncture hiss that it was gloved.

He was somewhere at my left now, somewhere in the deep darkness on Isobel's side.

I moved my arm from my side. Sweat released the skin reluctantly. My left hand groped beneath the pillow for the cut-throat razor – a present from Katya. I had never used it until now. It's handle was enamelled and cool. I rolled slowly over with a sigh to smother the sound. The breathing in the blackness stopped. With my right hand, I pulled out the blade.

218

Whoever was here was here to hurt me or my child. There was no chance that a shout would suffice to scare him away. There could be no 'Who goes there?', no bow-shots. I must attack or be attacked, defeat utterly or be defeated.

The wind wrapped itself like a whip about the house. The house hunched its shoulders and shuddered. I was glad that the intruder was now on Isobel's side, glad because hot, protective anger had replaced the vertiginous chill of a moment ago.

I rose slightly on my elbow. I transferred the open razor to my right hand. I gathered my knees up beneath me. As soon as he made a move, I must go for him, slashing and hacking at the curtain of blackness.

The wind growled, bit and worried.

And all hell broke loose.

Light glimmered at the window and was gone. There were two almost simultaneous explosions from below, the first a sharp crack, the second a deep bass boom which set the floorboards humming.

I threw myself over Isobel. Above me, a strong tenor voice snapped close at hand. 'Right. Don't move.' Muffled footfalls moved fast across the room. The door-handle rattled. The bedroom door swung inward and slammed into the wall. The wind charged in. The curtains woofed. Then the bare boards were beneath my feet. I crouched for a second, naked and uncertain. Isobel jerked up and her voice was high. 'What? Christ! What's . . .'

Those muffled footfalls thumped down the stairs, thumped across the hall. Two more of my ammonia tri-iodide booby-traps cracked like caps. The voice which had spoken in our room yelped, 'Fuck, what's going on here?', another voice from the kitchen moaned, 'Oh, shit, man!'

There were lights out there in the corridor, bobbing and shifting like Jack o'Lantern. 'It's all right,' my mother's voice called. 'You look after Polly.' Her slippered feet whispered on the stairs.

Polly started to scream. Somewhere in the background, Katya was yapping too.

'Ring the police,' I snapped at Isobel, and I was up and out.

God knows what doors or windows were open, but the through-draught howled and papers cackled. My mother was on the stairs beneath me when I reached their head. 'Wait!' I told her.

She turned up. Her face was very smooth and plush in the gaslight. 'You sort out Polly. See if you can get her hidden,' she whispered. 'I'll see what I can do.'

'You're sure?'

'Neil,' she was at the bottom now, gazing almost vertically up. 'How old am I?'

I nodded. I ran straight down the corridor and swung round the jamb into Polly's room. I had to come close to her to see her in the darkness. Her eyes were open. Her little fingers scrabbled at the eiderdown. She was set to screw up her face and do her best to outscream the gale, but she was intact.

'I whispered, 'It's all right, darling. Everything's OK.' I bent to pick up the current favourite among her soft toys – a rabbit with a hat – and tossed it into the cot as some form of consolation. I turned.

I stepped back out on to the landing. I stumbled on the runner and nearly sprawled headlong. I picked myself up and took the length of the landing in three strides. I descended the stairs three at a time, headed heedless towards the dancing lights from the study. My mother was ahead of me. I heard her voice, tremulous but strong.

I stopped at the study door. OK. Polly wasn't hurt so far. Isobel wasn't hurt. My mother was in there. I could hear her talking, taking charge.

That was all right. That would do. It looked as though my home-made bombs had caused some confusion, bought some time. If Isobel could raise the police now . . .

I turned and bounded back up the stairs. For Christ's sake, Munrow, keep your priorities clear.

I turned left on the landing. Even as I did so, Katya emerged from her room in a long, white cotton nightdress. She carried the tilley, whose light was bright and white. She was headed for Polly's room opposite. Her head jerked round as I emerged naked at the head of the stairs. 'What's hap –' she managed to get out before I clapped my hand over her mouth. She protested loudly, 'Mmm mmmm!'

'Shut it,' I hissed in her face. 'They're here. Downstairs. Come on. We can get you and Polly out over the roof. Come on. Quickly and quietly!'

I kicked open the door to Polly's room and pushed Katya in ahead of me. Polly stood howling over the vertical rails of the cot. Her shadow and those of the rails were giant on the wall and the ceiling.

'Darling, are you all right? It's all right, darling, it's all right, there . . .' Katya yodelled.

I pushed her to one side. I scooped up Polly with her blankets. 'Shh, darling one,' I growled into her hair. 'Come on now,' I whispered to Katya. 'Come on!'

I barged back out across the corridor and into Katya's room.

'Where's Tony?' Katya shrilled behind me.

'I haven't a clue.' I pulled open the glass door on to the roof and staggered under the gale's punch as I stepped outside.

The wind was cold on my naked skin. 'Get the hell out here!' I commanded. Katya stood on the threshold. Her night-dress puddered about her legs like a helicopter rotor. 'Come on, for Christ's sakes!' I grabbed her sleeve and pulled.

Polly's howling took turns to dominate with that of the wind. I shouted to Katya, 'Right! Jump off the roof and I'll hand her down! Run like hell, and I mean run! Babies fall silent if you run! Go down into the valley! Find shelter! Get to the village if you can . . .'

'Why are you bossing me about, Neil?' she shrilled back at me. Her lips were just inches from mine. 'I don't take orders from you, thank you! You created this mess, and if you think that Polly and I are going out there . . . !'

I reeled back, as much, I think, from astonishment as from the shove of the wind. Her crazed bitterness was such that even here, even now she was arguing, on a flat asphalt roof, with turmoil about us and death at our heels.

I grasped her arm. I tugged and pushed her to the very edge of the roof. 'Right! You jump or I push?'

'You wouldn't!' she shouted up at my chin. 'I'll walk straight back round to the door! You sort out your own problems, Neil! Don't involve me and Polly!'

'You are involved, for God's sake! You took that money, and Quinn wants to hurt me through Polly! Now go!'

I shoved hard, but she clung on to my arm and somehow swung round and broke free. She stumbled back on to her arse. The wind made her nightdress billow up. The tilley-lamp rolled on the felt.

In my arms, Polly reached out a grasping hand. She howled, 'Mahmee!'

And it was on to this farcical scene that Keith Gurdon strolled. He made much of strolling. He carried my gun under his left arm.

'Weel, weel.' His hair was slicked back off his brow by the wind, his leer exaggerated by the pulsing light from the hurricane-lamp which he held at head height. 'Domestic bliss, eh, Munrow? I'll be having that, you don't mind.' He nodded towards the razor in my right hand. I closed it and handed it to him. He pocketed it and turned to Katya. 'So, you must be Mrs Munrow. Won't remember me, will you? Oh, we have met, but you wouldn't remember.' He slung the lamp over his wrist and lowered a hand to Katya. She took it and stood.

She glared at him and me alternately as she tamed her skirts. Her teeth were gritted.

'And this must be the little darlin'.' Keith raised the gun-barrels towards Polly. I swung her away from him. 'Nice place you've got here, Munrow. Didn't expect the reception committee, I must say. But seeing as you're 'ere, Missis, I reckon as we'd be better off indoors, don't you? Come along, come along. Nice as you can.'

'Give me Polly,' Katya ordered. Her voice shook. I obeyed. Polly at once turned her face into Katya's breast and fell silent. I bent to pick up the fallen tilley. Keith shepherded us into the twin bedroom. He forced shut the door.

'I'll ... I'll just put Polly into bed,' Katya suggested. I marvelled at her submissiveness to a stranger after her bolshie-ness with me.

'No, no,' Keith objected. 'She's a nice little thing. Bring her down, fuck it, bring her down. Polly, is it? Ace. Just fucking ace. No. Everyone down in the lounge, nice and cosy. That's the best thing, and we can get it all sorted out. Bit of an accident, wasn't there? Gonna take some sorting.'

'Where's Tony?' Katya shivered, at the warmth, I think, not from fear.

'Oh, is that the arsehole's name?' Keith followed us down the corridor.

'Isobel?' I called towards our room. 'Isobel?'

'That the bit of cuff, is it, Munrow? You are a lucky boy. Wouldn't mind a bit of that and all. She's downstairs with the rest of 'em. Don't fret. Hadn't you better run along and get some clothes on, Munrow? Bad enough without having to look at your meat and two veg all night, thanks. Oh, and don't go all silly on us, will you? I'll keep Mrs Munrow and the babby here with me, so I'd advise you to be a good boy. Run along, then, and be quick.'

I needed no urging to be quick as I pulled on jeans and an old flannel shirt. I needed to know what had happened and was happening downstairs. I wanted to be back with my child. My hands shook, my stomach whimpered and my mouth was dry. I scanned the room quickly for anything which might serve as a hidden weapon, but, aside from bottles on the dressing-table, the room was bare.

Katya and Keith were talking softly when I returned into the corridor. They stopped as soon as they saw me. 'There,' Keith smiled his cockeyed smile. 'No, just saying, Munrow. Quite a bleeding houseful you got here, isn't it? Jeez, I mean, I was expecting just you and little babby here, perhaps the bit of skirt. Still, fuck up, but we'll sort it all out, I'm sure. We'll sort it out. That's it now. Down the stairs and into the nice warm lounge. As for your bleeding mother, Munrow – sheesh! See where you got your airs and graces, eh? Fuck me, I mean. Didn't blink when I told her about the mess. Me, I was set to puke.'

There was a blue-white flash and a bang. We all jumped. Polly said 'No?' and hid her head. Keith's hand flew from the banister rail. 'Jesus fuck, Munrow, what *is* this stuff?' he squealed. 'Your bright bloody idea, right? Yeah, well, not so fucking clever as it turns out. Jesus. Pitch darkness, one of these goes off, what do you expect a man to do? Scare the shit out of you.'

My heart sank. I was now fairly sure what had happened. Amiable Tony had heard the intruders and, big mastiff puppy that he was, had investigated. He had stumbled over one of my fireworks and someone, in the dark, thinking me to be the only man in the house, had acted precipitately. The big booming which had followed that first explosion did not give me very much hope for Tony's state of health.

He, least of all here save Polly, had deserved such a fate.

And another thought caused a lot of small creatures to abandon my hair and my neck and to scuttle for shelter in my arse. If Keith or his allies had fired on Tony, they must have killed or seriously injured him. All of them must now be confronting the prospect of life-sentences. They had nothing to lose, and there were four adult witnesses in the house. Lose those witnesses and there was a chance of escape. Leave them alive and there was no hope of a future.

We trudged down the steps into the drawing room. It was brightly lit. Someone had lit the big tilley and revived the fire.

'This is ridiculous,' said Katya. She padded over to the armchair closest to the fire. She set Polly down. She sat. 'This is just bloody ridiculous.'

I took in the scene.

My mother sat wrapped in a woollen plaid rug on the sofa. Wisps of her hair looped down at her temples. Isobel sat beside her. She wore my green silk dressing-gown very tightly tied about her waist. She looked up. She had been crying. 'Oh, thank God,' she smiled. She stood and moved towards me. 'I'm sorry. I'm an idiot . . .'

'Woah, there,' Keith stepped forward. He held out a halting hand. 'You heard what I fucking said, didn't you, doll? Just stay put and everything'll be OK. You fuck around with us, we have to make trouble, and I reckon we've had enough of that for one night, don't you?'

Isobel blinked wistfully at me for a moment, then nodded and shrugged. She retreated, narrowly avoiding Polly. She ruffled Polly's hair and sat again. Polly said 'Cuddle,' and stretched out her arms. She scrambled into Isobel's lap. Katya's lips twitched.

Quinn was not here.

Nor was Tony.

There were two other people here, though. I had seen neither of them before.

In the big bow-window, a tall man leaned back with his bum on the sill. He was perhaps my age. He was very lean, and good-looking in a gaunt, hungover Hamlet sort of way. His eyelids were heavy. The cheek which was turned towards me was thickly pocked. His honey-coloured hair was straight and thin. He carried a shotgun too casually for an expert. He smiled at me. His teeth were perfect, but yellow at their edges. His clothes were – hell – Juliette Greco, fifties left bank: suede walking boots, baggy brown cords and oversized black sweater. My gaze made him straighten and grin and jiggle from foot to foot. 'Hey, Neil, Neil, kind of a heel,' he said, and giggled.

At the far end of the room, her back to the sunroom, stood a woman. She was gnawing at a head of chicory. She must be – what? Fifty? Her face was pinched, her expression that of a mule on Friday evening. I guessed by her blinking stare that granny-glasses had been replaced by contact-lenses. Her hair was greying brown, but still hung down to her waist in the old hippy cascade. Her narrow, sloping shoulders, her stuff-you slouch, marched ill with that defiant sneer, that defiant tilt of the head. She wore a red kingsman about her neck, camouflage fatigues and military boots. She carried a cheap, but none the less unpleasant-looking, replica of a bowie knife. 'What are you looking at, man?' She jerked the big blade and chomped hard.

'Just wondering how you got here from Ibiza,' I shrugged.

'You what, shithead?'

'Or was it Bali? Let me guess,' my voice rang about the walls. 'Peer-pressure patsy, right? Fashion slave. Once a rebel, always a rebel. Hippy whore in an astrakhan coat with her knees behind her ears in tents from Pilton to Pokhara. Peace and love, man. Then, getting old, the circus has moved on, all the hippies have gone to work for Marks and Spencer, but the little exploited, rejected girl has sold her soul to the cause. Babies have been aborted. Marks and Spencer don't want her. And all she's got is a dose of clap and maybe a brat or two. Where can she go? Sure, they've got another movement just perfect for her. Militant feminism. Poor me becomes fuck-you. Then what? Crime, prison, more resentment – and all granny really wants is to sit down by the fire with nice old grandpa and knit socks, watch *Wheel of Fortune*; but she's fucked up every which way, hasn't she? How am I doing, darling? Nine out of ten?'

'Not even close, smartarse. Shit, where'd you find this guy, Keith?' She tried to smile through her snarl. 'I mean, fuck, talk about jerk. Shut him up for me, would you, and for good.'

'Easy, granny,' I taunted.

'Granny!' Polly cheered. 'I want a drink.'

'Please,' my mother reminded her.

'Oh, yeah, say "please",' granny jeered. 'Nice little girl.'

'Yeah,' the man in the bow-window was doing a sort of loose-limbed, on-the-spot jog. 'Nice little girl. Hey, sugar and spice and all things nice. What we do then, Keith? This wind, it really gets to me.' He shuddered. 'Hey, Lynn. This wind. It really gets to me, you know?'

'Sure, OK, Jake.' The woman's narrowed eyes never left me. She hated me.

I looked from one to the other. 'Oh, I get it!' I beamed. 'It's a package deal! Einstein Jake here is that unwanted brat, am

I right? You slightly overdid the acid during pregnancy, granny dear. Be more careful next time. Except there won't be a next time. Sorry. Silly of me. All withered up there now, aren't we? Too much oestrogen, too many drugs, too many men. Christ, what a life, justifying a childhood.'

'Keith,' the woman's mouth curled downward and her eyes were just dirty fingernails. 'You don't get on with it, blast the little shit, I'm going to do him right now.'

'Yeah,' Jake giggled, 'like I did, eh, Lynn? God. Like the devil. Poof! Flash of light, oh so bright. I didn't know it was just a big fat man.'

'Boy, do I like to work with professionals,' I shook my head slowly. 'So Einstein here shot Tony. That right, Keith?'

Keith shrugged.

'Yes, I'm sorry, Katya, dear,' my mother was precise, 'it appears that Tony is quite dead. Incredible, I know.'

'No,' Katya gasped and stared. 'No, this can't . . . This is a joke.'

'I would that it were, but it appears not. I can't see why these very peculiar people would want to joke about such a thing. He's in the kitchen.'

'Really messy, hey?' Jake smiled. 'Jesus, not my fault. What'd you do, you're all geed up, some guy comes in, flash of light, really bright, you're all uptight, big wham bang, like he's being really offensive, uncool, you know? No one even says there's other people here, big fat man, Chrissakes. No one tells me 'bout the big pig, big fat man. I think it's Neil baby here, maybe the devil. Jeez! So bang bang. What do you want?'

Katya covered her face with her hands. She said, 'No, no . . .' This, I knew from experience, meant that she could muster no tears.

I had found no source of courage. It was just that I wanted them angry with me and only me and that, in casting off concern for self-preservation, a sort of wild ebullience had filled me. I strolled over to Keith and faced him. 'OK, let's get on with this, Keith. Your battle's with me.' I turned to Isobel. 'Presume you didn't get through to the police?'

She shook her head. 'Line's down. That, or these little turds have done something. Dead, anyhow.'

'Like the big fat bastard,' Jake drooled. 'Dead, dead, hole in the head, splashing red . . .'

'Christ, you don't half pick 'em, Keith. Come on. Let's do whatever you've got to do.'

He nodded his smeared yellow head. 'Only thing is, it's not that simple any more, is it, Munrow? Shit, you have to have a cast of bleeding thousands, fucking bombs everywhere, fuck it. Make life difficult, you do.'

'It's a gift,' I told him. 'No, you've got no problem, Keith. Just drop Einstein in it. His prints on the gun. Everyone here gives evidence he did it all. No one else here. No one's going to miss him. So just do your worst and sod off, why not?'

Keith appeared to consider my suggestion. Soft light appeared on the old ivory of his eyes, but he shook his head. There was a tugging at the denim at my thighs. I looked down. Polly was staring up at me. 'Daddy, I want a drink!' she insisted.

'OK, darling.' I took her hand and led her towards the door.

'Hey! Where'd you think you're going?' the woman called after me.

I did not turn. 'To get my child a drink.'

Jake Einstein stood before me. I'd swear that he had crossed the room in just three strides. The gun's snout sniffed at my belly. 'Uh uh. No we don't,' he sang. 'Naughty Neil, trying to steal out of the salon and into the . . . Can't rhyme, have to mime.' He quaffed from an invisible glass in his left hand.

I smiled. I raised an eyebrow. I pushed the barrels to one side. 'Fuck off.'

'Naughty man!' Polly hit his knee.

'That's right, darling.' I led her up the steps. 'Horrid man.'

'Hey, you can't do that,' Jake whined up at me, 'he can't do that, can he, Lynn?'

'All right, all right!' The words curled from Keith's mouth like toothpaste from a tube. 'Jesus! How the fuck do I get into scenes like this? OK, OK. You all stay here. I want a word with this little fucker. Just everyone keep bleeding cool, will you?'

His footfalls played tag with their echoes. He caught up with me in the dark hall. The light from his lantern yawed. He grasped my sleeve and wrenched me around. 'You filthy fucker, Munrow,' he miaowed. 'You and that high-falutin' mother of yours. You're meant to beg. You're meant to bow to me. I've got the gun, haven't I? You see what happened to that big fart came to the door? Right. It's going to happen to you and all, and the little babby here. Think you can show me up, don't you? Treat me like shit, but you can't. You'll see.'

'Oh, yes, I can.' I pulled free of him and headed for the kitchen from habit, forgetting what lay inside. The locked door reminded me quickly enough and I doubled back into the utility-room. 'Because all you can do is kill me. I've taken that on board.'

'And your darling family.' Keith barred my way.

I was trying to lead him away from that line of thought. 'Sure,' I told him, 'if you want life, and I mean life, from a judge. As things stand, there's my wife's lover dead, me dead or injured, that's fine. Personal dispute. Jealous passion. They might just believe my mother's story or Isobel's, but I doubt it, and they'd find it hard to prove. Even if they did, even if they could prove it, it'd be – what? A burglary gone wrong. Murder, sure, but you'd be paroled in five . . .' I was extemporizing and failing to convince even myself. Keith was in terminal trouble unless he massacred the lot of us. I merely held out hope that he might clutch at a passing straw.

I wasn't going to give him time to see just how lacking in buoyancy that straw was. I sidestepped. He sidestepped, too. 'No, you don't . . .'

I scooped up Polly and barged straight past him, straight through him. I pushed open the door and stepped down into the utility-room. Behind me, Keith spat out ill-digested chunks of fury. 'That's it. I'll show the little bastard. Blast your fucking balls off, Munrow. Jesus, you should be crawling . . .'

The light from his lantern swung as though we were aboard a galleon. I put Polly down. I turned on the tap and filled a plastic mug with water. I handed it down to her. She did not, thank God, complain, but drank deep. Keith kept on spitting like a damp fire.

Again my eyes searched the room for a suitable weapon. There were weapons aplenty hanging from the hooks amid the coats or lying on the chest below – whips, curry-combs, skullcaps, croquet mallets and balls, dog-chains – but none of them accessible enough to be imperceptibly grabbed or small enough to be hidden.

Dog-chains . . .

My dog had not barked over the last twenty minutes. I remembered his heavy footfalls on the gravel as I had looked out of the window earlier, the long, low grunt with which he had subsided.

'Finished, darling?' I asked Polly.

'Yes, 'kyou,' she gasped and handed the mug up to me.

'Right.' I reached into the pocket of the Fermoy which hung on the wall. Keith's hand shot out to grasp my arm. 'What do you think you're doing?' he squeaked.

'Getting a knife.' I brushed off his hand and pulled out my Swiss Army knife. 'I want to see my dog.'

'Dog's dead,' Keith snarled. 'You put that knife back or I do you right now.'

'Get on with it, then, I don't care a toss.' Again I caught up Polly. Keith stood before me, one arm extended to the wall, the other pointing the gun directly at my chest. I span on my heel, unbolted the glass and wrought-iron door at the end of the room and stepped out.

Apart from two lights shining in the village below, the valley was dark. I could only just discern the swooping horizon and the swaying trees. I lowered my head against the wind, covered Polly with my jersey and walked quickly round the house.

Bracken lay on his side, just four feet from the spot where I had last seen him. A black speech-bubble sprouted from his throat. It made the gravel softly glisten. I knelt at his head. I reached down and touched the glistening blackness. It was cold and sticky. His silky fur rippled like breeze-blown barley. His soft eye was not wholly clouded. It moved up slow as a winter bluebottle to follow my movements.

I stroked his head. Behind me, Keith said, 'See? I told you he was fucking dead. Come on. You're coming in, and *now*.'

'Shut up, Keith,' I said softly. I ran my hand over the huge ribcage which bobbed fast and shallow. His tongue crackled once, and a long, deep groan seeped from him.

'Easy, lad,' I soothed. 'Easy, boy. Good boy, Bracken. Brave boy. There's a boy. There's a fine, bold lad. Jesus, but I'm sorry. Easy, now. Everything's OK. No more pain now. Good boy.' His tail shifted just inches. Gravel pattered.

I struck behind the shoulder.

The long legs stiffened and shook. The neck straightened. The teeth were bared. The underside of his upper lip glinted. Then he was still, and the last breath hissed slowly from him.

I pulled out the knife and blinked up at Keith over my shoulder. He stood six feet away, his hips thrust forward. 'You couldn't even get that right, could you, arsehole?'

He grinned and nodded. The flickering lamplight made deep channels of every line on his face, canyons of every hollow.

Polly's head shifted against my chest. She looked up at me. 'Bracky go nigh, nigh?' she asked.

'Yes, darling.' I hugged her close and kissed the top of her head, then slowly let her down on to the drive. 'Bracken's gone nigh, nigh.' I looked heavenward so that wind could cool my eyes. I wearily straightened.

I swung round and I flung myself at Keith's lurid, leering face.

I knew that my body effectively shielded Polly. I wanted to sink the blade into Keith's throat. Anywhere above the clavicle would do, I reckoned. Even if I missed with the knife, but none the less managed to knock him down before he could raise the gun, I was in with a chance.

It was the wind that undid me. It chose that moment to deliver one of its bolos from behind my back. I saw Keith's eyes and mouth drop open. His left arm rose and the hurricane-lamp arced through darkness. He staggered backward, off-balance, and then backward again as the wind crashed into him. The point of the blade hit something, tore something, but there was no cushion for my fall, no consoling weight and warmth beneath me, just cold air and hard gravel.

I rolled as I hit the floor, but then jockeys always do. Keith knew that. I saw the fluttering trail of flames from the hurricane-lamp, a few feet from my head, then something dark hurtled at me, faster than a high-speed train as you step on to the rails, and I did not scream because the pain was doing it for me. It was the pinball-machine when you break all records, all flashing lights and frenzied electronic noises. Icy mercury chased molten within my ears.

I must have rolled somewhere in there, because I remember seeing Keith's legs spread above me, his screaming face looking down, the gun once more raised above his head to strike, yet the next thing that I knew was that I was inhaling gravel and gasping in the smell of wet dirt while piercing pedal-steel chords rang in my temples. But I must not scream or moan. I knew that Polly was right behind me.

'You little bastard!' Keith was squealing, but a long, long way away, 'You cut me! Look, fucker, you cut me!'

I dragged my left hand up to my temple. The skin was hot and wet and pulpy to the touch. There were still all sorts of strange noises and echoes in my head as I pulled up my knees and straightened. I felt very sick, and it seemed that the whole world was being spin-dried by the wind. I kept my hand over the wound. Blood trickled down my sleeve. 'There, darling!' I gulped and very slowly stood. 'Daddy's fallen over!'

'Daddy fell down?' said the little voice behind me. I inhaled deep. Smiling was like drawing a line in treacle. I turned. Polly sat on Bracken's shoulder, apparently unconcerned.

'That's right, little one. Daddy fell down. Silly Daddy.'

She pulled herself to her feet and trotted unsteadily over to me. 'Silly Daddy,' she chortled.

I took her hand and turned to Keith. I had to set my feet wide to remain standing. 'Come on, shithead,' I croaked tremulously. 'You've fucked up enough lives. Let's do whatever it is. Let's get it over with. I'm tired.'

But something was wrong. I had tried to provoke him to anger and to violence. Anger I had succeeded in arousing, but he had not shot me when he could – even when his life was threatened – and his spluttering vituperations had now ceased. He hummed a tuneless 'pom, pom, pom' as we returned to the house, not for pleasure – that was clear – but to let me know that he had an idea, that he was once more in charge. He bowed low to allow me to pass ahead of him. He shut the door behind us and rubbed his hands. The hurricane-lamp had shed paraffin, but had not exploded, and still gave off sputtering light. I could see his gleeful gollum grin. I could see that the knife had drawn blood at his left shoulder but had then dragged uselessly down through the fabric of his shirt.

'Right, then,' he sidestepped past us and led the way to the hall again. 'Put the brat down, Munrow.'

I obeyed. 'She can't be here, Keith,' I said vaguely. There was still a lot of falsetto singing and bass drumming in my head. 'She can't watch this. Let's give her back to her mother, OK?' I turned hopefully towards the drawing-room door. There was desultory talk in there.

'That,' Keith snarled at my shoulder, 'is the last time you tell me what to do, Munrow.'

I reeled back towards him. The hurricane-lamp swung at the horizontal and Polly was in his arms. She wailed 'Daddy!' and her little legs cast scissoring shadows on the wall.

I lurched towards her. 'No!' I screamed. 'No! Leave her alone!' But I stumbled and my hands clutched at nothing.

'Whee!' Keith called as he scurried up the stairs. I stumbled again on the bottom step. I was still at the staircase's foot when he reached its head. 'Stay right there, Munrow!' he ordered. He laid down the lamp.

Polly had gathered breath. Her wail was strident and designed by nature to rend adult hearts. It worked. 'No, no, no . . .' I pleaded. Each word came out as a whimpered sob. 'No. No. Leave her!'

'That's better, Munrow. Now just stay there,' he gloated. The fluttering light from below made a giant grotesque of him, a floodlit gargoyle. I saw the jagged canines at the corners of his mouth. I saw those hated, strong fingers clawing roughly, inexpertly at Polly's chest. He held her high above the stairwell. She extended her arms, a miniature crucifix, and screamed. 'That's what I like to see, Munrow.' His clogged rough voice competed with hers. 'You want to play catch with your pretty little babby, hmmm?'

'No, no, please . . .' I felt my knees going. Sobs pummelled at my solar-plexus. 'No, please, Keith. Sorry. Do anything, but . . .'

He laughed. He lowered Polly and, with his left hand, clutched her to his chest. With his right, he reached into the pocket of his jerkin. He pulled out a length of binder twine. 'Now,' he spoke like a conjuror, 'shall we do a little trick?' His fingers flickered as they tied the twine.

He slipped it round Polly's neck. He sat her on the banister rail above the stairwell.

And he stood back, the end of the twine in his hand.

My daughter sat screaming with a noose about her neck and twenty foot of darkness beneath her.

I had never known that kneeling to beg was natural rather than customary. I knew it now. Al Jolson was a naturalist actor after all. My knees buckled. My arms extended. 'Please, Keith . . .' I whispered, 'Please no . . .' Polly just sat on the rail and howled. One of her fists was jammed into her mouth. In between screams, she fixed her eyes on me, mystified as to why Daddy did not stop this torment but merely knelt transfixed and weeping beneath her.

Behind me in the drawing room, I could hear Katya screaming, my mother rapping commands, then suddenly the full-throated roar of a gun, the shining echoes, the whimpering of women, but it was as if all that was on the fringes of my consciousness. I was watching my child.

'No, Keith,' I swallowed. I had eased myself up two steps in hope that I might catch her should he permit her to drop. 'No, please. Your fight's with me.'

'And this is the way to hurt you, isn't it? Now who's so fucking cocky, eh?' he bellowed. 'Or shall I give the little babby to Jake to play with? Not much brains, but plenty of imagination, our Jake. That's right, Munrow. Cringe like the filthy little crook you are. You try to lord it over people, this is what it comes to in the end.'

'All right, Keith,' I nodded and panted, my eyes always on Polly. 'All right. Yes, you're right. Please, Keith, I'll do anything. Don't hurt – don't torture her. I'll do anything. Please,' I whimpered, 'please, please . . .'

Polly screamed and reached out to me with both hands. The wind whined.

'All right, all right, Munrow.' Keith's arm encircled Polly and pulled her back. 'You've learned your lesson.' He unlooped the twine from round her neck. 'That's the ultimate price. Next time you argue with me, stand on principle, there'll be no going back. She gets it. Understand?'

'Yes,' I gurgled and nodded gratefully. 'Yes. Yes, OK. Sorry.'

He carried Polly down the stairs. I reached for her but he swung her away from me. Still she bawled. Still her little arms extended, seeking the warmth of a familiar, trusted body. Still her little legs stamped on the air.

'So everyone has their price after all,' Keith snarled beneath her screaming. 'You've got that message?'

'Yes,' I sniffed and nodded. 'Yes. Please, Keith, give her to me.'

'Nope. So, what are we going to do, Munrow,' Keith strode across to the study door, swinging his lamp. He used Polly's body to push his way in. 'Mr Quinn tells me you don't like to take responsibility for your own if it's not nice for your precious conscience. I'm told you refuse to do violence to protect them because violence offends your delicate sensibilities.'

'No. No, that's not true,' I panted. My heart and head were still pounding, my breath fluttering up and down. 'I'd do anything to protect them. I tried to do you, didn't I?'

'Not what I mean, is it? That's easy. We'd all do that. No, but some of us, not as lucky as you, we have to do nasty things sometimes to keep our children alive, our wives, ourselves, that sort of thing. We don't have the luxury of a clean conscience. Me, now, I've got no argument with your tart, have I? No argument with little babby here, come to that. Nah. Course I haven't. Question is, you're always so smug about the likes of us, have to do the dirty work – question is, are you prepared to grow up, hurt someone never did you no harm? We – we poor sods have to, don't we? Well, now you have to, too. I'm told, Mr Quinn said remember Charl-main, right? You understand? Learn what it feels like, be one of us, do the dirty work yourself, not just whinge and be all bleeding self-righteous.'

He put the lantern on the study mantel. He was full of himself now. His shoulders were back. His jerkin rustled as, carrying the howling Polly over to the drinks' tray, he picked up the Glenfiddich bottle with his free hand and raised it to his mouth. He tipped it almost vertical. He glugged for a few seconds, then sighed.

Polly's screaming was like the wind, violent blasts withering to whimpers as she sucked up breath, then returning with renewed power. Her face was red and glistening. Keith winced and wiped his lips on his sleeve. 'Right, what we do. Simple, really. You get your lesson and you get us off the hook. We're in a bit of a mess, aren't we? One guy splattered in the kitchen. Lots of witnesses. Best thing, really, massacre the lot of you and get out, but that's risky, isn't it? Forensics and all that. No, but you do the dirty work for us, that's different, isn't it? Your fingerprints on the gun, your wife's boyfriend dead, someone else who's obviously been killed by you . . . Looks suspiciously like a little domestic matter, doesn't it? Sure, you say, these nasty people made me do it. Think they're going to believe you? We say, yeah, we were there, sure. Check the records. Munrow's got eighty grand of ours. Of course we visited, even gave him a hard time, but no one got shot, not while we were there. Munrow just waited till we was gone, obviously cracked up, shot his mistress, or maybe thought this is a good opportunity to do away with the wife, get her money. Have to kill her fancy man and all, of course, blame it on us. No evidence to prove otherwise, is there? Only thing they can prove for certain is, you did a killing. So that lets us off the hook, doesn't it, and you learn what it's like, live with yourself.'

His words were impressionistic as music to me, a haze of vaguely persuasive ideas which chinked at my brain like a sculptor's chisels. They seemed to make sense, in that anything made sense. He and his friends might get away with it if I incriminated myself. Polly – and the others – might be spared.

And yes, I had found my price. Perhaps after all what I had seen as morality was no more than expediency generalized and theorized. Perhaps after all, for men like Quinn, men like Keith, the choices were fewer.

I took the point. I had been prepared to kill my assailant to protect Polly. I was prepared myself to die. How should I not, then, violate my own precious Christian conscience in the same cause? My cause was Polly's survival. I would die for it, as would any parent, but Keith was right. So much was easy. To kill for it was the hard part.

Keith sat on the sofa. 'So, you're one of us, now, Munrow.' He shouted to be heard above Polly's yelling. 'Just another poor fucking gofer because you want something and I've got it to give. You want your daughter's safety. OK. You got it. Listen. To make it more fun, you even get a choice, right? You kill *one* of the girls in there. Same gun, one cartridge. No bleeding Roman suicides neither. You take out one of them, or babby here gets splattered. And the rest of them. Crazed jockey cracks beneath the strain, kills wife, tart, baby, mother, self. So there you go. Your decision. The mother of your child or your bit of skirt. Take your pick.' He stood. 'It's time you knew what it feels like, Munrow. All yours now. You're the boss. I'll give you – what? Fifteen minutes should be enough. Shall we join the ladies, then?'

All heat had drained from my head and my chest as he spoke. The thumping in my temples now seemed to shake the whole house. The wound above my left ear played a hot snare. My whole body trembled. Tell me that I was trapped in a heavy disco – shit, tell me I was trapped in a major earthquake, I think I'd have believed you. I'd sooner have believed you.

I looked at the panic-stricken child in his arms. For her, I knew, I would go through hell.

For her, I was going to have to.

So here we are, as promised, at the razor-thin edge of morality and sanity.

It may seem strange to those who sit in comfort and pontificate on such things, stranger still to the childless, but I was never in any doubt but that, if no opportunity for escape should present itself, I would do it; not after watching my daughter teetering above a black oblong marked 'Rew $\langle\langle$'. Alternatives may occur to lateral thinkers. To me, who knows only how to think in terms of a grammatical, causal dynamic, the end justified the means and the means tended towards that end.

Oh, sure, the alternative that occurs to every armchair savage is that of heroism. It had occurred to me. I could have died happy as a hero, hot blood throbbing, war-drums, the warrior's scream silencing fears, doubts and pain, and for that, no doubt, I would have been honoured. Death – I hope – offers shelter from accusing beloved faces and from responsibility. I would have been OK. And in the charnel house that remained, they would find evidence that Neil Munrow had fought fiercely to protect his family. My every sin would be forgiven me. The slate, copybook and escutcheon would be wiped clean by one last mad moment. 'Always a good chap, for all his faults,' they would say at the memorial service, and

'Blood will tell,' and my brother, Donald, would sob, more for himself than for me.

But Quinn and Keith had it right in this at least: the hero has an easy ride. He does not have to vex his conscience. Like a blinkered horse, he looks neither to left nor right. He just charges and hopes that his chosen direction is the right one.

A contract to murder should, no doubt, be deemed unconscionable in that it is a contract to break one still more fundamental, but, looking at my child, at Katya and at Isobel as I walked in silence back into the drawing room, I found that parenthood, with its inherent and subjective brand of utilitarianism, was an imperative more binding than any social contract formalized in law.

So one of these women must die at my hand.

Polly ran at once to Katya, flung herself into her lap and at once resumed her thumb-sucking and hair-twiddling. 'What – what the hell was going on out there?' Katya demanded. 'Polly was shrieking the house down.'

'Yeah,' I nodded. I noticed, again vaguely, that the big Venetian gilt mirror above the fireplace was shattered and its frame spattered with caries. 'Yeah, she's OK now.'

Keith noted the damage too. 'You do that, Jake?'

'Yeah. All that screaming from out there, Jeez, this lot, scurrying round like headless chickens. Man, I had to do something. It was scary.'

Keith sniffed. He moved over to the grandfather clock in the corner. 'Yeah, well, watch it, right? Take it easy. That thing's not a toy. Remember what I told you, OK? Right. Now, Neil?' he said. He reached up and roughly swung the minute-hand round to quarter to four. The clock whirred and gave its somehow tinny but still resonant chimes. He pointed at the hour point. 'Got it? Set your watch.'

I licked my lips. I said, 'Yes.' My fingers shook as I turned the tiny gold knob on my watch.

I sat down on the sofa between my mother and Isobel. I took Isobel's hand in mine and squeezed it tight, then just sat forward and gazed into the dying fire.

239

'Well, I hope that we're close to resolving this ridiculous business,' my mother said grimly. 'The company is less than diverting and it's well past Polly's bedtime, and mine, as it happens.'

'We're close to resolving it, yes,' I said dully.

'Have you offered them the gee-gaws?'

'Yesterday. Too identifiable. Quinn thought I'd just ring the police, accuse him of theft.'

'What a nasty mind. Of course, we should have thought of that, but I must say, it never crossed my mind. Oh, dear.'

'God . . .' Isobel was suddenly crying.

I put an arm about her shoulders. She half-turned, rested her forehead in my throat, and sobs forced their way from her, shaking her whole frame.

'Cry, Baby!' Jake sang behind us. I turned my head. He was using the shotgun as a low-slung guitar. His eyes were closed. He shook his head and tunelessly mimicked Joplin's switchback vocal jerks. 'Cry-y-y-y-y . . . Hey!' He grinned over at the woman. 'Right, Lynn? Get it while you can, hey? Come on. We need music. All I need is music. Hey, Keith, come on. This party's farty. Let's do something. This wind . . . Hell, I hate this wind.' He stamped. His nostrils widened. His lips rolled downward. He showed the inside of a fat lower lip. 'Do something about it, for Christ's sakes,' he whined. 'I hate this house, I hate that jerk, I hate the whole thing.'

'You and us both,' I snapped. 'You're welcome to leave.'

'Don't talk to me like that!' He stamped and screamed, then the red in his cheeks fled, his legs started jiggling as though he needed a piss. 'Hey, let's have a party. This house is all stuffy. Jesus. "How sweetly did they float upon the wings of night, at every fall smoothing the raven down of darkness till it smil'd." Wow! Just listen. "Raven down of darkness till it smil'd." A-may-zing.'

'All right, main man.' The woman reached into a pocket in her fatigues. She pulled out a head of chicory. She tossed it across to him. He snatched it neatly from the air. 'Keep cool.

240

These people are like seriously tedious, but we'll be out of here soon. Just keep your eye on them.'

My eyes swivelled to watch Keith, but he was back at the fireplace, and the gun levelled firmly at the three of us on the sofa.

'Sure. 'Kay,' Jake sniffed and nodded two big nods. 'Right. Keep your mind on your driving, keep your hands on the wheel . . .' He forced the chicory into his mouth and chomped. He raised the gun barrels to the horizontal and aimed it at each of us in turn. 'Pow, pow, pow.'

'I'm sorry.' Isobel smiled up at me. She wiped her eyes on my sweater.

'Don't be bloody silly. It's all right. Everything'll be OK,' I lied.

'It's not that. It's just – if you knew how good it was to see you both back in one – well, two – pieces. God, all that noise. We didn't know what was happening.'

I kissed her. I smiled what I hoped was a soothing smile. I glanced over at the clock, then back at my watch in hope that they might disagree, but the old elephantine English beast and its slender Swiss descendant had struck up a co-operative relationship. Twelve minutes to go.

Still holding Isobel's hand, I turned to Keith. 'I've got to talk this over,' I said. 'I want a word with my mother.'

'So speak,' Keith shrugged. 'Your funeral.'

'I want some privacy, unless you want a mutiny on your hands.'

Keith shrugged. His finger remained still on the trigger-guard. 'So this is a big room. Jake, you stick close to them. Mister bleeding Munrow is tricky as a snake with shingles. Every word he says, anything odd, anything out of the ordinary, I want to know. And keep them both covered.'

I kissed Isobel again. 'Sorry, darling. I'll not be long.'

Katya said, 'I don't believe this,' three times.

Polly slept.

I stood. For a moment, the floor rocked. Jake did his bobbing, floating trick. He should have been on stage. He could really glide. The gun was an inapposite prop. 'Good night, ladies, good night, ladies,' he lowered his gaunt head, 'and no whispering with white lips or –' he made a slicing gesture across his throat, 'quietus, with, we need hardly observe . . .'

'A bare bodkin. Clever boy,' my mother droned as we walked over to the corner of the room.

This was perhaps our last chance. 'University?' I murmured.

'Oh, yes. Unquestionably. And theatre.'

'Drugs?'

'Yes.'

'Still?'

'Surely.'

'Her?'

'Maybe. You got her right.'

'Hey, you two.' Jake's voice was a lazy rest-stroke. 'No prattle, no rattle, and that'll be cool and we'll all grow fattle.' He giggled. He held the tilley-lamp high.

'Cute,' I said. 'Maybe Mabel Lucy Atwell did not die in vain.'

'Oh, lordly little jockey,' Jake went all Uriah Heep. 'Oh, mighty and magnificent little jockey. Permit me to salaam at your feet, Mister Jockey!' He bounded and knelt, Jolson-style, at our feet, but his eyes glittered and shifted, and the gun in his hand pointed steadily up at my gut.

I looked at my mother. She merely raised her eyebrows and turned her back on him.

'Oooh, that feels good, good, good!' Jake leaped to his feet with an acrobat's ease. 'Degrade me, beat me. I love it. I love it. But I've got the gun, Mister Jockey and Duchess, dear. Oh, I'm a lowly thing, a thing of shreds and patches merely, but I – can – do – damage, and I will!' he was suddenly roaring. 'Don't get me wrong! I am bored, little Mister Jockey-man! Watch it. That's all I'm advising. Watch it! Watchet . . .' he suddenly stopped and considered. 'A charming little Somerset port, I'm sure you'll agree, Duchess. Have we been there, played the queen there, even, mayhap, been obscene there? Have we?'

242

My mother sighed. 'Please be still, young man.'

Jake shuddered. His lower jaw dropped. He stared dully ahead. A deep voice from his stomach spoke. 'They don't know, they don't know. They never realize. Sure, I like to be abased. People do things to me. I let them. I like it. They deride me, they piss on me, they hang weights from my tits, they twist my balls and twist and twist. But I'm a joker, me. I like it both ways. When they're done, it's my turn. I pull out a sweet little blade, a lady's weapon, ladies from Hades, give them the same treat over and over. That's love for me. You don't know how loving I can be.'

'For Christ's sakes, shut it!' I bellowed at him.

His right nostril arose and tugged his upper lip with it. He raised his head and thrust his jaw towards me. He was a petulant little boy, uncertain whether he was going to cry or attack. 'You hear him?' He called across to Keith. 'You hear him? You gonna let him get away with talking to me like that?'

'Yeah, yeah, all right.' Keith was weary. 'Cool it, Jake, OK? It's almost over now.'

'Hey, just whose side are you on?' Lynn demanded. 'Whyn't you teach him a lesson for once and for all? I'm not standing here and having Jake insulted . . .'

She rattled on and Keith made appeasing noises as I drew still closer to my mother. Jake, instantly recovered, shrugged, placed the small lamp on the chest-of-drawers, plucked a Victorian album from the bookcase behind him and started to emit shrill, batlike squeaks of delight.

'I've got to believe they're serious,' I murmured to my mother. 'After Tony.'

'It's ridiculous.' My mother slowly shook her head. 'I mean, what do they want from you, for God's sake? What do they hope to get out of all this? They're facing life-sentences and they don't even seem worried.'

I shrugged. I looked down at my watch. Two minutes gone. My stomach keened. I needed a loo, but there was not time. 'I know what they want,' I said grimly.

243

'Oh, this dratted money.' She grimaced. 'Listen. Katya. Has she still got it, the cash?'

'I don't know. Look at her.' I waved a hand at where Katya sat blithe in the armchair. 'The woman's mad, you ask me. You've seen her. She's behaving like this is some silly prank that's keeping her from bed, and I'm all to blame. Christ, I mean, I don't understand. They've killed poor Tony. She doesn't even seem to have noticed.'

'We've got to drum it into her, then. When she knows the score, she'll pay what she can – she can't have spent half of it in this time – and I can write a cheque to make up the shortfall. Thirty, let's say. My bank manager will carry me for that much until the jewellery is sold . . .'

'I don't somehow think they're going to be accepting cheques, Mama. Katya's got to be our best bet. And if not . . . ?' I looked deep into her eyes, trying to convey images which were far from clear in my own mind – images of me flinging myself at Keith, of her lying over Polly's body, of Damascene blue barrels kicking like coming cocks, and, like coming cocks, engendering something far, far greater than they discharge, of spines buckling and limbs improbably twisting, of sheets of blood unfurling like sails.

'Oh, I'll do my best, of course, darling,' she said. 'If there's really no way out, we'll just have to fight.'

'There could be another way, love.' Again I looked down, then across at the clock. Just under ten minutes remained. Once more some giant grabbed me in both hands and shook me hard. 'Fighting, dying, that's easy, irresponsible . . . It's casting dice for lives. It's Polly I'm worried about . . .'

'Natural enough,' she nodded. 'It can be argued, of course, that adults matter more than children. Children are replaceable.'

'Sure. Not one's own, though. Bad morality, I know . . .'

'But fundamental, darling. OK.' She ran one hand down my scabbed and swollen temple. 'Don't worry. Whatever you do, I'll support you.'

'Whatever I do?' A laugh burst from me. 'Oh, God. The

worst of it is, I'd like to do this thing. Well, the results, anyhow, not the deed. That makes it more difficult to do. The guilt after . . .'

A giant shudder shook me. Again I looked at my watch. Nine minutes to deadline. I thought of Quinn's Charlemagne, his saintly ruler whose head must uneasy lie. No wonder power proofs the soul. That sad, silly, sensitive and lonely invertebrate could not withstand this again and again without growing a carapace. I sought refuge with my cheek against my mother's. 'Oh, God,' my moan was muffled. 'Haven't I done enough for that child?'

'Oh, it never ends.' My mother stroked the nape of my neck. 'Look at me.'

I raised my eyes. She was smiling, but tears streamed down her cheek and dribbled from her jaw. They were tears of pity, but not for herself.

'So, everything sorted then, Neil?' Keith was sitting on the arm of Katya's chair. His left arm extended along the back of the chair. His right hand held the gun which rested across his knees. The muzzles were inches from Polly's lolling head. Katya was yawning. Isobel looked up sharply, alarmed and quizzical as a puppy. Her shoulders were sagging now. She was tired.

'Yeah.' I dragged my feet as I walked to the centre of the room. Jake seemed to have acquired a new alertness. He took up his old position, covering the whole room, but his eyes shifted back and forth, projecting a glitter like a sword-fight. The gun looked small in those long, large hands. The clock behind him indicated that I had just seven minutes to go. 'We can pay the debt, OK?'

'Not interested.'

'What do you mean, not interested?' I demanded. 'Katya here has the money – some of it, at least, and my mother's prepared to pay you thirty grand more.'

'Yeah,' Jake sneered, 'she wants to give us thirty grand against the jewels. She's going to sell them, she says. Old bat.'

'Unfortunately,' Keith drawled, 'we've incurred some extra expenses. These two need paying, don't they? We thought the jewels would just about cover that. Sorry, Duchess.' He sniggered. My mother frowned at me and sighed.

'And I'm not paying.' Katya's voice rang clear in the silence. 'That money's mine.'

We all turned and gaped.

'I don't believe this woman,' Isobel breathed.

'You're telling us . . .' I swallowed and tried again as I took two strides to stand over her. 'You – you're telling me you'd sooner – it's a choice between Polly and eighty grand, and you'd sooner have the money? No. No, I'll not believe it.'

'Oh, stop being so melodramatic.' She smirked as she turned up to Keith. 'Dan Quinn's not going to hurt me or Polly. This is just show. He just wants to teach you a lesson for being so damned cocky.'

'Oh, yeah? And what about Tony?'

'That was . . .' she flapped her hands. Her eyes skittered this way and that. 'That was an accident. Your fault. Tony and I weren't meant to be here. If it wasn't for your childish explosives everywhere . . .' Again she cast a glance up at Keith.

'Katya.' I closed my eyes and prayed for a moment before I could trust myself to proceed. 'I don't think you understand. These people are here to do murder. They have already done murder tonight. We are witnesses. They are not going to spare you or Polly because of your winsome ways. I don't know what Keith here has been telling you, but he's having you on. Polly is their only way of getting at me. They're – going – to – kill – her. Do you understand?'

'It's just not true.' Her voice was high and girlish. 'It's not true, is it? Tell him.'

Keith just grinned. 'Jake,' he said calmly, 'give the gun to Lynn and take the brat.'

Katya got the message.

'You can't . . .' Her voice fluttered. 'Dan promised . . . Neil's the one at fault . . . He's the crook . . . He deserved it, but . . .'

She got to her feet, still clutching our sleeping child. She looked at each of us in turn. My mother, Isobel and I were stony-faced. The others grinned.

I had made no assumptions of order or reason since that gunshot had shaken the bedroom floor an hour ago. There were no surprises in chaos. But Katya, for her own reasons, had thought the whole business to be a game – a cruel game, but one with rules.

Chaos bulldozed her tidy living-space.

'No?' Katya squeaked and swung away from Jake's reaching hands. 'No, no, no, no, no?' Her face was white, her eyes wide and wild. 'No!' she howled. She sat because her legs had given way. The wind howled back at her and worried the house like a terrier with a rat. 'No,' Katya continued to murmur down to Polly. She rocked. 'No . . . no . . . no . . .' She looked up suddenly. Her eyes were filmy. 'Anyhow, I haven't got it,' she blurted. 'The money. I – Dan – Dan took forty back, and I've spent – and – the bastard – oh, Christ Jesus in heaven, my baby?' Her face crumpled and the tears seemed to jerk from deep within her. 'My baby, my baby . . .'

Jake was struggling with Katya. Polly was squirming and hitting out in half sleep. Katya's distress had commanded Keith's respectful attention. He had not lowered the gun, but he was watching her, not me.

I scuttled sideways round the back of the chair, out of the line of Keith's sight. If I could hook his throat with one arm, subdue the gun with the other . . .

'Don't even think about it, shithead.' The voice was so deep, so close behind me that I started and span. Lynn was grinning. The twin skull's eyes of the gun stared into mine, *mementi mori*, and behind them the glittering grey slivers of living eyes, foxed at the edges.

'Back off, fuckface,' she said gleefully, because we all do the cliches when we're holding the gun. Mind, as I'd discovered tonight, we do them when we're at the other end. There is no established etiquette in such circumstances. She sighted down the valley between the two barrels. I held my hands up and

247

out in protestation of innocence and powerlessness. One does, when a shotgun muzzle is two feet from one's nose. 'Keith,' she gloated, 'we've got . . .'

There was swirling movement behind me, a sound like a hoof hitting soft turf. I turned.

'No, Duchess. Think again,' Keith was advancing on my mother, the gun at his shoulder. She had made her move while I was blocking Lynn's line of fire. She backed until her shoulder-blades touched the mantel. She had chosen a bronze of a horse and a spaniel as her weapon. It dangled from her right hand. She was frightened, but never less than scornful.

That yellow head jerked. His forehead rammed into the bridge of her nose. Her head jolted back. Her back hit the mantel hard. Her eyes rolled upward. Blood sprayed from her nose and dribbled down her chest. She slid vertically down on to the hearthstone and sat, open-mouthed and staring at her feet. 'Oh,' she said sadly as she waited for the floorboards to stop speeding away from her. She blinked. 'Oh, dear. Sorry . . .'

Isobel was kneeling beside her, cooing to my mother with one breath, spitting fire up at Keith with the next. The khaki woman was laughing. It sounded like the last twist of water down the plughole.

'Now, sorry about that, Duchess,' Keith was munificent, 'but you got to learn your fucking place. I told you that. And your bleeding son. Now, we don't want no more bleeding heroics, do we?' He looked down at her. 'Christ, all that blood. Tell you what, Lynn, take her out of here, will you? I can't stand it.' He shuddered. 'Wait one. Keep them covered.'

He bent and added his strength to Jake's in wrenching Polly from Katya's grip. Polly awoke again and yelled, and my heart oozed hot treacle, not blood. Katya made a noise like an airlock and tightened her fingers, but said nothing. She just gulped and stared, apparently cataleptic. It was not that she fought. On the contrary, she just sat there rocking and drooling to her thrashing child, but her fingers clawed tight and snapped back into place as soon as they were released.

'Right,' Keith ordered Jake as they finally pulled my hollering child free, 'take her over there . . .' He pointed at the table in the bow-window. 'And if the clock's struck before Munrow here has made up his mind, just slit her throat, right?'

Jake nodded and smiled. His mouth made a delighted 'Yeah', but I could not hear him for Polly's screams.

And suddenly there was real desperation, real urgency in those screams which she hurled out, in her frantic twisting and kicking as she felt Jake's hands on her tiny body, saw his crazed eyes leering down at her.

He carried her ineptly over to the table and laid her down on her back. He pulled my razor from the back pocket of his jeans. 'Hush, little baby, don't you cry,' he giggled, 'I'm gonna put you in a pie . . .' I moved towards them, but found Lynn's gun nudging at my gut. Keith caught my eye and nodded towards the clock. Three minutes remained.

My mother's eyes were veering and apologetic as she stood and teetered. Lynn propped the gun up against the sofa and took her arm. 'Come on, old woman,' she snarled, then, 'Keith, I don't want to miss the fun, OK?'

'Sure, sure, OK,' Keith sighed and at least pretended to pray. 'Just get all that blood out of here.'

My mother suffered herself to be led, snuffling and gapelegged as though she were wearing nappies.

And Katya freaked.

Her arms closed about nothing. Her eyes snapped open. 'No!' she screamed. 'No, bring me back my baby! No! No! Where have you taken my baby? No! Let go! Bring her back! I need my baby! Polly! Polly! Naaah!' She fought Isobel, she fought me, she fought Jake as she screamed, with feet, teeth and clawing red nails. She spat, she wriggled, she kicked and she yelled. Polly shrieked in answer.

I have seen much of pain, but never agony so manifest as on Katya's face as she struggled against us and in the shrieking and cursing which made the house sing.

Keith slapped her hard, which only made matters worse. Any illusion that these were her allies had fled now.

Eventually, he pinioned her arms, but still she squirmed and howled obscenities. I knew that sound, the ringing shriek of metal on stone which had tormented and pursued me over three years, yet never had I felt such pity as now.

At another time I might have gloated, thought, 'Now you know what it feels like to have your child snatched away,' but not now. That scream spoke of a natural bond far deeper and more primal than mine with Polly. Katya would massacre for our daughter without my Hamletizing.

She strained against the hands until her throat was deeply channelled and her tongue lolled. Each intake of breath was a discord of French horns. Only when Jake stood before her, grinning, with the razor at Polly's throat, did she stop fighting and become suppliant. Keith stood back.

I nodded at my gun which he held in the crook of his arm. 'Is that it?'

'No, that one.' Keith indicated the cheap-looking Spanish gun which now leaned against the sofa. 'And careful, Munrow.' He pointed his – my – gun at me. 'Remember your little babby over there, and I can take two of you without moving.'

'Sure.' I nodded warily. I ducked beneath Katya's screams and bent to pick up the gun. 'Isobel, love,' I said, 'you come with me?'

Keith's eyes narrowed. 'Where you going now?'

'Just out there to the sunroom.' I jerked the gun. 'You can see us.'

Keith nodded.

I led Isobel to the double French windows. She frowned. She stepped through ahead of me. There was a long scratch like a zip down her left cheek where Katya had caught her. I shut the door behind us.

Katya's shrieking was muted, the moaning and woofing of the wind more distinct. We were in a glass capsule wrapped by the wind, high above the valley. The panes stuttered in their frames. The bare tendrils of clematis barely shifted.

'Sit down,' I told her.

She frowned at the gun, but she sat in a sunchair, her hands hanging loose between her legs. 'What is this?' Her voice buzzed in the glass. 'Neil?'

'I've got less than two minutes.' I leaned on the outer door-frame and gazed out into the night. Out there was fresh air and the sanity of the everyday business of survival, all just a fraction of an inch away. Maybe it was just fancy, but I thought that the sky at the horizon was lighter than in the heavens' vaults. Dawn would come for some. It would come, as ever, too late.

'I don't see an alternative!' I wailed. 'What am I meant to do? For God's sake, have I missed something out? Is there some brave course you can suggest? Please. OK, so I go out there, try to shoot Keith . . . Is that responsible? Even suppose I got him – and he's waiting for me – there's a whole bloody commando-course to do before I get to Polly. Oh, God. Is there a choice?'

'What are you talking about, Neil?' Isobel's voice was high and cool. 'Why have you got the gun?'

'It's absurd,' I croaked, and I could barely hear my own voice for the Royal Wedding clamour of bells in my head, the boxing of the wind. 'They say . . .' It came out as a sort of laugh. 'They say I've got to kill someone, or there's a blood-bath. You, Polly, everyone . . .'

She too laughed. It was a comic riot in there. 'You can't be serious,' she said, but her voice just faltered.

I took a deep breath. I looked up at the ravelment of bare clematis tendrils. 'I know,' I sobbed. 'It's absurd, but Tony . . . They mean what they say . . .'

'No. Come on. You're crazy, Neil. They're not going to kill the lot of us.'

'Why shouldn't they?' I howled. I turned towards her. She was all smeared and smudged like a pavement picture in the rain. 'Keith just says "do it", and Polly . . . Maybe they wouldn't, but I can't take the risk.'

My right hand shook on the trigger-guard as though I'd been using a pneumatic drill. Isobel looked to me and frowned, then she looked down at those twin tunnels to absolute darkness. She breathed sharply in. 'You can't,' her voice was like walking on crisps. She swallowed. 'No. You can't. You can't, Neil . . .'

'What the fuck am I meant to do?' It came from me in an elephantine screech. 'It's one life or two, maybe three . . .' I moved nearer to her. Something strange was happening to me. The drumming at my temples was of a piece with the sounds outside – the rustling of Isobel's dressing-gown, the persistent shrieking from the drawing room, the persistent belly-laughing of the wind.

'It's just not fair!' Isobel was shouting. 'Fight them, something!'

'I know, I know,' someone spoke with my lips.

'I came here to help you! No, Neil. No, you can't!'

'I know.'

'No, Neil?' she had raised an arm before her face as though it could deflect the blast of a twelve-bore. 'No! How – how – will you live with yourself? What about me? No! Oh, please help me. OK, so she's Polly's m-mother, but I'm – I'm no one's mother. I've never had the chance! I don't deserve it! No, Neil. No. I loved you. I helped you. No, please.'

'I know, I know,' I wept. 'I love you. I'm sorry.'

'Neil . . .' Her voice shook violently. Her eyelids were an oyster's shell. You could glimpse the flesh and the pearl. Her mouth was stretched wide in a silent scream of agony. She reached out over the barrels and her fluttering hand touched mine. 'Neil, no,' she groaned. 'Please, please, pleeease . . .' It ended on a little whiplash whimper.

I looked down. My finger was on the trigger now, and squeezing. The muzzles were mere inches away from that gleaming, beautiful but contorted face.

Something cracked like a great tree within me. A rapid succession of little staccato whines seeped from me, a huge sob, then a roar.

'No, Neil.' She was pushing at me now. 'No . . .'

I had dropped to my knees. I hugged her hard to me. I

252

kissed her damp hair and her eyes. 'It's all right,' I panted, 'it's all right.' But still she whimpered, 'No, Neil . . .' and struggled and shoved.

'It's all right,' I groaned, yearning for pardon. 'Please. It's all right.'

'No, no, no . . .' she drooled. 'No, Neil, please, please!' She wriggled out from under me. She escaped from the deckchair on to her knees. She shoved hard at me and stood. 'No – no – God, no . . .'

And she wrenched open the door and bolted back into the drawing room.

I hugged myself. My shoulders were raised and dropped by a vast piston. I was retching great gouts of air. I was rocking and squeaking, my eyes screwed up tight. I was broken. Quinn had proved his point. I was worse then a murderer. I was a murderer without the guts to do his duty.

From the drawing room came Katya's gasping and wheezing. 'Dan promised! He promised! Ring him! He'll tell you! He said that no harm would come to us! He promised! Neil would work for him, work for me. No harm would come to me or Polly. He couldn't do this! Ring him! Oh, let me have my baby back! Give me my baby . . .'

I pulled myself to my feet. I swallowed.

I picked up the gun. I walked into the drawing room, which tilted and veered. Katya was bent double in the arm-chair with her back to me.

I raised the gun to my shoulder. And I shot her.

Death is not glorious. Death by violence is not glamorous. No one reels and topples like Mexican extras.

It is smut and stink and splattering dirt and chinking bone. It is glowing skin turned inside out, healthy hair turned to matted tufts and wisps over shards and gobs of matter.

Death is not still. It is pulsing and twitching and bursting and slow suppuration thereafter. It is filth which can never be cleaned.

Death is not silent. After the boom and the ringing, there

was still pattering in the fireplace and a slow-puncture hiss and splashing on the wooden boards.

But it was done.

Never to be undone.

My child was motherless.

I had done murder.

I had judged and condemned.

Suicide was not even an option. Polly bound me to this earth while she lived.

In Japan, they say, you can buy an aerosol replacement hymen. Few things on earth are irreparable.

But no one could piece together the shattered mess of blood and brain, hair and bone. No one could re-inject the life, the soul. And no one could give me back the ignorance, or the innocence which had fled.

I would never sleep soundly again.

There was a long silence broken only by Isobel's gaspings.

I had dropped the gun and fallen to my knees. I had covered my ears. I wanted never again to stand, never again to open my eyes to hear. Even the darkness, though, did not protect me. I heard Polly's screaming. I heard her voice in later life. 'No, my mother died when I was two.' I heard myself trying to explain to her . . . 'I had no choice, darling . . .' I saw again Katya's bright, loving face at our wedding, felt again the gentleness of her kiss the morning after, remembered presents, parties, holidays, and Polly's birth.

I had smashed all this in a fit of terror and anger and of pity for a woman whom I loved more. If Katya had become a crazed bitch, how far was I responsible for the transformation? Had I then punished my own creation? Even if I accepted that I had had no choice but to kill, by what right had I imposed my passions on the choice? By what right had I spared the woman whom *I* loved and done this to the woman *I* hated? No matter that Katya had taken the money against my will, no matter that she had plotted with Quinn to enslave me. Even such crimes are not punished by execution.

'I could kill her . . .' spoken and overheard a thousand times . . .

I do not fear death; I fear dying. I did not mind Katya's dying: it was the fact of her death which was to be my albatross every moment of the rest of my life.

I did not at that moment know that I could bear it.

Behind me, Keith kept babbling, 'No, no, it was just . . . Fuck it, Jake, you realize what you've done, you shithead? You realize what you've bleeding done? I said unloaded, didn't I? Unloaded. Not . . . not this. Oh, Jesus.'

'Shit, man, I didn't know. I was scared, wasn't I? I had to protect myself. Shit, bombs and all that. This is too heavy for me, man. I'm out of here.'

I stood at last and, clinging my daughter to me, howled to heaven. Then I opened my eyes.

And turned my head and vomited.

There was a lot of activity, a lot of shouting. Isobel was wailing. Keith was hanging on to Jake's sleeve. I wiped my mouth and staggered between them. I opened one of the casements and leaned out, choking, while behind me the wind celebrated this latest triumph by goosing the furniture and scattering the Christmas cards.

'No, Jake, we're in this together. We've got to think . . .' Keith was arguing behind me. Isobel was just chanting a mantra, 'Oh, God, oh, God, oh, God . . .' again and again. Again I opened my eyes and let the watery wind wash over them. I did not care what happened to me. Maybe Keith had the gun trained on my back even now. I might not seek it, but I welcomed it should it come.

'Jesus, what sort of shit you've landed us in?' Keith persisted. 'You realize what's happened? You realize – oh, God, you berk . . . You deaf or what? What'd I say? I said, "Put him through the wringer, but when the time comes, hand him an *unloaded* shooter. Break him, not . . ."'

'I didn't know!' Jake was yelping like a soap-opera matron. 'All these people screaming, Neil here looking fucking dangerous, Jeez, I'm meant to stand there without a loaded gun? Let go, man. Let go! I'm splitting. It's your fucking mess.'

The words were rattling noise, no more. I have reconstructed, reinvented them. But their import entered my head like cartoon-strip blocks.

Katya need never have died.

I turned to the room. 'Dear God in heaven!' I screamed.

Isobel fell silent. She was sitting curled on the floor at my left. Her forehead rested on her knees. All modesty was long forgotten. 'Please,' I said. I plucked Polly's fingers from my sweater. I handed her down. She was too tired to object, and Isobel hugged her gratefully.

Jake was already somewhere out in the hall, calling urgently for Lynn. Keith stood staring, a childlike plaint in his eyes. 'Here, Munrow, you'll tell 'em, won't you? I said "unloaded". Shit, it was a game gone wrong, that's all . . .'

I threw myself at him without regard to the gun across his chest. I was snarling and swearing and babbling, my every muscle taut, my only thought – no, I had no thoughts, only pains and hungers.

Keith's eyes were wide and dirty-white. His twisted mouth dropped open to make a wedge-shape. His hands vaguely raised the gun, but he was too shocked to know what to do.

My shoulder hit him at chest height. I bore him back across the room. He fell back beneath me. His head hit the mantel just as my mother's had mere minutes ago. He grunted and slithered vertically down into the fireplace amid a swirl of ashes and sparks.

I held him down with my left hand. With my right, I pummelled that leering face. My knees were scorched by hot clinker. I did not care. I raised my fist again and again and brought it down with all my force, picking my targets, closing this eye, then that, smashing his nose, breaking the teeth, while between my legs his wiry form bucked and wriggled and behind me the legs kicked like those of a child in a tantrum.

When I had done, I looked down. The yellow hair was blackened and dusty. On his right-hand side, it was charred. The face was more even than it had been since my mount's hooves had started the work all those years ago. Both eyes were closed, but still he groaned and shifted.

I remembered the Swiss Army knife.

I reached into my pocket. I pulled it out. I opened it.

'No!' Isobel yelped behind me. 'No, Neil. You mustn't.'

Panting, I turned my head. She stood just two yards away. She looked unutterably beautiful with her cheeks all red, her eyes wet, her hair spread by the struggles and the wind. My dressing-gown had fallen open. The were two deep slivers of white from her clavicle to her belly-button, from the belt to her feet. Her open hand covered Polly's head, pressed it to her chest.

I looked at her for a full five seconds, just saying goodbye.

I returned to my task.

Murders are like millions. It's the first one that's hard.

'They've gone,' I said in the hall.

'Yes.'

'Just two-bit druggy punks.'

'Yes.'

'Wind's dying. Be back to normal soon.'

'I'm going to get dressed, Neil. We must call the police.'

'Yes. Don't touch anything. Especially the kitchen . . .'

'God,' she shuddered, 'poor Tony. You wouldn't get me in there if you paid me.'

'I'll have to ride down to the village. We can tell them . . .'

'Yes?' She was subdued and acceptant.

'Well, I mean, there were the threats, all that. Tony surprised them and got killed for his pains . . .'

'Yes?'

'And we rushed down, but they had guns and herded us all in the drawing room, then Keith panicked and the gun went off, and Katya . . .'

'OK.'

'So then I thought, shit, he's going to kill the lot of us, and I just attacked him.'

She led me wearily up the stairs. 'Yes. All right. Don't worry,' she sighed. 'I'll see it's all right.'

'Isobel, I'm sorry.'

'So am I,' she shrugged and shuddered. 'You did what you felt was right. I can't complain.'

'Was I wrong?'

'I don't know, Neil,' she was irritated. 'Only you can say that.'

But she bundled up her clothes and carried them to another room sooner than dress in front of me.

The birds chinked like chisels as I crunched out on to the gravel and blinked weary eyes at the tarnished silver sky. The world had been washed by the night's gale. It smelt like aluminium.

Lynn had proved as much a talking horse as her son. They had bolted together, taking Tony's car. They would be caught, and then Jake's story would be tested against mine, Isobel's and my mother's. My mother had come down, bloody and swollen. She had taken in the scene and concentrated on the important things first. We had put Polly to bed together. We had changed her nappy. We had soothed her. We had given her favoured toys. We had even brought a smile to her face. Then, with Isobel, we had sat in the study and worked out our story. Jake's tale should prove a selling-plater in a classic.

I averted my eyes from Bracken's corpse, a large, red caterpillar on the drive, and walked down the little track to the yard. With Bossy's heavy hunting-saddle over my left forearm and his bridle on my wrist, I went from the tack-room to the feed-room to fetch his morning scoop of oats.

I kept my horse-feed safe from rats in two large, unserviceable chest-freezers which Curry's had sold me at a fiver apiece. I frowned as I entered the room because it sounded as though the rats had somehow found a way into the left-hand freezer. There was a rustling in there, but I had neither the energy nor the interest to investigate. I opened the one on the right. The oats were running low, so I had to bend in deep.

It was then that the rat-rustling became a distinct thumping. I raised my head sharply. I said. 'What? Hello?'

There was muted shouting. Pimples appeared on the white metal front of the chest. I laid down the scoop, reached for a curry-comb and cautiously approached the freezer. I unlatched it. I flung up the lid and stepped quickly back.

'Bloody hell.' The man within puffed bran and blinked up at me.

I started back still further. I slipped on the floury floor. I had to prop myself on the open freezer opposite. 'No.' I shook my head fast as though to dislodge the sight from my brain. 'No. That's impossible. Stop it.'

'Well, right berk I look,' said Tony Wickham. 'Everything OK? Sorry, have you got a knife or something, cut these bloody things? No, last thing I knew, about an hour after we went to bed, Kati wakes me up, says she's heard something outside, says she can't sleep till I've gone out across the roof and checked it out. They must have seen me coming. God, I felt an idiot. Jumped down with just that little torch thingy, and there's this bugger pointing a bloody shotgun at me. Didn't see him properly. Couple of other buggers hanging about in the bushes too. Just told me to shut up – not that I could have made myself heard above that hellish wind – take me out here, tie me up and shut me in. And I'm, you know, trying to shake the buggers off, but the bigger one's quick and strong, seems to find it all very droll. Sniggering and singing. God, I have never had such a frustrating night. Oh, I bellowed a bit, but the air is pretty filthy in here, and you'd never have heard me up at the house. Surprised Kati didn't raise the alarm when I didn't come back. Still. Funny girl. Oh, God, yes, I'm sorry – you know they killed your poor old dog?'

'Yes.' I was still gawping. 'Yes, but, Tony, you're dead.'

'Not unless this is heaven or hell, and it don't seem much like either to me. I'll check my pulse for you in a second if you'll just cut me free.'

I winced. My head was hurting badly now. 'This is crazy,' I protested. 'Oh, for Christ's sakes, what is happening here?'

'Well, if you don't know, I certainly don't. You look pretty beat-up yourself.' He screwed up his face and strained against his bonds. 'Neil, please.'

I nodded. I reached up on to the shelf for an eighteenth-century bone-handled steel, now worn to a right-angled triangle. 'Sorry. Sorry. I'm just – well, shattered and shocked and . . .' I leaned down and sawed at the webbing which bound his wrists. 'I'm sorry, Tony. Katya. She's dead.'

He turned his large, dusty head to me. 'Kati? Come on. She can't be.'

'She is. I'm sorry.'

'No,' he argued with himself. 'No, it's not possible. She can't be.'

'I've seen her, Tony. She's dead.'

'But it was all a joke. She told me . . .'

'She told you what?'

'Well, not a lot, but she said – sorry, bit stiff – she said you were every sort of shit, didn't give her any money, all that, but this fellow she knew . . .' He clambered out of the feed-bin with my support. He frowned down at his open dressing-gown, his gaping, dusty pyjamas. He plucked and flicked at the bran in his chest-hair. 'Katya? No. It can't be.'

'Go on. What about this fellow she knew? Do you mean Quinn?'

'Well, she didn't tell me his name, but I assumed he was the same chap as we were talking about last night. I – what I understand – they planned to play some sort of trick on you. He paid some money into your joint account, she took it, gave half back, kept the rest and you got a nasty fright. She did need cash, you know. Small child, no house of her own and so on. But that was it. A silly gag. Put one over on you. She doesn't like you,' he informed me solemnly.

'Didn't.'

'Didn't.' He considered the word once it was out. 'God, you're not having me on, are you?'

'No, Tony. Those people you ran into last night were very nasty people. No silly gags. They were killers.'

260

Yes, my numb mind told me, but Tony was here, alive. I remembered Keith's face as the echoes of the blast had faded and died . . . A brutal, but silly gag . . . They had not been killers. Only I had knowingly done murder last night . . .

Keith had believed the gun to be unloaded. Quinn, I was sure, had instructed him in this. The idea had been to break my spirit but to leave the house corpse-free. I had believed the gun to be loaded but had still fired. I had not needed to kill Keith, but still I had done it. Any horseman could have told Quinn why. Sure, you can break an animal's spirit. Sometimes you will totally subdue him. If he is of noble spirit, however, you will simply turn him rogue. They had stripped me of pride and of the prospect of self-preservation. They had denied me the customary protection of law, courtesy and public opinion. They had wanted to show me the savage within the well-mannered, weak but moral man that I had become.

They had succeeded beyond their wildest dreams and their worst nightmares.

God, they had probably thought the whole grand illusion to be a killing joke as they planned it. Could they not see, these men who played violent and played with violence, that the true stripped savage within any one of us is a million times more dangerous than their posturing and bullying, that man had survived supreme and the Briton supreme among men simply because, in defence of his own, man is the nastiest and most resolute of creatures and the Briton more warlike than any other of his species? It was as if some absurd, Aleister Crowley-style sham of a shaman had accidentally summoned Satan himself. Keith and Katya had been way, way out of their league.

It felt very lonely, knowing that I had been the only murderer in the house last night.

'You'll find Isobel upstairs,' I told Tony. 'Look after her. I'm going down to fetch the police.'

'Right. Jolly good.' Tony looked bleary and bemused. 'OK. Help clean up. Nasty mess, that.'

'Yes. Better leave the drawing room. Damned sight nastier in there. No, leave everything for the police.'

Bossy was gassy and up on his toes as we set off down the hill, but he soon caught my mood and plodded weary as an old dray-horse. I dropped the reins and slouched in the saddle, let him find the way.

We rounded the bend at the bottom, and suddenly he planted his feet, threw up his head and snorted. I had barely gathered the reins and sat into him when he half-reared and swung to his right as though to gallop up the hill. I soothed, 'Hey, boy. Easy.' I drew him in, turned his head back and squeezed tight with my right leg. Crescent, he tittuped and strained, snorting his objections, but at least I had him facing forward and I could see what had caused his consternation.

It had not been a sight which had alarmed him. It had been a smell, below, thank God, the range of my senses.

I had forgotten the fallen branch.

So had Jake.

A bee that had flown into the windscreen of Tony's BMW might have looked a little as the car looked now. Its nose was broken and buckled. One wheel had done its best to jump the unexpected obstacle. The other had ploughed it, so the car lay skewed.

They had not worn seatbelts.

What remained of the front and rear windscreens was now milky. Through a jagged star of darkness, I could see from back here Lynn's head turned sideways on the dashboard between clawing hands. There were arms about her neck. I could not see Jake's head.

I assumed that it was now free of its frenzied, cockchafer buzzings. Maybe not. I was too tired to care. I solemnly swear that that was the only reason for which I made Bossy climb the bank and walk on. It did not at the time occur to me that I had reason to hope him dead.

I was unchanged, a civilized and sympathetic man. I was

not – I swear it – so steeped in blood as to leave a man to die for my own advantage. I swear it.

It was two days before the police left me alone, two days before they stopped battering me with questions of detail and with quizzical, knowing looks.

I fought them. I anticipated and repudiated their insinuations. Numb though my mind was, it sidestepped discrepancies, parried accusations and lumbered clumsy lunge with lunge.

Perhaps they had their suspicions of me, but principally, I think, they were just going through the motions. It was fun to put a jockey through the wringer. They had a dead villain and his victim. Both guns had my prints on them, sure. Why should they not? One was mine, the other I had wrenched from Keith when I jumped him, toted defensively about the house until I was certain that Lynn and Jake were gone. Experts hoovered the house with tweezers, but in the circumstances, forensic niceties were superfluous. The obvious conclusions were so much more probable than the truth.

They grilled Quinn, I heard. They caught up with Trevor Verulam in Spain and presumably gave him a hard time, too, but for all that Quinn and Keith had been seen together, there was no evidence that Keith had been acting on Quinn's orders. Keith was known to have a grudge against me. I was happy to accept that explanation. I repeated much the same non-specific guff that I had spoken on television. My family had been threatened. Bribes had been offered. Inevitably I had rejected these overtures with scorn. The night of the killing joke had been the consequence. Katya and Tony, forced to remain by the storm, must have been the first to hear the interloper. Tony had been confined. Keith had shot Katya. I, coming on the scene, had been justly enraged . . .

We were front-page news for three days. Johnny McIlroy's haphazard interview proved, after all, a major scoop. It was replayed on the national television news and in a major investigative report on the state of racing. That interview, my statement in the weighing-room, my subsequent assault on Quinn and the police's insistent attention, all served to ensure that Quinn was a busted flush. If he dropped a sweet-wrapper henceforth, he would be warned off if not arrested. He would fix no more races.

I could have destroyed him utterly. I chose not to. Quinn was my intimate now. I had my own plans for him.

I had my own plans for him.

I waited. I let him sweat.

I had somehow assumed that the police would clean up the gore at the scene of a violent crime. To my astonishment, they merely gave me the names of a few contract cleaners.

I engaged a nanny. By day, then, I was a cheery, affectionate, rough-and-tumble daddy. By night, with the whisky hot in my veins, I gazed at the spot where the chair had been and I brooded on damnation and cursed myself faster thither.

When the telephone rang, it was usually my mother, sometimes my solicitor. Sometimes I was not in.

Initially, I hoped that it might be someone else. At length I knew that for her, too, I had passed over the Styx.

She was at the inquest, though. She nodded to me. She vaguely smiled. She shuddered when she turned away. Nothing is nastier than cool politeness can be. They say that boiling water freezes faster than tap-water. I can believe that. Lukewarm relationships can cool, and so what? A hot one goes off the boil and you're instantly thirty below zero.

She skilfully edited her tale, yet told it with genuine horror in her voice and eyes. The court had no cause to doubt her or my mother. Katya was deemed to have been murdered by Keith James Gurdon. Said Keith James Gurdon had been lawfully killed by me.

'Lawfully' did not help a hell of a lot.

It was only then, in late February, that I drove up to Gloucestershire and made my way to Quinn's manor house. I had unfinished business with this man who had known me well enough to drive me to do murder.

And I knew that something else bound us, though I feared to know its precise nature.

I knew now that once I had been awakened and had gone downstairs, I knew now that in those first moments of that night's terror, Katya had had time aplenty to cross the passage and snatch up Polly. She had been emerging from her room just as I arrived back on the landing. Her face, I would swear, had been flushed and her hair tousled, but it had been cold, not hot from bed. I had re-lived every moment of that night a thousand times already. I remembered the cold of her skin beneath my hand as I tried to keep her from speaking, the wide, wide-awake eyes that had glared at me.

Tony had been gone some time by his account, but Katya had not called to any of us in alarm. Well and good, if she had been asleep all that time, but she had not. It was she that heard the suspicious something, she that had asked him to investigate – and then she had gone outside herself . . .

I remembered, too, her initial lack of concern as to Tony's welfare and her own. And I remembered her last, howled and blubbered words . . .

Oh, yes indeed, we had unfinished business, Mr Quinn and I.

The Cotswolds looked like a giant, abandoned slapstick set. The Crazy Gang had been and the ASMs on strike. Custard pies of snow had splattered the fields and now turned flat and pinkish grey. The trees were bare. Dark-grey cloud lay above the pale-yellow horizon like snow above a billiard table. It was cold and gloomy.

Quinn's house was not what I had expected. It was a small Cotswold manor not twenty yards from the main road. The garden, enclosed by yew, looked as though it had received no attention beyond mowing for many years. The house, too, though pretty enough, had an uncared-for, forlorn sort of air. The second-storey windows were blinded, the shrubs straggling, the creeper wild as a hobo's hair.

I had expected glitz. This was glitzy as Mrs Havisham's wedding-cake.

I parked outside the front door and calmly jumped down. I ran up the steps, rang and, for good measure, knocked with the unpolished brass knocker.

There was a long wait.

Stairs creaked. Footfalls clopped precisely but slowly across the hall. Bolts were shot. Plainly they were not expecting visitors.

The door opened inward. A small, stocky man with greying black curls blinked out at me. He smiled. His face was creased and friendly. He wore a dark-blue nylon jacket, lightly seasoned at the shoulders. 'Sorry, yes. Can I help you?'

This was the sonorous, fart-in-the-bath voice which I had heard on the telephone. It did not belong to the face or the frame.

'Yes,' I told him. 'I'm here to see Quinn.'

'Mr Quinn is busy, I'm afraid.' The man glanced over his shoulder into the perpetual twilight. 'You haven't got an appointment, have you?'

'No, but he'll . . .'

'I'm sorry. He won't see you. You really should have called, sir.'

'He'll see me. Tell him Neil Munrow is here. Tell him I've got his map.'

'His map, eh? Oh! Oh, yes. You're the jockey, right? I was sorry . . . Well, that was . . . You know, I'm sorry. Bad luck. And well done, sir. Like to see people have a go.'

'Thanks,' I nodded. 'Quinn?' I reminded him. 'Please?'

'Oh, yes, sorry. Well, I'll try, Mr Munrow, but I can only tell you that it's unlikely. Hold on a second.'

His eyes were on the door, which he held. He was uncertain as to whether he should be so brutal as to shut me out or whether – strictly, I was sure, in contravention of the rules – he should let me in. In the end, seeing as how I was a widowed hero and all that, he compromised. He left the door ajar and scampered very fast across the hall.

I pushed the door open and strolled in, breathing steam.

The walls were the colour of old mustard, the floor-tiles

266

dull mustard and Bristol-blue. There were foxed Herring and Morland prints on the walls – nothing special – and a fuzzy sub-Rothko abstract above the fireplace.

I wandered further in, wondering. I had not seen all of the house, but one thing was plain: here were no swimming-pools, Jacuzzis or executive gym. No house-party or orgy had been held here in decades, and the bonkettes of my imagination would have been as out of place as Happy, Sleepy and Co. with the Globetrotters.

I strolled further in. At my right, beneath a broken architrave unhappily adorned with Wedgwood-type classical figures, another door stood open. I peered in.

It was a kitchen where a kitchen should not be. It was fully equipped with modern electrical gadgets, some of which I had never seen before. There were four or five long cords like light flexes hanging from the ceiling.

I did not understand. This room must have cost forty grand to equip, but the room to which I returned looked as though it belonged to the widow of a Church of Ireland vicar.

I tried another door. Suddenly everything was clear.

The room was bright and light. The walls were papered with tiny pink flowers and curtained with large crimson roses. There were abundant flowers on the bedside table and the chest-of-drawers. The French windows gave on to another garden, a little garden with a cruciform path dividing smooth lawns filled with rose-bushes.

I walked past the bed and through a further door at my right.

I had been right, and wrong, all along.

There was a huge whirlpool bath. There was a massage bed. There was a swish stereo-system and a massive video-screen. Everything could be operated by remote-control. But it would not be operated by tanned, long-legged slatterns.

All this had been constructed, at enormous expense, for someone who could not use her legs at all.

'I suppose you are entitled, Munrow.' The voice behind me was still a mighty engine idling. 'Though I'd have killed anyone else who ventured in here.'

267

'You've done enough damage. Is that it?' I turned slowly. Quinn looked very old where he stood in the doorway. His grey sweater hung loosely about his torso. His hands hung loosely at his sides. He looked at me over the swollen bags of skin beneath his eyes as over unfamiliar bifocals. His face was grey. 'What? No bruisers to beat me up and dump me in the river, Quinn? Come on. What about your butler or whatever?'

'Nurse,' Quinn almost belched.

'So I'm meant to pity you? Because you have a disabled wife or something?'

'Wife and child.' Quinn raised his chin. 'And have you ever seen me ask for pity? Oh, no. I'm the smooth, rich manipulator, aren't I, Munrow? The audience is simple, so I give them a simple message. No. Muscular dystrophy, if you're interested. My wife did not realize until she was twenty-nine. My daughter was already born.'

'So? So there are tens of thousands in the same position, Quinn, and without your advantages. They don't do murder, man. You are demented.'

'Maybe,' Quinn shrugged and slowly shambled in. 'Maybe I am. Maybe I'm bad. A rogue born and bred. I suppose one should pity such a creature. Have you met horses like that?'

'Two,' I told him, 'out of thousands.'

'And the rest? The vicious ones? The wrong 'uns?'

'Men make them that way. Or tumours, physiological things.'

'You console me. You're singing my tune.' He turned back into the flowery, high-tech bedroom. I followed him. He sank on to the bed and picked up the remote-control console.

'I think you'd better leave that, Quinn,' I said sharply.

He looked up with a canine query in his eyes.

'Leave it. Put it down. I don't know what it can do.'

'Oh. Yes.' He laid it down gently and eyed it sadly. 'It can raise or lower the head or the feet. It can make the bed vibrate, stimulate sluggish circulation. No, I don't think I'm a rogue. Oh, yes, I worked for Rachman, but then, I was a bright, ambitious young kid, not many morals, OK, just doing what everyone else on the make seemed to be doing. It wasn't just Rachman. There were big, respectable concerns doing it on twice the scale. Rachman was the foreigner doing it. That was all. He got found out.'

'No fucking excuse . . .' I sneered. But I had used it.

'You've got my map, I hear? Ah, well. Little Munrow stays on the top of the pack. Luck of the draw. All right. And I did my best. I got lucky and I did my best. I went into straight business, read the world's classics, learned what you're meant to do, meant to feel, or pretend to feel. The first two marriages didn't work out. OK, that happens to the best of us, doesn't it, Neil? One was a blinding snob, despised me when the old me came out. My fault, of course. I just gave her surface, thought it would be enough. Then a neurotic, sex-mad girl, lovely but crazy. She loved me for the opposite. She wanted me to be the villain. Got a kick out of it. She liked the danger, liked to go slumming. She liked the hard boys in their leather jackets. I was moving away from all that, for God's sake, and she wanted stories of villainy in bed. And then I met Liz. She was a decent girl, beautiful, protective. She knew where I came from but forgave me. She loved all of me, hard as it may be for you to believe . . .'

He was rambling. His thick fingers plucked at the white counterpane as old men will pluck at the skin on the backs of their hands and watch it descending ever slower. 'And then,' he slowly shook his curly head. He sniffed. 'Then this happened. OK. I could cope. I liked looking after her. I had the money. It wasn't so bad at first. Walking-stick, then walking-frame, then wheelchair, then control of limbs, sphincters, starts to go . . . But the money ran out, didn't it?' He smiled sadly down at his lap. He took a deep breath and spoke on a quavering monotone. 'Wives had cost me, property market collapsed, I got done for a tidy fortune by this fucker – earl's son, stitched me up . . .' He shrugged. 'Do you know what it costs, Neil? To keep an invalid out of a home? And I would not have Liz in a home, not Liz or Clarissa. No fucking way.

My capital ran out five years ago. Liz . . . Her father left a trust fund. Not much, but we can scrape along on it. The house is hers . . .'

'I'm still not hearing choirs of angels, Quinn,' I told him. 'What about the clothes, the car, the flash bit?'

'Tools of the trade, Munrow,' he said as if it were obvious. 'Oh, I don't expect you to understand, but I decided I wasn't going to sit on my arse and sink singing 'Rule Britannia'. Leave that to you bleeding noblemen. The city wasn't the place for me. Full of brainless, toffee-nosed snotbags. No. I knew where I could make money. I turned back to the things I knew best: odds, and fixing the market. The racecourse. Sniff out needs, fulfil them, put a little pressure on here or there. So wrong? Maybe. You didn't fucking object when you wanted to buy that house of yours, did you? Oh, no. But anyhow you can't do that sort of business in jeans and a Morris Minor.'

'Goddamn it, Quinn,' I paced from the windows to the door, my eye always on him, 'we're not talking about the ethics of race-fixing now. You killed my wife.'

'Moot.' Quinn smiled a lopsided smile. He cocked an eyebrow up at me. 'I or you?' He resumed his slow plucking. 'Or Keith, perhaps? I certainly didn't intend to kill anyone, and for it to be murder, there must be intent. That's the same in the law-courts and at the Last Judgement. I didn't have the intent. Did Keith?'

'Keith thought the gun was unloaded,' I admitted.

'Silly arsehole. So, Keith had no intent to do murder. But you – you didn't think the gun was unloaded, did you? You fired in the belief that it would kill. Where does that get us?'

I rested my hands on the end of the bed. I snarled up at Quinn, 'I killed to save life. It was you and Keith . . .'

'Ah!' Quinn interrupted triumphantly. 'So you're admitting it at last. You will do anything for your own. To hell with the rule-book, is that it?'

'Of course that's bloody it,' I spat. 'I had no choice.'

'Oh, you had choice, Munrow. The average, weak, silly

little human would have fought and died sooner than kill because the word "kill" is so big and frightening. That would have been immoral, wouldn't it? Nice, proper, but immoral. Allowing others to die to spare your sensibilities. Man must impose his reason, act for the best. Sure, but the best, logically, would have been to allow the child to die, wouldn't it? Each of those other human beings was worth far more than a toddler, was capable of doing more good, had more invested in them . . . But you chose the sentimental course, the selfish route. She was your child, so others must go to the wall. I sympathize . . .' He waved a hand about the sick-room. 'Well, you can see that I sympathize. There's no difference between us. That's what I told Keith. Break him, put him through the wringer, I told him, make the little shit sweat, show him that, when he's subjected to the same pressures as us, he's not better than we are. And I was right, wasn't I? You obeyed orders, just like those people told to press buttons which give lethal electric shocks. That was the idea. Teach you not to be so effing self-righteous, teach you to obey orders. No one intended to kill anyone. Damn it, Katya had told me when she and the boyfriend were arriving, she gave me the photograph, she let us in.'

'You were there, then?' I resumed my pacing. 'I thought so.'

'Of course I was there, Munrow. You think Keith had the wit to set things up like that? No, that tree or whatever was down. We walked up from there. Katya was listening out for us. We hadn't expected them to be there, so she sent the boyfriend out by way of a warning. Get rid of the inconvenient witness. Then she came out herself to warn us of the change. I thought she'd want to get out. Not a bit of it. I'd had the idea by then, and she loved it. Just wanted to know that she'd be safe, and the child, that's all. Ironic, really, but it suited me down to the ground. So I told Keith, splash muck around in the kitchen – and bingo. You were in extremis where I wanted you. Then I went back to the car. But the fact that she was there, doesn't that show you? No one was

271

meant to die. If it hadn't been for Keith, no one would have. You'd have heard a loud click, and you'd have known that you were damned like the rest of us. You'd have joined the human race.'

'It wasn't just Keith.' I swung to face him. 'You snapped those slender threads of morality which keep us alive. Evil was let loose. Accidents happen which can't happen when there's order.'

He nodded. He spread his hands. 'I take the blame. It seemed like a perfect opportunity. A game. Beautiful, perfect, almost moral. Break you, scare Katya . . .' He shrugged. 'I'm sorry.'

I had forgotten vigilance now. I paced into the corner, rested my forehead against the walls and closed my eyes. 'It's still crazy,' I mumbled. 'Why me, for God's sake?'

'You made it all happen, didn't you?' His voice was almost cheerful. 'Sure, cast the blame on me if you will, but none of this would have happened if three separate people – Katya, Keith, me – had not hated you and hated you passionately. Do you not accept some of the blame?'

'But why?' I almost whined as the burden of that hatred sank on to my shoulders. I turned, my back to the corner. 'It doesn't make sense! OK, Katya's crazy . . .'

'And Keith's bitter and twisted. You were foul to him when he was down on his luck. Your horse trampled him. You represented everything he hated. You didn't have to call owners and trainers "sir". You had a famous jockey for a father, a duke's daughter for a mother. Of course you could afford to be smug and moralistic. Jesus. And me? Oh, shit, look at you. Sweet, holier-than-thou little Neil Munrow. I'm a yob. You're a fucking nobleman. I'm immoral. You're a fucking saint. You despise me. You show it in your every gesture, your every sanctimonious smile. Yeah, and on what grounds? You hooked horses for money – for my money – and, eventually, you killed for your child. So? I did some pretty filthy things for money. I've done all this for my child. We do these things, Munrow, nobleman and yob. The mon-

arch does shit, you know. Once – once, you know, at Cheltenham, after the Champion Hurdle, it was, Potomac, and I
came up to you, said, "Well done, Neil." That was all. You
just looked at me, raised your fucking eyebrows and your
fucking snotty nose and walked on. Oh, no. Neil Munrow
was better then me. You'd never sin, whatever the pressures
on you. Bastard. No, time came, I loved watching you
squirm.'

I wanted to weep for the absurdity and the pathos of it all.
I did not even recall the incident of which he spoke. Certainly
I had always despised him back in those palmy, easy, winning
days, but I don't think that I had ever deliberately cut him.
Perhaps I had had a drink too many. Of such tiny errors
come evil.

And I remembered – and wished that I didn't – Katya's
plaint, 'Oh, you're so good, so pure, so arrogant. Balls, you
are. If I have to listen to one more of your sanctimonious
bloody lectures . . .'

I swallowed the giant and jagged pill, but the cure came too
late. I wanted to howl, 'But can't you see? That's just my way of
protecting myself! In here, there's a confused and crying child!'

But maybe Quinn could say the same.

I moved over to the ladder-backed chair by the wall. I sat
heavily and leaned forward. I clasped my hands. 'OK,' I said,
'so you're crazy, so Keith was crazy, so Katya was depressed.
Are you telling me she deserved that torture?'

'Kati?' His affectionate smile rapidly turned into a sneer.
'Oh, Munrow, now I have you. I have your whole happiness
in my hands. Come on. You have the map. Call the police. I
knew something would undo me. It's OK. I've got the insurance all sorted out. Liz and Clarissa will be all right, provided
that I can meet with a fatal accident soon, and I can arrange
accidents, even on remand. I've wasted enough time talking
to you. Let's get on with it.' He picked up the telephone from
the bedside table. He held it out towards me.

'I want to know,' I said. It came out gruff. I had to clench
my fists to stop my fingers from shaking.

'No, you don't.' He jerked the telephone.

I shook my head. 'None the less.'

Quinn eyed me, appraising and amused. 'You're sure?'

'Come on, tell me, you twisted little man.'

'Oh, little man, is it?' Quinn was the cocky street-kid again. He laid the telephone on the bed beside him. 'All right, Munrow. On your own head.' He sat up straight. 'I liked her, Kati. She was like me in some ways, a fighter, a survivor. Cunning. I like that. But she shouldn't have blackmailed me.'

'Blackmailed? Oh, come on . . .' I scorned the idea.

'No. True. Bitch blackmailed me. Came into my room at the Grosvenor in Chester one night. You were going out with her at the time, but we hadn't had the pleasure of meeting yet. Whinged about you, how you didn't care for her. I felt sorry for her. Nice, you know, one up on the heroic jockey, fuck his girlfriend. Childish, maybe, but there.' He licked his lips. He gazed at the pink roses on the quilt, traced their form with his finger. 'I had the camcorder there. It's useful for recording races, and I like to bring back a record of the things I see on my travels. For Liz and Clarissa. That's how it happened. Few drinks. She'd never seen herself on one of these, so I suggested we filmed ourselves fucking, send it to the boyfriend, you, tee hee. OK, big joke. Didn't matter. I kept the film, wiped it before I came home. What I didn't know, sometime in those three days, while I was away at the races, she must have had it copied somewhere. I asked about contraception. She told me it was safe, she had a coil or whatever, but a few months later, she's back, pregnant, she says. Wants money, serious money. Or she tells Liz, tells the world. Oh, Liz would have forgiven the sex, the video, all that. It would have hurt her, but she's not stupid. No, the problem was, Liz would have insisted that we pay for the child. I know. It happened once before. She'd have insisted that we pay out of the trust fund. There wasn't the money. I said to Katya, "Christ's sake, why can't you have an abortion? Why can't Munrow pay?" She screams at the one, sneers at the other, says you could but you wouldn't. So.'

I gulped. The thought was battering at my brain but I would not give it admission. The portcullis had slammed down.

'Funny, really,' Quinn mused. 'Katya had thought I was rich as Croesus. She'd fallen for the myth, the image. My fault, really, I suppose. I told her the truth, she was furious, didn't believe me at first. God, I've often wondered, did she set out to get herself pregnant because I was rich and she was fed-up with you? Ironic stuff, eh?'

I looked at the harness above me. I looked at the pale-green carpet. I looked at the bedside lamp. I said quickly, 'This is ridiculous. It doesn't even start to . . . I mean, how was she going to prove it was yours? OK, the video . . .'

'Dated,' Quinn supplied. 'It's one of those camcorders, you know, that supplies the time and date.'

'OK, suggestive, but hardly proof. She was having you on, Quinn. She was going out with me. Of course I'd have paid. I was doing OK then . . .'

'Yes, she had to accept that in the end. But you wouldn't have paid if you'd known all the facts, would you? What if the child had been born rhesus negative and you'd got to know? You're positive, aren't you? Katie told me. So's Kati. I'm negative. She knew that. Two positives can't throw a negative, so what then? Definitive enough proof for you? You'd have kicked her out on her ear. You forget, Munrow. That's what gets me. You're a ruthless little shit by birth. How in hell d'you think your ancestor got his effing dukedom? By being a ruthless little shit is how. No, you'd have kicked her out. So we compromised. She'd introduce you to me, you'd ride to my orders, we'd share the profits . . .'

'When . . . ?' it came out as a sort of wood pigeon's coo. 'When was this?'

'Forget it, Munrow,' he ordered. The words had the finality of the bar which drops at the end of a pool game. 'In the past, that's all. Just accept. In the end, I had to be rid of her. Damn it, she'd come to my room, but still she blamed me. I had done it to her. Christ. Anyhow, I had paid her too much for too long. Then you decided to go straight for a while, so you weren't bringing in the cash. I had to pay her out of the trust fund. That couldn't go on. She wanted out from your marriage. One lump sum, she said, and that would be it. So I put a deal to her. It was a clever deal, a pretty deal. She steers you to the bank account at Slaughters'. I borrow eighty and pay it in. She keeps forty, gives me forty back. You're enslaved and earning nicely for me again. It could have gone on like that for years. But you wriggled, you resisted before you'd so much as earned back Katya's share. That left me and my family in the hole, didn't it? I couldn't have that. Still you thought you were better than me. It sickened me. You were born privileged, I was born poor. That's the only difference between us. You have a healthy child and I have a sick one. You had to learn, Munrow. You had to knuckle under . . .'

His lips twitched as he struggled to regain control of his resentment. At last he raised a hand to his brow and slowly, sorrowfully shook his head. When at last he looked up again, it was with red-rimmed, blinking eyes. 'You're not better, Munrow. You're as bad and bent as any of us, as Keith, as Kati, as me. Your principles are just reflexes conditioned by pressure and privilege. Free will? Bollocks. There's no such thing. Did you have free will that night? Have I had free will all my life? Of course not. And I tell you, if I'd been born in your position, I reckon I'd have made a damned sight better job of it.'

He shrugged. The gold signet flashed and the fingers flickered. 'I didn't want blood on my hands, Munrow. Believe me. We're just – all pre-programmed to survive as best we can. You, me, just the same. We have no choice, in the end.'

'When . . . ?' I croaked. A hundred voices were heckling from the dark corners of my head. I could not get the question out. Could Katya have had an abortion while we were living together? No. Quinn would not have continued to pay. Could she have conned him, then, with all that blood-group stuff? Yes. That was it. She was devious and greedy. She had wanted

Quinn, but he had scorned her, and she, knowing his weakness, had used it against him just as he had done with me. The question came up again. 'When . . . ?'

Quinn just looked me in the eyes and slowly shook his head.

I found myself nodding. I would sooner live with uncertainty than with unbearable knowledge. I was almost grateful to Quinn.

But I had come here to be ruthless, and I was not minded to show mercy. The time had come.

'So,' I said casually, 'the map.'

Quinn was shaken from his musings. 'Yes. Like I said. Something had to go wrong.'

I had pulled from my pocket the grubby little map which I had taken from Keith's leather jerkin. I studied it. 'A map of my house,' I said. 'Clear directions. Dining room, study . . . Your handwriting, I think. More than sufficient to send you down for life, wouldn't you say?'

I stood and strolled over to the bed. I held the map out to him. He took it with a shaking hand. He looked down at it and sighed.

'So?' he said at last. 'So what? Call the police. You're thinking of blackmailing me, too, forget it.'

'Nope.'

'What are you going to do with it, then?'

I shrugged. 'That's the only copy, Danny boy. You've got it. Tear it up, burn it, frame it, if you will. I'm giving it to you.'

His eyebrows rose at the centre. He looked ready to cry. His voice came out as a husky squeak. 'But why?' he implored an answer. 'Please. Why, Neil?'

'Because I'm not going to let you commit suicide, Quinn. Your wife and kid need you.' I grinned. 'Because every day for the rest of your life you are going to owe to my magnanimity.' I bent down inches from his ear. 'Because I can, yobbo,' I growled. I straightened and patted his shoulder. 'Just because I can.'

*

Polly is sixteen now, and the spit-and-image of her mother, though several people have said 'Yes, but she's like you too.' She has Katya's wide eyes which can be vulnerable one second, hard as marbles and fierce as lasers the next. She has the same sweet laughing mouth, which can too readily pout, too readily shriek if she is denied her way. She has even dyed her hair blonde, despite my mumbled objections.

As you sow, with children, so shall ye be poisoned. Seeking to pay my debt, I have indulged my baby, proudly shown her off, fiercely protected her, denied her nothing. At first she was loving and grateful, then petulant and demanding. Now she is frankly spoiled. Her ferocity and vindictiveness astound me, but I love her, and still must pay my dues.

I hung up my boots at the end of that terrible season. I was sole owner of the house and the yard. I even, paradoxically, inherited sixty thousand from Katya, who had not changed her will.

As a trainer, I prospered in a quiet way. I was able to pay for Polly to go to a good school – from which she has recently been expelled for unspecified sins – to take her on decent holidays, to buy her fashionable clothes. I have no life aside from racing and fatherhood. My love life has consisted in cynical, transitory encounters on the rare occasions that I have stayed away from home. That, to my mind, is 'safe sex'. I have not seen Isobel since the inquest. Polly wouldn't remember Isobel.

Polly has taken to walking in the night. From time to time, I hear her, padding in the darkness about my room. The first time it happened, I screamed, and Polly, awaking, screamed back and pummelled me and scratched at my face and called me 'bastard' and 'devil'. Usually I manage to steer her back to bed without waking her. Once she half awoke when I had pulled the blankets over her, and she grabbed my hand and placed it on her right breast and said, 'Mmmm. Like that. Snuggle,' just as Katya had. Once again I woke her and she screamed and lashed out and would not be calmed, but, calling me 'fucking devil' and 'evil, evil', writhed and kicked and snarled and dribbled and broke a bedside lamp on my head.

When she had appendicitis, I sent the nanny to the hospital. I did not wish to know details. Otherwise, I have been her constant defender.

It is, after all, only natural.